HEIRS OF RAVENSCAR

Barbara Taylor Bradford was born in Leeds, and by the age of twenty was an editor and columnist on Fleet Street. Her first novel, *A Woman of Substance*, became an enduring bestseller and was followed by twenty-one others, including the bestselling Harte series. In 2006 *The Ravenscar Dynasty* began an epic new family series around Ravenscar and the house of Deravenel. Barbara's books have sold more than eighty-one million copies worldwide in more than ninety countries and forty languages, and ten mini-series and television movies have been made of her books. She lives in New York City with her husband, television producer Robert Bradford. This is her twenty-third novel.

For more information and inspiration behind the Ravenscar series, visit www.barbarataylorbradford.com

Visit www.AuthorTracker.co.uk for exclusive information on Barbara Taylor Bradford

Books by Barbara Taylor Bradford

Series
THE EMMA HARTE SAGA
A Woman of Substance
Hold the Dream
To Be the Best
Emma's Secret
Unexpected Blessings
Just Rewards

Others
Voice of the Heart
Act of Will
The Women in His Life
Remember
Angel
Everything to Gain
Dangerous to Know
Love in Another Town
Her Own Rules
A Secret Affair
Power of a Woman
A Sudden Change of Heart
Where You Belong
The Triumph of Katie Byrne
Three Weeks in Paris

Series
THE RAVENSCAR TRILOGY
The Ravenscar Dynasty

BARBARA TAYLOR BRADFORD

Heirs of Ravenscar

HarperCollins*Publishers*

HarperCollins*Publishers*
77–85 Fulham Palace Road,
Hammersmith, London W6 8JB

www.harpercollins.co.uk

Published by HarperCollins*Publishers* 2007

I

A catalogue record for this book
is available from the British Library

ISBN-13 978 0 00 726269 4

Set in Sabon by Palimpsest Book Production Limited,
Grangemouth, Stirlingshire

Printed and bound in Great Britain by
Clays Ltd, St Ives plc

For Bob: For his loving support and generosity, and for always being in my corner.

Contents

PART ONE

The Deravenels

Dangerous Triangle

Edward was of a gentle nature and cheerful aspect: nevertheless should he assume an angry countenance he could appear very terrible to beholders. He was easy of access to his friends and to others, even the least notable. *Dominic Mancini*

When the Plantagenets started to kill each other the downfall of the dynasty began.

London citizen: 15th century

Ah, me, I see the ruin of my House!
The tiger now hath seiz'd the gentle hind;
Insulting tyranny brings to jet
Upon the innocent and aweless throne:-
Welcome destruction, blood and massacre!
I see, as in a map, the end of all.

William Shakespeare:
Richard III,
Act II, Scene IV

ONE

Yorkshire 1918

It was a compulsion, the way he came down to this stretch of beach whenever he returned to Ravenscar.

A compulsion indeed, but also an overwhelming need to recapture, in his mind's eye, their faces . . . their faces not yet cold and waxen in death, but still warm. Neville, his mentor, his partner in so many schemes and adventures; Johnny, the beloved companion of his youth. He had loved them well and true, these Watkins brothers, these cousins of his who had been his allies.

At least until a mixture of hurt feelings, overweening ambition, flaring emotions and dangerous elements had intervened and prised them apart. They had become sworn enemies, much to Edward's chagrin, a pain which had never ceased to trouble him. And now Johnny and Neville were dead.

Edward raised his head, looked up at the clear blue sky, blameless, without cloud, a sky that appeared so summer-like and benign on this icy Saturday morning in December. Unexpectedly, his eyes felt moist; he blinked back sudden, incipient tears, shook his head in bemusement, still disbelieving their tragic end, here on this bit of shingled beach at the edge of the harsh North Sea.

How unexpected, how sudden and abrupt it had been. Their motorcar had shot off the dangerous, winding cliff road, had plunged six hundred feet, rolling down the face of the cliffs, crashing onto the rocks below.

Neville and Johnny had been thrown out of the car onto the shingle, and had died instantly.

It had been a terrible and unnecessary accident, one which Edward knew had been caused by Neville's festering anger, frustration and bad temper. His cousin had been furious with *him*, and had been driving far too fast, spurred on by raging emotions he could not always control.

If only Neville had been handling the Daimler in a normal way, he and Johnny would be alive today, and perhaps they would have been able to reconcile their differences, end their quarrel, come to some sort of mutual rapprochement.

In a sudden flash of vivid memory, Edward saw Johnny standing before him . . . the serious Johnny, so sincere, so wise, full of the Watkins's brilliance; then the happy-go-lucky Johnny, light-hearted and carefree, his handsome face full of laughter and the pure joy of simply being alive. Edward snapped his eyes shut, remembering so much from the past. Memories that haunted him rushed at him once more, overwhelming in their reality.

After a few minutes Edward opened his eyes, and placed his hand on his chest. He could not feel the medallion through the layers of heavy winter clothes, but it *was* there, lying against his skin . . . Johnny's medallion.

Fourteen years ago, in 1904, Edward had presented a medallion of his own design to those men who had helped him in his fight to win back and take over the family business empire. The medallion was a badge of honour, in a sense, to mark their success. It was made of gold and bore the Deravenel family crest: an enamelled white rose on one side, the sun in splendour on the other, with the Deravenel motto *Fidelity unto eternity* embossed around the edge under the enamelled white rose.

Johnny apparently continued to wear his medallion despite the differences that had grown between them. This convinced Edward that Johnny Watkins had remained his faithful friend right to the very end, obviously a man torn between diverse family loyalties – torn between his influential older brother Neville, and Edward, his favourite first cousin.

It was his brother Richard who had discovered the medallion around Johnny's neck after the car crash, when he had opened his cousin's collar as he lay on the beach, the life seeping out of him.

Needing to determine Johnny's true condition, Richard had loosened his tie, pulled open his shirt, and had instantly noticed the glint of gold on his neck.

On the night of the accident Richard had brought Johnny's medallion to Edward, who had later removed his own identical medallion and fastened Johnny's around his neck. And he had worn it ever since and would until the day he died.

The following morning Edward had given his own medallion to Richard, as a token of his love and regard for his youngest brother. Richard had been thrilled to accept it, understanding how meaningful it was.

Easter Saturday of 1914. That was the day they had died. So much had happened since then . . . the War had erupted a few months later, in August . . . friends and colleagues had been killed on the blood-sodden fields of France and Flanders . . . he and Elizabeth had had more children . . . the business had grown in importance . . . there had been deaths, births, marriages . . . Richard had been quietly married to Anne . . . the eternal cycle ever repeating itself.

Four years ago two men he had revered and loved had died on this beach where he now stood. Yet, to him it seemed as if it had happened only a mere few hours ago. He could not forget that fateful day, or expunge it from his mind.

The sound of a horse's hooves thundering along the beach

interrupted Edward's melancholy reverie, and he turned his head, saw his youngest brother riding hell for leather down the beach.

Raising a gloved hand, Edward waved, stepped over to Hercules, his white stallion, and with lithe agility swung himself up into the saddle. Galloping forward, he rode to meet his brother.

As the two men drew closer and reined in their mounts, Edward knew at once that something was terribly wrong even before Richard uttered a word.

'What is it? What's happened?' he demanded, staring hard, his bright blue eyes sweeping over the younger man's face.

Richard, his voice tight with concern, said, 'It's Young Edward. Something's wrong with him, Ned, and –'

'*Wrong?* Do you mean he's *ill*?' Edward cut in peremptorily, instantly worried about his little son.

Richard nodded. 'Elizabeth thinks it's the influenza and she sent me to fetch you. Mother has already telephoned Dr Leighton. She spoke to his housekeeper. Seemingly, he and his wife are house guests of the Dunbars. He's staying at The Lodge for the weekend, and he's on his way already. He won't be long.' As he finished speaking Richard saw that his brother had gone extremely white.

'My God, the Spanish flu,' Edward muttered. 'It's lethal, you know that. Some of my chaps at Deravenels have been felled by it. It's certainly fortunate that Leighton is nearby.' Alarm filled his eyes, and he shook his head. 'Come on!' He rode off down the beach, galloping at breakneck speed, heading for Ravenscar.

Richard followed hard on his heels, catching up, riding alongside his brother, never very far from his adored Ned when he needed him.

TWO

Ravenscar stood high on the cliffs above the sea, which was glittering like polished steel in the brilliant light of mid-morning.

The house was built of mellowed, golden-hued stone, and was ancient, dated back to the sixteenth century and Tudor times. A pure Elizabethan house of fluid symmetry and perfect proportions, it had been home to the Deravenel family for centuries.

Built in 1578 by Edward's ancestors to replace the ruined stronghold still perched on the promontory below, it was a house which Edward had loved since childhood. He genuinely appreciated its overall beauty, cherished it for the meaning it had held for those Deravenels who had gone before, and those who would follow, once he had departed this world.

Now as he rode around the circular courtyard at the front and went on towards the stable block, he paid no attention at all to the grandeur and elegance of this stately dwelling, did not even notice the many windows sparkling in the wintry sunshine or the façade of honey-coloured stone aglow in that dazzling light so peculiar to these northern climes. He held only one thought in his head: his son. His heir. Edward, his namesake, whom he loved with all his heart.

Edward needed to see him. The very thought that his son had contracted Spanish flu filled him with dread. It was a virulent killer, had gone from epidemic to pandemic since it had broken out in the summer. People in Europe, England, and America, in many other countries around the world, had been laid low, and thousands had died.

Finally trotting into the cobbled yard behind the house, Edward jumped off his stallion, glancing around as he did, looking for the stable lads. Not one of them was in sight. 'Ernie! Jim!' he called, 'I'm back.'

Richard had followed him into the yard, and as he dismounted he said, 'I'll deal with the horses, Ned. Please go into the house, I know how anxious you are.'

Edward nodded and hurried off without another word.

Richard watched his brother stride towards the back door, anxiety ringing his face. People thought that Edward Deravenel held the world in his arms, and, in a sense, perhaps he did. Certainly he had everything any man of thirty-three could ever desire. Yet at this moment, Richard knew, his brother was truly vulnerable, filled with concern for his son. His great success, immense wealth and undeniable power could not buy the boy's recovery. Only God, and a good doctor, could do that. Silently Richard prayed that his little nephew would be all right. He loved him like his own, just as he loved all of his brother's children, most especially his niece Bess.

Taking the reins of the horses, he led them across the yard towards the stalls just as Ernie, one of the stable lads, suddenly appeared, looking worried.

'I'll tek 'em from yer, Mr Richard,' the lad said, then added apologetically, 'Sorry I weren't out 'ere when yer got back. It was Minnie, Mr Richard, that there young filly. Right skittish, that she is.'

Richard nodded his understanding as he handed over the reins. 'She has calmed down, has she?'

The lad said, 'Yeah, but can yer 'ave a look at 'er, sir? Mebbe there's summat really *wrong*. Yer knows wot, I think it's 'er front foot. 'Orseshoe might be loose. Mebbe she'll get real troublesome again.'

'Yes, I'll examine her foot, Ernie, but I must be rather quick about it.'

'Nowt but a minute, Mr Richard, it'll only tek a minute.'

When Edward had entered the house he had been struck by the overwhelming silence, and now, after throwing his outer jacket onto a bench in the gun room, he rushed down the corridor, frowning. Usually this part of the house was filled with constant sounds, familiar sounds . . . the clatter of pots and pans emanating from the kitchen, as well as cheerful laughter and the dominant tones of Cook giving orders to the kitchen maids. But unexpectedly there was not a single sound at this moment, and Edward was puzzled because it was not at all normal.

He paused when he reached the Long Hall, curious about the absence of Jessup. The butler was generally hovering around in this area, wanting to be of service, but he was nowhere in sight.

Edward shrugged, and had begun to walk towards the staircase when Jessup came hurrying out of the butler's pantry, asking swiftly, 'Do you need anything, Mr Deravenel?'

'No, but thanks anyway, Jessup. I'm on my way upstairs to look in on Master Edward. Have you seen him this morning?'

'Yes, I have, sir. A bit under the weather he is, poor little mite. But then he's a strong young fellow, isn't he, sir?'

'Yes, indeed he is. Please bring the doctor up immediately when he arrives, Jessup, won't you?'

'Oh, yes, sir, right away.'

With a slight nod Edward was gone, taking the stairs two at a time, heading for the nursery floor where the children spent most of their time. Striding rapidly down the corridor, he realized he could already hear the sound of his five-year-old son coughing before he even reached the bedroom, and he felt his chest tighten. He stood outside the door for a moment, filled with sudden apprehension, and took a deep breath to steady himself before going inside.

Elizabeth was leaning over their son, and she glanced around as Ned hurried to the bedside. 'He's feverish,' she murmured, smoothing the boy's red-gold hair away from his damp forehead, 'and exhausted from this frightful coughing.'

Edward moved closer and squeezed her shoulder, wanting to reassure her. When he leaned over the child himself, he was shocked, disturbed when he saw his son's appearance. The child looked as though he was burning up with fever and his blue eyes were glazed. Beads of sweat stood out on his face and Edward was more alarmed than ever, realizing that his son did not even recognize him.

He turned to his wife, asked quietly, 'Don't we have any cough medicine in the house? Surely there's something? Somewhere?'

'We gave it to him already, Ned, but I was afraid of giving him too much, over-dosing him. It is rather a strong syrup. Your mother then remembered the raspberry vinegar concoction she used to make for you and your brothers. She went downstairs to explain to Cook how to prepare it. She said she gave it to you when you were a child.'

'That's true. It's made of raspberry vinegar, butter and sugar, all boiled, and like a lot of those old remedies from the past it seems to work very well.'

'I hope so.'

Looking over at the bed, Edward remarked in a low voice,

'I think he'd feel better propped up against the pillows, rather than lying flat. It might help him, ease the congestion in his chest, if he were sitting up.'

Without waiting for her response, Edward gently brought their child closer to him, wrapping his arms around him, and said to his wife, 'Please move the pillows, Elizabeth, lean them against the headboard.'

She did so without a word; he placed the boy against them, kissed his forehead and straightened the bedclothes.

Edward looked towards the door as it opened to admit his mother, who was carrying a tray. Cecily Deravenel exclaimed, 'I'm relieved you're here, Ned,' and immediately put the tray down on a chest of drawers. 'I'm going to try and get him to take this syrup of mine. I also found another medicine downstairs that might be helpful as well.

It's that Creopin mixture, for inhaling. I bought it in London recently.'

'Is Creopin better than Friar's Balsam, do you think, Mother?'

'I'm not sure, Ned, we'll ask the doctor when he gets here,' Cecily replied, and began to attend to her grandson, spooning the raspberry mixture into his mouth.

After a moment, Edward touched Elizabeth's arm and whispered, 'Let's go outside for a moment, darling.' Taking her arm, he guided her to the door. Once they were in the corridor alone, he pulled her into his arms and held her close, stroking her hair. Against her cheek, he said, 'Do try not to worry. We'll get him well, Elizabeth, I promise.'

'Do you promise me that, Ned?'

'Oh, I do, Elizabeth, I do promise you he'll soon be as right as rain.'

Elizabeth let her body relax against his, comforted by his presence, his warmth and his love. When it came to his children's welfare she trusted him implicitly. Also, Ned's self-assurance, his confidence in himself, his belief that he could control everyone and everything had always made her feel safe. Some thought these characteristics reflected his arrogance. She knew otherwise; and no one knew him better than she did.

THREE

'**M**r Deravenel wishes me to take you upstairs straight away, sir,' Jessup explained to the doctor, after putting his hat and coat in the hall cupboard. 'If you'll come this way, please.'

'Thank you, Jessup,' Peter Leighton answered, and followed swiftly on the heels of the butler, crossing the Long Hall to the grand staircase.

Before they had reached the nursery floor, Edward, who had heard their voices, was standing at the top of the stairs, impatiently waiting for them.

'Good morning, Dr Leighton,' he exclaimed at the sight of the doctor, and added, 'Thank you, Jessup.' With a brief nod Edward dismissed the butler, who hurried off down the stairs.

As the doctor stepped onto the landing, he thrust out his hand and shook Edward's. 'Good morning, Mr Deravenel. So, Young Edward's poorly, is he?'

'Yes. My wife thinks it's Spanish flu. He's got a fever, a hacking cough. Earlier, there were flecks of blood in his hand-kerchief, my wife tells me. As you can imagine, we're extremely worried. I can only add that we are very glad you happen to be staying with the Dunbars this weekend, so close to us.'

'Very fortuitous indeed,' Dr Leighton answered, then asked, 'How are the other children? Are they showing any signs of infection?'

'No, they're not, but I would like you to see them, once you've seen Young Edward.'

'Of course, of course, that's understood, Mr Deravenel.' Dr Leighton gave Edward a smile of encouragement and continued, 'I'm afraid Spanish flu is extremely virulent, as no doubt you know from the newspapers and the radio, but it hasn't been striking down children or the elderly, as flu usually does. This new strain appears to infect young adults mainly. Mostly young men between twenty and thirty. As I parked my car in the stable yard just now, I noticed your brother, and I should point out that *he* could be a candidate for this particular virus. I think I ought to take a look at him also before I leave.' Then the doctor finished, almost under his breath, 'Unfortunately there seems to be no remedy for Spanish flu. No one knows how to treat it.'

Observing the look of apprehension crossing Edward's face, the doctor took his arm and murmured, 'Look here, there's no point in my beating about the bush, Mr Deravenel, you have to know the facts. But let us hope your little son has not contracted this terrible illness and that he either has a very bad cold or bronchitis. They're bad enough, I know, but at least they are treatable. *And curable.*'

'I understand, and please don't apologize for telling me the truth. However unpalatable the truth might be, I prefer to hear the worst, so that I know what I'm dealing with. I hate surprises. Let's go to Young Edward's room shall we? You can examine him and then check on the rest of the brood.'

When they entered the bedroom a moment later, Elizabeth and Cecily turned around, politely greeted the doctor and then stepped away from the bedside.

'I shall go along and look in on the other children,' Cecily announced. 'Give you a little breathing space in here, Dr Leighton.'

The doctor nodded, offered her a grateful smile as Cecily slipped out; Elizabeth moved closer to her husband, who was standing near the door of the bedroom, took hold of his arm, leaned into him.

Elizabeth explained to the doctor, 'The coughing seems to have abated, Dr Leighton, since my mother-in-law managed to spoon down a raspberry vinegar mixture.'

Peter Leighton glanced at her and nodded. 'It's often those old-fashioned remedies that work the best, you know.' As he spoke he took a stethoscope out of his medical bag, bent over Young Edward, noting at once that the boy was feverish and had a glazed look. He listened to his chest, then put a thermometer in his mouth, held it there for a few seconds.

After reading the thermometer, he said, 'His temperature *is* a bit high, but that's to be expected. I'm going to turn him over, Mrs Deravenel. I want to check his lungs.'

'Do you need my help, Doctor?' she asked, her eyes pinned on the doctor, a worried expression on her face.

'No, no, there's no problem.' Dr Leighton laid the little boy on his side, lifted his pyjama top and put the stethoscope on his back, listening acutely. A moment or two later he repositioned the child, and covered him with the bedclothes. After opening his mouth gently, the doctor used a wooden tongue depressor to look down Young Edward's throat.

Finally straightening, and turning to Edward and Elizabeth, Dr Leighton said, with some relief, 'He has bronchitis. It's not Spanish flu.'

Elizabeth put a trembling hand to her mouth and swallowed back a sob. She looked up at Edward, sudden tears of relief glistening on her blonde lashes, and attempted to smile at him without much success.

'You're certain?' Edward said softly.

'I am, Mr Deravenel. He has all the symptoms. Let me explain. Bronchitis causes obstruction to the flow of air in and out of the lungs, and interferes with the exchange of oxygen between the lungs and the blood, hence the hacking cough. The airways are continuously inflamed and diseased, and are filled with mucus. And sometimes, after a fit of coughing, flecks of blood appear in the mucus, from the strain of coughing. I'm going to telephone the chemist in Scarborough and prescribe an excellent cough mixture, as well as an expectorant and a fever powder which will help bring down the fever. The chemist will send his son up to Ravenscar with the medications. In the meantime, you can continue to give him the raspberry vinegar mixture until you have the cough syrup.'

'Thank you, Dr Leighton. Now, what else should we do for him?' Elizabeth asked.

'Keep him warm, but not hot. Aim for an even temperature, and let him rest quietly. Give him plenty of liquids, particularly beef tea and chicken broth – warm liquids are best,' the doctor explained.

Edward cleared his throat, looked over at the doctor and said, 'What about food? What should we feed him?'

'I don't think he's going to feel very hungry, Mr Deravenel, but if he is, you should give him very light things . . . fruit jellies, rice pudding, sago pudding, blancmange, custard, calf's foot jelly, soft boiled eggs, or scrambled eggs, things like that which are easily digested. And easily swallowed, obviously, since his throat is somewhat inflamed.' After glancing again at Young Edward, the doctor picked up his medical bag and led the Deravenels out of the room.

'I think someone should stay with the boy in order to tend to his needs,' Dr Leighton now informed them. 'I know you would prefer to be there yourself, Mrs Deravenel, but frankly you are extremely pale and appear over-tired to me. You need a rest, you know, we can't be having you getting sick. What about Ada, the young woman who assists Nanny? She has always seemed rather efficient to me.'

'Ada *is* good, but Nanny can manage on her own, I'm sure of that.' Elizabeth smiled for the first time that day as she added, 'And nine-year-old Bess has become quite the mother hen these days, so she can keep an eye on her little sisters. Also, the maternity nurse is still with us, looking after the new baby. We are well covered, Dr Leighton.'

'Excellent. Now, why don't we go along to the nursery, Mrs Deravenel? So that I can examine the other children.'

FOUR

Cecily Watkins Deravenel sat alone in the library. She had positioned herself on one of the large, comfortable, over-stuffed sofas near the fireplace, and was enjoying a cup of coffee, thinking about her little grandson. Everyone called him Young Edward, in order to differentiate between him and his father, but in her mind he would forever be Neddie. That was how she had always thought of him since he was born. He was the spitting image of his father when Ned had been a little boy.

He was such a beautiful child, her little Neddie . . . a Botticelli angel, with his red-gold curls and blue eyes, so bright and sparkling and full of laughter. He was a happy little scamp, but he had been rather late in arriving, this heir to the Deravenel empire, the fourth child after his three sisters, Bess, Mary, and Cecily (who had been named for her).

He was only five years old, having celebrated his birthday in early November, but there were times when he expressed himself so well she often thought she was talking to a much older child.

Cecily was filled with relief that he was not suffering from the dreaded Spanish flu. Bronchitis was bad enough; on the other hand, she had never heard of anyone dying of that disease. Yet people were dropping like flies all over the world, once they became stricken with this new strain of the flu virus. The newspapers were now saying that more people were dying of the flu than had been killed in the War.

At this moment the doctor was upstairs examining the other children; but she was certain none of them was ill. She had just spent the last twenty minutes with them in the nursery playroom, and they were boisterous, happy, and laughing, as they played with their toys. Yes, they were all very well indeed, including Richard, who was two years old, and Anne, the baby, born a few months ago. The latest arrival.

Her son might not find his wife Elizabeth a true soulmate, or even a companionable woman to be with – God knows, he spent as little time as possible with her – but he was obviously still attracted to her physically. Elizabeth seemingly held a tremendous allure for him when it came to their marital bed. Six children already, and Cecily felt sure there would be more to come in the not-too-distant future.

Although Cecily Deravenel had never liked her daughter-in-law, she had always acknowledged her great beauty. Some said Elizabeth was the most beautiful woman in all of England, with her silver-gilt hair that fell half-way down her back to her waist, her crystal clear, sky-blue eyes and that incomparable pink-and-white complexion which was without blemish.

She was thirty-eight now, and yet Elizabeth did not show her age: there was no sagging chin; no wrinkles; no crow's feet around her eyes. Furthermore, her figure was still perfect, had hardly changed in the eleven years she had been married to Edward. Everyone wondered how she did it, including Cecily herself.

The problem with Elizabeth Wyland Deravenel was her character. Right from the beginning Cecily had understood that her daughter-in-law was ambitious for herself and her family – and there were scores of *them*, as Cecily knew only too well. There was an arrogance inherent in her personality, and she was a snob. Cecily was well aware that her eldest son knew she had never believed Elizabeth Wyland was good enough for him. As Richard had once said, with great acerbity, 'She's not good enough to lick Ned's boots, Mother.' Richard was far too intelligent for the likes of Elizabeth. He had seen right through her from the start, and had detected her jealousy of him instantly. Richard knew she thoroughly resented his relationship with his eldest brother, was eaten up because he was Edward's favourite and his most trusted ally.

It was true, her daughter-in-law did have an extraordinarily jealous nature, and was constantly confronting Edward with rather vile and vulgar gossip about him, announcing that she knew all about his affairs with other women.

Cecily sighed to herself. Being nobody's fool, she had long ago acknowledged that her son adored women. At the same time, he was not the unmitigated womanizer his wife made him out to be. Not these days. In fact, as far as Cecily knew, and she was well-informed about everyone in the family, Edward only had one woman friend at the moment. This was Jane Shaw, a divorcee, who had been part of his life for a long time. Cecily understood that Edward was the kind of man who genuinely needed companionship from a woman, and Jane supplied this.

Will Hasling, Edward's best friend and a particular favourite of hers, knew Jane well, and he had always spoken kindly about her to Cecily, had convinced her that Jane was not ambitious, nor angling for marriage with Edward, that she was perfectly content to be his friend. And friends they were, apparently, enjoying a shared love of music, the theatre and art.

If Elizabeth were smarter, she would keep her mouth shut and stop berating Edward about non-existent affairs, Cecily suddenly thought. Knowing men the way she did, being unjustly accused generally pushed an innocent man into the arms of the first available woman. She's such a fool . . .

Letting her thoughts drift off, Cecily turned around at the sound of footsteps, and stood up when Peter Leighton came into the library, followed by Edward and Richard.

'I'm assuming that all of my other grandchildren are perfectly all right,' Cecily exclaimed, smiling at the young doctor.

'Indeed they are, Mrs Deravenel. I would even go so far as to say they are in blooming health. And, I must add, they are the most beautiful children I've ever seen.'

'Thank you, Doctor,' she responded.

Richard, moving forward, hurrying towards his mother, announced, 'Dr Leighton says I'm very fit, in great health.'

'I'm glad to hear it,' Cecily answered warmly.

Edward murmured, 'Elizabeth won't be coming down to lunch, Mother. She's exhausted herself, mostly with worry, I think. Anyway, Dr Leighton insisted she went to bed.'

'I quite understand, Ned.' Glancing at the clock on the mantelpiece, Cecily addressed Peter Leighton. 'I don't suppose I can coax you into staying for lunch, since I know you're houseguesting with the Dunbars. But perhaps you will partake of something – coffee or tea? Perhaps sherry?'

'You're so kind, Mrs Deravenel, but I won't, thank you very much. I must be getting along. The roads were icy this morning, and what is normally a fifteen-minute run in my motorcar took me forty minutes. So I'm sure you do understand that I must be setting off if I'm to arrive at The Lodge in time for lunch.'

'Yes, I do, Dr Leighton, and thank you so much for coming so promptly.'

'I shall return tomorrow, to check on Young Edward. In the meantime, Thomas Sloane, the chemist in Scarborough, is preparing the medicines, and as I just told Mr Deravenel you should receive them soon. He's sending his son Albert in the van. But do use the raspberry vinegar mixture if the boy is coughing excessively.'

'I will, and thank you again, Dr Leighton.'

Cecily shook his hand, as did Richard, and then Edward escorted him out into the Long Hall.

Richard sat down opposite his mother, and explained, 'Dr Leighton only gave me an examination because he was worried –'

'You look very well to me, Richard,' Cecily cut in with a frown.

'Yes, I know, and I *am* perfectly well. Seemingly young men between the ages of twenty and thirty are those most likely to catch Spanish flu. He thought I could easily be a candidate because of my age, that's all it was about.'

Cecily peered across at Richard. 'You don't have any symptoms, do you?'

'No, I don't. The doctor was merely being his usual efficient self.'

'I understand. I really do like Peter Leighton, and I was delighted when he took over Dr Rayne's practice. He's young and intelligent and caring. His methods are very *modern*, and he's most up-to-date with the latest advances. I approve of his approach.'

Edward walked in, a broad smile on his face. 'I was so glad to hear the clatter of pots and pans in the kitchen a moment ago. Earlier this morning, when I came back from my ride, the house was ghastly, so quiet, and the total silence rather eerie. In fact, Jessup just told me that Cook was most upset about Young Edward, hence the gloomy atmosphere in her domain. According to Jessup, none of the other staff were allowed to speak.'

'I know she can be quite a tartar at times,' Cecily murmured.

Walking across to the drinks tray which stood on a chest-of-drawers, Edward poured himself a glass of pale Amontillado sherry. Then went and stood in front of the French doors, staring out at the gardens and the sea beyond, lost in thought.

His mother said, 'Ned?'

'Yes, Mother, what is it?' He swung around to face her, his blond brows arching.

'It's the fourteenth of December today. Only ten days left until Christmas. I do think we ought to *consider* cancelling the festivities we've planned. Bronchitis lasts several weeks, even longer –'

'I'm not going to *consider* cancelling. I've already decided to cancel. *Immediately*. It must be done today. That will give the guests we were expecting some time to make other plans . . . well, hopefully. After lunch, I'll telephone Will, also Vicky and Stephen. They're like family and will understand. I'd better have a word with George, also.'

'*George!*' Richard exclaimed, gaping at his brother. He was thunderstruck. 'You didn't tell me you'd invited George, Ned. *How could you?*'

'I didn't. George invited himself and you know what our brother is like. And he also said that he was bringing Isabel and the children.'

'Why didn't you tell him he couldn't come for Christmas?' Richard cried irately, his pale face unexpectedly flushed.

Edward was totally silent.

'You know how upset I've been with him, and so has Anne. The way he treated her and blocked our engagement was appalling!' Richard shook his head. 'I don't want to see him. Or Isabel, for that matter. She plays along with him.'

'She's weak,' Ned muttered. 'She dare not oppose him in anything.'

'It was my idea,' Cecily interjected very softly, staring at Richard.

'*Why?*' Richard demanded, his voice rising. 'In God's name *why*? George has treated me most abominably these last few years.'

'I hoped you would both make up this Christmas, be friends again, loving brothers, the way you used to be.'

Laughing hollowly, Richard snapped, 'I wouldn't trust him as far as I could throw him, Mother.'

'He's your brother,' she answered.

'Tell *him* that!'

When she remained quiet, Richard continued in an angry tone, 'You always did stick up for him, even when he was a boy. And a mother's boy at that! Always clinging pathetically to your skirts, throwing himself at you, and hiding behind your skirts when he had committed some nasty little prank. You protected him then, and *I'll* never understand why.'

Cecily shook her head, and her voice broke slightly as she tried to explain. 'There was something about him that made *me* feel *he* needed protection. In a peculiar way, I was always a bit afraid for him, he always seemed so vulnerable . . .' Her voice trailed off.

'*Vulnerable*. That's a laugh.' Richard now turned to Edward, stared at him. 'George *betrayed* you, Ned. Not once, but many times. He went over to Neville's side, after Neville and you quarrelled. He entangled himself in Neville's plans to go along with Louis Charpentier and make a bid for Deravenels. And he fell for Neville's idea of putting *him* in *your* place. George thought he could *usurp* you. *His brother*. And then he married Isabel when he knew you were against it. If those are not betrayals then I don't know the meaning of that word.'

'It's all my fault, really it is, Richard,' Cecily said slowly, wanting to placate. 'Don't be angry with Ned. I am the one who begged Ned to forgive George for his transgressions, because I wanted to heal the family, make it whole again. I wanted to show the world a united front. We are a famous family, Richard dear. *We are the Deravenels*. I did not want to expose us to ugly gossip, tittle-tattle on the streets.'

'Didn't *I* matter then?' Richard asked, wonderingly, gazing at his mother. '*My* feelings weren't to be considered?' He looked from his mother to Ned. 'You know he betrayed you, and that

I have always stood by your side no matter what. My loyalty binds me. And yet you permitted George to block my marriage to Anne, which caused us great pain.'

Edward answered swiftly, adopting a cajoling tone. 'Because you were both so young I believed I had time to work things out with George. He was creating numerous problems, more serious than you'll ever know. Look, getting to the essence of it, he was demanding all of Neville's fortune because Isabel was the eldest daughter. He didn't want Anne to share in it, that's why he tried to block the marriage – because he knew you would fight for Anne's rights.'

'It's always about money or power with George, isn't it, Ned?'

'Too true. However, because you agreed to wait, I did manage to hammer out a deal with George, a deal you would accept. Let's not forget, I did get Anne her fair share of Neville's estate, Richard.'

'It was an iron-clad will, if I remember correctly,' Richard shot back. 'Neville Watkins never left anything to chance. Never made mistakes like that! And I also happen to know that the entire estate was actually left to Nan Watkins. Neville wanted his wife to have everything, and only after her death were the girls to receive their share.'

'I know that, Richard,' Ned replied in the same conciliatory voice. 'I had to enlist Nan's help, although you perhaps don't know this. I also had to give George a very handsome financial settlement, a huge amount, out of my own money, actually, in order to solve the problem finally.'

'I see.' Richard sat back, his expression still one of anger.

'And you did marry Anne,' Cecily pointed out in a quiet voice.

'Practically in secret, here at Ravenscar. A tiny wedding ceremony, with no guests except the immediate family,' Richard answered grimly, shaking his head. 'I just don't understand why it is that George has to be accommodated all the time. I really don't. And personally I think he's crazy. Let's not forget our cousin Henry Grant, who spent a lot of time in lunatic asylums . . .'

Ned threw back his head and guffawed, looked amused. 'Oh, Richard, that's a beauty! Are you suggesting that the bad genes carried by Henry Deravenel Grant of Lancaster might well be inherent in the Deravenels of Yorkshire, the true heirs of Guy de Ravenel? The *real* Deravenels, as we say about ourselves.'

If Edward had hoped Richard would see the joke he was wrong. His youngest brother shook his head, the grim expression making his mouth taut. 'I think George is crackers. Just consider the daft things he does at times . . . then you'll see what I mean.'

'Richard, really, I don't believe that is a very nice thing to say about George. He can be very kind, and he does mean well,' Cecily answered.

No, he doesn't, Richard thought, but said, 'If you say so, Mother. Let's close the discussion about George, shall we?'

Ned said, 'I am going to cancel the Christmas festivities, Dick, but if you and Anne wish to come for Christmas you know how much we'd love that, wouldn't we, Mother?'

'Of course. I haven't seen my grandson for ages. Perhaps Nan Watkins would like to come as well, rather than staying alone in Ripon.'

'I doubt that very much, Mother,' Richard said softly. 'She doesn't like to come to Ravenscar anymore, so I am led to understand. It reminds her of her tragic loss. After all, her beloved husband and her favourite brother-in-law Johnny met their deaths here.'

FIVE

London

'Why don't you tell him about the house, Ned? He really ought to know the true story, the full story.'

Edward Deravenel sat back in his chair, and regarded Will Hasling, his best friend. He and Will had been boon companions for many years, and colleagues at Deravenels for fourteen, ever since Edward had become managing director. And he trusted Will as he trusted no other man, except for his brother Richard.

Loyaulté Me Lie, loyalty binds me: That was Richard's adopted motto and he was ever faithful to it.

It was Richard they were talking about this morning, facing each other across Edward's desk, in his office at Deravenels.

'I never wanted to go into all the details,' Edward explained, 'about the house. Don't you think it would look strange? What I mean is, don't you think it could appear that I'm boasting about all the things I've done for him over the years? Signalling that he's obligated to me, perhaps?'

'He might think that, but frankly I rather doubt it,' Will answered, shaking his head emphatically. 'No, no, it won't look that way at all. It's ridiculous to even think that, Ned. And he *should* know. And once he understands everything, he won't continue to harbour a grudge and think that you put George before him . . . that is, *if* he does think that.'

'Actually, you're quite right, Will. I'll be frank with him.'

'Would you like *me* to explain the way things are?'

Edward couldn't help laughing. 'You know, that had crossed my mind, but I quickly dismissed the idea as being somewhat silly, since I haven't done anything wrong, quite the contrary, in fact.'

Continuing to chuckle to himself, Edward Deravenel pushed himself to his feet, walked across the floor to one of the tall windows, glanced down at the Strand, thinking how congested with traffic it was today. But then it was the Wednesday before Christmas, and London was busier than ever. This was the first festive Christmas in four years, now that the War was finally over. People were determined to celebrate, to have a good time, to rejoice that peace had come at last.

Christmas for his family was going to be exceptionally quiet at Ravenscar, but he didn't mind. He rather welcomed it, if the truth be known. He had cancelled all of the invitations which had been sent to friends, and everyone had understood his dilemma, understood that he was endeavouring to protect Young Edward. And them as well. Only George had been truculent, as usual. Quite vile, actually.

Turning around, Edward strolled back to the centre of the floor and stood there for a few seconds, a reflective expression settling on his handsome face.

Finally, glancing at Will, he said, very softly, 'The upset this past weekend was really my mother's fault, Will, in a sense. Her desire to unite the family does seem to cloud her normal good judgement. She simply can't accept that Richard cannot stand George anymore, or that Elizabeth detests him because he and Neville Watkins were responsible for the ruination of her father and brother. She would rather see George burning in hell than entertain him at Ravenscar. Unfortunately, my mother appears to brush everything to one side, keeps harping on about forgiving and forgetting, letting bygones by bygones. Because we are a family.' He shook his head sadly, and finished in a Cockney accent, 'That ain't the way it is, me old mate, now is it?'

'No. And George has always been Elizabeth's enemy since your marriage. He loathes her as much as she loathes him . . .' Will's voice trailed off. There was no point in reminding Edward that people disliked his wife. Very beautiful she might be, but she was not a very nice woman. Her ambition for her family knew no bounds. She had inveigled Edward into giving several of her brothers positions at Deravenels, and Anthony Wyland, her favourite, played a powerful role in the company these days. But this brother he liked, knew him to be a decent man, talented, and worthy of respect.

After a moment's silence between them, Edward changed the subject, remarked in a more buoyant voice, 'Jarvis Merson's been in touch with me. Yesterday evening. He's after us to start up again in Persia. Drilling for oil. In Southern Persia, to be exact. He wants us to buy another concession from the Shah. Because we're doing so well in Louisiana, he thinks we should begin expanding, now that the war is over.'

Sitting down behind his desk, Edward continued, 'It's not the right time, I know that, Will. However, I have decided to create a company, so that we're ready to go ahead when things are right in the world, once we have all recovered from this awful Spanish flu pandemic, and recouped from the War –'

'I agree it's too soon to think about oil in Persia,' Will interjected, leaning forward intently. 'There's far too much turmoil everywhere. I'm convinced we have to sit it out for the whole of this coming year. First, let's get through 1919, and then seriously consider drilling for oil in mid-1920. I believe that's when we should take the plunge. *Not before.* I know you've always had an odd rather compelling belief in Jarvis, and so do I, actually. He's proved himself a thousandfold with the creation of the Louisiana oil fields, so I don't doubt that he's probably right about Southern Persia. On the other hand, Ned, I've lately heard that some of the top brass at Standard Oil, and also Henri Deterding of Shell, don't fancy Southern Persia at all, don't believe there are *any* strikes to be made there. I do trust Deterding's judgement – he's a great oil man.'

'I've heard the same stories. However, I do trust Jarvis's nose for oil. He and his new partner, Herb Lipson, are an unbeatable team, in my opinion. Anyway, as I just said, I aim to start a new company. I want to be ready. I'm thinking of calling it Deravco. How does that sound to you?'

Will grinned. 'Sounds like an oil company to me. And it's short. And sweet, let's hope.'

There was a sudden loud knock on the door; Edward glanced across the room and called, 'Come in.' He immediately jumped up, a wide smile flashing across his face when he saw his brother in the doorway.

'There you are, Richard!' he cried enthusiastically. Grabbing Richard by the shoulders, he smothered him in a bear hug. 'Did you get my message about lunch?'

'I did. That's why I came down to your office, to find out what time you wish to leave,' Richard answered.

'Pick me up at twelve forty-five and we'll walk across to the Savoy Hotel,' Ned said.

When Richard and Will left his office, Edward sat for a few minutes, going through the papers on his desk. After perusing them conscientiously, and making notes on a pad, he sat back in the chair and stared out into the room.

His mind went to the oil business in Southern Persia, and he felt a little rush of genuine excitement. He had always believed that oil was the business of the future; he wanted Deravenels to own more than their stake in Louisiana, and Merson was just the man to make his dream come true. He had believed in Jarvis from the day he had met that bright if rather talkative young man. And he had been proven right in his assessment of him.

Yesterday, when he had been meeting with Alfredo Oliveri to talk about the marble quarries in Italy, Oliveri had suggested they look farther afield, perhaps investigate the quarries in Turkey.

Swivelling around in his chair, Edward gazed at the map which hung on the wall behind him. His father's map of the world, with all its little numbers written in so neatly. There was Persia sitting right next to Turkey. Perhaps they could kill two birds with one stone. He and Oliveri could go to Turkey to see about marble and then move on to Persia to see about oil.

Not yet, of course. Alfredo had pointed that out most vociferously. Europe was still in upheaval and disarray, and it was not possible to pursue the idea of buying Turkish marble quarries until travelling became much easier. And, as he and Will had just agreed, the same reasoning applied to oil.

Just the prospect of these trips gave him a boost, helped to dispel some of the irritation he was feeling about his brother George.

Opening his engagement book, Edward looked at the notations he had made in them last week. Always methodical, he wrote in his lunch date with Richard, and then frowned. He had arranged to see Jane tonight. For dinner. And he still had to buy a gift for her.

Today was the eighteenth, exactly one week from Christmas Day, and on Friday afternoon he was taking the train back to York and then driving out to Ravenscar. Tomorrow he had the private luncheon for his close friends in the company, a lunch he always gave across the street at Rules. Tomorrow night he was dining with Vicky and Stephen Firth. He had already bought their Christmas gifts, and also one for Grace Rose.

His lovely Grace Rose, growing more like him than ever, and

already almost eighteen. *Eighteen,* he muttered under his breath, and he wondered where all the years had gone.

Because of his plans for the rest of the week, he had no alternative but to find a present for Jane *today.* After his lunch with Richard he would go to one of the fine jewellers. She loved emeralds, and that was what he would get her . . . emerald earrings or an emerald brooch.

As he flipped through the pages of his engagement book, Edward suddenly realized with a sense of dismay that he would be in Yorkshire for almost ten days. *Ten days.* Rather a long time to be ensconced with Elizabeth. Perhaps there was a way he could rectify that. Just as he had managed to rectify the problem of George and the private luncheon tomorrow. He had not wanted him to come. Once he had cancelled the invitation for George and his family to visit Ravenscar for Christmas because of Young Edward's illness, George had behaved in his usual spoilt way. He had thrown a tantrum. To quiet George down, placate him, he had suggested that his brother should go to Scotland to represent him at a business meeting.

Edward smiled to himself, a smile that also held a hint of smugness. The ploy had worked. George had jumped at the chance to wheel and deal with the Scottish tycoon, Ian MacDonald. Good riddance, he thought, rather pleased with himself, and then got up, went to the cupboard on the other side of the room. Opening the double doors, he stepped inside and began to turn the dial of his safe, until it finally clicked open. Taking out a slim folder of papers, he closed the safe door and locked it.

A clean slate next year, he reminded himself. I want a clean slate next year. I've a lot of changes to make.

Richard and Edward sat opposite each other in the handsomely decorated Grill Room of the Savoy Hotel. After toasting each other with their flutes of Krug champagne, they had looked at the menus and ordered.

They had both chosen Colchester oysters, to be followed by steak-and-kidney pie, having similar tastes in food, as well as in other things. They shared a love of fine clothing, although Richard was much more conservative than his brother.

They enjoyed talking about books, English politics, and the coverage given to world events by the daily newspapers. They saw eye-to-eye on almost everything, because Edward had raised Richard after their father had been murdered in Italy, and he had imbued in the younger boy a love of justice and fair play.

Like Edward, Richard was a compassionate man who understood the pain and suffering of others, and was empathetic to their plight. Ned had favoured Richard since his childhood, spoilt him, made him feel special, and he had protected him in every way. And so naturally he was Edward's loyal ally, and defender, whenever that was necessary. Richard admired Ned, adored him.

The two brothers settled back in their chairs and sipped this finest and most expensive of all French champagnes. After a moment or two of silence, Edward leaned forward. 'Look, Dick, there's something I want to tell –'

Interrupting him swiftly, Richard exclaimed, 'Before you say anything, I must apologize, Ned. I was wrong to quarrel with you about George, last Saturday. I've no excuse really, except to say that I let my hurt feelings get the better of me. I'm so very sorry.'

'There's nothing to apologize for, Little Fish,' Edward murmured, affection ringing his face.

The use of this pet name from his childhood brought a smile to Richard's mouth, and he suddenly began to laugh. 'I'm a bit too old to be called Little Fish, don't you think, Ned?'

His brother joined in his laughter, then answered, 'No, because you're only twenty-two, my boy. However, it *was* my fault, truly.

I should have put my foot down when Mother asked me to permit him to come, after he had actually invited himself. I was indulging her need to bring harmony to the family.'

'I know. And I promise I will be quite *still* tomorrow at the luncheon . . . I won't say a word.'

'George is not coming to the luncheon.'

'Why not?' Richard sounded and looked surprised.

'He's going away this afternoon. In fact, as we speak he's boarding the train. He's on his way to Scotland.'

'Why?'

'I asked him to represent me at the meeting in Edinburgh which I had set up for this coming Friday. With Ian MacDonald, regarding his liquor empire. As you know, Ian has no heirs, and he approached me about a takeover some time ago. I'd actually made a firm date with him but cancelled two days ago, on Monday. I used the excuse of Young Edward's illness, not wanting to be away from him, etcetera, etcetera. I proposed George as my stand-in. Ian was a bit disappointed at first, but in the end he was all right with it. After all, George *is* a Deravenel.'

He doesn't always behave like one, Richard thought, although he did not voice this, remained silent, listening carefully to Edward.

'I then had a word with George –' Edward went on.

'And he agreed? Just like that?' Richard interrupted snapping his fingers together, giving his brother a doubtful look.

'He did,' Edward answered. 'Because I offered him an inducement that truly appealed to him. Actually, the offer was one George genuinely could not refuse.'

'And what was it?'

'*Money*. George's favourite commodity. I said he would earn a large bonus from the company if he managed to make the deal with Ian MacDonald, a deal which has to favour Deravenels.'

'And so you really want the MacDonald liquor business?' Richard sat back.

Edward shrugged, and there was a moment's pause before he replied, 'Well, yes, I suppose I do.'

'George could easily blow it, you know, if he mishandles the situation. He can be extremely volatile in negotiations.'

'I know that, and if he does, he does. As far as I'm concerned, the deal can go either way and I won't lose any sleep over it. Or the final outcome. The main thing is that I've got George out of my hair for the rest of this week, and also for Christmas.'

'What do you mean by *for Christmas*?' Richard asked, his voice puzzled.

'Ian had invited me to stay on in Scotland for Christmas. He wanted me to take the family up to his country estate for the holidays. I'd refused politely, because I had invited a number of people to join us at Ravenscar. Then, when I spoke to Ian on Monday I asked him if he would invite George and his family, because I had had to cancel the Christmas festivities due to Young Edward's illness.'

'And MacDonald agreed?'

'He did indeed. He is widowed, and his only child, his daughter, has three little girls ... I think when he invited my lot he was hoping to create a happy holiday atmosphere at his house in the Lammermuir Hills. So yes, he welcomed the idea of George and his family. I can be very persuasive.'

'We all know that, Ned.' Richard hesitated, opened his mouth to say something, and then stopped abruptly.

Edward looked at him alertly, and asked, 'What is it?'

'I was going to say once again that you *are* putting the deal at risk.'

'I'm fully aware of that.' A smile spread across Edward's face and he added, 'The deal is not particularly crucial to Deravenels, Dick. I wouldn't mind having Ian's liquor company, because it flows beautifully into our wine business. However, the main consideration was to remove George for the moment.'

Richard nodded, and looked off into the distance for a split second before saying, sotto voce, 'George has not gone off to Scotland so happily just because you've promised him a large bonus. He's a glutton for power, and you've just given him a big dose of it . . . by making him your representative.'

'Good point, Richard. But let's move on, shall we? As I mentioned earlier, I've something to tell you – I'd like to be done with it before lunch is served, if you don't mind.'

Richard merely nodded, wondering what was coming next.

'Two years ago, after you and Anne were married, Nan Watkins gave you a gift. Am I not correct?'

'You're talking about the deeds to Neville's house in Chelsea, aren't you?'

'It was never Neville's house, Richard. It was always Nan's house. Oh, he bought it right enough, and with his own money, but he actually bought it for Nan. He gifted it to her immediately, and the deeds are in her name, not his.' When Richard didn't speak, Ned asked, 'Well, they are because I saw them myself. Nan showed them to me.'

Richard sighed. 'Nan gave the deeds to Anne, and she merely glanced at them, and showed me Nan's letter. Then she put the déeds away.'

'So you never saw them?'

'No. Why? Does it matter? After all, Nan gave us the house.'

'No, she didn't, Richard. I gave you the house.'

Startled, Richard exclaimed, 'What do you mean?'

'Just before you were married, actually quite a few months before, I went to see Nan Watkins. I told her I wanted to purchase the Chelsea house from her because I wanted to give it to you and Anne. At first she didn't want to sell. She had actually had the same idea, and was going to give it to you both as a wedding present. However, I pointed out one thing to her, and it was this – that George, being the way he is, so dreadfully greedy, might object if she gave the house to you and Anne. I mentioned that he might actually try to get it away from you, by reminding her that Isabel and Anne are the joint heirs to Neville's estate after her death. And, therefore, Isabel was part owner of the house by rights.'

'You're correct, Ned! He could have done that! He's certainly capable of it, devious enough. And avaricious, as you say. So how did you persuade her to sell it to *you*?' Richard asked swiftly, filled with curiosity.

'I managed to convince Nan. As I reminded her, *my* knowledge of *George* is far greater than anyone else's in this entire world. I also explained that I would buy the house for you and Anne, so that George could never get his hands on it, and that she could still give it to you, as if it were her present to you both.'

'That was a nice gesture, Ned, and obviously she accepted. But I wonder why? Why didn't she tell us the truth at the time? That would have been more honest, wouldn't it?'

'I'm afraid I'm guilty again. I convinced her to say *she* was giving you the house, and to hand you the deeds Neville had presented to her years ago, so that everything would appear quite normal to you. And, of course, to George. In order to completely forestall George, in case he tried to make any trouble for you and Anne later, I had Nan's solicitors and mine draw up additional documents – a bill of sale, new deeds in my name, and a third legal document which gifts the house to you outright.'

'Do you mean you have given it to *us, Anne and me*, or actually to *me*?'

'Only to you, Richard. I couldn't take any chances. I didn't want Anne's name on any legal documents. In other words, I bought the house from Nan Watkins, and then, as the new legal owner, I gave it to a third party. All very legal. Essentially, what it did do was cut Anne and Isabel out, because I had bought it from their mother, who had every right to sell, because it was *hers*, not part of Neville's estate.'

For a moment Richard sat there in silence, looking slightly stunned.

Smiling, Edward took the thin folder he had removed from the safe, and handed it to Richard. 'Here are the deeds to your house. They would have always been secure with me, but I decided you ought to have them. After all, the house is yours.'

'You didn't give them to me before because you were protecting Nan, weren't you?'

'I suppose so . . . I didn't want to take the credit away from her. In a sense, she was only the innocent bystander, and she had wanted to give you the house anyway.'

Richard had taken the folder and he held it tightly for a moment, looking at it. But he did not open it. He put it on the floor next to his chair and then sat gazing at his brother, at a loss for words. Finally, he said softly, 'Thank you, Ned. You're the best brother any man could have.'

'And so are you, Little Fish: well trusted and well loved.'

SIX

Jane Shaw sat at her dressing table in the bedroom of her charming house in Hyde Park Gardens.

Leaning forward, she peered at herself in the antique Victorian mirror, brought a hand to her face, touching the fine wrinkles around her eyes with one finger. Crow's feet they were called. What an ugly name, she thought and sighed. There were also tiny lines above her top lip, hardly visible, but they *were* there, much to her dismay. And the lip rouge ran into those lines sometimes, she had begun to notice. Her jaw was not as taut as it had once been either, and she knew her neck had begun to sag, only slightly, but, nonetheless, this *was* visible.

Sitting back in the chair, trying to relax, Jane looked at herself again in a more objective way, and at once she was reassured that she was still a beautiful woman. A beautiful woman who was, very simply, growing older.

Ten years.

Not *many* years . . . not really. In 1907 ten years had not seemed much at all. Even in 1910 they were still a mere nothing in her mind. But today, in December of 1918, those ten years had assumed enormous proportions all of a sudden.

39

She was now forty-three.

Edward Deravenel was thirty-three.

She was ten years old than he was, and whilst this had not seemed too big an age difference between them before, it did now . . . because it was beginning to show.

It seemed to Jane, now that she focused on their ages, that Edward had not changed at all. He looked exactly the same, as handsome as ever. His hair was still that wonderful red-gold colour, burnished and full of light even on the dullest of sunless wintry days. His eyes, of an unusual cornflower blue, were still sparkling and full of life, and at six foot four he was an imposing man who appeared much younger than his years. He had kept his lean figure, had not put on weight: in fact, there was not an ounce of extra fat on him.

Rising, Jane walked over to the cheval mirror that stood in a corner, and removed her peignoir, stood naked in front of the looking glass, examining her body appraisingly.

Her breasts were still high, taut, a young woman's breasts, and her hips were slim, her stomach flat. She was pleased that her figure had not altered very much; because she was of medium height, she had always watched her diet carefully. As a consequence of this, her body was slender, and there was a youthfulness about her appearance. Nonetheless, the age difference between them was unexpectedly troubling her today.

Shaking her head, she turned away from the mirror, endeavouring to laugh at her own silliness. As she slipped into the white chiffon peignoir again, Jane reminded herself that no man could be more giving, loving and attentive than Edward.

The odd bits of gossip she heard about him from time to time actually pleased her, because the gossip was about *them* and their long friendship, and not about him and other women. The crux of the gossip was that, most miraculously, he was faithful to her.

Sitting down in the chair, she began to apply her usual evening cosmetics. A dusting of light face powder, a hint of pink rouge on her high cheekbones, and red lip rouge on her sensual mouth. She touched her blonde eyelashes with dark mascara, added the merest hint of brown pencil to her blonde eyebrows, and then picked up the comb, ran it through her wavy blonde hair. It was shorter than it had been for years, layers of waves that swept over her head and around her ears. This shorter cut was the latest style, and it suited her, added to her youthfulness.

After putting on silk stockings and underwear, Jane went to the wardrobe and took out a tailored, dark-blue silk dress. It had a V neckline and loose floating sleeves. As finishing touches she added several long ropes of pearls, pearl earrings, a sapphire ring and matching bracelet.

Now stepping into a pair of dark-blue suede court shoes, she hurried out of the bedroom and went down the stairs to the parlour.

A perfectionist at heart, Jane wanted to be certain that everything was in order before Ned arrived to spend the evening with her. She was worried about him because of Young Edward's illness. Ned was concerned about his little son, who was his heir, and he tended to fuss about him rather a lot. But she fully understood why this was so. Jane knew what a genuinely good father Edward was, devoted to all of his children, who did seem to keep coming along on a regular basis.

Pushing open the mahogany door into the parlour, she smiled to herself. Several of her women friends were extremely curious, incurably nosey about their relationship. They had no compunction about asking her outrageous personal questions, especially about Edward's wife. They said Elizabeth was mean and selfish, but Jane did not care.

She simply laughed in their faces and told them nothing. What did she care if he slept with Elizabeth from time to time? She was fully aware that most married men who had mistresses also had continuing sexual relationships with their wives. Usually because they had no option.

Being pragmatic by nature, Jane tried not to worry too much about things she could not change. It was a waste of her valuable time. And certainly she had no control over Edward Deravenel, or what he did when he was not with her. She knew he loved her, and he saw her several times a week, frequently even more when he was in London, and she knew how much he enjoyed her companionship. He took pleasure in her quick mind, her wit, and, of course, her knowledge of art.

It was to her that Ned owed his extraordinary collection of Impressionist and Post-Impressionist paintings. She had spent years searching out the best for him, including Renoirs, Manets, Monets, Gauguins, and Van Goghs.

Her eyes flew around the blue room. She was pleased to see that everything was in its given place. The fire was burning brightly, the softly-shaded lamps were turned on, cushions had been plumped, and the hot-house flowers Ned had sent her earlier were filling the air with the heady scent of summer. Glancing across at the table in the far corner, she noted that the bottle of champagne was already in the silver bucket, with two crystal flutes on a tray next to it.

Well done, Vane, she said to herself, thinking of the former parlour maid, whom she had promoted to be the under-housekeeper. The young woman was doing extremely well and she was pleased about this.

Edward Deravenel always felt an enormous sense of relief when he arrived at Jane's house. He knew that the moment he walked in the tensions of the day would instantly evaporate, and he would relax, become totally at ease with himself. It had been that way since he had first met her.

They were highly compatible in every way. She gave him pleasure and satisfaction in bed, and delighted him out of it.

Intelligent, articulate and full of knowledge about many things, she also had a unique quality about her – a lovely tranquillity surrounded Jane. Not only that, the calm atmosphere and well-ordered household met with his approval. Edward loathed chaos, and insisted on his own homes in London, Kent and Yorkshire being run perfectly.

Even though he had a door key he always rang the bell before inserting the key in the lock and going inside. Usually it was Mrs Longden, the housekeeper, who greeted him, but she was nowhere in sight. It was Jane who hurried forward tonight, a happy smile on her face.

'Ned, darling!' she exclaimed, reaching up to kiss him on the cheek. 'Oh, goodness, your face is *cold*. It must have turned chilly.'

He laid his briefcase on a hall bench, brought her into his arms and held her close for a moment. 'There's an icy wind all of a sudden,' he explained, releasing her, struggling out of his coat and scarf.

'Didn't Broadbent drive you here?' she asked, looking up at him quizzically.

'Yes, but there was an awful lot of traffic tonight, and I got out on the corner. It was easier to walk a few yards into the square, rather than having him struggle through that madness. I sent him off for his supper, and he'll return in a few hours. By then the traffic will have lessened.'

As he spoke, Edward put his coat, scarf and briefcase in the hall cupboard, and together they crossed the hall, heading in the direction of the parlour.

'Mrs Longden's off tonight: it's her sister's fiftieth birthday, which I'd totally forgotten about.'

'Oh, Jane, why didn't you tell me earlier? I could have taken you out to dinner.'

'That would've been nice, Ned, but I know how much you enjoy dining here, and to be frank, so do I. Vane can serve us, and Cook has made some of your favourites – roast chicken, a cottage pie, and she managed to get an excellent smoked salmon from Fortnum and Mason. How does that sound?'

'You're making my mouth water,' he said, laughing, following her into the parlour.

It was Edward's favourite room in the house, intimate and inviting, decorated in various shades of blue with touches of brilliant yellow throughout. Over the years Jane had collected exquisite decorative objects and all were well displayed, with flair, but it was the art which captivated. Jane had an excellent eye, and the paintings she had bought over the years, as well as those which Edward had given her, were superb. They enhanced the parlour, gave it even greater beauty.

Jane hurried across the floor to the circular table in the corner, and picked up the bottle of champagne. 'Would you like a glass of your favourite Krug?' she asked, turning, smiling at him. 'I think I will.'

'Grand idea,' he responded, going to stand in front of the fire, warming himself, his eyes resting on her as she poured the champagne.

A moment later, as she approached, he suddenly thought of Lily. Almost from the first moment he had met Jane she had reminded him of Lily Overton, who had died so tragically. His darling Lily. For a split second a flicker of sadness clouded his brilliant blue eyes.

Jane, who was particularly observant when it came to Edward Deravenel, saw the sudden shadow on his face, and as she handed him the flute of sparkling wine she asked quietly, 'Young Edward *is* all right, isn't he, Ned?'

'Oh yes, he's getting better. Much better. I spoke to the doctor before I left the office, because the boy still has an awful cough, and Leighton told me that's not unusual with bronchitis. Apparently it lingers. And Young Edward is eating better. Also, my mother tells me he's finally lost that rather disturbing glazed look.'

'I'm relieved for you, darling. He's obviously on the mend, thank goodness.' Jane retrieved her own glass of champagne and came back to the fireside. She and Edward touched glasses and took a sip, and then she sat down on the sofa close to the fireplace.

Lowering himself on a chair opposite her, Edward remarked, 'I spoke to Vicky this evening, before I left Deravenels, and I was so pleased to hear that you finally accepted her invitation for tomorrow evening.'

'I hesitated at first, because I didn't want to intrude –'

'How can you say such a thing?' Edward interjected, sounding surprised. 'Why would you think you're intruding? You're one of my oldest friends . . . we've known each other for ten years.' He grinned at her. 'Or had you forgotten how long it's been?'

'Of course not. It's just that . . . well, you and Will and Vicky go back years –' Jane broke off, shook her head. 'I've always told you I never want to embarrass you, or be an embarrassment, and you know the reasons why.'

'I do,' he replied, an amused smile touching his mouth. 'I'm a married man and you're my mistress. However, you must remember, my darling, that Will and his sister are two of my best friends. They are not my wife's friends. They never have been. They are part of my coterie, shall we call it, not hers. It is *you* they care about, Jane, not Elizabeth. But let's not go into all those hatreds now. Let's get back to the point – I'm happy we'll be together tomorrow night.'

Jane nodded. 'I am too. But –'

'Why have you stopped? Say what you started to say.'

'Vicky told me Grace Rose will be there.'

'I know that.' He burst out laughing when he saw the troubled expression in Jane's eyes, and shook his head. 'Darling, do you think she doesn't know you're my mistress? Good Lord, of course she does. She's eighteen and very clever, and very much my daughter . . . quite sophisticated, not at all naive. You know,

Vicky and Stephen have been wonderful parents to her, have brought her up to be a lady, and she's had an extraordinary education. She's just lapped up knowledge, and has also become quite the historian. I'm extremely proud of her. Don't you have any concerns about Grace, my dear. *She's* on my side, and she always has been.'

'Yes, I am being rather silly, aren't I?' Jane drank her champagne and began to laugh. 'It's been one of those days for me. Being silly.'

'What do you mean?'

'I suddenly looked at myself in the mirror tonight and decided I looked old. And then I started to think about the difference in our ages. I *am* ten years older than you, after all, Ned.'

'You don't look it! Anyway, you know I've always preferred older women. And everyone knows I like blondes best, especially blonde widows.' He grinned at her. 'Or divorcees. Ten years is not that much, you know.'

Jane realized it would be better to let this topic fade away, and she smiled and said, 'I have a surprise for you.' Putting down her glass of champagne, she went to her desk and returned to the fireside with an envelope, which she handed to Edward.

'What is it?' he asked curiously.

'Something I found for you, if you want to buy it.'

'Aha! a painting, my Jane! That's what it is, isn't it?'

She nodded and sat down, looking at him expectantly.

Edward took the photograph out of the envelope, and stared at it, caught his breath as he took in the unique beauty of the Renoir. It was marvellous, a painting of two young girls aged about sixteen or seventeen. They were wearing identical orange dresses with black fronts and trimming, sitting on a window ledge against a backdrop of blue sky. Both had hair of a burnished red-gold, swept up on top of their heads. Their gaze was directed at a book they were reading.

'It's absolutely marvellous!' he exclaimed, looking across at

46

Jane. '*Glorious*. And the girls remind me of Grace Rose and Bess. Except that these two young ladies look as if they are the same age.'

'It's called *Les Deux Soeurs*. Renoir painted it in 1889. And you're quite right, they are the same age I think. Look at the skin tones, Ned, the beauty of their faces. It's an incomparable painting. I fell in love with it when I saw it.'

'Which gallery has it?'

'It's in private hands. It was brought here to London at the outset of the war. For safety, I suppose.'

'And now the owner wants to sell it?'

'Apparently. If you *are* interested I can take you to see it on Friday.'

Edward frowned. 'I was going to go to Ravenscar that morning. But I'll tell you what, Janey, I'll take the late afternoon train instead. We can see the painting in the morning hopefully, and then we'll have lunch. How does that sound?'

'That's perfectly fine. So you do want it, do you?'

'Of course I do. It's wonderful. How much is it?'

'I don't know. I knew you wouldn't be able to resist it,' she said, nodding, smiling. 'I was sure it would remind you of your own little redheads.'

'It does, and as usual your instincts were right. You second-guessed me perfectly. Thank you, darling. And now I have a surprise for *you*.' Rising, he hurried out of the parlour, got his briefcase, opened it and took out a package.

He held this behind his back as he returned, and handed it to her with a bit of a flourish once he stood in front of her.

'What is it?' she asked, staring down at the package covered in dark blue wrapping paper and then looking up at him.

'Open it and see.'

Tearing off the paper, Jane found herself holding a dark blue cardboard box. Lifting off the lid, she saw that the box held a jewellery case made of very dark blue velvet. Once she was holding the case she glanced up at him again, shaking her head. 'By the looks of this, you've been very extravagant again. Oh, Ned, you do spoil me so.'

'No, I don't. Open it.'

She did. Her light eyes widened when she saw the lacey bib composed of diamonds interwoven with aquamarines. For a moment she was stunned and gazed at him speechlessly. Finally she said softly, 'Darling, it's just . . . beautiful.'

'As are you. I was going to get you an emerald brooch or emerald earrings, and then when I saw this I immediately thought of your eyes . . . they're the same colour.' He picked the necklace up, held it in front of her so that it caught and held the light. 'Look, Jane, your eyes are this colour exactly.'

Edward slipped the necklace in his pocket, took hold of her hand and pulled her to her feet. 'I want you to try it on. Immediately. *Now*. It won't work with this dress, so come on, darling, let's go upstairs. I want to see it on you.'

She made no protest. He hurried her out of the room, up the stairs, and into the bedroom, and he went on swiftly, 'Take off your dress, Jane. I want you to put this on.' As he spoke he took the necklace out of his pocket. 'Hurry up, I can't wait to see how it looks on you.'

Laughing, she did as he said, and in a second stood in front of him in her underwear.

Circling her, Edward went and stood behind her, put the necklace around her neck, fastened it, and guided her across to the dressing table, pressed her down into the chair. 'Look at yourself, look how the stones reflect the colour of your eyes.' She leaned forward, staring at herself in the mirror, and he leaned over her shoulders, regarding her reflection.

He murmured, 'The necklace is perfection, and so are you.'

Turning her head, she gazed up at him, and her eyes filled. 'Thank you, thank you for this lovely, lovely gift. I will treasure it forever, Ned.'

'As I will always treasure you, Jane. Please remember that, especially when you start getting strange ideas, start thinking you're too old for me.'

In a few long strides he had crossed the bedroom floor. He locked the door, took off his jacket, threw it on a chaise longue, and then as he turned around, walked back to her, he began to unbutton his shirt. 'I'm now going to prove that you're *not* too old, that I still desire you.'

Jane met him in the middle of the floor, her eyes on his. 'Can you unfasten the necklace, please?'

'No, I can't,' he whispered, and took her in his arms, pulled her closer, so that her cheek rested against his bare chest. 'I want you to wear it tonight. All night. But I will unfasten this,' he added; his hands fumbled for the hooks of her bra. 'Let's find that bed of ours,' he said against her hair. 'It's a matter of some urgency.'

Jane now saw that he did indeed have a strong need for her, that he wanted her; she shed the rest of her clothes, followed him. He was undressing as quickly as she had. A moment later he took her in his arms, held her tightly. His mouth found hers and he kissed her deeply, passionately, his tongue on hers, his hands sliding down to her breasts. When they broke their long kiss he led her to the side of the bed.

They lay down together, catching their breath. Eventually Edward propped himself up on one elbow, looked down into her face. 'Jane, my beautiful, beautiful Jane, you're such a silly girl.' He lowered his face to hers, added, 'You'll never be too old for me . . .' Leaving the rest of his sentence unfinished, he kissed her once more.

Edward lay on top of her, pushed his hands under her buttocks and brought her close to him as he entered her. It was the same as it always was with them. Desire and an overwhelming need. Passion. Urgency. They swiftly found their familiar rhythm, clinging to each other as they soared together, filled with ecstasy, and the pure joy of being together, possessing each other so completely and with total abandon.

At one moment Edward stopped abruptly, raised himself up to gaze down at Jane.

She stared back, perplexity crossing her face.

He said with a small smug smile, 'The aquamarines are indeed the colour of your eyes, especially at a moment like this.'

He lowered himself onto her once more, his face against her neck. 'Oh, how I love you. Love *you*, Jane. I'm yours. Just as you are mine. Come now, come to me. *Now*.' And she did, calling his name. He echoed her, cried out, sank against her breasts, sighing, 'Oh Jane, oh Jane.'

They remained joined together for a few minutes. It was Edward who moved first. He took a pillow and placed it against Jane's chest. 'The necklace is a little sharp against my skin,' he told her, his voice low. 'There, that's better ... with the pillow between us.'

'I can take it off, darling.'

'No. I want you to wear it tonight. I know you'll find a dress that has the right neckline.'

'I will.'

There was a long silence, a lovely quietness between them that lasted for a while. It was Jane who broke it finally when she suddenly said, 'What did you do about the dog?'

'Dog?' Edward asked, puzzled.

'Don't you remember, I suggested you buy a dog for Young Edward. He's always wanted one, or so you once said, ever since he was very small boy. I told you I thought it would be a lovely Christmas present.'

'Oh, my God! The dog! I'd forgotten about it. I was going

to buy it in Scotland for him . . . a West Highland terrier, he loves that breed. Damnation!'

'You can still get one, Ned. At Harrods. They sell dogs.'

'I'd have to take it with me to Yorkshire. That's a bit of a nuisance.'

'I'm sure they'll send it up for you. In a van.'

'What a good idea. What on earth would I do without you? I'll go over there tomorrow morning, and pick one out, arrange for it to be taken up to Ravenscar. Well done, Janey, well done. You've saved my bacon again.' Pushing himself up, he leaned over her, kissed the tip of her nose. 'This necklace *is* a bit dangerous,' he murmured, touching it with one finger, and starting to laugh. 'I'm surprised I don't have a raw chest.'

'I did volunteer to take it off.'

'I know, but I didn't want you to . . . You know . . . I like to make love to women wearing *only* jewels and nothing else.'

'*Women!*' she exclaimed. 'Now what other *women* wearing only jewels do you make love to, Edward Deravenel? Tell me *that.*'

'Only you my sweet, only you,' he answered swiftly, telling her the absolute truth.

Jane was wise enough to make no further comment, even though she did believe him. She was well aware he was faithful to her. The whole world knew that, including his wife. She wondered if this troubled Elizabeth. Didn't one other woman in a married man's life pose a threat? Whereas many women in a married man's life could be so easily dismissed. She let these thoughts slide away from her, and instead asked, 'By the way, why did you send George off to Scotland? You never did say.'

'I wanted to get him out of my hair. He'd invited himself for Christmas at Ravenscar, and to please my mother I'd acquiesced. And then when I cancelled our Christmas festivities, told the guests they could not come, he became very obstreperous. Because Young Edward was ill I'd decided to cancel my trip to

Scotland. It then occurred to me that I could get rid of George by sending him up to Edinburgh to negotiate the deal with Ian MacDonald. The deal for his liquor business. Killing two birds with one stone, really.'

'Isn't that a bit dangerous?' she asked, pushing herself up on the pillows. 'Allowing him to be the voice of Deravenels?'

Edward looked at her intently. 'He can be a bit volatile, I know that, even in business discussions. But I promised him a large bonus if he pulls it off to my satisfaction. He'll be careful how he handles himself because of the prospect of money.'

'I hope he doesn't make a mess of it,' she murmured, thinking out loud.

'Funny thing is, Jane, Richard said the same thing to me earlier today,' Ned said. 'If it doesn't work, I won't care too much, you know. George *is* strange at times, but more of a nuisance I'd say than anything else.'

'No, he's not a nuisance, Ned. He's a threat.'

'Why do you say that?' he asked, frowning to himself. Will Hasling had made the same comment several times in the last few weeks.

Jane answered in a thoughtful voice, 'I think he's in competition with you. I've always believed that George sort of . . . well, *fancies* himself, thinks he can be you, thinks he's as good as you, as clever as you, and he's not. Everyone knows how brilliant you are.'

'It was Neville who put those ideas in his head, a long time ago. Obviously they've taken hold. Now that the War is over perhaps I can ship George off somewhere. To America, perhaps.'

Jane laughed. 'On a *permanent* basis, of course. Don't you think that would be a good idea?'

'Yes. And I've got an even better idea,' he murmured, leaning towards her, kissing her fully on the mouth, and moving even closer. 'I want to make love to you again, before we go down to dinner.'

'What about the necklace –'

'To hell with the bloody necklace,' he interrupted, smiling at her. 'I don't care if I do get a few scratches as long as I can have you in my arms. You, Jane, my one true love.'

'Oh Ned –'

He cut off the rest of the sentence by placing his mouth firmly on hers.

SEVEN

Amos Finnister sat in his office at Deravenels on the Strand, giving Will Hasling his entire attention. There was an expression of concern on his face as he listened to the other man.

'And so,' Will continued, 'I would appreciate it if you could do a bit of digging, Amos. In your usual discreet fashion.'

Nodding, Amos asked, 'Do you think Mr George has fallen in with a bad lot? Is that it, Mr Hasling?'

'Yes. And a dangerous lot, at that. The drinking, the whoring are bad enough, well that's George's nature, I'm afraid: he's always been a bit of a libertine. It's the drugs that worry me, and the gambling. He's losing a lot of money on a regular basis, *a great deal*, in fact. Very troublesome.'

'If I might ask, how did you find this out?' Amos gazed at Will steadily.

'Someone came to me, warned me.' Will nodded, and murmured, 'Thank God.'

'I'm assuming it's someone you can trust, Mr H?'

'It is, actually, Amos, and there's no good reason why you shouldn't know. It came from one of my brothers – Howard.

When he was at Eton he became extremely close to a boy called Kim Rowe-Leggett, and, in the way of old Etonians, they've stayed close friends over the years. Rowe-Leggett is a stock-broker in the City these days, quite well-known, and very successful. Anyway, he likes the occasional flutter on the ponies, and he sometimes gambles, on a small scale, at one of the newer London gambling clubs. He's a member of Starks, Julian Stark's place, another old Etonian. To get to the point, my brother told me that according to Kim Rowe-Leggett the gossip about George is rampant. Naturally I'm perturbed. Not only about his gambling losses, but the drugs.'

'I don't blame you.' Amos shook his head. 'Mr George is a great worry to Mr Deravenel, as you well know. And more than once in the last few weeks he's asked me to keep an eye on him. You know what I mean . . . he wants me to keep track of what his brother does in his spare time, but in a . . . casual way, unobtrusively, shall we say?'

Will rubbed his mouth with his hand, frowning. 'I wonder if Mr Edward has heard any of the gossip about Mr George? Has he said anything to you?'

'Not really. When he does express concern it's in a . . . well, a mild way. He doesn't get excited, or anything like that. And he's said nothing about gambling or drugs.'

'It's bound to get back to him sooner rather than later, especially if there is a demand for payment of the gambling debts. Julian Stark might come to Mr Deravenel if he doesn't get satisfaction from George.' Will sighed. 'I have to tell him, Amos. I really do. He and I have never had any secrets from each other in all the years we've worked together here at Deravenels, and even before that, when we were at Oxford.'

Amos sat back in his desk chair and stared off into the distance, an odd look settling on his face.

Will Hasling noticed this immediately, and asked, 'What is it, Amos? You're looking peculiar.'

'Can it wait until after Christmas? What I mean is, Mr Edward is a bit worried at the moment, as you well know, about his little boy. And it *is* the holiday season . . . the annual lunch tomorrow and then the dinner at your sister's tomorrow evening.'

'I see what you mean.' Will became reflective for a moment or two, weighing the odds before remarking, 'I understand exactly what you're saying, but we all know that he *detests* surprises. If the gossip comes to him from someone else, he's going to be furious with me for not telling him, preparing him in advance.'

Sitting up straighter in the chair, Amos agreed, exclaiming, 'A point well taken. I reckon you will have to have a word with him. To quote my late father, forewarned is forearmed.' Leaning forward across the desk, Amos added quietly, 'Mr Richard said to me only last week that he believed his brother George was not suitable for Deravenels and shouldn't be given any power in the company. That he had very poor judgement.'

Will was not at all surprised by this confidence. He had long been aware that there was bad blood between the two brothers. Richard was devoted and loyal to Ned, and would lay down his life for him, but he loathed George.

Will had known Richard since his childhood, and he loved him, admired him. He was of good character; a stickler for discipline and a bit straitlaced. He was also very hard working, talented in business, and Edward was especially pleased that he had settled in so well at Deravenels. Will knew that.

Of late Richard had become unusually critical of George. Will recognized that Richard had suffered because of George who had tried to block his marriage to Anne Watkins in the meanest way. Will stifled a sigh. He had never quite understood why Ned had not intervened sooner, rectified the situation, not allowed it to drag on.

Rousing himself from his thoughts, realizing Amos was waiting, Will continued. 'Do you think Richard knows any bad gossip about George? Has he mentioned anything to you?'

'No, he hasn't. However, he might have heard *something*. Last week, out of the blue, he did make a remark – he said his brother was venal.'

'He certainly hit the nail on the head.'

'In my opinion George Deravenel is a dyed-in-the-wool trouble-maker.'

Will gave Amos a long look, murmured, 'He's also . . . *dangerous.*'

'Oh, I know *that*. Ever since he became entangled with Neville Watkins, and *his* machinations all those years ago, I've been suspicious of him. To tell you the truth, I've not trusted him since then.'

'And neither have I.' Will Hasling rose, walked towards the door, explaining, 'I must get off, Amos, my wife is waiting for me at the Savoy Hotel. We're going to the Savoy Theatre tonight.'

'I understand. Have a pleasant evening, Mr H.'

Will swung around when he reached the door, and stared hard at Amos. 'I *will* have to speak to Mr Edward as soon as possible. I must inform him about everything, prepare him. And please do a bit of digging, won't you? Who knows what you'll turn up.'

'You can depend on me. If there's anything to find, I'll find it.'

There was going to be trouble. He could smell it in the air already. And he knew it in his bones for sure. For as long as he could remember, Amos had relied on his intuition, coupled with his insight into people. He also had a knack of knowing what made people tick, understood why they did the things they did, recognized their motivation. All of these gifts, because that's how Amos thought of them, had helped him when he was a copper on the beat, policing the streets of Whitechapel, Limehouse, and other areas of London's East End.

And they had continued to work for him during his years with Neville Watkins; nor had they disappeared when he had joined Deravenels, to head up the Security Division. A wry smile touched his mouth. No such thing as a Security Division until *he* had been hired to 'watch my back', as Edward Deravenel had so succinctly put it at the time.

These days this was no longer necessary. Most of Edward's enemies were dead; some were living abroad but had been rendered powerless by Edward Deravenel's success as head of the company. Deravenels had always been a huge global corporation; he had turned it into an operation which was bigger than ever and made more money than it had in its entire history.

His was a household name, not only in England but around the world, and he was considered to be one of the most influential tycoons in the City. Some said he was even more important than his late cousin Neville Watkins, who had been the greatest magnate at one time.

Amos now remembered that once he had told Mr Edward he wanted to retire. Edward had thrown a fit. Or something tantamount to one. He had gone berserk. That was the only word for it.

'I want you here by my side for the rest of your life, and mine!' Edward had declared heatedly. 'I will not *countenance* talk of your retirement, and that's that. Don't bring it up again, Amos. And besides, always remember that men who retire invariably fall apart and die.'

Amos had been a little stunned by these words at the time, words so emphatically uttered, and yet he had also been immensely flattered. He realized then that he had a most special place in Edward Deravenel's life and in his heart, just as his boss did in his.

Loyal, devoted, discreet and protective, Amos Finnister was also calm and cool under any circumstances. And he was so extraordinarily trustworthy that Edward Deravenel had never bothered to hide any aspects of his extremely complicated life from the former private investigator, who was usually at his side.

It was quite common knowledge at Deravenels that Amos Finnister was very close to the managing director, but no one knew just how close. Except for Will Hasling, who was even closer to Ned, being his longest and dearest friend.

These three men worked in harmony together, and had for years. They trusted each other implicitly, and were totally discreet about each other, revealing nothing to colleagues or family. Once, rather laughingly, Edward had said that they were like The Three Musketeers, and in a certain sense that was true.

The relationship between them worked for a number of reasons. Edward and Will, though aristocrats, were not snobs; they were affable, accessible, natural, and democratic in their attitudes. Amos Finnister knew he must never overstep the line. He was well aware of his place in the order of things. And he was never over-familiar. He knew how wrong that would be.

These three had been hand-in-glove for a long time. They thought alike, after years in each other's company, and acted in a similar manner when confronted by problems. And they could usually second-guess each other.

Amos rose, walked up and down the office for a few seconds, stretching his long legs. And thinking hard.

Will Hasling was a lot more troubled that he was letting on, Amos was convinced of that. And he also knew, without a shadow of a doubt, that Will would tell Edward everything tomorrow morning. And Edward would want *him* on it immediately.

Amos stepped over to the window and looked out. It seemed like a nice night, with a clear, dark sky, no clouds at all, and a galaxy of stars.

After locking his desk and taking his overcoat from the cupboard, Amos left his office and went down the stairs. He crossed the imposing, soaring marble lobby of Deravenels, as usual admiring its grandeur, and stepped out onto the Strand.

The thoroughfare was busier than he had seen it in a long time. Taxis, motorcars and omnibuses crowded the road, and the pavement was congested with pedestrians, mostly moving swiftly, hurrying about their business. It struck him immediately that he must walk. He had no alternative since it would be hard to find a cab in this mess.

Anyway, he did enjoy walking; it reminded him of his days on the beat, he supposed, and he usually did his best thinking when his feet were moving. Buttoning his topcoat, he set off at a brisk pace.

Tonight he was heading to the Ritz Hotel in Piccadilly. His old friend Charlie Morran was staying there, and they were to dine in the elegant Ritz Restaurant, which was one of the best in London. He had sometimes eaten there with Edward Deravenel, and he knew it quite well.

The hotel itself was palatial, with marble floors, rich carpets, crystal chandeliers, handsome dark-wood furniture, potted palms and huge arrangements of flowers. It was a particular favourite of the rich and famous, a rendezvous for the most well-known people in London ... the aristocracy, socialites, famous actors, actresses, and writers, members of Parliament, politicians and heads of state ... the crème-de-la-crème of the world.

Amos's thoughts remained focused on Charlie as he strode out towards Trafalgar Square. He had not seen him for over two years; the young man had been at the front in France, fighting for King and Country.

When war had broken out in August of 1914, Charlie had immediately booked passage on a ship from New York to Southampton, and had come home to England to be a soldier. 'I'm determined to do my bit,' was the way he had put it to Amos when he had first arrived in London, adding, 'I want to stand up and be counted, fight for what's right and just. So here

I am, and I'm going to enlist in the British Army this week.'
And he had.

Charlie had come back to London alone; his sister Maisie
had already left America the year before. In 1913 she had gone
to live in Ireland with the man she had just married.

Amos had grown very proud of Charlie and Maisie, and of
the success they had achieved over the years. Within a few
months of arriving in New York, where Charlie had constantly
insisted the streets were paved with gold, the two Cockney kids
from Whitechapel had found work in the theatre. And eventually they had become stars on Broadway, as they had always
wanted. And why not?

They could sing, dance, and act, and both were clever mimics,
quite aside from being exceptionally good looking. Talent and
looks. The best combination. It was really no surprise to Amos
when Charlie's letters kept arriving very promptly with news of
their continuing triumphs.

They had sailed away from Liverpool in 1904; then their love
of London lured them back. They made many visits home over
the ensuing years, and Amos had been delighted to see them
whenever they arrived on his doorstep.

It was a happy day for Amos when the famous letter came,
announcing Maisie's marriage to her young Irishman, who, as
it turned out, was the eldest son of Lord Dunleith, an Anglo-
Irish landowner with a splendid Georgian mansion called
Dunleith and vast acres surrounding his county seat.

All of these thoughts were swirling around in his head as
Amos tramped towards Trafalgar Square. There were a good
many people circulating in the area, and especially around the
statue of England's greatest hero, Horatio Nelson. Revellers were
singing and waving the Union Jack and dancing. Some were
shouting, 'We beat the Hun!' Obviously they were celebrating
because it was the end of the war, not because it was Christmas,
which was still a week away.

At the other side of Trafalgar Square somebody let off a Catherine wheel, and bursts of sparkling lights rushed up into the night air. More and more fireworks began to explode for a wonderful display of colour and brilliance, and there was applause and laughter and more songs.

Unexpectedly, a clear soprano voice rang out above the din. The woman began to sing *Land of Hope and Glory*, and after the first verse other people joined in, and soon everyone was singing. Including Amos, who discovered he had a funny lump in his throat. He felt an enormous swell of pride, and realized he was as sentimental and patriotic as the rest of them were.

Eventually, he moved on, walking through the square, heading West to Piccadilly and the Ritz Hotel.

Thank God the fighting has ended, he thought. For the first time in history, a war had exploded and engulfed the entire world, destroying the old order of things. He understood that nothing would ever be the same again. But thankfully the world was at peace tonight, after four years of hell and millions of young men dead, mowed down before they had had a chance to live.

EIGHT

Whwhen he reached Arlington Street, just off Piccadilly, Amos crossed over to the other side where the entrance to the Ritz Hotel was located.

Nodding to the doorman, attired in a uniform of dark blue and black top hat, he pushed through the swing doors and entered the lobby.

Glancing at the large clock on the wall, Amos was gratified to see that he was not late. It was exactly seven o'clock. After depositing his overcoat in the gentleman's cloakroom, he went into the promenade area where English afternoon tea was served without fail every day of the week.

He stood glancing around, and a split-second late he spotted Charlie coming towards him. *Slowly*. He had an extremely bad limp and was using a walking stick, leaning on it heavily. A captain in the British Army now, having received many promotions, he looked very smart in his officer's uniform and Sam Brown belt.

Amos lifted his hand in a wave, and Charlie waved back. Hurrying forward to meet him, Amos's step faltered slightly as he drew closer to his old friend. But he quickly recouped, took a deep breath, and continued down the plush carpet, hoping Charlie hadn't noticed.

Pushing a smile onto his face, Amos thrust out his hand when they came to a standstill opposite each other, and Charlie grasped it tightly, held on to it for a moment.

Amos felt his heart clench and he had to swallow hard. The young actor would never act again, not with that ruined face. One side was badly scarred by burns, the skin bright red, puckered, and stretched tightly over the facial bones. The scars ran from his hairline to his jaw, and looked raw.

As if he had read Amos's thoughts, Charlie said evenly, 'I'll have to find a new profession, I'm afraid, Amos. But at least *I* got out alive, and you know what, the doctors thought they'd have to amputate my leg, but they didn't. Somehow they managed to save it for me.' His voice wavered slightly as he added, 'I've been one of the lucky ones.'

Amos was choked up, but swiftly took control of himself, impressed by Charlie's courageous attitude. 'I know you've been to hell and back, but you're home now. And you're safe.'

Charlie smiled faintly. 'Aren't you a sight for sore eyes, old friend. Come on then, let's go to the restaurant, shall we? Have a drink, toast each other, and reminisce about old times.'

'Best idea yet. And how's your sister Maisie?'

'She's tip-top, very cheerful, feeling better because Liam is steadily improving, and every day. He was so shell-shocked he was like a zombie for a long time. Then he started weeping a great deal, and constantly woke up screaming in the night. And I know why . . . it's the memories . . . they don't go away.' Charlie shook his head. 'Too many walking wounded who probably won't ever get better. The walking dead, I call 'em. Might as well be dead, the kind of lives they're going to have. Well, I shouldn't say that, should I?' He endeavoured to adopt a more cheerful tone, and finished, 'Maisie's a wonder, and she's convinced that Liam will make a full recovery. She sends you her love, by the way.'

'I received a Christmas card from her the other day, and she told me she hopes I'll go and visit them at Dunleith. In fact, she suggested we go together.'

'We'll do it!' Charlie announced, and nodded to the *maître d'* who had come to greet them, and was waiting to usher them into the restaurant.

'Good evening, Captain Morran, very nice to see you tonight.' The man glanced at Amos, and smiled, 'Good evening, Mr Finnister.'

Amos inclined his head. 'Good evening,' he replied, feeling certain that the *maître d'* remembered him from the times he had come here for lunch with Edward Deravenel and Will Hasling.

They followed the head waiter across the room. When he showed them to a table near the window overlooking Green Park.

'I'm glad I was able to get a room here,' Charlie volunteered, looking across the dinner table at Amos. 'The hotel seems to be very busy, no doubt because of the Armistice, and Christmas, of course. But I'm an old client and they were most obliging. I'm sure you remember that once we could afford it, Maisie and I stayed here whenever we came to London. Mostly to see you, Amos, you know.' Without waiting for a comment, he rushed on, 'Believe me, this place is a helluva lot better than the trenches. Take my word for it.'

'I do. I can't imagine what you boys went through over there. Nobody can. Hell on earth, I'm certain, and I've no doubt that it was bloody horrific –' Amos cut himself off as a waiter appeared at the table.

Charlie looked at Amos and asked, 'Would you like champagne? Or something stronger?'

'I'll have whatever you're having, Charlie, thanks very much.'

'Then it's champagne.' Charlie said to the waiter, 'I'd like a bottle of *pink* champagne, the best in the house.'

'That would be Krug, sir. I'll bring it right away.'

When they were once more alone, Charlie leaned closer to Amos and said in a low voice, 'The constant shelling, the mustard gas, the hand-to-hand fighting, it was bleedin' awful. But it was the bloody mud that got to us. Sometimes we sank knee-deep in it, and it slowed us down, I can tell you. One of my lads suddenly hit on the idea of using our rations to make a solid floor in the trenches.'

'Rations?' Amos's eyebrows shot up questioningly.

'That's right . . . tins of Fray Bentos corned beef, our daily rations. Hundreds of tins went under our boots, helped to keep our feet dry, and at eye level, so we could see over the top of the trenches. Spot the Germans as they came at us. It was horrible, like glue, that mud, and then there was the incessant rain, the bombs exploding, the men dying all around us . . .' Charlie let his voice fall away. He pressed his lips together, struggling to keep his emotions in check, but it was a struggle for him.

Amos, regarding him worriedly, noticed that Charlie's dark eyes were suddenly moist, and he reached out, touched the younger man's arm quietly, lovingly. 'There, there, lad, take it easy. Perhaps we shouldn't be talking about this –'

'It's all right, honest,' Charlie cut in with swiftness. 'It's better to talk about it really, especially with an old friend like you. I know you understand how I feel, you always have.'

Amos said nothing, but thought that Charlie had never been through anything like this before, but then who had? It had been a war of such magnitude, horror and brutality that it defied description.

Charlie suddenly coughed behind his hand, and swallowed. Then before he could stop himself he went on talking. 'I saw my men die around me, all of them. I lost the whole battalion. I'm the only survivor.' His voice broke on these words, and he pulled out a handkerchief, blew his nose, sat back quietly, pushing the memories of his men away.

Amos, aware that Charlie was trying to control his distress, motioned to a waiter, and when he came to the table, Amos said, 'Could we have some water, please? And the menus . . . we've been waiting for those. We'd like to order.'

Nodding, the waiter hurried off.

After a moment or two, Charlie turned to Amos and made a face. 'Sorry, old mate, very sorry. Usually I'm fine, quite all right most of the time, and then suddenly I get upset, sort of overcome. My apologies. I didn't intend to inflict this on you.'

'You're doing no such thing, don't be daft,' Amos answered, and then seeing a bevy of waiters descending on them, exclaimed, 'Everything's coming all at once.'

Within minutes they were alone again, and lifting their flutes of champagne; they clinked glasses. 'Here's to the future!' Charlie said.

'The future!' Amos echoed, and took a sip.

A silence fell between them as they both scrutinized the menu, and then Charlie looked over the top of his, and said, with a smile, 'Lots of delicious things to choose from, and I must confess, they all tempt me. A lot better than the grub I was getting in the army hospital at Hull. Bloody foul it was.'

Amos laughed, relieved to see that the old Cockney cheerfulness was surfacing in Charlie. 'I must say it does read like a repast for a king. Well . . . I fancy the Colchester oysters, or perhaps the Morecambe Bay potted shrimps, and then saddle of mutton with redcurrant jelly, or roast beef and Yorkshire pudding.'

'D'yer think they knows 'ow to mek Yorkshire pud 'ere? Me old muvver used ter say only the folks from up the Dales could do it proper, and that's right, innit? No, this ain't the place fer it.'

Amos burst out laughing. 'I thought you'd forgotten all your Cockney, Charlie, seeing as how you're speaking like an officer and a gentleman tonight.'

Charlie laughed with him and took a long swallow of his pink champagne, enjoying it. 'Not only tonight, but all the time really. Didn't you ever notice on our trips home before the war that Maisie and I were speaking differently, like this, not falling into Cockney slang at all?'

'Come to think of it, yes, I did. But occasionally you sort of, well, *lapsed*, shall we say?'

'Not often. However, there was a really good reason why we decided to speak properly, after we'd arrived in New York. And it's this . . . they didn't understand Cockney there. I mean, what Yank would know that apples and pears means stairs, and rosy lea is a cup of tea?'

'That's understandable. But let's face it, a lot of the English don't understand it either,' Amos pointed out.

'That's because you've got to be born within the sound of Bow Bells to understand Cockney and speak it proper-like. And that's St Mary-le-Bow Church where the bells are, but I know you know that. And listen, Mum once told me another fing, that rhyming Cockney slang was invented so that nobody else could understand it. Only Cockneys. It was a way to outwit the rozzers, coppers like you, Amos, and anybody else trying to listen in to a private conversation.'

'A secret language! I'll be buggered.' Amos grinned.

So did Charlie, who announced, 'You do manage to cheer me up, you really do. It's the first time I've had a laugh in months and months.'

Before Amos could answer, the *maître d'* came over to the table to take their order, and once he had left them alone, Amos leaned closer to his old friend. 'I just wanted to say something, and it's this. I'm here to help you, in whatever way you might need me. If I can help you in any way, you know I am ready, willing and able to do so. I don't suppose you need money, because you were a successful actor, a star, but –'

'No, no, I don't need money!' Charlie interrupted. 'I have a good business manager in New York, and he's done very well for me, taken my money and quadrupled it over the years. And Maisie's money, too. A' course, she doesn't need money. After her father-in-law died last year, Liam inherited the title and quite a fortune. He was the only son, you see. I'm proud of her, Amos, because she's been running that estate ever since she married Liam. Lord Dunleith was sick, and a bit decrepit, and she took over because Liam was at the front, and Lady Dunleith was dead. She's quite remarkable, I think, our Maisie.'

'I agree with you,' Amos murmured, and pushed away thoughts of the past and things he had no wish to remember. Changing the subject, he asked, 'What do you think you'll do, now that the war's over? Or are you just going to be a gentleman of leisure.'

'That's not for me, doing nothing!' Charlie shook his head vehemently. 'I can't act anymore, not with this ruined face. But I could direct or produce, and perhaps I might even write for the theatre. Something will turn up.'

'I know it will, you've always been very enterprising. But isn't there anything you can do about the scarring? I mean once your face has properly healed?'

'Maybe. One of the doctors at the hospital in Hull told me that skin can be grafted, and that there are certain new methods, special treatments being developed. I shall just have to wait until I've healed. Perhaps then I can see someone.'

At this point two waiters arrived with trays of food. There were Colchester oysters for Amos and paté for Charlie, which they promptly served, and then brought plates of toast and brown bread.

'I'm glad we're having dinner together tonight,' Charlie remarked at one moment. 'I couldn't wait to see you. As long as I've known you, you've always made me feel tons better.

It's comforting to have a really close friend, someone you can trust.'

'Yes, it is. And I can say the same for you, Charlie.'

It was after they had finished the main course of roast beef and Yorkshire pudding, and were sipping their glasses of St Emilion and relaxing, that Charlie suddenly sat up straighter in the chair.

'What is it?' Amos asked, following the direction of his gaze.

'A friend's just coming into the restaurant. That officer over there in the entrance. The one on crutches, with those two women and another man. Do you see him?'

Amos nodded.

'He lost a leg, after he was severely wounded in the third battle of Ypres.'

'Were you in the trenches with him?' Amos asked.

'No, I wasn't. I didn't know him then. We first met at the military hospital in Hull, and then again at Chapel Allerton Hospital in Leeds, when I had a problem with my leg. As you can see, they took his, amputated above the knee. I was much luckier, they saved mine. Do you mind if I go and say hello to him?'

'Yes, go and speak to him, Charlie. I'll just sit here and enjoy the very good claret you ordered.'

'Cedric's a nice chap, and he was very helpful to me.'

Amos frowned. 'What did you say his name was?'

'Cedric.'

'And his last name?'

'I didn't say, but it's Crawford. He's Major Cedric Crawford. Why do you ask?'

'I just wondered, that's all.'

Excusing himself, Charlie walked across the restaurant, intent on speaking to the man with whom he had become good friends in the two hospitals in Yorkshire.

Amos stared after him. He felt as though he had just been hit in the stomach with a brick. Could the major on crutches be none other than the same Cedric Crawford who had lived with Grace Rose's mother, Tabitha James? And who had abandoned Grace Rose? Who had turned her out into the streets to fend for herself?

He didn't know. But he certainly aimed to find out.

NINE

As he waited for Charlie to return to the table, Amos glanced around the restaurant. It had filled up as the evening had progressed and there was quite a din . . . voices, laughter, the clatter of dishes and bottles, the clink of ice . . . all the sounds of a busy place, in fact.

There was a wonderful festive feeling here tonight and an air of celebration about the other people present who were dining at the Ritz. He noticed many officers with their wives, parents and families; some of them were wounded and his heart went out to those men. His eyes swept around the room once more, and he thought how truly fortunate they were. They were alive, safely home, and Christmas would be a good one for them this year. The world was at peace. But so many had died. *Millions.* The flower of English youth was gone, a generation wiped out.

Several times he sneaked a glance at Major Cedric Crawford, who was talking animatedly to Charlie. They both looked pleased to see each other.

Amos realized he would have to handle the situation with care and delicacy. He knew full well that men who had lived through similar experiences during a war, and became friends,

72

always bonded, were blood brothers under the skin. And Charlie and Crawford had suffered horrific wounds in the Great War, had been in two hospitals together. There was bound to be an enormous closeness between them; in fact it was quite apparent that indeed there was, from the manner in which they greeted each other with such enthusiasm.

Amos averted his face, glanced towards the window and the view of Green Park, and then spotted Charlie hobbling back to the table.

'Your friend appears delighted to see you, Charlie,' Amos remarked as the other man sat down.

'He was, and I was happy to see him, too. He's a nice chap, Cedric, and he was always kind to me, very helpful.'

'I'm glad he was. Tell me, is one of those good-looking women his wife?'

'No, they're both his sisters. Rowena, that's the dark-haired one, is actually Cedric's twin, and she's not married. The blonde is the eldest sister. Her name is Daphne. The other man at the table is her husband, Sir Malcolm Holmes, who's some sort of industrialist.'

'I've heard of him. So Cedric is from a prestigious family, then?'

'Very much so, Amos.' Leaning forward Charlie confided, with a huge smile, 'Cedric is going to be awarded the Victoria Cross. Just imagine that. What an honour . . . his sister Rowena just told me. She's very proud.'

'Well, that's very impressive indeed. The Victoria Cross is the highest recognition for valour in the face of the enemy that anyone can get. Did you know that?'

Charlie shook his head. 'I didn't, but he bloody well deserves it, from what I've heard about his actions in the Battle of the Somme, just after Verdun. Saved a lot of his men, took great risks to do so.'

'So he told you about his feats of bravery, did he?' Amos's

eyes searched Charlie's face. He was also wondering if there were two Cedric Crawfords in the world . . . but it was such an unusual name, wasn't it? Hardly likely that there would be two of them, although you never knew. Could be there was. No, he thought. Cedric Crawford who had been a guards officer and a gambler before the war surely had to be this man.

Charlie exclaimed, 'No, no, he wouldn't boast about his courage, he's not that sort. No, no. It was a surgeon at the hospital in Hull who mentioned his bravery to me one day. Apparently Cedric arrived at the hospital with quite a reputation as a hero . . . he got seven of his men out of a trench under heavy bombardment from the Germans, shepherded them to safety, then went back and carried out first one wounded Tommy, and then a second. That was in 1916 . . . the summer when General Haig sent in British troops to help the French. That first day the British troops were just mowed down . . . 20,000 dead, Amos, 20,000. And another 40,000 wounded or lost. It was on the second day that Cedric came to the rescue of his men.'

Amos nodded, said nothing, stunned by the size of the losses. It was almost impossible to conceive . . . 60,000 men either dead or wounded. He sat up straighter and looked at Charlie, who was still talking about Cedric.

'After that violent summer, he went on to fight at Ypres. Funny thing was, I was at Passchendaele, and so was he, but we didn't know each other. That was in 1917 . . . bloody wholesale slaughter it was. Those of us that got out alive, well, we sure as hell must've had a guardian angel watching over us.'

Amos could only nod, wondering how on earth he could broach the subject of Cedric Crawford, suggest that he was the man involved with Tabitha James. There were no two ways about it, they certainly sounded like two different men to him. But, in actuality, what did he *really* know about Cedric Crawford? Not much. He only had a bit of disjointed information from Grace

Rose, a little girl who had been four at the time, plus a few comments from a woman who supposedly had been Tabitha's friend, but was not all that well-informed. Nor had she been worried enough to rescue Tabitha.

'You're lost in thought, Amos. You look troubled. What's wrong?'

Amos stared at the young man for whom he had always had great affection, and wondered where to begin. Clearing his throat, he asked in a casual tone, 'Is your friend a professional soldier?'

'I don't believe so, but he was in the guards at one time. Then he got out, he didn't say why. He lived in Paris for a bit and then he went to America. You know what, he actually saw me in a show on Broadway, and he remembered me and Maisie, believe it or not. It was a Billy Rose show, a wonderful revue.'

'Does he like a flutter?'

'You mean on the ponies? Or in a gambling club?'

'The latter. Does he?'

'I think so, but listen here, what's all this about? Why all the questions about Cedric, Amos?'

I know I can trust him, Amos thought, and said, 'I'd like to speak to you in confidence.'

'You know you can. Go on then, what's in your noggin?'

'I think your friend Cedric Crawford probably might have known, actually been a friend of, Tabitha James, the real mother of Grace Rose.'

'Get on with you, Amos, you can't be serious!'

'I am. I know it sounds a bit far-fetched, fantastical even, but certainly Tabitha knew a man by that name. Do you think there are two Cedric Crawfords in London?'

'I don't know, but I very much doubt it.' Charlie shook his head. 'After all, it's not a name like John Smith, is it?' He drew closer to Amos. 'Refresh my memory a bit . . . I know you found Grace Rose in Whitechapel, in terrible circumstances.'

75

'She was living in a cart, I think it might have been a discarded costermonger's cart, in a cul-de-sac, and she was dressed as a boy.'

'That's *right*! Now I remember, you told me all about it when I came back for the first time with Maisie. You took him to Lady Fenella's, to Haddon House, and when they washed all the dirt off of him he turned out not to be a him, but a her. How's she doing?'

'You've got a good memory, Charlie, and she's doing wonderfully well. But going back to her childhood, when I found her she told me her mother was dead, and then later her mother's old friend, a woman called Sophie Fox-Lannigan, explained to Lady Fenella that Tabitha James had been living with a man called Cedric Crawford, a guard's officer and a gambler. And that when she went to see Tabitha one day, she'd disappeared. They all had. It seemed a bit of a mystery to her.'

Charlie frowned, looked suddenly worried. 'And you want to ask him if it was *him*, is that it?'

'Well, yes. You see we just don't know where Tabitha is buried, and it's always troubled me, and Lady Fenella. You see, when Grace Rose was four she said her mother was buried in Potters Field, but nobody's ever believed that, it didn't sound right. And she isn't, we checked. It would be nice to know the truth, especially for Grace Rose . . . that's all there is to it, I promise you, Charlie.'

'Do you think he knows?'

'He might. Then he might not. It's just possible he moved out, moved on, left Tabitha James before she died.'

Charlie took a deep breath, then blew out air. 'I wouldn't want you to upset him, Amos, he's been through such a bloody lot.'

'I understand that, and I would never create any problems. But I would like to talk to him, yes. Can you arrange it?'

'I could, I suppose,' Charlie answered, sounding reluctant.

'But will you?'

Charlie nodded. 'As long as you handle him with kid gloves.'

'I will, word of honour. And don't tell him why I want to see him, let's not alarm the man, make him think I want to blame him about Tabitha. Because I really don't, I assure you of that.'

'I can ask him as we're leaving if he can dine with us tomorrow –'

'I can't tomorrow, Charlie,' Amos interrupted. 'As a matter of fact, I'm having supper with the Forths, you know, the couple who brought Grace Rose up. But apart from that, I've no other commitments, I'm free.'

'Shall I suggest Friday?'

'That suits me fine.'

'And where should we go? Come back here? Or do you have a particular preference?'

'We can go wherever you want, Charlie, pick any place you like, just so long as you understand I'm doing the inviting and I'm doing the paying.'

Charlie grinned. 'Let's have dinner here. It's nice and convenient for me, and also for Cedric. He lives in Queen Street. With his sister, Rowena.'

'I'll book the table when we leave tonight. And remember, let's keep this nice and easy, Charlie. He mustn't know why.'

'Mum's the word.'

TEN

'I always know when it's going to rain,' Will Hasling said to Alfredo Oliveri. 'My shoulder gives me hell.'

'It's the same for me, my arm feels as if it's in a vice. Never mind – better to have aching wounds than be kicking up daisies in a foreign cemetery,' Alfredo pointed out.

Will grinned. 'Very true.'

The two of them had both suffered minor wounds in the Somme in 1917, and had been shipped home on a hospital ship, then treated at a military hospital in London. As soon as they could, both men had returned to work at Deravenels, and were extremely relieved to be safely back in their old jobs. They had worked with Edward since he had taken over the company in 1904, and were his key executives.

Alfredo paused just before they reached Edward's office, and put his hand on Will's arm, stared at him intently. 'He's not going to like what you're about to reveal to him.'

'You don't have to tell me, I know that, and I'm going to suggest he deals with everything after Christmas, when George is back in London. Giving his brother a rollicking on the telephone won't be effective. He's got to dress George down face to face, don't you think?'

'I do,' Alfredo replied, and sighed. 'He hasn't discussed the MacDonald situation at great length with me, but I'm making the assumption he's a trifle indifferent to the deal.'

'You're right, as usual. For him it's a take it or leave it deal. He'd like to own the liquor company, but if he doesn't get it he won't cry.'

'It struck me earlier that he might have set a trap for his difficult little brother. If George blows the liquor business out of the water he's in trouble, and most certainly can then be *demoted*. What say you?'

Will began to laugh. The Italian part of you is certainly quite Machiavellian, Oliveri. I mustn't forget that.'

Alfredo merely smiled, and walked on down the corridor. He stopped at Edward's office, knocked, then walked in, followed by Will Hasling.

Edward was hanging up the phone. 'Morning, you chaps!' he exclaimed cheerfully when he saw them, an affectionate look crossing his face. He had worried about these two men so much during the war, filled with fear for their safety, and had vowed to cherish them for the rest of their lives when they came back.

'I know you've got to go and see a man about a dog,' Will began, 'but I've something I need to talk with you about.'

Edward chuckled. 'I am indeed going to see a man about a dog. Or I was. However, because of my work here today I've asked Mrs Shaw to go to Harrods to pick out a Westie for Young Edward, and she agreed to do it.'

Alfredo began to laugh, suddenly realizing the play on an old and very familiar saying. 'Will you take the dog with you to Yorkshire tomorrow?' he asked. 'You can ship it, you know, that's no problem.'

'So Mrs Shaw told me, and that is how it will travel . . . in a van, by road, special delivery for Master Edward Deravenel from Harrods. He'll love it because he'll feel very important.' Leaning forward, he now asked, 'So, Will, why are you here?' He glanced at Alfredo. 'And you, Oliveri? You're both standing there with such glum faces I'm assuming that you're about to deliver bad news.' Edward, looking very handsome in a dark blue Savile Row suit and cornflower-blue tie, sat back in his chair, his eyes focused on his executives. 'And for God's sake sit down, the two of you. You might as well be comfortable when you give me the dire news.'

'You assume correctly,' Will said. 'It's about George. He's in trouble.'

'How unusual,' Edward said in a sardonic voice. 'What's he done now? I know he can't have killed my deal with Ian MacDonald because that meeting is not until tomorrow.'

'That's so,' Will agreed, and went on, 'You're about to get hit with his gambling debts, and Amos can fill you in better than I can about those. But the gossip is rampant, all over town, so Howard tells me.'

'Gambling debts! Why am I going to get hit with them, for God's sake? He can bloody well pay his own gambling debts,' Edward exclaimed, his voice rising angrily.

'Let me start at the beginning,' Will said. 'A few days ago my brother told me there was gossip out on the street about George's gambling, whoring, and drug-taking –'

'He's taking drugs?' Edward shouted, his face turning red as the fury erupted. Although he was blessed with an affable nature and was calm most of the time, Edward did have a famous temper that struck terror in everyone. 'I'll have his guts for garters!' he shrilled, jumping up, his temper getting the better of him. 'And why does he have debts in the first place? I'll skin him alive, the little sod! Bringing dishonour to our name. *A gentleman* takes care of his obligations, and he's well aware of that.'

'You know what George is,' Oliveri murmured softly. 'And I

have a suggestion to make . . .' Oliveri paused, staring hard at Edward.

'Go on, then, tell me,' Edward snapped, and immediately shook his head. 'I'm very sorry, Oliveri, I'm not angry with you. Do excuse me.' He sat down.

'Don't have to explain, I understand. Getting back to the bad lad, I think we should send him off on a few trips, get him out of London, and away from all the temptations of the flesh, etcetera.' Alfredo sat back, eyeing Edward, his expression serious.

'Where can we send him?' Will asked, glancing at Alfredo swiftly, frowning.

'First of all, if the deal with Ian MacDonald proceeds, he can take charge of it, and he'll be back and forth to Edinburgh for quite a while. Otherwise, he can go to Spain, which was neutral during the war: travel is still relatively easy. He could look into the Jimenez situation. They do want to sell their sherry business, remember.' His gaze still fixed on Will, Alfredo finished, 'They make the best sherry in the world, let's not forget that.'

'George certainly won't,' Edward interjected. 'I should think he'll jump at a job like that. But it's a good idea, keeping him travelling, I mean. But what's this about drugs, Will? And what is he taking?'

'Howard didn't know, but he's promised to find out for me. I suspect it's either cocaine, or possibly he visits those opium dens in Chinatown, down Limehouse way.'

'Bloody fool!' Edward shook his head, stood up again, paced for a moment, and then he addressed Will. 'You said Amos has investigated all this, knows more.'

'He does. I spoke to him earlier. I'd asked him to do a bit of digging for me yesterday, and he did find out a few things last night. I told him to come in around ten thirty –' Will stopped at the sound of a loud knock on the door. 'I'm sure this is him.'

'No doubt,' Edward agreed, and called out, 'Come in!'

'Good morning,' Amos said to the room at large; they greeted him in return. Hurrying over to the desk, he waited until Edward was seated behind it before taking the empty chair at the other side.

'What did you find out?' Edward asked.

'The promissory notes are held by three clubs. Starks, The Rosemont, and the Gentleman's Club. Starks is owed the most money, and Julian Stark is personally holding the notes. I heard last night from one of my contacts that he is going to come and see you himself, to demand payment.'

'Is he now? Well, we must forestall him. He's a big gossip. Do you know how much my brother owes Starks?'

Amos nodded. 'I do. Thirty thousand pounds.'

Edward was flabbergasted, and his face paled. 'What an idiot he is!' he cried, his rage surfacing.

'Don't lose your temper again,' Will murmured in soothing tones. 'He ain't worth it, Ned, and it's only money.'

Endeavouring to calm himself, Edward muttered, 'It's the principle.' Then he addressed Alfredo. 'I'm going to write a personal cheque for that amount, a cashier's cheque, and I'd like you and Finnister to take it to Julian Stark after lunch. I know you won't mind doing that, will you? And get those promissory notes.'

'That's not a problem, we can handle this bit of business in a few minutes.' Oliveri glanced at Finnister. 'Isn't that so?'

Amos nodded, then looked over at Edward. 'The other two gambling clubs are each holding notes for five thousand pounds.'

'I see.' Edward was livid, and his anger showed on his face which had now lost all of its colour completely, was paler than ever. 'I'll write those two cheques as well, and you can drop them off, can't you, Amos? Oliveri?'

'Yes, and I'll get the promissory notes,' Amos replied and Oliveri nodded.

There was a sudden silence in the office. Will thought a pin dropping would be like a bomb going off, and he held himself perfectly still, waiting for a further explosion from Ned. But he said nothing. Nor did anyone else speak.

Forty thousand pounds was a fortune, Will thought, turning over the amount in his mind. How had George Deravenel managed to lose so much? *Drink? Drugs? Total* stupidity? Well he was stupid. Will had always known that. A pretty boy, spoiled by his mother and sister Meg before she had married and gone to live in France. George. All that silky blond hair, those unusual turquoise blue eyes. But dumb yes . . . beautiful and dumb. Poor eyesight, couldn't pass the test to join the army. He thought he was Ned, or, more correctly, thought he could *be* his big brother. That was not possible. Edward was brilliant; he couldn't hold a candle to him. George was his own worst enemy, Will understood this. He was always heading for trouble of his own making.

Will looked at Amos, as Edward was saying, 'So tell me, what did you find out about the drugs, Amos?'

'I went to a lot of clubs late last night, and I think the drug-taking has been exaggerated,' Amos explained. 'He might have tried reefers at times, also cocaine, but I don't believe it's a problem. Liquor is. He drinks a lot. He's on the road to becoming an alcoholic.'

'Just as I thought.' Edward nodded. 'Thank you, Amos, for sniffing around. I'm going to have to decide what to do with Master George, when he returns to London.' He gave the three men a warm smile. 'But I'm not going to let him spoil Christmas. Lunch at Rules at one o'clock, and please, gentlemen, I don't want any discussion about this matter in front of Richard.'

ELEVEN

Grace Rose finished wrapping the last of her Christmas presents in gold paper, tying the gauzy gold ribbon into a lavish bow. After adding a small spray of gold-painted holly and a bunch of tiny gold bells, she put it to one side on the table. Then, very neatly, she wrote on the small gift card: *To dearest Bess, with much love from Grace Rose*. Once she had tied the card onto the ribbon she sat back, regarding her handiwork.

There were nine presents all beautifully wrapped and ready to be sent off to Ravenscar. Six of them were for her half sisters and brothers, and three were for her adult relatives, Aunt Cecily, Aunt Elizabeth and Uncle Ned.

Uncle Ned. *Her father*. She loved him the most except for her parents, Vicky and Stephen Forth. They had adopted her, brought her up since she was four years old . . . fourteen years of love and devotion they had given her, and they had given her a life, one that was truly wonderful, and which she wouldn't have had without them.

In her mind Grace Rose associated Vicky and Stephen with love, for that is what she had received from them, and continued to receive unstintingly. They had never demanded anything in return but she had responded to them with utter devotion, love and obedience.

Within the first few weeks of her arrival in this house the three of them had become as close as any parents and a child could be. And right from the beginning she had fallen into their ways, had adapted easily to their lifestyle, been comfortable in their world of courtesy, good manners, cosseted comfort, and undeniable wealth and privilege.

There were moments, like right now, when she thought about the courage they had shown . . . they had been so very brave to take her in, make her their daughter.

She, the urchin child, existing on the streets of Whitechapel, living in an old cart, alone, scared witless and forever hungry. An urchin child dressed in ragged boys' clothes, which were far too big, and covered in grime and dirt. A little girl who had been thrown away without a second thought, until Amos Finnister had found her and taken her to Lady Fenella and Vicky Forth at Haddon House. The three of them, and Stephen as well, had saved her life. She shuddered to think about what would have happened to her if Amos had not gone into that cul-de-sac on that particular night to eat his meat pies. And found *her*. She might not have lived to see the year out.

Rising, Grace Rose stood up and went over to the looking glass which hung above the fireplace in the parlour, staring at her reflection. What she saw quite pleased her, even though she didn't think of herself as being beautiful; she now decided that she looked attractive. She especially liked her red gold hair, which she thought of as her best asset. It fell to her shoulders in curls and waves, and was constantly admired by everyone. Her eyes were unusual, very, very blue, and she knew – everyone knew – that she looked exactly like Edward Deravenel. Even her slender nose, rounded chin and broad forehead were inherited from him.

Grace Rose had first met him fourteen years ago, in this house, when he had rushed into the library looking for Amos and Neville Watkins. The minute she set eyes on him her heart had done a little leap inside her, and she felt a lovely surge of happiness. It was *him*. Her father, looking just the way her mother had described him to her. Tabitha had told her he was strong and tall like a tree in the forest, with eyes as blue as the sky above, and hair the colour of the autumn leaves. She had recognized him.

She had smiled at him and he had smiled back, and she knew deep down inside herself that she was his, and he was hers, and there would always be something special and unique between them. And it had been so.

Her thoughts swung to Tabitha . . . her first mother. A little sigh escaped her. She was still perplexed about her mother's fate; Tabitha had gone away one day and never come back, and *she* had gone out into the streets, running as fast as her little legs would carry her. Her need to escape that hovel of a house had propelled her as far away as possible.

Now she knew as much as Vicky and the others knew about Tabitha James. Her first mother had been born Lady Tabitha Brockhaven, the daughter of an Earl; she had fallen in love with her music teacher, Toby James, and had eloped with him. But they had never had any children together. *She* had come along later, fathered by Uncle Ned when he was only a boy, then her mother had moved and had lost touch with Edward Deravenel.

Vicky, her adoptive mother, had told her about her background, given her all the facts that were available when she was fourteen, at which time Vicky had believed she was old enough to know everything. But even Vicky had admitted rather sadly that it was not very much.

'It's all right, Mother,' Grace Rose had responded at the time. 'I'm glad to know who Tabitha really was, but you and Stephen are my parents and that's more than enough for me. And Uncle Ned has always acknowledged that he's my biological father.'

Grace Rose turned her back to the fireplace and stood warming herself for a few minutes, thinking about Edward Deravenel. He had always been honest and straight forward with her. He had taught her so many things over the years, imbued in her a sense of honour and fair play, told her about justice, and taught her to have integrity in all things. 'And here is something else,' he had said quite recently. 'Follow your own dreams. Don't put them aside for anyone or anything. Because sometimes people and events will . . . betray you. Be your own person, Grace Rose, go your own way, and always be true to yourself.' That day last summer she had promised him she would do as he said.

He was coming to the dinner party tonight, and she was excited that he would be one of the guests. He was bringing Mrs Shaw. She liked Jane Shaw, who was a beautiful, gracious, gentle person. And she fully understood why this woman was Uncle Ned's mistress. He needed a woman to be nice to him. She had often noticed, when she was at Ravenscar for holidays in the summer, that Aunt Elizabeth could be mean to him, unkind really. And she shouted at him, which frightened the younger children. Another thing she had noticed was that Aunt Elizabeth paid more attention to the two boys than the little girls. Bess, her very dear friend, had confided that her mother was really only interested in the two boys because they were 'the heir and the spare'. There were times when Grace thought that Bess was not particularly attached to her mother, and this saddened her. Having a loving mother was the most wonderful thing.

It seemed to her, all of a sudden, that Elizabeth Deravenel was not well liked in the family; certainly Aunt Cecily disliked her, she had picked up on that ages ago, when she was much younger. Grace Rose loved Cecily Deravenel her grandmother, if unacknowledged as such.

'Well, there you are, Grace Rose,' Vicky exclaimed, pushing open the door of the parlour. Glancing over at the table she then nodded approvingly. 'I see you've wrapped a lot of presents, darling. Good girl.'

Grace Rose beamed at Vicky. 'I have, Mother, all of those which you are sending off to Ravenscar. Is Fuller going to take them to the post office tomorrow?'

'Actually, he isn't, after all. Uncle Ned just telephoned me about something, and in passing I asked him if he would mind taking them, if we packed them up in a small case, of course, and he said he would be happy to do so. We can do that job after lunch. In the meantime, I have some very good news for you.' Vicky waved the letter she was holding, and continued, 'My friend Millicent Hanson has written back to say she will be delighted to have you to stay with her next spring and summer. Therefore you will be able to attend some of the courses at Oxford.'

'Oh, how wonderful! Thank you, Mother, for writing to her. I'm so happy.'

Edward was in a foul mood, and he knew exactly why. He was blazing mad with George, and for some reason he was finding it hard to rid himself of the anger. Usually he managed to toss things off, especially things which had to do with George's bad behaviour. This mess with the gambling debts was another matter entirely.

In the first place, there was the question of honour. George had been brought up properly, as a gentleman, and ought to know better than to leave debts of this nature unpaid. It was a disaster for his reputation, and also damaging to the family name.

Leaning back in the chair, closing his eyes, he asked himself why George hadn't paid the clubs immediately. Was he short of money? Edward doubted that. He earned a good salary here at

Deravenels, received quarterly director's fees, and his wife Isabel had a huge allowance from her mother. Nan Watkins was a millionairess many times over, and had been extremely generous to Isabel and George. Actually, in his opinion, they had money to burn. On the other hand, thirty thousand pounds owed to one club and five thousand each owed to two other clubs were hefty sums. Forty thousand pounds.

Then there was the matter of the drinking. It had startled Edward to hear that George was considered an alcoholic. He hadn't realized it had gone that far. As for the drugs, he wasn't certain about that at all. But who knows, he now thought. Perhaps he is on something addictive, other than the drink.

Edward accepted that George would have to be dealt with very sternly when he returned from Scotland, and he also decided that George was going to pay back the forty thousand pounds *he* had just laid out. He had no intention of funding his brother's bad gambling habits; quite suddenly he wondered if he could have George's memberships to the clubs cancelled. Or perhaps he could have George banned. How he wasn't sure, but it might be worth a try. And he would put the fear of God into George after Christmas. Yes, he was going to deal with a lot of things in the new year, he had made that decision days ago.

Now he must throw off this foul mood. Immediately. He had to push a smile onto his face and go across the street to Rules. He didn't want to put a damper on the lunch he was giving for his special colleagues at Deravenels. It was almost Christmas, the first Christmas they would be able to celebrate properly, because finally they were at peace. There would be a few faces missing at the lunch: Rob Aspen and Christopher Green, who had died in France fighting for their country. They would be remembered fondly by everyone, himself most especially.

Rising, Edward went over to the cupboard where the safe was housed, and opened it. He stood there for a moment, and then he made a decision. He took out two large envelopes, locked the safe, went back to his desk and placed the envelopes in a drawer. This he locked. Pocketing the key, he went to get his overcoat and scarf. It was almost one o'clock. Time to go.

TWELVE

Vicky Forth was an optimist. She had been all her life; even as a child her attitude had been positive.

Her glass was always half full, never half empty; tomorrow would be a much better day than today; the future was full of promise and success. Her nature induced her to forge ahead with her projects, undaunted and full of bravery. If any adversity occurred she looked it straight in the eye, and moved right through it, as if it didn't exist.

Her husband Stephen, who loved, adored and encouraged her in her work, said she was a woman warrior out to conquer the world by doing good deeds. And this was true. Vicky had touched many lives. She loved helping others, most especially damaged women down on their luck, in need of care, counselling and encouragement. She wanted to help them have better lives.

Her optimism had served her well over the years, and she suddenly thought of this now as she looked at some of the dresses in her wardrobe, wondering which one to wear tonight.

How right she had been to encourage Grace Rose to be optimistic, to set her sights on Oxford University. Women were not yet admitted to membership of the University, but they could attend lectures and take courses.

Grace Rose would be able to do all of the above, and would be safe, well looked after by her old friend Millicent Hanson, now widowed, who had a lovely old house in Oxford. It had been an inspired idea to write to her.

In the letter Vicky had received today, Millicent had said she would be delighted to have Grace Rose living with her whilst she pursued her studies; Vicky was relieved, happy for her daughter, who was a wonderful student. She hoped to be a historian one day.

Finally, Vicky selected a stylish, dark-rose coloured silk dress with three-quarter length sleeves and a narrow skirt which fell to the ankles. It had a V-shaped insertion of beige lace at the front, and this made for a unique neckline. She had only worn it once before, and she decided it would be perfect for the dinner party tonight. It had style, but it was not overly dressy for a dinner at home, especially since the men were not wearing black tie.

After putting on the dress and stepping into matching rose-coloured silk pumps, Vicky went back to her dressing table, selected a pair of pearl-and-diamond earrings, and a matching brooch in the design of a flower. After adding the jewellery, she moved across the floor with her usual willowy grace, stood staring at herself in the cheval looking-glass in one corner of the bedroom. Nodding to herself, she decided she liked her appearance. Yes, she would do.

Now in her mid-forties, Vicky Forth looked like a much younger woman; her dark chestnut hair was glossy and thick, with only a hint of silver threads here and there. The few wrinkles she had around her eyes and mouth were hardly visible, and because she was full of *joie de vivre* there was an amazing sense of youthfulness about her. Her energy and enthusiasm added to her attractiveness. Both men and women were drawn to her, found her to be a warm, kind and compassionate woman. Edward Deravenel had always said hers was the best shoulder to cry on because she had so much sympathy to give.

Turning around, Vicky hurried towards the door, just as it flew open to admit her husband Stephen.

A smile struck his face when he saw her. 'How beautiful you look, Vicky!' he exclaimed, coming into the room, closing the door. He paused to kiss her, held her away from him, smiling broadly, nodding his approval.

'Hello, darling,' she said, smiling back at him.

'You're dressed rather early, aren't you, my dear?'

Vicky shook her head. 'Not really, I do have a few things to check with Cook, and Fuller. Also, a short while ago Ned telephoned. He asked to come a bit earlier, before everyone else. He wants to talk to us, so I said it would be all right.'

'What does he want to talk to us *about*?' Stephen asked curiously.

'Grace Rose.'

'What about her?'

'Apparently some years ago, after he had taken over as head of Deravenels and was making money, he set up a trust for her. It will not be hers until she is twenty-one, but he wishes to bring the relevant documents tonight. He thinks we should now hold them for her until she comes of age.'

'How odd. Why?'

'He didn't actually explain everything, Stephen darling, but he did mention that he was putting many of his affairs in order between now and the end of the year.'

'I see. Well, then, I'd better get a move on, darling, change my shirt and suit, dandy myself up for your dinner party.'

'Our dinner party, Stephen,' she corrected. 'Ned said it would only take fifteen minutes or so. He suggested Grace Rose could entertain Jane whilst we have our discussion in the library.'

'I know Grace Rose will enjoy that, but will Jane?'

'What on earth do you mean?' Vicky frowned in puzzlement, staring at her husband questioningly.

'Grace Rose has become amazingly forthright lately. Whilst she is not in any way rude, in fact she's extremely polite and well-mannered, I do find she really does speak her mind these days. Or hadn't you noticed?'

'Yes, of course I have,' Vicky responded. 'On the other hand, she makes her somewhat startling comments so casually and with such panache, such good humour, I'm quite certain no one takes offence.' Hurrying to the door, she added over her shoulder, 'But I must go down. I have to make sure everything is in order. Don't be too long, will you?' She glanced at the carriage clock on the mantelpiece and pointed out, 'It's already ten past six, and Ned and Jane will be arriving at six-thirty. The other guests are due at seven.'

'Who else is coming, by the way?' he asked swiftly. 'Just refresh my memory again. You never did give me a final list, as you normally do.'

'Oh sorry, so sorry, Stephen. Yes, well, it's only family, really. There's Ned and Jane, and us, that makes five, plus Fenella, Amos, and my brother.'

'Isn't Kathleen coming with Will?'

'No, I'm afraid not. He telephoned me this morning. She's fighting an awful cold apparently, and he said they both thought she ought to stay at home. She doesn't want to spread germs. So I agreed. What else could I do? Anyway, a lovely flower arrangement and a note of apology arrived this afternoon from Kathleen. She's a sweet woman, very thoughtful.'

'Yes, she is. It's all this blasted rain we're having, if you want my opinion,' Stephen grumbled. 'It's been raining cats and dogs for days. No wonder people are catching colds, becoming ill.'

Vicky burst out laughing. 'Let's not complain about the English weather, my sweet! The war is OVER. That's quite something to be happy about, isn't it? To hell with the weather, I say.'

He chuckled, and headed over to his dressing room. 'Give me ten minutes and I'll be down,' he muttered as he disappeared through the doorway.

Smiling to herself, thinking how awful her life would have been without him, Vicky closed the bedroom door behind her and went downstairs. She wanted to check on Fuller, to make sure he had taken the champagne to the library; she had selected Krug, knowing it was Ned's preferred brand these days.

Dear Ned. He had always been her favourite and one of her dearest friends. They had known each other for donkey's years, and had become very close as time had passed. He was her brother Will's best friend, and she fully understood why these two had bonded years before.

She had helped Ned to get through his grief and despair after his mistress Lily had been killed in that horrendous accident. Well, she added to herself, that was no accident, it was cold-blooded murder. Margot Grant, Edward's bitter enemy, in his fight for control of Deravenels all those years ago. She had had Lily Overton murdered. And she had gone scot-free, had never been made to pay for it. No, she *had* been made to pay, actually. In the worst way. The Frenchwoman had lost everyone and everything. God's will, no doubt.

A shiver ran through Vicky and goose flesh sprang up on her arms and the back of her neck. She had been in the landau with Lily that fateful day in Hyde Park, had been thrown out with her and could have easily been killed herself.

Lily . . . her best friend, so beautiful, and far too young to die. And the unborn baby killed, too, Ned's child which she was carrying. Vicky knew she would never forget the sight of Lily laying there on the grass, the pale blue silk of her dress covered in bright red blood. That image was indelibly printed on her mind; it never faded.

Pausing on the staircase, Vicky took a deep breath and endeavoured to throw off these dire memories of that most miserable day, and then she went on down slowly, calming her thoughts before their guests began to arrive.

Almost at once she bumped into Fuller in the downstairs hall. 'Good evening, Madam,' he said, inclining his head. 'I'm just about to put the grog in the library.'

'Thank you,' she answered, noting that he was holding a silver bucket full of ice. 'Everything else is in hand, isn't it?' she asked. 'All the fires going?'

'Oh yes, Madam, all shipshape. We're ready to set sail.'

'Thank you, Fuller,' she murmured and walked along the corridor towards the kitchen, shaking her head. Before joining them last year Fuller had been head butler in the house of a former admiral in the Royal Navy, now deceased, and he tended to speak in somewhat nautical terms. She and Grace Rose found it amusing, but at times it irritated Stephen: only the other day he had complained that he felt as if he were living on a damned battleship!

Her answer had been to quickly point out that Fuller just happened to be an excellent butler, the best they had had in years.

Opening the kitchen door, Vicky put her head around it and asked, 'Do you need me for anything, Mrs Johnson?'

The cook turned swiftly, holding a ladle in her hand and it hovered in mid-air for a moment. Putting it down, she said, 'Evening, mum. No, there're no problems. All's well 'ere, we're shipshape, and on time. Dinner will be ready at eight bells, as you requested.' Cook compressed her mouth hard, swallowing her sudden laughter. She steadied herself and blurted out, 'Seems I'm pickin' up Fuller's jargon, mum, sorry, ever so sorry, mum.'

Trying to keep a straight face herself, Vicky answered, 'Just make sure the mulligatawny soup is very hot. You know Mr Forth likes the soup to be *scalding*.'

'Yes, mum, and everything else! I knows he prefers his 'ot food 'ot, and so he should, mum.'

Laughing, Vicky made her way to the drawing room and went in. It was her favourite room in the house, and she glanced around, admiring it for a moment. The walls were covered in pale-yellow silk, and yellow-and-cream striped taffeta draperies hung at the windows, billowed out like ballgowns, the way she liked them to be.

Against the pale-yellow backdrop there was a mélange of bright colours, mainly clear blues and reds in the upholstery fabrics on the various antique French chairs and large comfortable sofas. The fire was blazing, the porcelain lamps shaded in cream silk offered a welcoming glow, and there were bowls of fresh flowers everywhere. Perfect, she thought. The room looks just perfect.

The ringing of the doorbell made Vicky start, and as she hurried across the antique Aubusson carpet she heard Fuller's footsteps echoing in the marble hall. She hoped he wouldn't say welcome aboard, as he had been known to do sometimes. On the other hand, if he did, she knew that Edward would simply chuckle.

THIRTEEN

Grace Rose had been given the task of entertaining Mrs Shaw while her parents and Uncle Ned had some sort of business meeting in the library.

She was glad they had asked her to keep Jane Shaw company because she really liked her. There was something about her that was intriguing and special; also, Grace Rose knew that Jane Shaw liked her in return, and there was a certain ease between them.

That this woman was truly lovely to look at was obvious; that she was charming, kind and extremely intelligent a bonus, Grace Rose thought, impressed by her knowledge of art and sculpture, her willingness to answer questions whenever Grace Rose asked. Jane knew a great deal about certain artists and their work, most especially the French Impressionists and Post-Impressionists, and she was happy to share.

The two of them were seated in the yellow drawing room, chatting generalities. At one moment, Grace Rose couldn't help thinking that Jane Shaw looked perfect in this perfect room tonight. She was wearing a most elegant and fashionable sapphire-blue velvet dress, and sapphire earrings which exactly echoed the particular blue in some of the fabrics her mother had chosen for the room. She ought to be painted in here, Grace Rose thought, and it should be called *Portrait in Blue*.

After another brief discussion about a recent art exhibition at a well-known gallery in Chelsea, with Jane doing most of the talking, they fell silent. But it was a compatible silence, not awkward at all; the two of them were comfortable with each other and had been since they had first met some years before.

Looking across at Grace Rose, Jane took the lead again, and murmured, 'I hear you love your studies, and your uncle told me you are extremely dedicated and disciplined. He thinks that's admirable, and so do I.' Settling back in the French bergère, Jane took a sip of champagne and then smiled warmly at the younger woman.

Grace Rose nodded, her face full of eagerness. 'I've always loved school, Mrs Shaw, and I'm really happy today because it will soon be possible for me to live at Oxford with a friend of Mother's, and attend courses at the University.'

'That's wonderful! Congratulations! History is your subject, isn't it?'

'Yes. At this moment I'm particularly interested in France, and in French kings.'

'What an extraordinary coincidence. I've always been partial to French history, and although the English are not supposed to like Napoleon Bonaparte, I must confess I've always had a sneaking admiration for him. In many ways he was a genius.'

'And probably the greatest general the world has ever known,' Grace Rose remarked.

'Except when he invaded Russia,' Jane pointed out, eyeing her young companion acutely.

'That's true . . . but it was mostly the weather that scuttled him,' Grace Rose replied. 'I was thinking in terms of strategy when I said he was the greatest.'

'I understand, and many agree with you. But tell me, which particular king intrigues you the most?'

'To be honest, I'm more taken with the mistresses of kings. You see, that's what I'm studying at the moment. *Mistresses*. I find them fascinating –' Grace Rose broke off, remembering that Jane Shaw was Uncle Ned's mistress. She chastised herself silently for having embarked on such a controversial subject. 'Oh, dear, I'm so . . . s-s-sorry,' she stammered, looking chagrined, and then flushed in embarrassment.

Jane couldn't help laughing when she saw the woebegone expression on her face, and reaching out she patted her arm, said very softly, 'Don't apologize, my dear, I know you know that I am Uncle Ned's mistress.'

'Yes,' Grace Rose replied, nodding. 'The whole world knows –' She broke off again, looking even more flustered than ever, and cleared her throat.

'I'm very sorry, Mrs Shaw, I keep saying the wrong thing. I don't mean to give offence.'

'And you haven't, I promise. Tell me why you love mistresses so much that you want to study them?'

Suddenly feeling undeterred, realizing Jane was obviously inter-ested to hear her opinion, she rushed on. 'Those I've been reading about are all extraordinary women. They played such enormous roles in history. Most were influential in politics and government, whilst caring about their kings, and what they did says so much about the times they lived in. We learn from them. Their rela-tionships were usually about power. In most instances, I think.'

'Absolutely!' Jane exclaimed. 'And money. And position. As well as social ascendency, and, in another sense, social accept-ance and *supremacy*.'

'I love mistresses, I mean as a subject,' Grace Rose continued. 'They're much more interesting to read about than most of the queens. Frequently, the king cared more for his mistress than his wife.'

Struck by the girl's openness, and an unusual honesty that was quite breathtaking, Jane began to chuckle, her expression amused. After a moment, she asked, 'And which mistress are you concentrating on at the moment, Grace Rose?'

'Diane de Poitiers, the mistress of Henri II of France. She met him when he was a little boy, only twelve. This was just after he had come back to France, after being held in captivity by the Spaniards. He was a hostage, along with his brother, while his father went free. He was depressed and shy at the time, and she befriended him. Actually, she became his protectress, and was very kind to him, a steady influence. She mothered him quite a lot, too. I believe that she made him feel safe and secure. That was important to him, I think.'

'Yes, you're right, it probably was.'

'Diane seduced him when he was seventeen,' Grace Rose announced. 'She was twenty years older than he was, but he never left her. She was his mistress for his entire life. He died before she did, but when he was alive he doted on her, much more than on his queen.'

'Ah yes, the famous Catherine de Medici. A woman scorned at the outset of her marriage. Henri II was too preoccupied with Diane, I do believe, to be bothered with his wife.'

'You seem to know quite a lot about Diane, Mrs Shaw.'

'Yes, I do,' Jane answered and a small smile flickered at the corners of her mouth, her eyes twinkling with amusement.

Grace Rose felt her own mouth twitch and she began to laugh softly. And Jane Shaw laughed with her. And it was at that moment that these two women bonded forever. The mistress and the illegitimate daughter. Outsiders, in a certain sense, and yet so close to this most dominant man in their lives, closer than most others whom he knew and cared about.

Grace Rose shifted slightly on the sofa, and remarked, 'Then you must know that Henri II gave Diane the crown jewels. Just imagine that. And also that most palatial of châteaux, Chenonceaux.'

'I did know that, yes. And I'm also aware that she held her

power for almost thirty years. Yet she was wonderfully kind to the king's whole family, to the queen when she was desperately ill, and Diane virtually brought up the royal children.'

'And those children happened only because Diane persuaded the king to visit his wife's bed, pointing out that he needed an heir.'

'My goodness, Grace Rose, you've done your research well. Diane is your favourite, is she?'

'Yes, but there's one other mistress whom I admire, and would have liked to have known.'

'And who may I ask is that?'

'Agnès Sorel,' Grace Rose told her. 'She was the mistress of Charles VII in 1444. He was so smitten with Agnès that he made her his *official* mistress. By that I mean he created an actual official position, and for the first time in French history. *Maîtresse en titre* –'

'And who is the *maîtresse en titre*?' Edward asked from the doorway, striding into the room, a look of considerable amusement on his face. Although the two women did not know it, he had been standing there listening to them for several minutes.

Grace swung her hand, and exclaimed, 'Oh, goodness! Uncle Ned! I was just explaining to Mrs Shaw that I am currently studying mistresses.' Once again she instantly became flustered, and hurried on, 'What I mean is – er – er French mistresses, I mean the mistresses of kings –'

'But only French kings apparently. Are you not interested in English kings and their mistresses?' He chuckled. 'Too dull, I suspect, the English, eh?'

'Oh, no, not at all. I know a lot about English kings. There was Charles II and Nell Gwynne, and –'

'Yes, my dear, I know, I was just teasing you.' He walked over to the sofa, stood behind her, his hands resting on her shoulders affectionately, whilst looking across at Jane quizzically.

Jane smiled at him. 'I was thoroughly enjoying our discussion,' she murmured with warmth and genuine sincerity. 'Grace Rose is going to be a marvellous historian, Ned. She has all the right instincts. She's obviously not afraid of research, and she has a nose for sniffing out the truth, I think. None of us were around to witness events hundreds of years ago, so historians have to weigh the written evidence, go with their instincts.'

'I have always been impressed,' he murmured, obviously pleased by Jane's comments. He remained standing where he was, for a moment lost in his thoughts.

Jane caught her breath; seeing them together like that in such close and intimate proximity was tremendously revealing. There was no doubt whose daughter she was – that red-gold hair and the brilliant blue eyes. And they both had the same pink and cream complexion. Yes, Grace Rose was Ned's spitting image and the vividness, the vibrancy of their looks was startling.

I want to make her my friend, Jane thought all of a sudden. And I will be *her* friend, protective of her if that is necessary. And that way, no matter what happens, I will always have a little bit of Ned.

Vicky said, from the doorway, 'Everyone seems to be arriving at once! Come along, Grace Rose, I hear Fenella and Amos in the foyer.'

'Go along,' Edward said, standing away from Grace Rose. 'Go and greet your old friends.'

'Oh yes, I will!' she cried and jumped up.

Edward watched her go, and then he turned to Jane. He walked over to her, pulled her to her feet, kissed her on the cheek, led her to the fireplace. 'She takes one's breath away with her bluntness, I'm afraid. I hope she didn't say the wrong thing, or embarrass you?'

'Of course not. Frankly, I found her refreshing.' Jane hesitated, and then murmured in a low voice, 'I would like to get to know her better, Ned.'

'Then you shall,' he promised.

'There isn't anything wrong, is there? I mean you're not ill are you, Ned?' Vicky asked sotto voce, looking at him intently.

He was seated on her right at the circular dinner table, and he glanced at her swiftly. 'Of course not. I'm in perfect health. Why do you ask?'

'Because you decided to give us those documents tonight. It was so unexpected, Ned, out of the blue. I can't help, well . . . worrying, wondering if things are all right with you.'

He leaned to her and said quietly, 'I suppose the war and the flu pandemic have affected me a little, in the sense that they've made me realize I'm mortal like everyone else. When one is very young, one thinks that life is endless, that we'll all live forever. But, sadly, that's not true. We're all vulnerable.'

Now Ned flashed her his most brilliant smile. 'I'm truly not ill, Vicky, dear. I don't intend to keel over for donkey's years, and I promise you there's only one reason I've given you and Stephen the documents. And that's because you *should* have them in your possession as her parents. That's all there is to it. Also, I've been rather efficient lately, and these last few weeks I've been putting a lot of my other personal business in order.'

Vicky nodded, leaned back in her chair, filled with relief. She gave him a warm and loving smile. 'You've been so good about her all these years, and good to her. Just as you've been good to everyone you care about.'

'I just try to do my bit, the best way I can, that's all,' he answered with a light shrug of his broad shoulders, and then he turned to speak to Fenella who had asked him a question about Young Edward and his health.

With the worry about Ned now totally erased from her mind, Vicky relaxed completely, and glanced around the table. She saw that everyone was having a good time, enjoying being together. Fuller had just served the Sole Colbert a few moments before, and there were several comments about how delicious it was, and she was pleased they liked Cook's food.

After a moment, she realized Jane Shaw was trying to get her attention, and she asked, 'Is everything all right, Jane? You are enjoying the fish, aren't you?'

Jane smiled. 'It's delicious, and I just wanted to say how special your table looks tonight, Vicky, with all your beautiful china and silver. You know how much I love your little red box, as you call it.'

'Thank you. Everybody does – I suppose it's cosy, intimate, rather a nice place to be on a wintry night.'

Smiling, Jane nodded, and went back to her food.

Vicky eyed the room which she had decorated about five years ago, just before the war, flattered by Jane's comments. It *was* a little red box, with crimson silk brocade covering the walls and hanging at the windows, the Victorian chairs around the table covered in a deeper red velvet, the Turkish carpet underfoot a mélange of reds, pinks and navy blue. The fire burning brightly and the many candles in their tall silver candlesticks added to the warmth, intimacy and elegance of the room on this cold December night.

Vicky usually gave this dinner party every year, just before Christmas. And even during the war she had kept up the tradition. It was always the same people who came, old friends and relatives. It struck her suddenly how clannish they all were, but then the Deravenel family in particular had always been somewhat addicted to their family and oldest friends. All of their lives they had been intertwined with other branches of the family, and most especially the Watkins clan, who were their first cousins. She supposed it was because of shared beliefs and ideals, a particular philosophy, a way of life that drew them into each other's orbit. And loyalty and friendship and constant support were essential elements in their relationship.

She thought of her sister-in-law Kathleen, not present tonight because she had a cold. She was Ned's cousin, sister of the late Neville and Johnny Watkins, both killed in that awful car crash at Ravenscar four years ago. She missed her presence. When he had arrived tonight Will had told her that Kathleen was really quite sick. 'But not Spanish flu,' he had added swiftly, observing the look of apprehension crossing her face, 'Just a heavy cold.' Will loved and adored Kathleen, and it had always been a very solid marriage, much to Vicky's gratification.

Fenella's voice brought her out of her reverie, and she looked across at her old friend, who was saying, 'How is Charlie feeling, Amos?'

'He's relieved he's safely home, happy that the war's over, Lady Fenella, and he sends his best to you, to everyone. But he has been wounded, has a really bad leg injury and he limps, uses a cane. But at least they saved his leg. Also, one side of his face is scarred. I'm afraid it was burned.' Amos shook his head, looking suddenly worried. 'However, he is very cheerful, I must admit, and looking forward to doing something else in the theatre, perhaps producing or writing.'

'Is he that badly scarred?' Fenella asked, frowning, all of her attention on Amos.

'As I said, it's only one side of his face that was burned. And the scars are still healing. He told me he might be able to do something about it later, once he's really better. There are apparently new methods for treating burns.'

'Yes, that's true,' Grace Rose interjected. 'Actually, skin-grafting and that kind of special surgery goes back to ancient times.'

'I didn't know that!' Vicky exclaimed. 'You're a fountain of knowledge, darling.'

Fenella had a thoughtful expression on her face when she looked across the table, said to Vicky, 'Jeanette Ridgely made a remark to me the other day when she came to help out at Haddon House. Her son was an officer at the front, and he's home now, also wounded. She said he wished there was somewhere wounded soldiers could go, to have some sort of relaxation and recreation, talk to other Tommies. He said that was what his men needed. A place more like Haddon House than a public house, where inevitably many of the men just got drunk.'

'That's an interesting idea.' Vicky glanced at the others, raising a brow. 'Don't you agree?'

'Yes, I do,' Stephen answered, always ready to back his wife in her projects.

Fenella nodded. 'We could talk to her next week, if you like, Vicky, I know she's volunteered to do two days at Haddon House. I think such a place would be quite marvellous for the wounded men who are now coming home.'

'Like a club,' Stephen suggested, sounding enthusiastic. 'Not the many working men's clubs that have sprung up all over, more like a recreation centre, don't you think?'

Will nodded. 'A place where they could meet up with other solders, have refreshments, play cards, read . . . somewhere to go, to get them out of the house, from under the feet of their wives or mothers.'

'It's an excellent idea, in my opinion.' Edward addressed Fenella and continued. 'If you decided to do it, Fenella, I'll certainly write a cheque, give you a donation to such a cause.'

'Why thank you so much, Ned, but I hadn't really thought of doing it, not until this moment anyway. But we'll see.'

'I'll match Ned,' Will promised.

'Count me in,' Stephen announced. 'We must show appreciation to our wounded, they risked their lives for us, and you know damned well the government won't do much to help the returning wounded.'

'Well, how lovely of you all,' Fenella murmured, thinking of the way she and her aunt had started Haddon House years ago. They created a safe haven for abused women and much to their satisfaction it had done wonders in the East End, saved many helpless women from terrible fates.

Vicky glanced at the door. 'Ah, here is Fuller with the main course.'

Fuller and two parlour maids came into the dining room, carrying large tureens of lamb stew. Once everyone was served they departed, although Fuller returned within seconds to pour the red claret into the fine crystal goblets.

'Your dinners are always the best,' Edward said at one moment, turning to Vicky. 'I've loved this stew of yours for years.'

Vicky inclined her head, pleased. 'Thank you,' she said with a smile. After a moment she added, 'If we did open such a place for wounded soldiers, shouldn't we have a canteen? To serve a good lunch to them every day.'

'I can see this project, which was only just suggested a minute ago, is growing in magnitude,' Will murmured, staring at his sister. 'The first thing you must do, Fenella, and you too Vicky, is sit down and figure out what such a place is going to cost. Certainly before you do anything else.'

'Of course you're right, Will,' Fenella agreed. 'In fact, I must do quite a lot of thinking first, before we get to that stage. We're very busy at Haddon House. We'd need quite a few helpers for such a project . . .' Her voice trailed off.

'I know we'd soon have lots of volunteers,' Vicky said in a confident voice.

Edward laughed. 'Always the optimist, my dear Vicky.'

After dinner, when everyone was drinking coffee and liqueurs in the drawing room, Amos edged towards Edward.

Edward, attuned to Amos after all these years, gave him a quick glance and inclined his head. Excusing himself to Stephen, he took several steps in Amos's direction.

'What is it, Amos? You look as if you need to speak to me, and quite urgently.'

'I do need to have a word, sir, but it's not urgent. I can speak with you tomorrow morning, if you'd prefer.'

'I can't tomorrow morning, I'm afraid,' Edward answered, remembering the appointment Jane had made for them to view the Renoir painting.'How about now? Shall we step outside into the hall?'

'Yes, Mr Edward, if that's all right.'

'It's fine.' He went over to Stephen, who now stood near the window, and muttered, 'Finnister needs a word with me. Excuse me for a moment, will you?'

'Of course.'

Following Amos out, Edward said, 'Too much staff clearing up out here. Let's step into the library.'

'Good idea, sir.'

Once they were ensconced in the library overlooking the garden, Edward asked, 'What's on your mind? You look worried.'

'No, I'm not worried. It's like this, sir. Last night I had dinner with Charlie at the Ritz, and he went to say hello to another officer, who'd just come into the restaurant. A major he'd been in two different hospitals with. When he returned to the table I asked him who the man was, and he said he was a friend by the name of Cedric Crawford.'

Edward was so startled to hear this name from the past he simply gaped at Amos for a moment, genuinely dumbfounded. Finally, he said, 'The Cedric Crawford who lived with Tabitha James? Is that who you mean? Well, I suppose you do: after all it's quite an unusual name.'

'That's right, sir, and I don't think there are two of them.'

'So you're obviously planning to do something about this, knowing you as well as I do, Amos.'

'I'm taking them both to dinner tomorrow. I hope to establish his identity at least.'

'And then what?'

'I thought I would ask him about Tabitha James.'

'Will he tell you the truth? We both agreed she wasn't murdered, because if she had been the police would have been involved at the time, whatever Grace Rose said when you found her. After all, she *was* only four.'

'I'm hoping he can tell me what Tabitha's fate really was, and also where she's buried. I think that would be a good thing for Grace Rose to know, Mr Edward. Set her mind at rest.'

'She's talked about this to you, hasn't she?' Edward murmured, as perceptive as always, and understanding Grace Rose as well as he did.

'Yes, she has. I've even taken her down to Whitechapel at different times, with Mrs Vicky's permission of course. And naturally she's been to Haddon House over the years. Nothing's ever been hidden from her. Mrs Vicky has always believed in telling her the truth.'

'And rightly so. It would've been silly to keep things a secret.' A reflective look settled in Edward's eyes for a moment, and he stood holding the brandy balloon, staring into its amber depths. At last he said, 'Find out what you can, Amos. It will be quite interesting to hear what he has to say. But don't expect too much, because perhaps he doesn't know much of anything. After all, he could have left her. Or she could have left him . . . it's all something of a mystery . . . and one we might never fathom.'

FOURTEEN

I n all his years as a policeman and then a private investigator, Amos Finnister had learned about people and knew
how to read them. He had a psychological insight into most,
and usually understood the motivations of others. This aside,
he had acquired a certain charm. He was at ease with people
from all walks of life, and they were at ease with him. Certainly
he had a way with them, handled them with expertise and
finesse.

And this was most apparent on Friday evening, when Charlie
and Major Cedric Crawford dined with him at the Ritz
Restaurant. As it turned out, he discovered that the major was
the perfect English gentleman, well mannered and genial, and
from a distinguished family. And Charlie was being himself
tonight, *playing* the perfect English gentleman as he had done
so often on the stage in London and New York.

Amos knew how to make people relax, and by the time they
were halfway through dinner he had the major laughing, and
sharing stories, some of which were hilarious. And as Amos
joined in the general hilarity, told stories himself, and chatted
mostly about inconsequential things, he listened and watched,

trying to observe the major surreptitiously in order to properly weigh him up.

By the time they had eaten the main course, Amos felt comfortable enough to broach the subject of Tabitha James. At a given moment he glanced at Charlie, a quizzical expression on his face, and Charlie gave him a quick nod.

After taking another sip of the good French wine he had ordered, a Châteauneuf-du-Pape, Amos put down his glass and leaned back in the chair, not wanting to appear intrusive or in any way threatening.

Speaking in his ordinary, neutral tone, Amos said, 'I wonder if you'd mind my asking you something, Major?'

'No, not at all. What is it you'd like to know, Finnister?'

Having worked out a simple story before dinner, one based on truth, Amos had it ready and on the tip of his tongue. 'Before I begin I'd just like to explain something . . . I'm wondering if you happen to know a friend of mine.'

The major's eyes were glued on Amos. 'Who would that be?'

'Lady Fenella Fayne. Have you ever come across her?'

'No, I haven't, I'm afraid. But I do know who she is, I think everyone does. Great philanthropist, so I've read, and a woman who has devoted her time, energy and money to helping women . . . women at risk, shall we say? I believe she's the widow of Lord Jeremy Fayne.'

'That's correct, and her father is the Earl of Tanfield. Some years ago Lady Fenella tried to find a friend of hers from Yorkshire, where she herself comes from originally – a lady friend who had disappeared in London. She did manage to find out, through another acquaintance, that her friend had ended up living in the East End, in Whitechapel or thereabouts, and that her friend had been acquainted with a gentleman by the name of Cedric Crawford. That wasn't by any chance your good self, was it Major?'

Cedric Crawford nodded at once, showing no signs of embarrassment or reluctance to admit to knowing the woman Amos was referring to. 'I did know a lady who lived in Whitechapel by the name of Tabitha James. I knew her quite well, actually. You see, she was an extremely close friend of a fellow guards officer, Sebastian Lawford. At one moment I did believe they were going to marry – they were very much in love. But unfortunately that did not come to pass.'

'And why was that, Major, do you know?'

'Oh yes, I'm afraid I do. Tabitha James became very ill. Actually, she had contracted consumption, and then she was felled by double pneumonia. Before I knew it, she was dead and gone.'

'I see. So you went to their home in Whitechapel, did you?'

'It was Tabitha's home, in point of fact. She wouldn't move to a better place for some reason – though, with all due respect, Seb had tried to install her in a cottage that was more than comfortable. I have no idea why she was so obdurate.' He shook his head, and finished, 'It was all very sad because she was obviously a genuine lady: what I mean is, a woman of breeding.'

'She was indeed. She was Lady Tabitha Brockhaven, and her late father was the Earl of Brockhaven,' Amos informed him.

It was obvious that the major was surprised; Amos thought he looked thunderstruck, even a little disbelieving. He waited, wanting this information to sink in.

Cedric Crawford frowned, and he sounded dubious when he eventually asked, 'Are you sure of that, Finnister? I mean . . . a *title*? Goodness me.'

'Yes, I am sure. Absolutely. Anyway, a moment ago I mentioned Tabitha's home. You did go there then?'

'Oh yes, quite a few times. It was in 1904, the spring I think. Yes, that's correct. You see, I was about to travel to Europe with my father and my two sisters. We were going to the family villa in the South of France, and then I was moving to Paris. Permanently. I wanted to be a painter and my father had agreed I could attend the Beaux Arts. In fact, he was footing the bill.'

'But you were a guards officer, weren't you?' Amos probed.

'Oh yes, but the old man, well, he was a good sort, my pater, he let me do what I wanted, more or less. So he put up no resistance when I resigned my commission. His father had been rather a bully, so I was led to understand, and Father sort of –' Cedric paused, shrugged, 'tended to go the other way. Indulged me. Spoiled me rotten, I expect. Anyway, he agreed with me that I wasn't cut out to be a soldier.'

'But you rejoined the army when war broke out, and you were both wrong as it turned out, weren't you, Major? Since you must have been a very dedicated soldier from what Charlie tells me. You performed great acts of courage, so much so you are about to be awarded the greatest honour in the land, the most prestigious medal a soldier can receive for valour in the face of the enemy . . . the Victoria Cross.'

The major looked suddenly bashful, and he merely nodded, turning pink. He took a sip of his red wine.

Amos now leaned across the table, and asked the question he'd been holding back. 'In the spring of 1904 did you come across a little girl living with Tabitha?'

'Good Lord, yes, I'd forgotten about her for a moment. Tabitha did have a daughter. A toddler. Yes, yes, *of course*. Now what *was* her name . . . I've got it! She was called *Grace*.'

'You don't happen to know what happened to Grace, do you?'

'Not really.' The major rubbed his hand over his forehead, frowning slightly. 'You know, now that I think about it, the last time I saw the child was the last time I saw Tabitha.'

'Can you remember what happened that day?' Amos sat back, sipping his water, and waiting, a sense of excitement growing inside him. His eyes rested on the major reflectively. He was very intent on arriving at the truth.

'I remember it was quite a nice day,' Major Crawford began. 'Sunny, if a little cool. I went to Whitechapel with Seb Lawford because he wanted to persuade Tabitha to move to a better place, a decent cottage which he had found in Hampstead, near the Heath. He asked me to help him move her things, and we arrived in a hansom cab. Tabitha was there, but she wouldn't agree to move or leave that . . . hovel. She was stubborn. We both noticed how dreadfully ill she looked, and she was coughing . . . coughing her heart out. Seb sent me to talk to the woman who lived several doors away, down the street. She had a teenage daughter who apparently sometimes looked after Grace. He wanted her to come to the house and watch Grace whilst we took Tabitha to the hospital. I can't remember the girl's name, but she agreed, and she came back with me. As I recall, I gave her a guinea to wait until we returned. Then Seb and the girl helped to get Tabitha into some of her clothes, and he and I carried her out to the hansom, and we took her to the hospital.'

'Which hospital was that, Major Crawford?'

'The one on Whitechapel Road, it's called Royal London Hospital. Very old place. Naturally, they kept her in the hospital, she was so very ill.'

'And what happened after that?' Amos asked quietly.

'Seb returned to Tabitha's place in Whitechapel, and I took a hansom cab back to my father's house in Queen Street in Mayfair. We left for France about five days later.'

'But you said Tabitha died. You must have seen your friend Sebastian Lawford before you left, didn't you?'

'He came to see me only two days after we had taken Tabitha to the hospital. And yes, she *had* died, she had a virulent case of pneumonia, not to mention consumption. It was her lungs, I think, they were horribly congested, she had trouble breathing.'

'At that time, did he mention the little girl Grace?'

'No, he didn't say anything, and I didn't think to ask. We, that is the family, were going abroad for three months, and I was packing for a much longer stay in Paris. It was somewhat chaotic, I'm afraid –' Cedric Crawford broke off as if suddenly something had occurred to him. 'What happened to the little girl, Mr Finnister? I hope nothing bad.'

'No, not really, thank God.' Amos cleared his throat, went on, 'When Lady Fenella was looking for Tabitha, I know she checked all of the hospitals in the area, because I helped her. But she didn't find Tabitha registered. Don't you think that's a bit odd?'

'Yes. But then again, no, I don't. You see, she was using the name Mrs Lawford . . . Mrs Sebastian Lawford . . . Seb thought using his full name would offer her protection in that rather rough area of London. Anyway, he had a pet name for her, as well. He always called her Lucy. I've no idea why, but what I do know for a certainty is that he registered her as Mrs Sebastian Lawford, Christian name Lucy. I was standing right next to her when he spoke to the nurse.'

'I understand, and so will Lady Fenella. Everything has become clear. Tell me, Major, did Sebastian Lawford invite you to the funeral? Or tell you where she was buried?'

'No, he didn't say, but I couldn't have gone because of the problems of the family leaving, and, as I said, my father's house was chaotic until the day we left.'

'I think I would like to meet Sebastian Lawford, if you would help me to locate him. Do you know where he is, Major?'

'Yes, I do.'

'And where is that, if I might ask?'

'In a grave in France. He was killed at the battle of Ypres, the third battle. He died in my arms, Mr Finnister. So you see, I can't help you with that. So sorry.'

'You *have* helped me. You've given me the name of the hospital, and hopefully they will be able to tell me where Tabitha James, or rather Mrs Sebastian 'Lucy' Lawford, is buried. I'm certain they will have that on record.'

'Is it important, knowing that?' the major asked curiously.

'Oh yes, very much so,' Amos murmured, and added, 'Thank you again, Major, thank you.'

It wasn't unusual for Amos to go to Deravenels on Saturday, even though the offices were closed over the weekend. He often went in to tidy up his paperwork, and do other small jobs, which he couldn't attend to during the week.

But on this Saturday morning he had a specific purpose when he arrived at the grand old building on the Strand. The uniformed commissionaire touched his cap, said 'Good morning, Mr Finnister. Weather for ducks, ain't it, sir?'

Amos grinned at the older man. 'Good morning, Albert. And indeed it is the right kind of weather for our fine feathered friends.' As he spoke he closed his umbrella, then hurried across the grandiose marble entrance foyer and up the staircase.

The reason he had come to the office was to list the names of cemeteries in the vicinity of Whitechapel, and make a few telephone calls.

His first call was to the Royal London Hospital, Whitechapel, where he quickly discovered the records office was not open on weekends; this was an answer he had fully expected. He then dialled Ravenscar, and when Jessup, the butler, answered, he announced himself, spoke to the butler for a moment or two, and then was put through to Edward Deravenel.

'Good morning, Amos,' Edward said. 'I'm assuming you have some sort of news for me.'

'Good morning, sir, and yes, I do. It was the right Cedric Crawford, as we had thought on Thursday, but he was not the man involved with Tabitha James.'

'How strange!' Edward exclaimed. 'That friend of Tabitha's, Sophie whatever her name was, seemed so certain about Cedric Crawford.'

'According to Lady Fenella, yes, she did. But according to the major it was his fellow guards officer, Sebastian Lawford, who was the man in question. And I do believe Major Crawford.'

'And an easy mistake, I suppose, to muddle Crawford and Lawford,' Edward commented.

'That's right, Mr Edward, and the major kept referring to him as *Seb* last night. Seb Lawford or Ced Crawford, what's the difference when you don't actually care about the facts?'

'And Sophie didn't, is that what you're saying?' Edward asked.

'Yes, I am, sir. And let me tell you everything I learned.' He then proceeded to relay all of the information he had garnered from the major the night before.

'Well done, Amos!' Edward exclaimed. 'Now you've got something to follow up.'

'I do, but it will have to be on Monday. I telephoned the hospital and I can't get into Records until Monday, and I know Somerset House is closed at the weekend. They have a registry of all births, marriages and deaths in Great Britain, so I'll be able to track her death certificate now that we have the correct name. Well, the name she was using.'

'Thank you for going to all this trouble, Amos, you've done a splendid job.'

'There is something else, sir. Er, er, Mr Deravenel?'

'Yes, Amos, what is it?'

'Once I have all the information would it be all right for me to tell Mrs Forth?'

'Absolutely! She'll be happy as I am to know everything, it's been such a troubling mystery all these years. And I'm sure she will agree that Grace Rose should be told . . . it's an ending for her, Amos, and it will finally put her mind at rest, knowing what happened to her mother.'

'I agree, sir. I will telephone you on Monday as soon as I have been in touch with the various organizations involved, and then I'll talk to Mrs Vicky.'

'That's a good plan, and thank you again, Amos –' Edward paused for a split second, then finished, 'And how strange life is, really. All of this came about by coincidence, because Charlie met another soldier in hospital. Truly amazing, Amos.'

FIFTEEN

Ravenscar

S he was in charge. Her grandmother had told her so, and this pleased Bess Deravenel. But she should be in charge, shouldn't she? After all, she was nine years old, the eldest, the first born. Everyone was aware that the heir was more important because he was a boy. But this did not trouble her. She had always known that she was her father's favourite, and therefore she was very special. He had said that to her when she was small.

Her father had recently bought her a cheval mirror, and had it placed in the corner of her bedroom, so that she could view herself full length. Now she went over to it, stood staring at her reflection, her head on one side.

Bess decided that she looked very nice, and was most appropriately dressed for the Christmas Day lunch. She had chosen the dress herself, because Nanny was fussing about the other children, and had told her to use her own judgement. She liked doing that, it made her feel very grown up. And so she had picked out a dress made of royal blue velvet with a gathered skirt almost to her ankles, long sleeves and a beautiful white lace collar and cuffs. Her white stockings and black shoes were an excellent choice, Nanny had said a few moments ago.

Returning to the dressing table in the bay window, Bess took the small brooch out of its black velvet box. Earlier that morning they had all opened their Christmas presents in the library, where the huge Christmas tree stood, and this brooch had been a gift to her from her father. It was a small bow made of diamonds. Her mother had seemed annoyed, and Bess had heard her say to her father that it was much too expensive for a child, and he had retorted, 'Not for a child of mine, Elizabeth,' and walked away looking even more annoyed than her mother. She was used to them. They often quarrelled; she had grown up with their quarrels and often wondered why her mother said the things she did when she knew he would be instantly angry.

Carefully, Bess pinned the brooch at the neckline of the dress, saw that it fitted in neatly between the two sides of the collar. She touched her hair, arranged the curls away from her face, and nodded to herself. Her hair was the same red gold as her father's and her eyes the same bright blue. She looked like him, just as Grace Rose did. She was very disappointed Grace Rose wasn't coming for Christmas. It was all because of Young Edward's bronchitis. None of the guests were coming; her father had cancelled the festivities. 'God help us,' Nanny had said to Madge, the nursemaid, the other afternoon. 'I don't know what we'll do without family and friends here, they usually act as a buffer between them.' She had shrunk back from the door, hoping Nanny hadn't seen her. And she knew exactly what Nanny had meant, and agreed with her, although she could never say so. Nanny would think she had been eavesdropping.

Jumping up off the stool, Bess ran across the bedroom floor and opened the door to the corridor. In the distance she could hear Nanny's voice coming from the direction of Mary's bedroom, which she shared with little Cecily, because Cecily was afraid of the dark. Wondering if there was some sort of problem, she flew down the corridor and pushed open the door of Mary's room.

Nanny turned around swiftly and exclaimed, 'Now, now, Bess! Please don't run down the corridors. It's simply not ladylike. And how many times have I told you *that*?'

'Every day, Nanny. Sorry. But I thought you might be in need of me. To help you.'

Nanny, a trifle spherical in shape, with apple-rosy cheeks and twinkling brown eyes, compressed her mouth to hide her smile of amusement. 'I think I can manage,' she answered and turned her attention to Cecily. The six-year-old look on the verge of tears.

'Why are you crying, Cecily?' Bess asked, going closer to her younger sister, staring at her. 'It's Christmas Day and we're going to have a wonderful lunch.'

'I'm not hungry,' Cecily answered, her lip quivering. 'I don't like this fwock.'

'Let's not have baby talk, missy, it isn't suitable,' Nanny murmured, and finished tying the pale blue taffeta bow on top of Cecily's blonde head.

'Your dress is beautiful, and it's the same colour as mine,' Bess said. 'Look at me.'

Cecily did as she was asked, and nodded. 'It's the same colour. But I don't like this fwock.'

'Yes, you do, Cecily. And say frock. Just look at Mary, she's wearing blue too and not complaining. We match. Now isn't that nice. And we are sisters, you know. I think Nanny's been very clever, choosing blue dresses for the two of you. We blend.'

Mary said, 'But you chose your own, 'cos Nanny told us.'

'Now, now, Mary, speak correctly. Say *because*, not 'cos. Rather common, that way of speaking,' Nanny pronounced, frowning.

'Not suitable,' Bess added, using one of Nanny's favourite expressions.

Nanny turned to look at her, peering over the top of her glasses. 'We're not being cheeky are we, Bess?'

'Oh no, Nanny, I'm never cheeky to you.'

'That's all right then. At least I've taught you something.'

'What's suitable and what's not suitable,' Mary cried, and began to laugh. The eight-year-old had a very happy nature, and she began to prance around, singing, 'The Blue sisters. We're the Blue sisters. Look at *us*. Blue like Boadicea. Blue, blue, blue!'

Bess said, 'Now stop this, Mary, we must hurry, and we must help Nanny.'

'Everything is in hand, missy.' Glancing around, Nanny realized suddenly that Richard was missing. 'Oh my Heavens, where's little Ritchie? Oh dear, where has that child gone?'

'I'm here,' a small voice said, and Nanny was more horrified than ever when she saw a blond head peeping out from under the bed.

'Ritchie, please come out at once!'

He did so and scrambled to his feet. Nanny looked him over, her eyes seeking out the merest speck of dust. But there was nothing on him. Straightening his black velvet jacket, Nanny muttered, 'Well, at least we know the maids here are thorough.'

Cecily said, 'I want my red fwock.'

'Stop saying fwock!' Mary cried, echoing Bess.

'Nanny,' Bess said, 'What about Young Edward? Is he coming down for Christmas lunch? Or is he too ill?'

Nanny beamed. Young Edward was undoubtedly special to her, and she exclaimed, 'Oh yes, indeed, your father helped him to get dressed and he took him downstairs a short while ago.'

'Then we'd better go at once,' Bess announced. 'Father must be waiting for me.'

'He's waiting for *all* of you,' Nanny replied, giving her a pointed look.

'I want the baby,' Cecily muttered. 'Where's Anne?'

'The nursemaid has her, she'll be taking her downstairs in a moment.'

'Is she wearing blue velvet too?' Mary asked, eyeing Nanny solemnly.

'Don't be silly, child. Of course the baby's not wearing blue velvet. She's wrapped in a bundle of frothy white lace right now.'

Bess said, 'Where's Grandmother?'

'Mrs Deravenel is downstairs also.'

'You like her, don't you, Nanny?'

'Yes, I do.'

'But not Mother. You don't like *her*.'

'What a dreadful thing to say, Bess,' Nanny said reprovingly. 'Of course I like your mother. She's a beautiful lady, and very kind and considerate to me.'

'But not to my father,' Bess mumbled.

Nanny threw her a cautionary look. 'This conversation is not suitable, not suitable at all, and I won't have it,' Nanny said. There was a warning note in her voice.

Picking up on this, Bess said softly, 'I'm sorry, Nanny. I won't do it again.' Edging closer to the nanny she whispered, 'The little ones, *they* don't understand.'

'You'd be surprised what they understand,' Nanny shot back pithily. 'Very well, let us go downstairs to join your parents and your grandmother. Stand up straight, Ritchie, you're looking like a rag doll.'

Richard looked up at her, and yawned. Then he said, 'I'm hungry, Nanny.'

'I am too,' Mary announced. 'I could eat a horse.'

'That's a vulgar expression, Mary. Please refrain from using it.'

'A pony then . . . I could eat a pony.'

Richard laughed with Mary and Cecily, and they giggled all the way down the corridor.

Bess threw Nanny a sympathetic look as they followed behind. 'What can you do with them?' Shaking her head, Bess added, 'But then they're so young.'

Nanny averted her face so that Bess wouldn't notice the mirth bubbling to the surface. They were priceless, these children, far too grown-up for their own good. And they had seen far too much, witnessed too many quarrels that had verged on the violent. But then the mother was to blame. Poor Mr Deravenel. She couldn't help sympathizing with him. Fancy being married to that cold, nasty woman, and he so good and kind and handsome. Poor man. Oh, that poor man.

Bess made everyone stop at the top of the stairs, and looking at Nanny and then at her siblings, she said, 'Grandmother put me in charge of you, so you must do as I say. We will walk downstairs *sedately*. And then when we get to the library you will stand in line. Like I put you yesterday. And we will sing the Christmas carol.'

'I'm hungry,' Richard wailed.

'No food for you, Ritchie,' Bess warned, 'not 'til after the carol has been sung.'

'Be careful, Ritchie,' Nanny warned. 'Come, let me take your hand, and we'll go down together.' The two-year-old, who was as blond as his brother, clung to Nanny's hand tightly.

The three girls followed behind.

Once they reached the Long Hall Bess saw Jessup waiting. 'We are going to sing our carol first, Jessup,' Bess explained.

'Yes, Miss Bess. Mrs Deravenel, that is your grandmother, told me that lunch could not be served until after you had done your rendition. And she herself will play the piano for you.'

'Thank you.' Bess gave him the benefit of one of her radiant smiles just as her father so often did.

'Don't forget to stand in a proper line,' Bess hissed as they arrived at the doorway leading into the library. Ushering her siblings forward, she said, 'Here we are, Father! We are going to sing a carol for you, and Mother.'

Bess turned and smiled at Cecily Deravenel, and added, 'And Grandmama is being very kind. She is going to play the piano for us.'

'How nice, Bess!' Edward smiled at her. 'I hadn't realized we were going to be treated to a Christmas concert before lunch.'

'Oh but Father, it's only *one* carol,' Bess exclaimed swiftly, suddenly looking worried. 'Because, well, I had to teach the others the words . . . they *had* to know it by heart.'

'How very clever of you, Bess, clever of you all, actually.' His eyes swept over his four children standing in a row in the doorway near the small piano, which Jessup had moved in from the music room yesterday afternoon, as he always did at Christmas. How beautiful they were, his children, with their bright blond and red gold hair. Four pairs of eyes of varying shades of blue stared back at him.

He turned his head, looked at Elizabeth and smiled warmly.

She was momentarily taken aback, since she had so irritated him earlier with her comments about the diamond bow. Wanting peace on this very special day of the year, she smiled back at him, then leaned closer, touched his hand, showing her affection. She felt a movement next to her and turned to Young Edward, who had drawn closer to her on the sofa. 'Are you all right? Are you warm enough?'

'Oh yes, Mama. I just wish I could sing the carol too.'

'I know. You don't like being left out of anything, I realize that. Next year. You can sing next year, darling.'

Cecily rose from the chair and walked across the room to the piano, stopping for a moment to let one hand rest on Ritchie's head for a moment.

He loved his grandmother, and turned his eyes to her face, gave her a huge smile. 'I'm hungry, Granny.'

'So am I, sweetheart.' She bent down to him. 'And we shall

have turkey, stuffing and mashed potatoes in a few minutes. After the carol. Very soon, I promise.'

Bess looked at her siblings, and murmured. 'Cecily, you must stand next to me, because you're taller than Mary. Come along all of you, make the straight line like yesterday.'

Ritchie asked, 'Am I here?'

'Yes, you're the last.' Bess took her place at the head of the line and said to her grandmother. 'We are ready.'

'I will play a few bars and then I will start the carol,' Cecily said and promptly did so.

A split second later four young voices rang out:

'*Hark, the herald-angels sing*
Glory to the new-born King,
Peace on earth, and mercy mild,
God and sinners reconciled.
Joyful, all ye nations, rise,
Join the triumph of the skies;
With the angelic host proclaim,
"Christ is born in Bethlehem."
Hark, the herald-angels sing
Glory to the new-born King.'

'Thank you, children, that was wonderful!' Edward began to clap, and so did their mother, grandmother, Young Edward, Nanny and Madge, the nursemaid, who stood near the window with Anne in a wicker perambulator.

'Well done, all of you!' Edward beamed at them.

Bess, Mary, Cecily and Ritchie beamed back at him. They all bowed low and then ran across to their parents, laughter filling their faces with happiness.

Mary and Cecily made for their father, as usual wishing to claim his attention.

Bess shepherded Ritchie to their mother, who bent forward,

kissed the top of his head. 'Thank you,' she murmured, acknowledging Bess who stood before her. 'Your father is correct, you did very well.'

Bess offered her mother a tentative smile.

Elizabeth rose, glided across to the window area of the library, where Nanny stood with Madge, the nursemaid.

'Enjoy your Christmas lunch, Nanny, and you too, Madge. Cook has everything ready for you both in the downstairs dining room. Also, I had Jessup put a small cot near the fire, just in case you wish to take Anne out of the baby carriage.'

'Thank yer, mum.' Madge bobbed a curtsy.

'That is most kind, Mrs Deravenel, thank you very much,' Nanny said, and touched Madge's arm to indicate they should leave. She wanted to tell the children to be on their very best behaviour, but the two younger girls were caught up with their father, clinging to him, and Bess was already moving in his direction.

Bess was Nanny's favourite, but because she abhorred favouritism she kept this a secret, treated everyone equally. But Nanny constantly worried about the nine-year-old girl, who was far too old for her years, not close enough to her mother, and far too possessive of her father.

What a strange family they were; still, she was accustomed to them by now. She had been here for eight years, and had brought Bess up, and the other little ones as well. They were sweet children, very beautiful, and she loved them dearly. It was the adults in this household who bothered her. At times she thought they were out to destroy each other.

She shook off this troubling thought. It was Christmas Day of 1918. The war was over and they were at peace. The whole world was at peace. And everyone said the World War which had just drawn to a close was the war to end all wars. She certainly hoped so.

SIXTEEN

Elizabeth was fully aware that she had said the wrong thing that morning, when she had told Edward the diamond bow brooch was too costly a thing to give to a child.

He had instantly taken umbrage, made an acerbic comment and walked away. She ought to have known better: she had come to realize this as the day had passed and turned into evening. He had always favoured Bess, spoiled her, made it clear nothing was too good for her.

And of course he detested any comment that smacked of criticism of him. Why hadn't she kept her mouth shut? She didn't know . . . but then she was always making remarks that he took the wrong way. She never did this with anyone else, only him. Was it some kind of nervousness? she wondered.

It wasn't very long ago that her brother Anthony had told her she was a fool, that she made a fuss about things that didn't matter. 'Forget about winning a battle,' he had said in a cold, reproving voice. 'And concentrate on winning the war. That's the only thing that matters . . . One day, Lizzie, you will wake up and find you've killed the goose that lays the golden eggs.'

He was so annoyed with her she hadn't dared to reprimand

him for calling her Lizzie. Instead she had stuttered something about not really understanding what he meant.

'For an intelligent woman you can be truly stupid at times,' he had said in that cold, disdainful voice of his that denoted his fury. 'You're argumentative for one thing, and complain about his other women, when there are no other women –'

'Then what is Jane Shaw?' she had cut in, glaring at her brother.

'She's his mistress, that's what she is, and you know it and I know it. She's not *other women*, as you put it.'

'What are you saying? That I should accept her?'

'Yes, I am indeed. Turn a blind eye, like other women of our class do, women whose husbands have mistresses. Which is half the population of this country I should think, perhaps even more. And remember this one important fact: a woman who has been with a man for a long time as his mistress has obviously not made any impossible demands, has not sought marriage, not wanted more than the relationship she already has. Jane Shaw has not rocked the boat. Don't you rock it, either.'

'It hurts my feelings,' she had mumbled. 'I want him to be faithful to me.'

'Oh, for God's sake, grow up, Elizabeth! Does he neglect you physically? Stupid question. He's obviously very attentive to you since you're always having babies, one after the other. So, does he beat you? Come on, does he? Are you hiding something from me? Does Ned hit you?'

'No. He doesn't beat me, or anyone else for that matter. Edward happens to be a gentle person.'

'I've understood that for a long time. I also know that he keeps you in lavish style, in luxurious homes, permits you to spend whatever you want to spend on clothes, and other trinkets, and literally covers you in jewels. You should have no complaints, my dear.'

'It's just that, well –'

'It's not *just* anything. Unless I might add that you are just being rather stupid, in my opinion.' Her brother had leaned closer to her, and said in a low voice, 'The longer he remains in this relationship with Jane the better it is for you ... why can't you see that?'

'I'd prefer him not to have a mistress at all.'

'Grow up! That's not going to happen, not with a man like Ned. And if he didn't have a mistress – I must qualify this and say that if he didn't have a mistress like Jane – then you would have to contend with *a lot of women*. Women who might not be as congenial as Jane, shall we say? Women with ambitions who may very well wish to become the second Mrs Edward Deravenel.'

She remembered now how much this last comment had upset and disturbed her, and if they had not been lunching at the Ritz Hotel she might have started to weep. Somehow she had managed to control her emotions, and had simply kept her head down, searching for a handkerchief in her handbag, saying nothing.

It was Anthony who had started to speak, this time in a gentler tone. 'I don't want you to cry, I can't stand it when a woman weeps.'

'You haven't been very nice.'

'I have told you the truth, the way things are, Elizabeth, and believe me, I am only thinking of *you*, and your welfare,' he had said then, taking hold of her hand. 'You have a wonderful life, Elizabeth, a charmed life, and a young, handsome husband, who is tremendously successful, and a wealthy man. One who treats you like a queen and allows you to spend money like ... a drunken sailor, for heaven's sake! He is incredibly generous. He is also a marvellous father and adores his children. And I know for a fact he has no intention of leaving you, so just give him some slack, won't you?'

'Yes, you are right, Anthony. Everything you say is correct.

I will keep my mouth shut, I promise you. I won't badger him about anything.'

Anthony had nodded and finished, 'There is no doubt in my mind that he has never contemplated divorce, Elizabeth. After all, he loves you.'

You would say that, you work for him, she had thought that day, but she had managed to swallow those mean words, knowing they were inflammatory.

Now, tonight, sitting alone in her bedroom at Ravenscar on Christmas Day night, she knew that those had been unkind and ridiculous thoughts. And very unfair to her brother, who was a most decent and honourable man. And he would have said exactly the same thing, even if he had not worked for Edward. I was being mean-spirited, she chastised herself, and she was tremendously relieved those words had never left her mouth. The last thing she needed was to antagonize her favourite brother, who wanted only the best for her – happiness, security and contentment.

Leaning back on the chaise longue, Elizabeth wondered how to make amends to Ned. She must do this. *Tonight*. She did not want her thoughtless comments about the gift for Bess to fester inside him. He had been civil this morning, and at lunch, but then the children had been present. Even at dinner he had been pleasant enough, if somewhat uncommunicative for him. He seemed to have been in a reflective mood, now that she thought about it. After dinner he had said goodnight to herself and his mother, gone into the library and firmly closed the door behind him. Cecily had gone to her room, and she had had no alternative but to accompany her mother-in-law upstairs, to go to bed herself.

Elizabeth glanced at the French clock on her dressing table, and saw that it was almost eleven. He still had not come up to bed. Or had he? Had he gone to his own room? Even when he wanted to sleep alone, in his bedroom next door to hers, he usually came in to say goodnight, to chat for a moment or two before retiring.

Rising, she swept across the floor, stood at the door into his bedroom, listened. All was quiet. There was no sound at all. Gently, she turned the knob and opened the door a crack. The lights were on, the bed was undisturbed, and he was nowhere in sight.

Was he downstairs in the library, nursing a drink and a grudge? She did not know. How could she? Now she must sit and wait for him to come to bed. She *must* talk to him, clear the air.

After Jessup had thrown more logs on the fire in the library, and poured him a Calvados, Edward Deravenel had stood for a while in front of the fire, in his usual way, sipping his apple brandy and thinking. He had so much on his mind at the moment he actually didn't know where to begin to sort it all out. Some things he had accomplished already: Richard had the deeds to the Chelsea house and George had been rendered impotent in that regard; the Forths were holding the documents for Grace Rose's trust until she was of age. Edward was pleased he had created the trust for her. She would always be independent because of it, would never need to ask anyone for anything.

And he had done the same thing for Jane Shaw. She had her own trust, which he had created six years ago, and like Grace Rose she would have financial security whether he was around or not.

He smiled as he thought of Jane's surprise last Thursday, when he had given her the trust documents. He had gone to pick her up to take her to the Forths' dinner party, and when he arrived he had handed her a package tied with red ribbon. 'Another little Christmas present,' he had explained.

Of course she had been happy as well as startled, and then she had wept when she understood what the package contained.

'Don't cry Jane,' he had murmured in a soothing voice. 'I'm not dying, or leaving you, or going anywhere. I just want you to have the documents in your keeping, since they pertain to you, your life and your future, if you outlive me.'

Being an intelligent and sensible woman she had immediately understood their importance, and she had put the papers in the safe, after thanking him profusely for thinking of her welfare. That safe also contained the deeds to her house in Hyde Park Gardens, which he had bought for her a long time ago, and given to her immediately.

Once she had wiped away the tears and repaired her make-up, they had gone off to the dinner party Vicky and Stephen were giving and had had a lovely evening together. Jane had fallen in love with Grace Rose that night and wanted to get to know her better. And this had pleased him enormously; he liked the idea of these two women becoming good friends.

At the beginning of December, Edward had sat down at his desk one day and drafted a new Last Will and Testament. He thought about this as he took a long swallow of the cognac and seated himself in a chair near the fireplace.

As soon as he returned to London after Christmas, he would make an appointment to see his solicitors, and go over his new will with them, have the old one redrawn at once.

He had not changed many things: rather he had refined the bequests, made things truly clear, not wishing anything to be misinterpreted by the use of poor language.

One of his main concerns was for Elizabeth, she who was so extravagant. He wanted his wife to have everything she would ever need because he did care about her, whatever she thought. He had also taken special care to provide extremely well for his four daughters, Bess, Mary, Cecily, and Anne, so newly arrived.

They each had their own trust funds, giving them total independence. That was the way he wanted it.

Edward was prone to worry a lot about the women in his family and his life, and what would become of them when he was dead.

Being essentially a pragmatist blessed with foresight, he believed he should attend to such matters the moment they arose in his mind. He wanted everything to be up to date, and absolutely legal.

As for his two sons, Young Edward and Ritchie, they were well taken care of as his two male heirs. The eldest would inherit everything, the houses in London and Kent, the money, and Ravenscar, and he would become head of Deravenels after his death.

But what would happen if he died before Young Edward was old enough to run Deravenels? This particular thought had long troubled him. If Young Edward was still at school, only a boy, then George would be the next in line, as far as the management of the company was concerned. But he was hardly the person to be in charge; George had no judgement, was untrustworthy, totally incompetent and apparently on the way to becoming a drunkard, if he wasn't one already.

Furthermore, George had always been greedy, jealous, divisive, and contrary. Overweeningly ambitious, he was petulant when he didn't get his own way. The troubling part was that his brother had always wanted to be him, as long as he could remember. Then there were the betrayals and the treacherous acts, far too many for him to excuse or forget. Although he had forgiven him, hadn't he? Because George was his brother and should be forgiven for his transgressions.

Not anymore, Ned thought. George deserved nothing. Then it *would* have to be Richard. He would add this particular proviso to his will next week. Richard, his Little Fish, his true and loyal brother, always his favourite. He could run Deravenels if it was necessary, until Young Edward came of age and took over. Yes, that was the solution. And his eldest son would have some true and good men to help and guide him as well as Richard. Will Hasling, Alfredo Oliveri, Anthony Wyland, his uncle, and of course there would be Amos Finnister to watch his back.

Edward began to laugh. *He was only thirty-three.* He would be thirty-four on April twenty-eighth this coming year. Far too young to die, surely? He laughed again. He knew he would have a long life.

Rising, he went to the table in the corner, where Jessup had placed the tray of liqueurs, and poured himself another Calvados, added a splash of soda water.

Returning to the fireplace, he sat thinking about his good friends for a few moments, wishing they were here. He was used to having them around him, those male friends of his who were so devoted to him and he to them. He was lonely, not used to this solitude and lack of male company.

Edward Deravenel, like most aristocratic young men who had been born in the Victorian era, was a traditionalist, had grown up in a world dominated by men. It was a special world built around class, wealth, public school, university, private clubs, and for some the British Army, the Royal Navy, entering the church or going into politics. There were rules and regulations, codes of behaviour, codes of honour, codes of dress. These young men were raised to be gentlemen who knew how to treat their elders, their superiors, their parents and women. Bad manners, shoddy behaviour towards women, bad debts, gambling debts, cheating at cards, drunkenness, and despicable behaviour in general led to a man being blackballed, gave him a bad reputation, earned him the names of blackguard, bounder, cad, and worse.

All of Ned's close friends were gentlemen, just as he was. They spoke the same language, led similar lives, had the same standards and beliefs, and would become the Establishment one day, the ruling class, as their fathers had before them. He missed them all tonight, felt lost without them. He could hardly wait to return to London, to be with them. Rising, he went and turned off the various lamps, returned to the chair, sat sipping the brandy, drifting with his thoughts, half asleep, half awake, lost in a world of his own.

SEVENTEEN

There was the slightest of sounds, like a long, drawn-out sigh, and he heard it vaguely, half dozing, sprawled in the chair in front of the fire. He was relaxed, feeling at ease and comfortable in his shirt, his jacket and tie discarded over an hour ago.

There it was again . . . the long sigh, this time followed by another curious whispery sound. To him it seemed like the swish of silk, faint yet intriguing.

Unexpectedly, the scent of gardenias floated across to him on the warm air, and he struggled to sit up in the armchair, rousing himself.

The library was awash with moonlight, and as he blinked and adjusted his eyes, he saw her standing in the doorway. *Elizabeth*. Lamplight from the Long Hall was shining behind her and her curvaceous figure was a tantalizing silhouette quite visible through the smokey-grey chiffon peignoir she was wearing. Her waist-length silver-gilt hair was loose, flowing around her face.

To him it was still the most beautiful face he had ever seen, absolute perfection, as if sculpted by a great artist from flawless marble. She was pale as a ghost tonight, and seemed to float before him like a spectre. Suddenly, she turned, locked the library door, then took a step forward, simply stood there, her arms at her sides, staring at him intently, not saying a word.

She had come to seduce him, he knew that at once.

Edward immediately felt the heat flooding through him; even his face was suddenly hot. He could not take his eyes off her, he was mesmerized.

Finally, he rose, went to meet her in the middle of the floor. She stared up at him, he looked down at her, their blue eyes met.

'What are you doing here?' he asked, and was surprised how hoarse his voice sounded, hoarse with desire.

'I'm seeking my husband.'

'He is here.'

'Is he waiting for his wife?'

'He is.'

'Does he desire her?'

'He does.'

'She is yours. Only yours.'

Edward reached out his hand, enclosing her long, slender fingers in his, drawing her closer. Putting his arms around her, he lowered his mouth to hers, savoured her, breathing in the perfume of her.

Elizabeth clung to him, her dearest husband. The man she loved, the only man for her. She ran her hands into his thick red-gold hair, pressed her body to his, let her tongue slide into his mouth sensuously, the way he liked. Instantly, he was aroused. She felt his erection against her body and her heart lifted. This was the right way, as her mother was forever telling her. This was the true way to win him back, to make him wholly hers again.

'Enslave him,' her mother had recently told her. 'He's a sensual man, sexually driven, very potent. Give him everything he wants from you. You are his wife, the mother of his children, so be his lover as well.'

Elizabeth remembered her words now. She slid her hands down onto his shoulders, his back, and finally they came to rest on his buttocks; she pressed him into her.

He was excited, and he muttered against the long silky hair, 'Let's go upstairs.'

'No, no, let's stay here.'

He released her without a word, took off his shirt and other clothes; she came to him, slid her peignoir over her shoulders, let it drop to the floor. And still they just stood there staring, their eyes locked, as if they had never seen each other before.

He was amazed by her tonight. How unusually beautiful she was, and she seemed very young, like a young girl, untouched, innocent even. She was five years older than him, yet she was like a girl tonight.

Watching Ned, aware of his eyes roaming over her, Elizabeth could hardly contain herself. He was so masculine, so tall and broad chested, with long legs. She had once told him he was an Adonis, and he had laughed, but it was true.

He took hold of her hand, led her closer to the fire, and they lay down together on the thick rug. Taking a handful of her silky blonde hair, he kissed it tenderly, leaned over her, kissed her throat, her eyes and finally her mouth. His kisses were gentle at first, but as he realized her excitement was growing, felt the heat of her, he grew greedier and more passionate.

She was trembling in his arms, and whispered his name against his ear. 'Oh Ned, oh Ned, I want you . . .' He lifted himself onto her so that he could look down into her eyes. And he said in a low, almost inaudible tone, 'I do love you, you know . . .'

'Prove it, Ned, prove it.'

He did so, taking her to him in a way he had not done for the longest time. And Elizabeth gave herself up to him entirely, recognizing that he was different tonight. Tender and loving, yet bursting with a raging desire that verged on wildness. She abandoned herself to him, as he was doing with her, and she knew she had won him back. With great skill and expertise, much of it learned from him, she held him in her thrall, fed his desire for her all night. Elizabeth so inflamed him they reached heights they had not reached for years. Their quarrels and differences forgotten, at least for this night, they were man and wife again, loving each other without restraint.

Edward felt a sudden cold wind blowing across his body, and he sat up in bed with a start. He saw immediately that he was in his own bedroom; the window had slipped the latch and banged back and forth against the wall. Icy cold North Sea air filled the room.

Jumping out of bed, he closed the window, and glanced around. Moving across the floor, he peered into Elizabeth's bedroom; it was in total darkness, the way she preferred, and he could see she was fast asleep. Closing the door quietly, he went back and sat down on his bed. He had a raging headache and his mouth felt dry. It was a hangover . . . he had a hangover from the large quantity of cognac he had drunk last night, just before she had come downstairs, and seduced him on the floor of the library. Thank God she had had the sense to lock the door, because he hadn't even thought of it.

Laughing, shaking his head, Edward stood up, went through into the adjoining bathroom. Running the tap, he filled a glass with icy water and drank it down, and then reached for the shaving soap and his razor.

Elizabeth had set out to seduce him last night, very purposefully, and she had of course succeeded. Not that she had had to try very hard. He had found her most alluring, and had been an extremely willing and enthusiastic partner. And because for once she had not said the wrong thing and annoyed him, they had enjoyed a night of flawless lovemaking.

If only she kept her mouth shut more often, things in general would be so much better between them. As it was, she forever made rather mean statements which, very simply, always got his goat.

Edward stopped shaving for a moment, the razor hovering in mid air, as a sudden truth rushed at him. Elizabeth, intelligent and also clever in so many different ways, was actually *dense*. That's it, he muttered under his breath, unexpectedly seeing his wife objectively, with great clarity. Certain things just didn't penetrate her brain; she was insensitive to other people's feelings, he realized.

Sighing, he continued to shave, pondering Elizabeth. She was one of the most aggravating people he knew, and she was so inflammatory at times he became infuriated with her. But he would never leave her because he wanted a normal family life, and also there were the children. They had six now, and he loved them dearly and they needed him, needed both their parents, in fact.

Also, to be scrupulously fair, his wife did have certain qualities and assets which were important to him. She was still sexually exciting to him even after eleven years of marriage; he was always drawn to her in the most sensual way. There was another thing – she didn't mind having babies, even if she didn't pay too much attention to them after they arrived.

He paused again, staring at himself in the mirror, wondering if they had just made another baby last night. It wouldn't upset her, and it certainly didn't bother him, not in any way. Large families had been popular in the Victorian and Edwardian periods. And big families were still looked upon with great pleasure and pride.

This aside, his wife was considered to be a world-class beauty, and indeed she was. She had enormous style in dressing, was chic, wore clothes well, carried herself with confidence and panache; he loved having her on his arm. She had also learned, much to her credit, how to run the Berkeley Square house. He did not worry about his house by the sea in Kent because Mrs Nettleton, the housekeeper, took care of it with efficiency, whilst his mother handled the running of Ravenscar with her usual skill, and enjoyed doing so. The estate itself now actually made money; she held the reins firmly, made sure that Alan Pettigrew, the steward, carried out all of her instructions exactly.

Elizabeth, under his tutelage, was now a polished and charming hostess, but there *was* a downside. He now decided he must try to turn a blind eye to this if he could. She was argumentative, and managed to ruffle feathers very often; she said the wrong things to people who frequently took offence. He *had* tried to break her of this irritating habit without much success. 'Her mouth's always open and her foot's always in it,' Will was forever telling him, and this was the truth.

Exciting though she was in bed, Elizabeth was, unfortunately, deadly dull out of it. Nor was she at all interested in any of the things which claimed his attention and were relaxing to him.

Well, of course, he had Jane Shaw for companionship, enjoyed their shared interest in art, music and books. He focused on Jane for a moment; she was such a good person, and she was entirely happy with their relationship exactly the way it was. Marriage did not interest her. Not marriage to him or any other man. She had been married once, and that seemingly was enough for her. Certainly she had told him this many times.

Will, his best friend and greatest confidante, constantly told him to accept his life as it was, had said only the other day,

'Stop worrying so much about both women. You treat them extremely well, the same way you treat everyone in your family and your life well. You've nothing to chastise yourself about.'

He hoped that was true.

EIGHTEEN

'Ah, there you are Ned, darling,' Cecily Deravenel said, putting her cup down on the saucer. 'Good morning.' 'Morning, Mama,' he answered and smiled at her as he walked across the breakfast room. He stopped at her chair, kissed her cheek, and went on towards the sideboard.

An array of silver tureens were lined up on hot plates, and he lifted the lids, saw a selection of mouth-watering food: grilled sausages, kidneys, bacon, mushrooms, and tomatoes, as well as scrambled eggs, and kippers. 'Good Lord, Cook *has* done us proud!' he exclaimed, and taking a plate he selected grilled tomatoes and sausage and came back to the table.

Just as he was sitting down next to his mother, Jessup came hurrying in, bringing hot toast and a fresh pot of tea on a silver tray. 'Good morning, sir,' Jessup said, and brought the small tray to the table, placed both next to Edward.

'Good morning, Jessup,' Edward murmured. 'Splendid day, isn't it?'

'Yes, sir, it is. Very sunny and clear, no sea fret this morning. But it's chilly, Mr Deravenel, as usual.' The butler now brought glass dishes of butter and strawberry jam and set them next to the toast rack.

Edward nodded, took a piece of hot toast, spread butter on it, saying as he did, 'Are we ready for Boxing Day, Jessup? Is everything in place?'

'Oh yes indeed, sir. Cook's done up some lovely boxes of tasty food for the estate staff – turkey, ham and beef, pork pies and Christmas cakes; and Mr Pettigrew has filled the money boxes with sovereigns.'

Edward nodded. 'Excellent. I don't like to neglect the estate workers, they deserve to be well taken care of, Jessup. And look here, you might want to add a bottle of wine to each of the boxes prepared for the tenant farmers. They're a good lot.'

'I will, sir.' Jessup looked at Edward's mother and asked, 'Do you need anything else, Mrs Deravenel? Can I get you something more?'

'No thank you, Jessup.' She took a small card from her jacket pocket, and handed it to him. 'Here are the menus for Cook for lunch and dinner today. Oh, and please tell her that Lady Fenella is coming for tea this afternoon. The usual afternoon tea will be fine, Jessup, and please remind Cook that Lady Fenella has always loved her mince pies.'

'Yes, Madam.' Jessup hurried out.

'I'd forgotten about Fenella,' Edward said, turning to his mother. 'She's coming with Mark Ledbetter, isn't she?'

'Yes. I know you cancelled all the festivities, Ned, but she did so want to come over this afternoon, I didn't have the heart to say no.'

'It's not a problem for me, Mother, really not. And I cancelled the houseguests because Young Edward was ill. Anyway, I'm thrilled with his progress, he's so much better. And Fenella's presence isn't going to affect him.'

He sipped his tea, then continued, 'I need to go over something with you, but we can do it later.'

Cecily groaned. 'You always do that, you know, say you want to discuss something, and then immediately put it off, until later you say. Just as your father did. Tell me *now*, Ned, please don't procrastinate.'

'I want you to take the company papers out of your vault at Charles Street. I need to look them over.'

Cecily sat up straighter on the chair, staring at him, her brows drawing together in a frown. 'Is there something wrong? Is there a problem, Ned?'

He shook his head. 'No, not at all, Mother. I just need to look at the company rules.'

'I see.' She opened her mouth, shut it, and pondered for a moment before saying to him slowly. 'Is there a problem with that relative of Henry Grant's – Henry Turner, the fellow who lives in France? The Grants are not breathing down our necks again, are they?'

'No, no, of course not! And as for Henry Turner, he's a youngish chap, about seventeen or eighteen. No trouble for us. He's been living in France for years, not sure what he does. But he has no claim on Deravenels, if that is what you're intimating, Mama.'

'I'm not intimating anything, actually, but I do know that some years ago he was heard to say he was Henry Grant's true heir.'

Amused, Ned laughed, then cut into one of the sausages. 'Heir to what, though? As I just said, he has no claim to Deravenels. Besides, he's a rather *dubious* heir, if you ask me. His father was Henry Grant's half brother, so Henry Grant was his half uncle, I believe.' Edward started to laugh again.

Cecily shook her head. 'Yes, you are right in everything you say, darling, but as you are well aware, he who laughs last laughs the longest. You are sure this fellow Turner doesn't have any plots up his sleeve?'

'Don't be silly, Mother. Now, allow me to explain something.

I want to look at the company rules for a very specific reason. I want to know whether I can change one of the rules.'

'I doubt that you can!' she exclaimed, leaning closer to him, searching his face. 'And what rule do you want to change, anyway?'

'The rule pertaining to who is eligible to inherit Deravenels.'

'What do you mean? It's the first born of the current chairman! Or, as in your case, managing director. Young Edward is your heir, and then Ritchie, if Young Edward has predeceased him.'

'I understand that – just as I was my father's heir. But things *can* happen, life is unpredictable, and I want to be sure that if there is no *male* Deravenel to inherit after me, that a *female* can inherit.'

'A woman run Deravenels! My God, Edward, what are you thinking of! I can't imagine the Deravenels board sanctioning that! Good heavens, no! And don't forget there *is* a board of directors, you are a little bit hampered, you know.'

'I do know. But times are changing. And also life is truly unpredictable, as I just said. So I would like to know that Bess *can* inherit, if she is the only Deravenel old enough to step into my shoes, if there is no male heir.'

'Why wouldn't there be a male heir?' Cecily suddenly looked nervous, her face taut.

'I'm quite certain there will be, but what if something terrible should happen to the boys?' Edward shook his head, gave her a long look. 'I remember very well what you said to me one day, here at Ravenscar. 'Has nobody ever told you that life is catastrophic, Edward?' Those are the exact words you uttered that day, fourteen years ago, when you told me my father and brother, my uncle and my cousin had all been killed in Italy.'

Cecily was silent, and then she slowly nodded. 'Yes, it's true. I did say that.' She sat back in her chair. 'Perhaps there *is* some way to change the rule about women. It's very old, of course, but there are some people who would say that it is now anti-quated, truly out of date.' Cecily closed her eyes for a moment, thinking; when she opened them she smiled at her eldest son. 'I have a feeling that *you* could actually do it, pull it off, providing the board went along with you.'

A sense of relief surged through him, and he said softly, 'I can be very persuasive, Mother, very persuasive indeed.'

'Oh, I know that only too well, you don't have to tell me,' she replied, and gave him a sharp look.

There was a sudden racket outside; a dog was barking, a child was crying, and someone was shouting. He thought it might be Bess. Then he heard Mary screaming, 'No! No! Stop it!'

Edward jumped up, exclaiming, 'What in God's name is going on out there?' He opened the French doors of the breakfast room, stepped out on the terrace, and ran down the steps leading through the tiered garden. In his anxiousness for his children, his haste to get to them, Edward did not notice the steps were covered in ice, and he slipped, falling hard, rolled down the flagged steps, unable to stop himself. When he reached the bottom, near the patch of lawn at the edge of the cliffs, he did not move, lay perfectly still.

'Father! Father!' Bess shouted, and ran towards him, at the same time calling out, 'Mary! Mary! Fetch Jessup. Find Nanny. Go on, go! Do as I say.'

'What about the dog?' Mary cried tearfully.

'Give the leash to Cecily. Just go!'

Now reaching Edward, the nine-year-old girl knelt down on the ground next to him, touching his face. 'Father, Father. Open your eyes.' Edward groaned, but no words left his mouth.

'Father, Father,' Bess said again, panic rising in her. 'Please speak to me.'

Still he did not answer her. She took hold of his hand, waiting for Jessup, and praying her father was not dead.

NINETEEN

Nanny stood in the middle of the wood-panelled parlour in the nursery, counting the chairs around the circular table where the children ate their meals. She counted seven and stopped.

'There's a chair missing,' she announced, surveying her brood. 'Where is it? Does anyone know?'

'It went away,' Cecily announced non-committally, quickly glancing at the fireplace.

'And where did it go?' Nanny asked, her eyes narrowing slightly.

'Don't know,' Cecily muttered.

'I see. Well, well, well, do chairs walk away by themselves, I wonder? I don't think so. So who took it?'

'Bess,' a little voice piped up, and Nanny's brown eyes swooped down on Ritchie.

'Thank you. And where is Bess, Mary? You always know everything, so, where did Bess go?'

Mary sat straighter in her chair, puffing up with a hint of sudden pride. 'When she put me in charge, she said she was going to see Father. Is he dead?'

Cecily gaped at her elder sister and promptly burst into tears.

Nanny went to her at once, bent over her comfortingly and said, 'No, he's not dead. Just a bit hurt.' Straightening herself, she glared at Mary and exclaimed, 'You mustn't say such things. Don't upset the younger ones, Mary dear. You know they take everything you say *very* seriously.'

'Yes, Nanny. Sorry, Nanny. Not suitable.'

Nanny made no further comment, hurried into the adjoining nursery and said to Madge, 'Please keep an eye on them. I'll be back in a moment.'

'I'll be right 'ere, Nanny, don't yer worry,' the nursemaid replied, fussing with the baby's lacey dress as she placed her in the bassinet.

Although she rushed down the corridor, Nanny took the stairs more slowly as she descended to the main bedroom floor. Her name was Joan Madley and she was a splendid down-to-earth no-nonsense Yorkshire woman who had spent her life looking after other people's children. Everyone knew she was the best nanny in the world, with the finest reputation.

As she stepped onto the landing, she spotted Bess at once. She was standing outside her father's bedroom door, and with her was Young Edward, who was seated in the missing chair.

'Children, you must come back to the nursery with me at once!' Nanny cried. 'The others are waiting for you . . . it's time for your morning snack.'

'We're waiting for the doctor to come out,' Bess said in a subdued voice. 'He's going to tell us how badly Father hurt himself when he fell down.'

'I understand. But we can't stay here. I promise you we'll know very quickly. Your mother, or your grandmother, will come to tell us immediately.'

'Grandmama says I'm a blessing in disguise,' Young Edward announced rather proudly.

'And what –' Nanny began.

'No, no,' Bess cut in swiftly. 'She didn't say *you* were a blessing in disguise, she said your bronchitis was. Because if you hadn't got it, then Dr Leighton wouldn't have been arriving here this morning to see you. And just when Papa fell down the garden steps. Very convenient, his coming then, so Grandma said.'

Young Edward appeared to be crestfallen when he answered. 'But it's the same thing, isn't it?' He glanced at the nanny. 'I like being a blessing.'

'And so you should, and you are, my pet. Everyone knows that. But let's not . . . *camp* outside Papa's door, it's really, well, it's really rather common and it won't do. It's not suitable.' She reached out and took his small hand in hers and he dutifully slid out of the chair. Looking up at her, he asked in a worried voice, 'He's not going to die, is he?'

'No, of course not! Don't be a silly goose. He's probably just a bit bruised.'

'Do you go to live with the angels when you die, Nanny?'

'Let us not have all this talk about dying, Young Edward,' Nanny answered in a brisk voice. 'It's exceptionally *morbid*. Nobody's dying around here, least of all your father. He's young and strong.'

Bess beamed at her. 'He's not going to die because . . . it's . . . not suitable,' the nine-year-old girl said, using Nanny's farourite expression, and started to laugh.

Nanny and Young Edward laughed with her and Nanny took the chair and they went back to the nursery floor for their morning snack.

'You don't know how lucky you've been, Mr Deravenel,' Dr Leighton said, putting his stethoscope and other instruments back in his black leather bag. 'You could have killed yourself, you know. Taking a fall like that, with your weight and height, you could easily have broken your neck. Or done something equally fatal.' The doctor shook his head. 'I'm surprised you have no serious injuries, hardly any injuries at all.'

'I'm just as surprised. When I felt myself slipping I tried desperately to break my fall, and I think that's when I twisted my arm and shoulder. But it's so amazing, Dr Leighton. I seem to have got off with only a few scratches.' Edward pushed himself a bit further up on the pillows, and added, 'I expect I'll be badly bruised tomorrow, though.'

The doctor nodded. 'Later today, I should think. Your back in particular will be sore, and you'll be very much aware of that shoulder. But it's not broken, thank God. You've got off scot-free, I'm glad to say.'

As he turned to leave, he noticed Edward's clothes thrown on the sofa, and remarked, 'Lucky thing you were wearing your riding togs. The leather boots protected your legs, they surely did.'

'It was also lucky you were coming here to see Young Edward. Lucky for me, that is. Thanks so much for attending to me at once.'

'No problem, and your son was so much better on Christmas Eve I wasn't too worried about him today. But I decided I'd come over anyway, since my wife and I are still at The Lodge with the Dunbars. Eric Dunbar and I studied medicine together, and his parents like us to come over from Scarborough for the weekend, whenever we can. They think we cheer him up.'

'How is Eric doing?' Edward asked, swinging his legs to the floor. 'I heard he was back from the front and had some bad injuries.'

'He lost a leg, actually. But as he says, as long as he's still got two arms he can practise as a doctor when he's really better. It's amazing how brave and cheerful he is. *Amazing*.'

'All of the wounded are,' Edward murmured, and instantly thought of Fenella. She was coming to tea today and he decided he would talk to her further about the idea of creating the recreation centre.

Peter Leighton paused in the doorway. 'I want you to take it easy, Mr Deravenel. You're going to feel a bit tender for a few days, and all over, I suspect. Also, that headache of yours will linger. Just keep on taking the aspirins, and rest. No hectic activity. And one other thing – if you feel at all ill, whether it's a pain in your extremities or your back or head, or nausea, whatever it is you must telephone me at the Dunbars. I shall pop in tomorrow morning anyway, just to check on you. But remember, I am only twenty minutes away.' He walked to the door, and added, 'And now I think I had better go and look for my young patient. I'll find Jessup downstairs, no doubt?'

'Yes, you will, and my wife is bound to be waiting for you in the library. She will take you to see the boy. He's most likely in the nursery. And thanks again, Leighton, for being so caring and diligent.'

Cecily Deravenel had been badly shaken, and even now, in the middle of the afternoon, she was still experiencing a sort of aftershock. That was the only way she could describe it to herself.

Her eldest son could have so easily been seriously injured or even killed this morning. He could have suffered a broken neck, a broken back, or some kind of fatal head injury. Anything was possible when one took that kind of tumble down a steep flight of flagstone steps.

And how unexpectedly it had happened, just like that, in the blink of an eye. That was the most frightening thing. Here one moment, gone the next.

Cecily was kneeling in a pew at the front of the centuries-old Deravenel private chapel up behind the house. She had come there a short while before to offer grateful thanks to God for protecting her son. Now, still holding her rosary, she murmured additional prayers of thanks for all of her blessings, which were many, and the safety of all of her children.

Soon her thoughts returned to Edward, and for a moment or two she dwelt on the conversation she had had with him over breakfast, when he had spoken of wanting to change the rules, and so ensure that there was always a Deravenel at the head of Deravenels. *Even if it was a woman.* She wondered if he could possibly sway the board, persuade them to add the new rule which would favour the female sex. She had no answer for herself. She hoped it would come to pass.

A small sigh escaped Cecily's lips, and she sat staring at the beautiful carved altar with the figure of Christ on the cross as its centrepiece. What an uncanny coincidence that had been this morning – he had been speaking about his heirs and then within the space of a few minutes Ned had rushed outside and fallen down, almost killed himself. *Unbelievable.*

If anything happened to Ned, something untimely when he was still in his prime, there would be a vacuum at Deravenels. No head of the company. Young Edward would probably not be of the right age to take over. Cecily knew in her heart of hearts that Edward would never favour George, never in a million years. It would be Richard who would come to power, who would safeguard the trading company, until Young Edward was old enough to take over as managing director in his uncle's place.

Poor George. There was something about him that had always touched her heart and made her his defender. It was odd how he had always run to her as a child, run to her as if he needed protection from the world, physically clinging to her even during his early teens. And she had responded to his need in the way a mother would, with love and reassurances that she would protect him, that he would be safe.

But she knew he wouldn't be safe forever . . . she had long had a premonition of a bad destiny, had known within herself that George was fated. It seemed to her that he tumbled into trouble constantly, trouble he brought on himself. He had a dreadful way of putting his foot in it, a knack of enraging Edward, and she fully understood why *he* ended up in a fury with his younger brother. At the same time, she felt sympathy for George . . . It struck her that he was something of a bumbler . . . making a mess without meaning to do harm . . . upsetting people . . . causing them terrible hurt. There had even been moments over the years when she had believed George was truly self-destructive.

Not long ago he had antagonized his mother-in-law, and she had heard all about it from Nan Watkins herself. Nan had come to visit her at the Charles Street house in London several months ago, and had poured out her woes. Nan had suggested in no uncertain terms that George was something of a wastrel, and that he was wasting *her* money, inasmuch as it was George who was spending the large allowance she gave to Isabel.

She still remembered how startled she had been, and also irritated with George. Nan had been good to her daughter and son-in-law, who apparently was abusing her goodwill and her generosity.

That day Cecily had tried to console Nan, who was genuinely upset, and had suggested she talk to George in a firm, no-nonsense way. 'You just have to make him see sense,' Cecily had finished. 'Or cancel the allowance you give Isabel, force George to support his wife and live within his means.' Nan had agreed, and left it at that.

Cecily now wondered what had happened, since Nan had never confided in her again. George, her charming and handsome son, was a bumbler, a wastrel, half-witted at times, and quite incorrigible, really. Yet he was her son, and she did love him. Just as she loved Edward and Richard, but somehow these two seemed much more capable of taking care of themselves . . .

Rising, Cecily crossed herself, turned and slowly walked up the aisle, wondering what would become of her sons and their families. And on this Boxing Day of 1918 she had no way of knowing that disaster hovered over the Deravenels, and that ultimately catastrophic events would change all of their lives. Irrevocably. And so much so that nothing would ever be the same again.

TWENTY

Mark Ledbetter had not been to Ravenscar for a long time, but even so he had not forgotten the spectacular view from the library windows.

As he and Fenella were ushered into the room by Cecily Deravenel he did his best to curb the sudden urge to rush over to them to look out, to take pleasure in that unique vista.

'It's lovely to see you both,' Cecily was saying, and then her face broke into smiles. 'Ah, here's Bess, your greatest admirer, Fenella. And Nanny with the other children.'

A moment later Fenella and Cecily were surrounded by the youngsters, all clamouring for attention, and Mark took the opportunity to walk to the other end of the room.

He stood in front of the set of French doors, looking out at the vast panoramic view of the North Sea and the flowing coastline of cream-coloured cliffs that stretched endlessly before his eyes. The sea had a metallic shine this afternoon, painted with great rafts of sunlight. The sky, often so moody and leaden on this unique stretch of the northern coast, was a radiant periwinkle blue with only a few scraps of white cloud floating on high.

The ancient house, built on top of the cliffs, had an extraordinary vantage point, and now, as he continued to stare out of the windows, he saw two great ships on the far horizon, ploughing their way through the turbulent waters. It was windy today, and the North Sea was restless, crested with white foam.

Turning around, Mark allowed his eyes to sweep the room for a moment, admiringly, taking in the soaring shelves of books, the memorable paintings on one wall, and the handsome antiques made of dark, ripe woods. There were comfortable sofas and chairs arranged near the huge stone fireplace where a log fire was blazing. It was a pleasure to be in such a well-appointed room.

His eyes settled on Fenella, who was momentarily preoccupied with the group of youngsters, and he had to admit he had never seen such beautiful children in his entire life. To him they might have just stepped out of a portrait by one of the great classical portraitists of the eighteenth century, such as Thomas Gainsborough, George Romney, or Sir Joshua Reynolds.

As young Deravenels clustered around Fenella, a hint of regret touched a corner of Mark's mind, and he suddenly wished she had had children. Most certainly hers would have been as lovely as those who now circled her, affectionately demanding her attention. But her husband Jeremy had been killed when he was young, early in her marriage to him. Fenella was a beauty with her liquid grey eyes, so translucent, her silky blonde hair shimmering around her softly-contoured face. And she was willowy, tall, with enormous elegance. And yes, her children would have been as lovely as she was.

Mark focused on the five Deravenels; he was enamoured of them at this moment. A long time ago, when their father had been a bachelor, Edward Deravenel had frequently been called the Golden Boy by many of his contemporaries. And his children were certainly golden, with their polished good looks, their vividness of colouring – that glorious red-gold hair, the shining

159

blue eyes. He saw that each one of them had a perfect little face, beautifully sculpted, the features fine, delicate, aristocratic. How innocent they were, and precious. Children so lovely that they were breathtaking. They must always be properly protected . . . it was a dangerous world out there . . .

He tore his mind away from his inner thoughts when Cecily came to him. 'I'm so sorry, I didn't mean to abandon you so abruptly, Mark. I was hoping to prevent the children from taking Fenella for themselves.'

Mark laughed. 'But it seems they have.'

'Yes, indeed. How is your mother?'

'She's quite remarkable, and she sends you her best wishes, and her love. She told me to remind you about the *fun* you and she and Fenella's Aunt Philomena had on Christmases long ago, when you were all single young women . . . debutantes together.'

Cecily started to laugh. 'We did indeed, and I think we were . . . well, to tell you the truth, I think the three of us were quite *incorrigible*.' Clearing her throat, she continued, 'Elizabeth will join us shortly. She had to take a telephone call just as you were arriving. Ah, and here is Ned, *finally*. Walking rather badly, I'm afraid, after his fall.'

'He had a fall?' Mark frowned, staring at her. He was obviously taken by surprise and it showed in his dark brown eyes suddenly full of concern.

'Yes, he did. This morning. He tumbled down the steps outside the breakfast room.'

Edward, leaning heavily on a stout walking stick, came slowly towards them, and as he stopped in front of Mark and his mother, he offered the other man his hand, along with a rueful smile.

'Excuse me, I see Jessup hovering. I believe he wants to speak to me,' Cecily murmured, and hurried towards the doorway, leaving the two men alone.

'How did you manage to fall?' Mark inquired, peering at Edward, concern still registering.

'I went arse over tit on the flagstone steps outside which were covered with ice. My own fault. I wasn't paying attention. There was a hell of a rumpus going on outdoors . . . with the children. They were shouting, screaming and the dog was barking. So yes, like a worried, doting father I rushed out, and I was rather hasty I must admit as I plunged down those steps. I hadn't even thought of *ice*.'

Mark eyed him quickly, noted the black eye, the grazed cheek, and the heavily bruised chin. 'You must have taken quite a tumble,' he exclaimed.

'I did, and I was frightfully lucky.'

'I'll say. I hope you've seen a doctor.'

'Yes. As a matter of fact, Young Edward has had a bout of bronchitis, and our local doctor happened to be arriving here to check on him this morning, when Jessup and two of the stable lads were bringing me indoors.'

'He gave you a thorough examination?'

'Indeed he did. But I promised him I would go to Guy's Hospital when I get back to London in a couple of days, to see Michael Robertson who looked after me years ago. Would you mind if we sit down over there on the chairs, Ledbetter? This wonky leg is giving me the gyp.'

'Let's sit, of course,' Mark agreed at once.

'So tell me, when are you going back to the Yard?' Edward asked, once they were comfortably settled in two armchairs close to the fireplace. 'Will Hasling told me you are to be given quite a big promotion.'

'I am, yes. Actually, it's going to be announced relatively soon. I shall become Police Commissioner of the Metropolitan Police Force at Scotland Yard.'

'Congratulations!' Edward leaned back in his chair, smiling at the other man. 'I'm pleased for you. It's a worthy promotion.'

Mark laughed. 'I know, but I wanted to go back anyway, to be frank. I have rather missed the Yard, to tell you the truth.

My War Office job was all right, and I had to do it, but I found myself bogged down in paperwork at times.'

'So, there you were, dealing with paper, and we all thought you were dealing with spies,' Edward remarked, his tone jocular.

'I was in a way, but not exactly face to face,' Mark explained, smiling. 'In other words, whilst I *was* with the British Secret Service, I wasn't out in the field.'

'You probably thought your wartime job was boring, but surely safer, wouldn't you say?'

'Indeed it was, Deravenel, and I must admit I did feel I was making a contribution to the war effort.'

At this moment Elizabeth arrived, looking extremely beautiful in a beige wool suit and several strings of fabulous pearls. 'Do excuse me,' she exclaimed, thrusting her hand at Mark, who had risen. 'I'm sorry I wasn't here to greet you. I had to speak to my mother on the telephone.'

Mark nodded his understanding, and then glanced over at the children, who were nearby and still surrounding Fenella. 'They are all very beautiful, Elizabeth, and such a credit to you.'

'Thank you.'

Cecily returned to the library, followed by Jessup and three of the parlour maids who were pushing tea trolleys, which they stationed near the piano at the entrance to the room.

Edward said, 'I think Jessup is going to announce tea is served at any moment.'

Fenella, having broken free of the younger set, hurried to sit with Elizabeth and Edward, and after kissing them both, she said to Ned, 'Oh, poor you, your poor face. Your mother told me about your dreadful fall.'

'The least said about that the better. I was an utter fool, Fenella, the way I rushed outside without thinking, and all because of the dog barking and Mary screaming. It turned out to be nothing, actually.'

Fenella smiled at him. They had known each other for years,

and she had always been his great defender and advocate; she loved him like a brother. 'Oh yes,' she murmured. 'I heard all about the dog from Young Edward.'

Ned began to laugh. 'Can you imagine such a name for a dog? *Macbeth*?'

They all chuckled, and Fenella confided, 'I understand from its little owner that when he said he wanted to choose a Scottish name, because the dog was a West Highland terrier, it was Nanny who suggested Macbeth.'

'That's right.'

Cecily joined the four of them once more, and murmured softly, 'I think Jessup wishes to serve tea. Perhaps you would like to come and sit over here, Fenella, with me. And Elizabeth. Nanny will look after the children. Over there.' She nodded her head in the direction of the windows. 'Where they can have their own little tea party.'

Taking a deep breath, Fenella rose, took a step forward, announced swiftly and very unexpectedly, 'I, rather, *we* have something to tell you all. Mark and I have just become engaged.'

As she spoke Mark also stood up, stepped over to her and took hold of her hand. 'That's one of the reasons we wanted to come over to see you today, to give you our news,' she finished, her eyes sparkling, her smile radiant.

Edward, Elizabeth and Cecily all offered them their heartfelt congratulations, and then Elizabeth exclaimed, 'Thank goodness you're not going to be an old maid left on the shelf after all. As everyone thought you would be.'

There was a sudden silence.

Ned threw his wife a furious look, and his mother's expression was one of utter dismay mingled with embarrassment.

Fenella Fayne had always known that Elizabeth disliked her, mostly because she was jealous of her relationship with Ned. But being a woman of true breeding, a titled woman in her own right and well brought up, she never stooped to other people's levels. She was also a calm person, and controlled. Finally, smiling widely at them, she said in a clear, steady voice, 'Between widowhood, starting up the Haddon House charity, and the war, I seem to have been somewhat preoccupied until now.'

Ignoring Elizabeth's jibe, Mark put his arm around Fenella, and looked down at her, then said lovingly to the others, 'I've been pestering her to marry me for years and she has finally said yes at last. To my utmost joy.'

Cecily hurried across to Fenella and hugged her affectionately, and then turning, taking Elizabeth's arm, she eased her up from the chair, and said to her daughter-in-law, 'Perhaps we should get the children organized, so that our guests can have afternoon tea in peace.'

'But Nanny's in con –'

'Come along, Elizabeth,' Cecily ordered in the sternest of voices, hurrying her forward, throwing a pointed look at her son as they moved towards the windows where Nanny was settling the children.

Fenella sat down on the sofa and looked at Edward intently. 'There's something I did want to ask you, Ned darling. I do hope you will allow your girls to be my bridesmaids? I would love it if you would. Please say yes.'

'But of course I say yes,' he cried, his bright blue eyes lighting up.

She offered him a happy smile, and the swift look they exchanged signalled his dismay at his wife's words, and her total lack of concern about them. They had always been able to read each other's thoughts and they understood each other.

In a lower tone, she now asked, 'I would like Grace Rose to be a bridesmaid as well, if that's all right with you. I do love her so, and she's very special to me, you know.'

'That is a marvellous idea! And I certainly don't have any objections. And I know Vicky won't either, she'll be happy.'

'I haven't asked her yet, Ned. In fact, we haven't told anyone we're getting married, you're the first to know.'

'I had to tackle her father over Christmas,' Mark announced. He sat down next to Ned and added, 'I was certainly relieved when the Earl gave us his blessing.'

Jessup arrived, ushered one of the parlour maids towards them, looking at Edward questioningly, who nodded. The maid was pushing a tea trolley, and came to stop at the fireside; Jessup poured cups of tea for them whilst the maid handed them small napkins and plates. Then she offered a large plate of tea sandwiches, including smoked salmon, egg salad, cucumber, tomatoes, and ham and cheese.

A ringing telephone took Jessup away from them for a few moments, and when he returned to the library he hurried to Edward, whispered something to him. Edward nodded.

'Thank you, Jessup,' he replied, and offered his hand to the butler. 'Help me up, would you, please?'

Once he was on his feet, Edward said to Fenella and Mark, 'So sorry, an urgent telephone call. I won't be too long, I'm sure.'

Edward limped across the library, leaning heavily on his cane. He picked up the phone which stood on a small table in the Long Hall.

'Deravenel here,' he said. And then he listened acutely, and in some astonishment, as a barrage of words flowed down the wire from Scotland. And without pause.

Finally, the caller stopped to draw breath and Edward answered in the most conciliatory voice he could muster, 'I understand everything you're saying, Ian, and I am in total agreement with you. At this moment I have guests. But I believe we can sort this out tomorrow, I'm quite sure of that.'

After Ian MacDonald agreed to speak with him the next day, the Scotsman hung up abruptly, without saying another word, not even goodbye.

Edward stood there for a moment. Stunned. His face was white with fury. He took several deep breaths, trying to calm himself before returning to the library. But it was quite a while before he felt able to do so.

Twenty-One

London 1919

'I'm sorry to have brought you in on a Saturday, Amos,' Edward apologized. 'But I do really need your assistance.'

'That's all right, Mr Edward,' Amos answered. 'To tell you the truth, I'm glad to be here, I've nothing better to do. So, how can I be of help, sir?'

'I want you to break into one of the offices. The only thing is, it mustn't look like a break-in. If anyone can do that, you can.'

'Beg pardon, sir, but I'm assuming it's Mr George's office you want me to break into, isn't it?'

Edward laughed a little hollowly. How well Amos understood the lay of the land around here. 'It is indeed. Let's get started, shall we?'

Standing up, Edward strode across the room, followed by Amos, who was explaining, 'I just have to pop into my office to collect my kit, sir. Give me a jiffy.'

Edward nodded, and continued on down the corridor in the direction of his brother's office, thinking about George. He had gone into hiding, so to speak, but Edward knew very well where he was – huddling behind the skirts of the women in his family, his wife Isabel and his mother-in-law, Nan Watkins. Little good that would do him. What a fool he was, a blithering idiot who didn't have the brains he was born with. After speaking with Ian MacDonald several times and receiving a full report about the débâcle in Edinburgh, Edward was fully aware that he had to render George powerless. And immediately. A demotion was all there was for it. Edward grimaced to himself; if he could get his hands on George at this moment he would cheerfully strangle him.

He leaned against the door jamb, waiting for Amos, who was now hurrying down the corridor. 'Don't push yourself, Amos,' Edward muttered. 'There's plenty of time. No one's likely to arrive here on Saturday, and something of a holiday Saturday at that.' It was the fourth of January, and people were still celebrating the advent of the New Year, *1919*. The beginning of the peace, and a year when anything and everything was possible, so the politicians were pronouncing at any rate.

Unrolling his brown leather pouch, Amos knelt down on the floor, and inserted an implement in the lock. After a bit of jiggling around, there was a click. Amos looked up at Edward and grinned. Rising, the older man turned the knob, and opened the door, exclaiming, 'After you, Mr Deravenel.'

Edward walked in and paused. 'My God, he must smoke a lot, this room stinks.'

'He never has a cigarette out of his mouth these days, sir. In all my life I've never seen anybody smoke like he does.' Amos shook his head. 'He's an addict, if you ask me.'

'What do you mean?'

'He has what Mark Ledbetter used to call an addictive personality, Mr Deravenel. When the Chief Inspector was a copper, that is.'

'I saw him over the holidays,' Edward said, looking at Amos swiftly. 'He's become engaged to Lady Fenella.'

'Oh sir, I *am* pleased about that! Lovely lady she is, and so philanthropic and caring.' Amos smiled and nodded, and his eyes grew very bright. 'I couldn't wish for her to have a better man than the Chief Inspector. Good chap, salt of the earth, sir.'

'He is indeed.' Edward closed the door and walked across to George's desk, reached for the top drawer and grabbed the pull. The drawer didn't budge. It was locked. He tried each one in the large Georgian partners' desk only to discover all of them locked.

'Well, Amos, my friend, you have quite a task here, I'm afraid. I need to look in all of these drawers, so get to it, do your tricks.'

'No problem, won't take but a minute.' Even as he answered Amos was kneeling down, inserting an implement and within minutes opening the top centre drawer, then the next and the next. Once they were all open, Amos got up and waved his hand at the desk. 'All yours, sir.'

The top drawer was full of unpaid bills. Appalled at the amount of money George owed to tailors and merchants, Edward put them back carefully, and slowly went through more drawers. He gaped in surprise when he saw the gun in a bottom drawer. 'Amos, come and look at this. There's a pistol here.'

Loathing guns the way he did, Edward had no desire to pick it up nor to examine it.

Amos stared down at the gun and shook his head in bafflement. 'God knows why he needs this thing, Mr Edward. Anyway, it's a Smith and Wesson for your information.' Amos lifted his foot and pushed the drawer closed.

Edward searched the other drawers and found nothing except an address book filled with many women's telephone numbers, plus the numbers for various nightclubs in London. He then crossed the room, opened some of the cupboards and found nothing of any interest. 'Well, that's it, there's nothing, better lock all the drawers.'

'Right-o, sir. Excuse me, sir, but were you looking for something specific?'

'No – well, yes, actually. I was looking for *something*, anything that might be . . . incriminating in some way.'

Amos threw Edward a look, and then set about locking the drawers.

A few minutes later they left George's office; Amos locked the door, and they walked down the corridor together in total silence.

At one moment Edward paused and looked at Amos, his eyes puzzled. 'Something nags at the back of my mind, and I can't quite put my finger on it. To be honest, Amos, I really did expect to find something in his office, something of vital importance, but I can't for the life of me think what it is I'm looking for.'

'If you do remember, let me know, sir. I can open the office door in a jiffy, as you just saw.'

Edward sat in his office, looking at the memos he had received from Oliveri and Will Hasling the day before. These two executives, who were the closest to him, had powerful positions within the company, and had finally finished their surveys of the world-wide business the company had done for the entire year of 1918.

When they had presented the papers to him yesterday they had been thrilled to announce that it had been an extraordinary year, exceptional, despite the war. Or perhaps, in part, because of it, Edward thought, leaning back in his chair.

Deravenels, the greatest trading company in the world, was truly riding high. Profits were up tremendously, and it seemed to him that they couldn't possibly do better. A small smile struck his face. Of course they could, and would. There would be a huge boom now that the world was at peace.

He leaned forward, shuffled through the papers, focused for

a moment on two divisions – mining and the vineyards in France. The latter had had some problems, but not because of the war so much as bad weather. But the wine division was as profitable as it had been for hundreds of years.

And their mines around the world were flourishing. Everything was doing well, and one day in the not-too-distant future there would be oil in Persia. He was convinced of that. It was his dream. After a moment of studying the memos, he put them back in a drawer in his desk, and locked it.

The business was in fantastic shape, thank God. He had turned it around in the fourteen years he had been at the helm. Nobody could fault him, and he was rather proud of his accomplishments, especially when he thought of the muddled mess he had discovered once he had removed the 'Grant lot', as he called them. Also, his personal affairs were in good order. The trusts for the women in his life were finished; he had an appointment to see his solicitors next week to make the changes to his will; and his mother's financial affairs, which he had handled for years, were also in perfect order.

He was starting the new year right. Except for George. He pushed aside thoughts of his brother, now a bigger liability than ever. He would deal with him next week. Richard leapt into his mind, and he reminded himself yet again how wise he had been to buy that house from Nan Watkins. Richard and Anne were safe; they held the deeds.

Bending down to the bottom drawer of his desk, he unlocked it and took out the photograph of Lily, and straightened up. Rising, he carried it over to the window and studied it in the bright daylight. How beautiful she had been, and so loving, sincere, and warm-hearted. A good woman. His first Mistress, the one woman he had truly loved, and who had meant so much to him. Her death had devastated him, for such a long time. Her murder, the murder of their child, he corrected himself.

Lily had loved him in return, with all of her heart. And in

death she had protected him, made him a very rich man. Her entire estate had been willed to him – the money, the houses, and much of her jewellery and antique furniture. It was Lily's fortune which he had increased over the years, that he had used to create the trusts for Grace Rose and his daughters, and to buy the Chelsea house from Nan. He knew Lily would be happy if she knew what good use he had made of her legacy. And perhaps she did know. He stared down at the photograph of her again . . . and he certainly knew how much he had missed her all these years. He cared very much for Jane Shaw, and she was a blessing to him, but she could never replace Lily. No one could. Elizabeth least of all.

Elizabeth. How she had infuriated him on Boxing Day; those mean words she had uttered to Fenella when she and Mark had come over for tea had cut him to the quick. *Her mouth always open, her foot always in it*, he thought, remembering Will's comment. She was a jealous woman, no two ways about that. And on Boxing Day night they had had a terrible quarrel, all because he had said she was silly to be jealous of his relationship with Fenella, who was more like a sister to him than anything else. He had gone on to add that they were, very simply, just platonic friends, known each other for donkeys' years. But Elizabeth couldn't seem to accept that, and she had accused him of a romantic liaison with Fenella.

'There's more self-love in jealousy than love,' he had retorted coldly when she had calmed down, paraphrasing de La Rochefoucauld to her. She had glared at him angrily and flounced off, and they had not been on very good terms since then. So be it, he thought, and went back to his desk.

There was a knock on the door, and Amos put his head round it. 'Can I have a word, Mr Edward?'

'Yes, come in Amos.' Edward laid the photograph in the bottom drawer and locked it. 'What is it? You sound worried.'

'I am, sir. I'm concerned about that damnable gun in Mr

George's office. I just don't like the idea of guns around here. Guns are dangerous.'

'Too true, but I can't do much about it.'

'I could remove it, sir.'

'Yes, you could. But I don't think you should. I don't want him to know that someone can get in and out of his office and his desk, and with ease. That must be our secret, Amos.'

'I understand, sir. So I won't remove the gun then. No problem.'

Edward nodded. 'That's a good chap, Amos. I'm about to leave. I have to meet Mr Hasling at the Savoy for lunch. And I doubt that I'll be back this afternoon. So I will collect Grace Rose and you tomorrow, at Mrs Vicky's.'

'Thank you, sir. She's excited, Grace Rose. She can't wait to go to her mother's grave.'

'It will mean a certain kind of ending for her,' Edward murmured. 'I'm so glad you were able to help her in that.'

TWENTY-TWO

Will Hasling realized the moment Edward Deravenel walked into the Grill Room of the Savoy Hotel that his friend and colleague was carrying new and heavy burdens.

Their close friendship of over twenty years was unsullied by any quarrels or disagreements, and he knew Ned as well as he knew himself; perhaps even better than he knew himself. And after all of these years of closeness he could read Ned like a book. He suspected that it was George who was at the root of the trouble, and the cause of Ned's glum expression.

'Am I late?' Edward asked a split second later, sitting down opposite his dearest friend.

'No, you're not. I arrived here early in point of fact, and I was certainly rather surprised to see how busy the Grill is today, a Saturday, after all.

Edward glanced around the Grill Room, and nodded. 'Very busy, but probably with hotel guests. I don't see any familiar faces.'

'That's true,' Will agreed. 'I thought I might have a glass of champagne. Does that appeal to you?'

'Yes, why not?'

Will signalled to a waiter, who came over immediately, and Will asked to see the wine list, then he looked across at Edward and asked, 'What's wrong? Is it to do with erstwhile brother George?'

'It is, naturally. As you well know he didn't show up this week, as he was supposed to do, and instead I had that silly message from him via Isabel, that he had bronchitis and couldn't come to the phone.'

Will half-laughed, half-snorted. 'You told me, and I was utterly amazed at his gall. But surely you're not worried about his absence?' Will stared at Edward quizzically.

'No. I'm worried about what happened in Scotland with Ian MacDonald. I didn't tell you about the débâcle that occurred up there, because I wanted to tackle George first, get his side of the story, face-to-face. But since he's done a bunk, and is still in Yorkshire ensconced at Thorpe Manor with Nan, I thought I ought to fill you in today.' Ned paused as the waiter returned with the wine list, which he gave to Will.

After flicking through the list, Will ordered a bottle of Krug rosé champagne. Turning to Ned, he picked up their conversation. 'I suppose he blew the deal, didn't he?'

'Well . . . sort of . . . but actually not quite. I have been able to satisfy MacDonald that I am serious. However, I believe it entails your going to Scotland this coming week, to settle matters with your usual diplomacy and skill. Richard will have to go with you, since MacDonald wants a Deravenel present at the final negotiations, and obviously George is not welcome.'

'Naturally I'll go, but what happened?' Will began to frown, perplexity ringing his face as he stared at Edward intently. 'The last I heard everything was going beautifully.'

'That's true, it was. The first meeting on the Friday before Christmas was handled well, and that weekend MacDonald took George to some of his distilleries outside Edinburgh. The problems developed on Monday, the twenty-third of December. George apparently became tough with MacDonald, and extremely so, according to the Scotsman, who had the good sense to let the matter drop for the moment. He didn't want to argue with George at that time. He thought it would be more sensible, and wiser, to continue business matters after Christmas. If you remember, I told you George had been invited to stay with MacDonald and his daughter and her family in the Lammermuir Hills. Seemingly, George behaved rather badly over Christmas, got drunk, became arrogant and boastful, as only he can. And on Boxing Day he stormed off, after demanding a car and a driver to take the family back to the hotel in Edinburgh. That was when I received an irate telephone call at Ravenscar from a very angry Ian MacDonald.'

'And our George does a bunk, rushes back to England, but not to London, to Yorkshire instead, unable to face you, I've no doubt.' Will shook his head. 'He's such a fool. Doesn't he understand that we all see through him? He's so transparent it's pathetic.'

Edward smiled faintly. 'He's in a bit of a funk at the moment, I should think, since he has made a bloody mess of things.'

'But MacDonald is still prepared to negotiate, I'm assuming?'

'Yes, he is, Will, and actually, if the truth be known, I can't imagine why George was even arguing about money. It was a very reasonable deal, as far as I'm concerned. Why he wanted to antagonize MacDonald in the way he did I'll never understand. *The price was fine.*' Edward compressed his mouth, looked away, and then turning back to face Will, he explained, 'MacDonald reported everything to me verbatim, and I'm absolutely sure he told me the truth. I've know him for years and he's an honest man. As for George, he should have discussed everything with me, especially if he had any doubts whatsoever. But in his usual conceited, arrogant and bumptious way, he wanted to play the big shot. Little good that'll do him.'

'It's all about power with George,' Will volunteered. 'He wants to wield it. *Powerfully*. He's got an inflated opinion of himself and his abilities, and he just plunges on like a wild pig in a forest looking for truffles, with absolutely no thought.' Will paused, turned to the waiter who had arrived with the champagne, and thanked him.

A moment later, Will touched his champagne flute to Ned's, and went on swiftly, 'But please explain one thing to me. You said at the outset, weeks ago, that you didn't really care whether you made the deal or not. So why do you want it so much now?'

'I don't,' Edward replied. 'No, that's not what I mean. Let me explain.' Ned leaned across the table, staring at his friend fixedly. 'I think acquiring the MacDonald operation would be good for us in the long run: it certainly will help to boost the wine division. The deal for me hangs on two things – the price MacDonald wants for the company, and the output at the distilleries. That's why I need to know more about the distilleries. But all of that aside, George has put me in an impossible situation.'

Will nodded, sipped his champagne, said nothing as he waited.

Edward murmured, 'I'm embarrassed, if you want to know the truth. That George behaved in the way he did is quite unconscionable. To become abusive with an older man, to behave like an ignorant lout, to make demands on his host, well, quite frankly, it makes my blood boil. He is after all a Deravenel. And we are gentlemen. *Supposedly*.'

'I understand, but George doesn't,' Will informed him. 'George is all about George. He's been thoroughly spoilt, if you don't mind me saying so. By your sister Margaret and also your mother.'

'I know how Meg babied him when they were growing up together, and yes, Mama does tend to come to his aid most of the time, and yes, he has a total misconception about himself.'

'I know you loathe it when you feel the Deravenel name has

been besmirched, and I do understand why you think MacDonald needs to be . . . well, shall we say appeased, catered to a little bit. He has to be brought into the fold, so to speak,' Will said.

'Exactly.'

'And you think I can do that?' Will now asked, settling back in the chair. 'With Richard's help.'

'Without his help, actually, Will, but MacDonald wants a Deravenel present at the meetings.'

'All right then. I shall go and do my damndest to get you the MacDonald Distillery Company, be assured of that. And I shall enjoy Richard's company. We always get on well, and have since he was . . . your Little Fish.'

Edward smiled. 'He's the loyal one, the caring and cautious one, my Little Fish.' He sighed, and gave Will a long, careful look. 'George has a gun in his office drawer.'

'Good God!' Will sat up straighter. 'What for?'

'I don't know. I'm sure he doesn't intend to go around the office, shooting people. Perhaps it's in the office because he doesn't want it in his home.'

'But why does he want a gun at all?'

Edward shrugged, bafflement settling on his face.

'How do you know he has a gun in his office drawer?' Will now thought to ask.

'Because I had Amos break into his office this morning, and he also picked the locks on George's desk drawers.'

'What were you looking for?'

'I honestly don't know. But somewhere at the back of my mind there's a vague remembrance of . . . *something* . . . something to do with . . . plots . . . takeovers. I just can't put my finger on it.'

Will became very still. He stared at Edward and said slowly, quietly, 'I think maybe I can help you there. I remember, long ago, Johnny Watkins talking to me about Louis Charpentier, John Summers and Margot Grant . . . he was muttering on about

. . . plots making strange bedfellows. Somehow we got onto the subject of Henry Turner, Henry Grant's nephew . . . Johnny said there would always be somebody prepared to stake a claim on Deravenels. You were in the room with us, perhaps that's what you remember, albeit only vaguely.'

'I think perhaps you're right, Will. I know that George wants to be me, to run Deravenels, to own Ravenscar, to have all that I have . . . money, power, privilege . . . and he would certainly make a deal with the devil. *Henry Turner*. My mother mentioned him over Christmas, and I suppose the name has stayed in my head. George is treacherous by nature. You know that as well as I do. He's not to be trusted.'

'You've got to do something about him, Edward,' Will now said in a low tone, adding, 'And immediately.'

'But what? That is the question.'

'Send him travelling as Oliveri suggested.'

'Not on your life!' Edward answered. 'I have to keep him right under my nose, where I can see him, hear him at all times. That's the only solution.'

'So, that settles George then. Shall we order lunch?' Will suggested, smiling for the first time that morning. But his smile hid his true feelings. Having George before his eyes did not mean that Edward would be safe from harm. George Deravenel was a born schemer, a troublemaker, greedy and ambitious. As long as he was around at Deravenels, working in the company, Ned was vulnerable. Will knew he had to watch Ned's back. And so must Amos. There was trouble brewing. Will could sense it, almost smell it . . .

TWENTY-THREE

Grace Rose stood at the edge of the grave, staring at the white marble headstone. Engraved in gold at the head of the stone were the words REST IN PEACE & LOVE. Underneath, also engraved in gold letters, was the name: *Tabitha 'Lucy' Lawford*. And below that, a single line which read: *The beloved of Sebastian Lawford. Died 1904.*

There was no doubt in Grace Rose's mind that this was the burial place of her birth mother. She had no recollection of Sebastian Lawford, nor had the name Cedric Crawford rung a bell with her when Amos had mentioned it over the years. But Tabitha was such a unique name, she surely knew this genuinely was her mother's grave.

Then again, when Amos had visited the hospital recently and looked at the records, and later the death certificate, he had seen the notation that Tabitha Lawford had been laid to rest in the Brady Street Cemetery in Whitechapel. This was the area where the hospital was located, and where they had lived. Her memory of those early days was vague; she had been such a little girl, and she barely remembered Tabitha. She was also aware that if she had not been in possession of the photograph of Tabitha, she would not even have been able to see her mother's visual image in her mind's eye.

As she stood there, flanked by Amos Finnister and Edward Deravenel, Grace Rose understood quite clearly that she felt no emotion for the person buried here, because she had no recollection of her. All she was experiencing was a terrible aching sadness for Tabitha, a young woman who had obviously been led by her heart and not her head, which in turn had pushed her into a downward spiral and a life of sickness and despair.

Her mother was Vicky Forth, in her heart and in her mind. It was she who had brought her up for the past thirteen years, who had loved and nurtured her, made her what she was today – educated, cultured, well mannered, and self confident, a young woman with a sense of her own self-worth, and of her rightful place in the world. A young woman of breeding and gentility.

Turning her head, Grace Rose looked up at Edward Deravenel, her real father. She did not blame him for her mother's downfall; he had been but a boy when he had become involved with Tabitha when she was in her twenties.

Ever since discovering she was his daughter, he had shown her love, treated her with kindness, gentleness, and made her understand how much he cared about her and her welfare. And he had acknowledged her to the world, made no secret of their relationship as father and daughter, even to his own family. She was proud to be part of him, and part Deravenel, to have his bloodline, even though she thought of Stephen Forth as her father. After all, Vicky's husband had helped to bring her up, been a true father to her in the best sense of that word.

And then there was Amos Finnister, who stood on the other side of her. What a good soul he had been all those years ago when he had found her living in a decrepit old cart in

Whitechapel, a little ragamuffin of a boy who, to everyone's surprise, turned out to be a girl.

Grace Rose smiled inwardly, imagining everyone's astonishment when her feminine little body and red-gold curls had been revealed. Of course Amos could have left her to her own devices, gone on his way after sharing those delicious meat pies. But he hadn't. He had been a responsible and caring human being, and had taken her to the only place he knew she would be safe: Haddon House. Here she had fallen straight into the loving hands of Vicky and Fenella Fayne.

Amos had cared about her ever since then, remembering every birthday, Christmas and special event all these years, bringing presents, and a lot of love to her. Somehow he had managed to cleverly piece together Tabitha's story and had isolated the places of significance in her last days on this earth. And here *she* was today, because of Amos, looking at her mother's final place of rest.

Suddenly Edward said, 'Are you all right, Grace Rose?'

Looking up at him she murmured, 'Yes, I am, Uncle Ned.' There was a slight pause before she added, 'But I can't really remember her.'

'Well, it *was* long ago, you know, and you were just a little girl of about five when Amos found you.'

'I can see her face in my head, but I know that's because I have the photograph,' Grace Rose admitted.

'I realize that,' Edward answered. 'She was very beautiful, you know, much more beautiful than she looks in the picture. And a sweet person, a loving young woman, very gentle . . .' He let the rest of his sentence go.

Amos said, 'You know where she rests, Grace Rose, and so you must have a sense . . . of resolution, don't you?'

'I do, Amos, I do. I worried what had become of her. I sometimes even thought she was still alive and that one day she would come and claim me.' She shook here head. 'How could I have ever thought that?'

'It was a normal thought,' Amos reassured her. 'And quite logical. You didn't know where she had gone . . .' He lifted his hands helplessly, shrugged. 'So why wouldn't you believe she was still alive somewhere, and one day come to find you.'

'Yes,' was all Grace Rose said, and stepped closer to the headstone, touched the flowers she had brought, which were on the grave. 'It's a good thing Mother insisted I bring a vase for these, isn't it, Amos?'

'It is indeed.'

She reached out, put a gloved hand on his arm. 'Thank you, Amos, thank you for everything . . . for all the good things you've done for me, for as long as I can remember.'

He merely smiled at her, his dark eyes full of love.

'And you too, Uncle Ned, thank you for your love and kindness, and for never denying me or my birthright.'

A lump came into Edward's throat, and he put his arm around the eighteen-year-old. Touched by her words, he murmured in a husky voice, 'You're part of me, Grace, and that I would never deny . . .'

Within minutes Grace Rose and the two men were hurrying out of the Brady Street Cemetery, heading for Edward's Rolls-Royce which was parked nearby. As they approached, Broadbent, Edward's chauffeur, was getting out of the car, opening the door to the backseats.

'We'll return to Mrs Forth's, please, Broadbent,' Edward said, and ushered Grace Rose and Amos into the back of the car, quickly got inside after them.

It was one of those bitterly cold, grey January days with a drizzling rain that seemed to penetrate the bones. Not such a nice day to visit a cemetery, Edward thought, as he settled in the back seat, but then when is it ever *nice*? The weather really didn't have anything to do with it. These occasions were always sad, filled him with melancholy. He knew that this was not only to do with Tabitha, but rather all of the other deaths which had caused him great sorrow . . . his father and his brother Edmund, Uncle Rick and his cousin Thomas, and those other two cousins he had grown up with and loved: Neville and Johnny Watkins. And he still missed Rob Aspen and Christopher Green, who had been so important to him – vital executives at Deravenels who had died so bravely in the War.

Edward pulled himself out of his sorrowful thoughts as Grace Rose announced, 'I shall come back from time to time, to leave flowers, Uncle Ned.'

'Yes, you should do that, whenever you feel the need.' He took hold of her hand, squeezed it, and added, 'My mother constantly reminds me that life is for the living, Grace Rose, and you must remember this too. It is important to occasionally think of those we loved who have died, but we must also live for today, and the future, not look back too much, you know.'

'I understand,' she murmured, and then taking a deep breath, she went on in a more spirited voice, 'I am so happy I'm going to be a bridesmaid at Lady Fenella's marriage, and that you've given your permission for Bess, Mary and Cecily to be bridesmaids as well. Mother told me we're going to wear pale blue taffeta dresses and wreaths of cornflowers on our heads.'

He smiled at her. 'I can't wait to see my bunch of golden-haired beauties walking down the aisle behind Fenella. I shall be so proud of the four of you. And you'll certainly make a pretty picture.'

She laughed, and leaned forward, looked at Amos sitting on the other side of Edward. 'Mother told me that you are coming to the wedding, too, Amos. Won't it be a wonderful day?'

'It will indeed,' Amos responded, glad to see the happy smile on her face after the mournful expression she had worn at the graveside. The terrible worry she had struggled with for years had now been alleviated, obliterated finally. Thankfully, she no longer believed Tabitha James was going to suddenly appear and snatch her away from Vicky and Stephen Forth. He knew that this had become part of the girl's problem, as well as her concern about what had really happened to her mother – Mam, as she had called her – who had just disappeared into thin air.

A silence fell between them for a short while, until Edward looked at Amos and said cryptically, 'The matter we were dealing with yesterday should be completed today after all, if you don't mind popping into the office later, after tea with Mrs Forth. I'd like you to retrieve the item from the bottom drawer and all of the papers from the top middle drawer. I fully intend to go to the office very early tomorrow, Amos, at about seven o'clock. We could have a meeting, just the two of us perhaps, at that time?'

'No problem, sir, and I will pop in tonight, as you suggest,' Amos answered, full of relief that he had been given permission to remove the gun. The thought of a firearm in the office filled him with alarm, especially since it was in the desk of George Deravenel, who was so erratic.

The three of them were silent after this, and when they did speak it was about trivial, unimportant things. The Rolls-Royce pushed its way through the traffic in the East End, as Broadbent drove it steadily towards Piccadilly and on to Kensington where the Stephen Forths lived.

The moment Grace Rose saw Vicky standing waiting for them in the drawing room she flew across the carpet towards her.

Vicky, smiling warmly, opened her arms and held Grace Rose tightly as she came into them, knowing how nervous the girl had been about this visit to the cemetery.

Grace Rose clung to her for a few seconds, and then finally pulled away, looked into Vicky's beloved face, and said, 'I'm all right, Mother, truly I am. I'm glad I went there because I know where Mam is now, and I'll never worry about her again.'

'That makes me happy, Grace Rose, and certainly there are no reasons for you to look back and be troubled. You can forge ahead, think of Oxford and the future.'

'Yes, I can, and I will. I told Uncle Ned that sometimes I will go and take flowers to her grave . . .' She let the rest of her sentence drift off.

Vicky nodded. 'That's a really splendid idea, and I shall come with you, and so will your father. Won't you, Stephen?'

Smiling broadly, Stephen Forth walked over to Grace Rose and Vicky. 'I will indeed. And we would have gone with you today, darling. But you didn't seem to want that.'

Grace Rose turned to him, kissed his cheek. 'I felt I had to be grown up about it, that's all,' she murmured, and laughed, her happiness apparent and contagious.

Stephen laughed with her, then hurried to greet Edward and Amos who were walking into the drawing room together.

As he always did wherever he was, Edward Deravenel strode over to the fireplace and stood with his back to it. 'It's very damp and chilly out there, good to be here in this lovely room of yours, Vicky, and I wouldn't say no to that cup of tea.'

'Then you shall have it at once,' she replied and glided out, returning a moment later. 'It'll be here in three shakes of a lamb's tail,' she reported, grinning at him, then turning to Amos said, 'I'm sure you're looking forward to a cup of tea also, aren't you, Amos?'

'I am indeed, Mrs Vicky. There's nothing worse than English drizzle, it dampens the spirit as well as the topcoat.'

'That it does,' Vicky agreed, laughing, and sat down on the sofa.

Stephen joined Edward in front of the fire, and confided after a moment, 'I saw Churchill the other day, at the club. Looking well, and in good spirits again, thank heavens.'

'Glad to hear it. What's Winston going to do? Did he tell you?' Edward asked, his curiosity apparent.

'He's still going to be a Member of Parliament, I'm certain of that. There'll be an election this year, you know, but Lloyd George is safe, and I'm absolutely certain Winston will win his seat at Dundee once again,' Stephen answered, full of confidence, his voice positive.

'I have to agree with you there.' Edward nodded emphatically, then compressed his mouth. 'Pity he got blamed for Gallipoli. It was not entirely all his fault, in my opinion.'

'That's true, Ned. But look here, he was First Lord of the Admiralty at the time, and he did conceive the naval attack on the Dardanelles.' Stephen stopped, shaking his head, and finished, 'But then what can one expect? You know only too well what politicians are like, and Churchill does have his enemies. But then, don't we all, old chap?'

'All too true, Stephen, but my money has always been on Churchill. I have enormous respect and admiration for him, as do a lot of people I know. We've not heard the last of him, mark my words, and he'll turn out to be a godsend to this country of ours one day, you'll see.' They continued to talk politics, standing near the fire.

Before long, Fuller and the parlour maid came into the drawing room pushing tea trolleys laden with food. They were soon busy serving everyone cups of tea, small finger sandwiches, hot scones with strawberry jam and clotted cream from Devon. And everyone exclaimed on how delicious the food was.

Friends for years, the Forths and Edward chatted about many worldly things, while Amos and Grace Rose sat together on a sofa, sipping tea, and talking about her move to Oxford in the not-too-distant future.

TWENTY-FOUR

'Y ou've certainly recovered rather quickly from your bout
of bronchitis, haven't you? Quite remarkable,' Edward
said in an icy voice, staring across the desk at his brother
George. 'It was my understanding that this ailment lasted for a
month. At the very least.' Edward's eyes raked over the other
man.

'It was a cold,' George mumbled, looking down at his hands,
unable to meet Edward's direct and very fixed scrutiny.

'How fortunate for you,' Edward murmured, and leaned back
in the chair, still studying his brother. After a moment he went
on, 'Tell me about your adventures in Scotland.'

'Not much to tell.'

'Oh, but I beg to differ, George. I think there's a lot to tell.
When you telephoned me on the Friday before Christmas, the
twentieth of December to be precise, you reported that the deal
was well underway, and said also that you did not foresee any
problems.'

'I didn't.'

'They just came along, did they? One by one, is that it?'
Edward's voice, though soft, echoed with sarcasm. When George

made no response, and still avoided his gaze, Edward probed, 'What about the distilleries? You visited them the following day, so I understand from MacDonald. Were you not impressed?'

Hearing this particular word, and not smart enough to pick up on Edward's scathing tone, George exclaimed, 'That's it . . . I *wasn't* impressed. No, no, not at all, and the price was all wrong anyway.'

'*Really*. That's extremely interesting. And tell me, how *was* your Christmas? I know you went to MacDonald's country house in the Lammermuir Hills. Did you and Isabel and the children enjoy yourselves?'

'Oh, it was all right, a bit dull actually.'

'I see. Is that why you left earlier than expected? On Boxing Day?'

'No, no, we left on Boxing Day because Nan was ill. Isabel wanted to get back to Yorkshire, to see her mother, to make sure she was all right.'

'But Nan has tons of servants, and her cousin's husband is a doctor in Ripon. Surely there were plenty of people to keep an eye on her, look after her.'

George shook his head, swiftly averted his face.

'Hubris!' Edward cried, banging his hand down so hard on the top of his desk that the crystal inkpots rattled on the silver tray and George flinched, suddenly aware of his brother's roaring anger. Fear punched him in the stomach. He swallowed and tried to speak, but discovered he had completely lost his voice.

'Look at me when I'm speaking to you, damn you!' Edward shouted, suddenly jumping up, his face cold, his fury spiralling. 'It's quite plain to see that you've not had bronchitis, but indeed you *are* ill. You're suffering from *hubris*. In fact, you've got a bad case of it.'

Baffled, and still at a loss for words, George gaped at his brother, wondering what he meant, and growing increasingly nervous.

A grim smile played around Edward's mouth, and leaning forward over the desk, he snapped, 'Obviously you don't know what hubris means. It's from the Greek, and it denotes overweening pride, enormous presumption. It also means flying in the face of the gods, tempting the gods with arrogance.'

'I still don't know –'

'Shut up! And listen for once in your life! I sent you to Scotland to negotiate with Ian MacDonald. But you didn't do that. Instead, you destroyed the deal. So it's flown out of the window. Furthermore, we have now acquired an enemy. As if we don't have enough already. You got sloppy drunk, behaved like a dolt, a lout, and insulted a man old enough to be your father. Then you demanded a car and driver from your host, packed up your family and went back to Edinburgh. Where you lingered for several days.'

'No, I did not! I went to Yorkshire. And straight away,' George shot back.

'You're a liar, George, as well as an idiot. Nan told me exactly when you arrived at Thorpe Manor, and, I might add, she was also somewhat startled to hear she had been ill. She told me she was in blooming health, actually.'

'She's recovered,' George answered lamely, running his hand through his blond hair. 'I think she had a touch of food poisoning.'

I'd like to poison *you*, Edward thought, but said, 'Pull the other leg, little brother, it has bells on! What's the matter with you, do you think I'm a dunce? I checked everything out, so don't even attempt to deny one single thing.'

'You spied on me!' George shouted, forgetting himself, once again prepared to stand up to his brother, the brother he envied.

'Keep your voice down,' Edward snarled, and lowered himself into his chair. He opened his desk drawer, took out some papers, and announced in a voice dripping ice, 'I've paid your gambling debts. You owe me forty thousand pounds. I want it immediately.'

Stunned, taken unawares as he was, George sat up straighter in the chair, and gazed at his brother. He flushed bright red, and sudden fear rushed through him. He was totally undone, thought he was going to be violently sick.

Ignoring his brother's silence, knowing full well he was flabbergasted, shaken, Edward waved the promissory notes in the air, and continued, 'These are the notes you signed. I've redeemed them. Once I have your cheque, and when it has cleared the bank, you may have them. I think you should know that I have informed the three clubs in question that I will not pay your gambling debts ever again. I wrote to them, explaining that I cannot be responsible. I do believe they have automatically cancelled your membership, because of bad debts. You've been blackballed. So, little brother, what do you have to say for yourself?'

'I wish to know why you are meddling in my affairs,' George cried excitedly, endeavouring to recoup once more, full of bluster all of a sudden.

'I wasn't meddling, just protecting *our* name to some extent. There was so much gossip about you and your debts, your whoring, your drinking and drug-taking I had to do something. However, I do believe *you* should do *something* about these.' Reaching into his desk drawer yet again, Edward removed a pile of bills. 'I think you had better settle these, pay what you owe these merchants and your Savile Row tailor. I won't tolerate any more scandalous gossip about you.'

'How did you get my bills?' George yelled, jumping up, his own fury bursting out of him. 'How did you get into my desk? It's locked.'

'I broke into it. And whilst we are talking about your desk, why do you keep this in it?' Edward dangled the gun on one finger.

Aghast, George sat down heavily in the chair. For a moment he was befuddled, and he shook his head as if he didn't understand what was happening, and then he looked at his brother.

In that moment he felt the blood drain out of him. He was sunk.

Ned's eyes were blue ice, and his expression was one of genuine rage. 'It's for . . . for . . . my p-p-protection,' George stammered, gulping, pushing back incipient tears, knowing he was totally at his brother's mercy. He also knew he didn't have a leg to stand on, and yet he nevertheless imagined he could somehow bluff his way out of this unexpected trouble.

Taking a large brown envelope off the desk, Edward dropped the gun into it, and went on in a cold voice, 'This is going to be put in a safe, where it will remain forever. As I said, please pay your household bills immediately and attend to your tailor. Furthermore, I expect to have a cheque on my desk tomorrow, for the forty thousand you owe me.'

George nodded. He was white as bleached bone, and trembling inside. He hated Ned, truly detested him. He must find a way to ruin him, so that he could take over and run Deravenels, as he was supposed to do. And he knew he would run it far better than his odious brother.

'You don't seem to have much to say for yourself.' Edward frowned, appeared puzzled. 'Aren't you ashamed, George, or sorry for this latest trouble you have caused, and the havoc you have wreaked in Scotland? Good God, man, you're almost twenty-six, married, a father, and you are also a Deravenel. You must show some responsibility, and a little pride as well, I might add.'

'How dare you lecture me!' George ranted. 'Who do you think you are? You're not God!'

'No, I'm not. But I do know exactly who I am. My name is Edward Deravenel. I am head of the Deravenel family, Head of Deravenels, and I am your older brother. I am also the man you work for. In other words, I am your boss. And let me tell you this, if you weren't my brother I would dismiss you at once.'

'You can't sack me. I'm a director of this company, and a Deravenel.'

'Oh, but you're wrong. I *can* give you the sack. I can do almost anything I want within certain boundaries, as managing director. I am not going to send you packing, George, for the very reason you are my brother. And a married man, the father of children. So, I am going to be lenient. I will overlook your behaviour towards Ian MacDonald, and hopefully I will be able to get the deal back on track. But I will not overlook the money you owe me. I want that cheque tomorrow.'

'I don't know where to get forty thousand pounds,' George wailed, his blue-green eyes sparkling with tears again.

'Obviously, you will have to go to your wife. Isabel is the other Watkins heiress, and her mother is an enormously wealthy woman. Surely the two of them will give you a loan?' A red-gold brow shot up. 'What do you think, Georgie? Will the ladies help you out?'

'I don't know,' George answered, his voice shaking. He rose, started to leave the office.

'Don't be in such a hurry, little brother. You'd better take these bills with you. Perhaps your mother-in-law will settle them for you. And as quickly as possible.'

George stepped over to the desk, grabbed the bills, and threw Edward an angry look. A second later the door banged behind him. What a strange thing it is, Edward thought, his eyes still on the door, that such a wonderful looking young man, with the most beautiful face, those blue-green eyes, almost turquoise, and marvellous head of blond hair, can be so rotten and mean-spirited. And he is rather stupid, not at all like Richard. Those two were only a few years apart, and had grown up together, mostly at Ravenscar. They had often defended each other, and he knew that deep down they cared for each other. And yet George had always tried to lord it over Richard, and *he* had felt the need to protect his Little Fish. Greed, ambition, envy, and arrogance, those were George's true characteristics. *Hubris.* Just the word to describe him. Whereas Richard was loyal almost

194

to a fault, very stubborn, courageous, and of a serious bent. Thank God for my Richard, Edward thought: he will be loyal to me forever. I have no worries about him. He's True Blue.

Rising, Edward walked across the room, knocked on the door to the adjoining office, where he knew Will would undoubtedly be at his desk.

'Good morning, Ned, come in, come in,' Will exclaimed, smiling. 'I heard raised voices. You were giving George a dressing down, weren't you?'

'I was. He's so dense, really rather stupid. I was talking to him about the Scottish deal, I don't think he got it at all. Although he did look a bit afraid at one moment, he suddenly came back at me, full of piss and vinegar. And he actually shouted back.'

Will laughed. 'You don't have to tell me that – I heard him. You know very well I've always thought he was three bricks short of a full load.'

Ned began to laugh with Will. '*Only three?*' He sat down in the chair opposite, and began, 'Let me pose a question. Do you think the board will permit me to change one of the rules?'

'I don't really know, to be honest. It depends what the rule is,' Will replied.

'Women can work here as secretaries, receptionists, and telephonists. But only a woman who is a born Deravenel can hold an executive position, and also be a director of the company. However, she cannot be a board member. Only men can sit on the board. Also, even a Deravenel woman cannot be head of the company –'

'And that's the rule you want to change?' Will cut in, biting his lip, suddenly appearing worried. 'My God, it's a bit radical, isn't it? And anyway, why do you want to change this rule?'

'Because I know, and you know, that women are as competent and responsible as men, and just as clever. We all have the same brain power, and to be frank, I sometimes think some women have more brains than men. In fact, I know quite a few formidable women. But look here, Will, I have four daughters, if we include Grace Rose. I want to be absolutely certain that any of them can be on the board, and be managing director or chairman, rule the roost in other words, if that is ever necessary. I have two sons, but what if I didn't have Young Edward and Ritchie, and I died? What then? Who would inherit?'

'I don't have to think twice about that. *George would.*'

'Correct, and it should be my brother Richard, really. But never mind this for the moment, let's stay on one subject. I have studied the rules, which my mother got out of her vault for me, and I think it comes down to this – if a dozen board members out of the seventeen members vote in favour of the change, then the new rule, whatever it is, can indeed be added.'

'Are you sure? Really sure, Ned?'

'I am. And Mama is an expert on these rules. She studied them for years, because of my father's problems at Deravenels. She agrees with me. But will the board members go along?'

'I feel certain they will. I can think of six right off the bat . . . Oliveri, Anthony Wyland, Frank Lane, Matthew Reynolds. They are certainties, and my vote makes five. You yourself can vote, so that is six. And there are six others I can guarantee, they'll do as you want. Maybe everyone will, actually. After all, you're the goose that lays the golden eggs.'

'Thanks for that,' Edward laughed. Stretching out his long legs, he steepled his fingers and brought the tips to his mouth, looking reflective for a moment, then lifting his head finally he focused on Will Hasling.

'What is it?' Will asked. 'You look as if you're about to ask me something quite momentous.'

'Not really. But it's certainly important. What do we know about this chap Henry Turner, who lives in France?'

'Not a lot. He's a sort of pretender to the throne of Deravenels, I suppose, on the Lancastrian side that is. You know very well his half-uncle was Henry Grant. His mother is Margaret Beauchard, and she was married to Henry's half-brother Edmund Turner . . . I think that's correct.'

'You're absolutely right. But is that *all* we know, though?'

Will nodded. 'I'm afraid it is.'

'I wish I could send Finnister to France, but no one can travel just yet . . .'

'I'll do a bit of digging, and as soon as we are able we'll send Amos to gay Paree.'

Once more, Edward laughed. 'You always manage to bring a smile, cheer me up.' Ned stood. 'I'd better go along to see Oliveri. Let's have lunch, the three of us. All right?'

'I'll book a table at Rules. Shall I invite Richard? We can go over our travel plans, and the Scottish deal.'

'Good thought.'

TWENTY-FIVE

Alfredo Oliveri was the first to arrive at Rules, and as he was shown to their usual table and sat down, he focused his mind on George Deravenel.

That he was a problem was known; that he now appeared to be dangerous was a new element that had to be put into the equation. Alfredo had been as alarmed as Amos and Edward when he had heard about the gun, a somewhat bizarre accessory to take to the office under any circumstances. It smacked of violence to him.

Leaning back against the banquette, he pondered the current situation, wondering what they should do with George within the company. Having once thought it would be a good idea to send him travelling, to get him out of Edward's hair, he now realized he would only make a mess of Deravenel business abroad. It would be foolhardy not to have him in their sights at all times.

His mind began to work as he contemplated a variety of solutions. Oliveri, now in his early fifties, had been at Deravenels for over thirty-four years. When Edward had taken over the company fourteen years ago, Alfredo had already been working there for twenty years, having begun as an apprentice. At that time, he was considered part of the old guard. He was certainly that now, one of the old-timers who had become part of the very modern present.

Having started out in the mining division, now he was head of that division on a worldwide basis. All of their mines around the globe came under his aegis . . . diamond mines in India, diamond and gold mines in South Africa, and other mines in South America and Asia that produced emeralds, sapphires and rubies; their opal mines in Australia were a new and successful acquisition.

He and Edward Deravenel had first met in Carrara, when Edward and Neville Watkins had come to investigate the murder of their fathers and brothers. Will Hasling had been with them. At that time, Oliveri was overseeing the Deravenel marble quarries in Italy, and he had quickly made it known to the three men that he had much more of an affinity with the Yorkshire Deravenels than with the Lancashire Deravenel Grants. Edward's father had been good to him over the years, and seen that he got the proper promotions when they were due him.

Alfredo had helped them as much as he could in Carrara, and had then come to London almost immediately, ostensibly to check in with the head office and his boss, Aubrey Masters. But he had really come to see them, and he had soon become their spy inside the company.

Apart from being one of the greatest experts on mines and mined stones, he was a tireless worker, and a pleasant, amiable man with a talent for getting the best out of people. Everyone liked him; as an executive he was revered.

Most people thought of him as more English than Italian. Certainly his looks were English. Pale of complexion, his face was scattered with freckles and when he had been a young man he had the brightest of red hair, which had earned him the nicknames of 'Carrot Top' and 'Red'. Now his hair was a sandy colour, a sort of salt-and-pepper grey with a hint of faded auburn underneath. He was a nice looking man, always well dressed, although not as elegant or as fashionable as Edward and Will.

Alfredo was happily married to an Englishwoman, had two sons aged twenty-two and nineteen, and he loved his family wholeheartedly. His mistress, a very demanding one, was Deravenels. The Mining Division and its continuing success throughout the world consumed him.

Edward was wont to say that Oliveri had given his entire life and most of his love to the company, and whilst this was true to a certain extent, Oliveri knew full well that Edward Deravenel had done exactly the same thing. He was certain his employer could not have made the company so enormous, bigger than ever, and such a great institution if he had not. And this was a bond that forever bound them together.

'A penny for your thoughts, Oliveri,' Edward said, staring at one of his favourite executives, a man he now considered a true friend as well as a loyal and devoted colleague of long standing.

Oliveri stared up at him, and answered softly, 'Pondering George.'

'That's not surprising.' Edward sat down next to Oliveri on the banquette. 'I'm holding my breath, waiting to see if he brings me a cheque tomorrow.'

'He will. He'll more than likely go to Nan Watkins to ask her for the money,' Oliveri volunteered, and then looked towards the door as Richard walked in, looking agitated, very nervous. The younger man was still wearing his overcoat, and his face was pinched, worried.

Edward followed the direction of Oliveri's gaze and jumped up swiftly as Richard hurried forward. Edward knew him so well, knew at once something was amiss. Richard's face was white as chalk, his slate-grey eyes filled with alarm.

'Good Lord, Dick, what is it?'

'I just ran into George. He . . . accosted me, and that's the only word for it. And in the lobby of our building. He was shouting at me like a maniac saying that he would kill you one day. And then he screamed, "Tell him I'll find the money somewhere, and do whatever I have to do to get it." Then he ran out into the street. I watched him rush heedlessly across the Strand. He almost got knocked down by a motor car. I couldn't believe his behaviour.'

Edward shook his head, a sad and knowing look clouding his blue eyes. 'He gets more incomprehensible by the day. There's something wrong with him. And if Nan won't help him, he'll get the money he owes me from Mother. He'll go with a sad story and ask to borrow from her, and she'll give it to him; she's always protected him since he was a child. Now, Dick, calm down, catch your breath, you're very upset. And do go and take your coat off.'

'I'm all right, honestly, Ned, I'll be fine in a moment. And I won't take my coat off, since I can't have lunch, actually. As I told Will earlier, I have a bad tooth. I must go to the dentist, I'm in terrible pain. I made an appointment early this morning, and I can't miss it. So sorry about lunch.'

'That's all right, just take care of yourself and get that tooth attended to right away.' Edward went back to the banquette.

Richard offered Oliveri a faint smile. 'Sorry for bursting in like that, didn't mean to upset.'

'It's fine, no problem,' Alfredo answered, and announced to no one in particular, 'Ah, here's Hasling.'

Richard took his leave after greeting Will and hurried out, and Will sat down, murmured in a low voice, 'Well, I suppose you already know about the scene in the lobby. Apparently a rather loud scene at that.'

Edward sighed deeply, thinking of George, who worried him no end. 'Richard just came to tell us. I do think George is daft in the head . . . at least some of the time.'

'Most of the time, if you ask me,' Will raised his hand, beckoned the waiter. 'Let's have a glass of claret, shall we, chaps? It's a cold day, and I for one need a drink.'

The other two men agreed with him, and Will glanced at the wine list, ordered, and then sat back and regarded Edward and Alfredo. Both were sitting opposite him on the banquette. Will's face was serious, and when he spoke his voice was somber, somehow seemed to hold a warning.

'You are part of a dangerous triangle,' Will said, directing his gaze at Edward. 'Extremely dangerous indeed, and I'm not talking about women and your private life, Ned. I'm referring to your brothers and yourself.'

Taken aback by this unexpected comment, Edward simply stared at Will. After a moment, he said, 'Continue, please.'

Lifting a finger, Will drew the shape of a triangle in the air. 'You, Ned, are at the top of the triangle, at the very tip. Your two brothers are at each side, at the bottom. Let's consider George first. He is envious, petulant, ambitious and treacherous by nature. *You* know that, we all do. He envies you, wants to *be* you, and he would stab you in the back to get what he wants. You know how easily Neville Watkins led him into *his* intrigues and acts of treachery against you. Let's put you to one side, for the moment, and consider Richard. He and George were close when they were children, but Richard is your *favourite*, and therefore George is angry with you, and with Richard. And he envies him. He is also hostile towards him because Richard did, finally, marry Anne Watkins, the other Watkins co-heiress, along with George's wife Isabel. George truly does begrudge Anne's share of Neville Watkins's fortune, and that's the real reason he endeavoured to stop Richard's marriage to her but you surely do know all this. Finally, Richard, for his part, is utterly devoted to you, loyal to you beyond reason, and he's a hard worker, intelligent, clever, even formidable in certain ways, and all of these attributes anger George, too.'

'In other words, I can't win . . . George is dead set against me for many reasons, not the least of which is for . . . just being me?'

'In that you are correct,' Will agreed. 'Good, here is the waiter with our glasses of claret.'

After toasting each other, it was Oliveri who looked at Edward and said quietly, 'He's tried your patience for years, and some-times he goes too far. Mistakenly, I recently said we should send him travelling, but that is not a good idea. We need him where we can keep an eye on him.'

'I agree,' Will exclaimed. 'No more trips for Master George.'

'That's right.' Edward took a long swallow of the red wine, and went on, 'I've little or no confidence in him now, not after his behaviour in Scotland. Thank God Ian MacDonald really wants to make this deal. If he didn't, we'd be out, that's a certainty.' He gave his closest friend a long stare and asked, 'So tell me, Will, what do I do? Should I say aloud those famous lines? 'Who will rid me of this turbulent priest?' Is that it?'

Oliveri chuckled. 'Better not.'

Will shook his head. 'There is nothing you can do about George, Ned, honestly there isn't. But I do suggest you watch your back, and I'll watch it also and so will Oliveri and Amos.'

Edward smiled.

Will said a trifle vehemently, 'No, don't smile. Please don't, Ned. I am very, very serious. George is a born intriguer and exceedingly treacherous. I've never trusted him. There's many a murder that gets passed off as an accident, always remember that. Now, shall we order lunch?'

'Do you honestly think George would commit fratricide?' Edward asked, frowning, looking momentarily concerned, his eyes troubled. 'Surely not, Will. I am, after all, his brother.'

'That's true,' Will responded noncommittally. 'I think I shall have the grilled plaice. What about the two of you?'

'The same,' Edward said.

'I might as well have the fish too.' Oliveri sat back, sipped his wine, and wondered how to murder George without getting caught.

Julian Stark, owner of Starks, the gambling club, looked startled when his secretary put her head around the door and said, 'Mr George Deravenel is here, Mr Stark. He says he doesn't have an appointment, but will you see him for a minute, or two?'

'Send him in, Gladys,' Stark answered at once, wondering what this was all about.

A moment or two later he found out. After greeting George Deravenel in a neutral voice, he asked, 'And what can I do for you?'

'Nothing, nothing at all, Stark. But I might be able to do you a favour.'

'Oh, really. What kind of favour?' Stark asked.

'I'll get straight to the point. I have a good tip, a good business tip. Not for you, actually, but for your brother, Alexander. I know he's a financier in the City, that he has some big clients. I'd like to pass on some information about a deal that's not yet actually on the market yet, so to speak. But it will be and very quickly.'

Puzzled, yet intrigued, Stark nodded. 'What is the deal, Deravenel?'

'The MacDonald Distillery Company is up for grabs.' Reaching into his jacket pocket, George took out an envelope and handed it to Julian Stark, leaning across the latter's desk to do so. 'Everything is here – all the details.'

Staring at the envelope, Stark put it down on the desk and asked, 'Why are you bringing this to me? After all, I banned you from my gambling club.'

'Old school tie and all that . . . and you were always decent to me when I was a member, held my notes for the longest time.'

Leaning back in the chair, Julian Stark, a shrewd judge of character, instantly understood what this was all about. But he decided to play George along for the moment. 'And what do you want in return for this so-called important information?'

'Nothing, nothing at all,' George answered, and stood up. 'The information came into my hands, and I thought I would pass it on to you. Do what you like with it.' George walked across to the door, and turned around, his hand on the knob. 'Thanks for seeing me at such short notice.'

He left the office without another word.

Julian Stark stared at the door, shaking his head. What a treacherous bastard George Deravenel was. He was convinced this was a deal George's brother Edward was working on, and now the disgruntled little brother was trying to scuttle it for some reason. Sighing, Stark opened the envelope, read the two sheets of paper, and then reached for the phone; he found the number he wanted in his address book, dialled it, and asked, 'Is that you, Howard?'

'Yes, it is, Julian. How can I help you?' his old friend asked.

Stark told him about his encounter with George Deravenel, and added, 'Do what you want with this information, but personally, in all good conscience, I think you ought to inform Will. Edward Deravenel should know about his brother's treachery. I consider him to be a blackguard.'

'It's done,' Howard Hasling answered, and hung up.

TWENTY-SIX

Jane Shaw stood at the French windows of the blue room in her house, looking out at the garden. It was vivid with spring flowers on this sunny March afternoon . . . purple, yellow and white crocuses, narcissi, pale and delicate, and a parade of bright yellow daffodils, rows of them, glorious, she thought. 'Dancing and fluttering in the breeze,' she said aloud as she turned away, smiling to herself. She had always loved that famous Wordsworth poem which had suddenly jumped into her mind.

Crossing the room, she went to the fire, lifted the poker and stirred the logs, then bent down, threw on several more. Although the bad winter weather had suddenly disappeared and spring was here, it was still quite cold outside today despite the sun, and there was a wind.

Glancing at the carriage clock on the mantelpiece, she saw that it was almost three forty-five, later than she thought. Leaving the blue-and-yellow room, she crossed the hall and went looking for the housekeeper, and found Mrs Longden in the butler's pantry going over some lists.

'I hadn't realized how late it was, Mrs Longden,' she said,

with a smile. 'Mrs Forth and Mr Deravenel will be here shortly. I'm assuming everything is prepared.'

'Oh yes, Madam, it is, of course. And do you wish Wells to serve tea immediately? Or should we wait a short while?'

'We can wait for a few minutes, I think, let everyone settle –' Jane broke off as the doorbell pealed, and Mrs Longden exclaimed, 'I think we have an early arrival, Madam, I'd better go and answer the door.' As she spoke she hurried off, and Jane followed more slowly, knowing that it was more than likely Vicky who was arriving, not Edward. He had told her on the phone earlier that he might be late this afternoon and not to wait for him to have their afternoon tea, and he would get there as soon as he could.

As the door opened Vicky Forth stepped inside, looking beautiful, the personification of elegance, as she usually did, smart in her dark purple wool coat trimmed with astrakhan and a purple felt cloche hat with a satin band trimmed with a small bunch of artificial violets at one side.

Jane glided across the floor and the two women greeted each other, embraced, and Vicky said, 'The weather's frightfully treacherous today, my dear. Quite cold, and the wind is biting.'

'I could tell how windy it is outside from the trees blowing in the garden,' Jane answered, as Vicky slipped out of her coat and gave it to the housekeeper to hang up. 'But at least the snow has gone.'

The two women walked into the blue room, and Vicky murmured, 'I came early, so we can have a few more minutes together. To discuss *that* party. The famously fantastic party we're planning.'

Jane nodded, looked suddenly gloomy, as she led her friend over to the fireplace. 'I think the whole thing might be rather a problem, to be honest. Sit here, darling, near the fire, it's lovely and warm.'

'I know what you're going to say, Jane, it will be a problem because Elizabeth will more than likely find out.'

'There's no question in my mind about that. She will, because there's so much awful gossip in this town. And she'll make a fuss.' Jane sat down opposite her friend, and continued, 'You went to see Fenella today, didn't you? How is she?'

'She's been very ill, but she's much better, and yes, I popped in this morning. She sends you her love. She's happy to be out of the hospital and back at home at the Curzon Street house, it's much more comfortable, obviously. She's going to be fine. Double pneumonia is perfectly dreadful, but she has the best doctors, and she's a very strong woman basically.'

'I know . . .' Jane left her sentence unfinished, and sighed. 'I suppose she knew about the things Elizabeth was saying about her before she became ill and went into hospital.'

'Yes, she did, but you know what Fenella is like – she rises above that sort of nonsense, and just gets on with it, does her job, leads her life without paying too much attention to the rest of the world. By that, I mean people she isn't close to, and quite rightly so.'

'I understand, and yes she is rather clever to do that.' Sitting back against the cushions, Jane added, 'All right . . . so, what to do about the birthday celebration for Ned?'

'I'd really love to have a party for him,' Vicky exclaimed enthusiastically. 'He's going to be thirty-four, such a lovely age for a man – well, for anyone, actually – and you know he so enjoys being spoiled by his friends. What day of the week is the twenty-eighth of April, Jane? I'm afraid I forgot.'

'It's a Monday, and I've always thought that it would be difficult for him to attend our party on that date, because of his family, particularly the children, who do so adore him. If we do go ahead and give it, then it will have to be on another evening. Either before or after the twenty-eighth.'

'Knowing Ned, he won't care if the party is before or after

his birthday,' Vicky murmured, thinking out loud. 'So for the moment the date doesn't matter. The thing is what kind of party are we going to give? Where shall we have it? And who are we going to invite?'

'Let's think about the guests first, Vicky,' Jane responded, trying to shake off her gloomy mood. She pushed on, said, 'We'll all be there, obviously. *His lot*, as he calls us, but who else? What other friends do we invite?'

Vicky pursed her lips. 'You know that better than I do, surely, my dear.'

'There are a few people he likes, whom we see sometimes but, to be honest, I'm not sure he would want to have the kind of large and fancy party we were originally planning. Nor would he want to have it in a public place, like the ballroom of the Ritz or the Savoy –' Jane stopped, shook her head. 'I think I have it. Ned loves *his lot*. *Us*. You and Stephen, Will and Kathleen, Amos, Grace Rose. What he would appreciate the most would be a small dinner at your house, or we can have it here. What do you think, Vicky?'

'I believe you're right. Also, it's safer in the long run . . . why give *her* titbits to gossip about. She's done enough damage –'

'But you said Fenella didn't care –' Jane cried, cutting in peremptorily, 'and only a moment ago, I might add.'

'She doesn't. However, I think Elizabeth's tittle-tattle, silly as it is, just besmirches Edward's name yet again. Why can't she keep her mouth shut about him, he's her husband –' Vicky stopped abruptly, staring at Jane, looking apologetic.

'I'm so sorry, darling, I didn't mean to blurt that out.'

Jane laughed. 'I know you didn't mean any harm, and let's face it, he *is* her husband.'

'Don't you ever get jealous, Jane?' Vicky asked, suddenly curious, gazing across at her best friend. 'You certainly never show it. You're the perfect lady.'

'There are moments when I do have a stab of it, naturally,

but I know exactly what he genuinely feels for me. I'm aware I give *him* comfort, warmth, much love, and support, and he needs that from me. He doesn't get that at home. And besides, I prefer things to remain the way they are.'

'But why?' Vicky couldn't help asking, her eyes wide, questioning.

Leaning forward, pinning her eyes on Vicky, Jane explained, 'If I wanted to, I could probably entice him into my arms permanently, induce him to leave her, even get a divorce. But he's a family man at heart, loves his children, enjoys being with them, and inevitably he would begin to miss them, and he'd start to feel remorseful, guilty and that would upset me. Because he'd want to be running to see them, and there would be havoc, chaos everywhere, tears and recriminations, and quarrels. It would be far too complex to handle. This way, being his mistress, he comes to me willingly, needing me, desiring me, and he knows very well he can have *me* and his children. In a sense he does have the best of both worlds, and that's all right with me. And before you say it, I know he sleeps with her, because the children keep arriving. He's that kind of man, you know. He'd always have women whomever he was married to . . . anyway I do know he is faithful to me.'

Vicky smiled. 'You remind me so much of Lily Overton, Jane. You are very much like her in many ways. Oh, let's change the subject, here's your butler with the tea.'

Vicky sat quietly on the sofa, listening to Jane and Edward chatting about a painting; they then moved on to more mundane subjects, spoke about his busy day at the office, her day, what they had each done. And planned to do later in the week.

She smiled to herself. They sounded like an old married couple, rather than mistress and lover. Their conversation echoed the kind of chit-chat she had with Stephen every night, when he came home from the bank.

It suddenly occurred to her that they were exactly *that* . . . except for a piece of paper declaring the legality of their union. Ned's peace, contentment and relaxation took place here in Jane's house, where he lived a rather domesticated life with her. It certainly did not take place in Berkeley Square with Elizabeth.

She shuddered at the thought of his wife, a vile woman, a shallow woman, concerned only with her looks, her clothes, her jewellery and the vast amount of money required to buy her expensive baubles and fripperies. She wasn't a particularly good mother, had neglected Bess and the other girls since they were born, was quite obviously only interested in the two boys, most especially Young Edward: because he was the heir to Deravenels and all that belonged to Ned.

Vicky dreaded to think what would happen when she told him the things Elizabeth had been saying about Fenella. Jane and she had agreed, before Ned had arrived, that she would be the one to tell him, since she had heard most of the gossip.

Dropping her eyes, Vicky stared at his shoes, polished to a gleaming finish. They looked like glass. Handmade. No doubt he had his own last at Lobb's, the renowned shoemaker. Her eyes took in the navy-blue suit. Impeccable cut. Savile Rowe perfect. The latest style. Shirt a crisp white Egyptian cotton. From Turnbull and Asser, more than likely. A bright blue silk cravat, tied in a fashionable knot, and the colour of his eyes.

A perfect specimen of elegant and handsome masculinity, she thought, and remembered how impressed she had been all those years ago, when her brother Will had introduced her to Ned. It wasn't his gorgeous looks that had captivated her so much as his charm, good-natured affability, and, more than anything else, his absolute self-assurance. It was a self-assurance that was truly *his*, he had been born with it, had not acquired it like so many other people did. It was the self-assurance some mistook for arrogance. But he wasn't an arrogant man, far from it.

Will had told her over the years that Edward had run Deravenels with a very sure hand from the beginning, even though he was only nineteen and not experienced in business. He had charmed those executives in the company who were inclined towards the Yorkshire Deravenels, and cleverly enlisted their help to learn about the business. They had followed Oliveri's example, and taught him as much as they knew about their divisions. By the time he was twenty-one he knew everything there was to know about the company started by his ancestor, Guy de Ravenel, hundreds of years before. The executives who had clustered around him had force-fed him information like a goose being force-fed for *foie gras*.

'He remembered everything,' Will had explained to her. 'And still does. He's got a photographic memory, and a relentless capacity for work. And he taught me everything I know, and that's why I'm a successful executive at Deravenels today.'

Vicky sat back, her mind still on Edward. He might have been considered a playboy in the past, and a womanizer, but he was neither today. He had been with Jane Shaw for over ten years, and had never strayed, to her knowledge. For the most part, the gossip about him had to do with his faithfulness to her, not his sexual adventures with other women. The only other woman in his life was his wife. Vicky pondered this for a moment. He apparently still found her physically enticing, because he kept making her pregnant. That was *it*, though, there was nothing else between them. Vicky was aware of this. The relationship he had with Elizabeth out of bed was frighteningly barren. They had nothing in common.

'You're very quiet, Vicky,' Edward said unexpectedly, glancing at her. 'I hope you're not worrying about funds for the recreation centre, now that Fenella and you have decided to go ahead with it. I have a cheque for you for ten thousand pounds, and I'll give it to you before you leave.'

Momentarily startled, Vicky stared at him, then exclaimed, 'Oh Ned, how generous you are! Thank you so much. Fenella has put up the same amount, and so have I. Stephen and Will promised to match you to the penny, and Fenella's Aunt Philomena has already given us twenty thousand, so we have seventy thousand pounds to start us off.'

'I'm delighted. Congratulations. It's such a good cause, a centre for wounded soldiers. I promise you I'll get a few more donors for you, and I'll give you more myself later.'

'Thank you. I'm so grateful, and Fenella will be, too.'

'How is she doing? I went to see her last week. She said she wasn't sure she was going to have the marriage in June, because of her bout of pneumonia. But frankly I thought she looked so much better. Anyway, she was talking about a July wedding instead,' Edward finished.

'She has decided to stay with June,' Vicky informed him. 'But it will be later in the month rather than the beginning.'

'I'm glad to hear it, since I was planning a trip abroad in July, providing we can travel to the continent by then.'

Jane glanced at Vicky, then at Edward, and said, 'Darling, Vicky wants to speak to you – about a rather sensitive matter. If you've finished your tea, I'll ring for Wells and have everything removed.'

'Yes, do that. I've finished.' He frowned, turned to Vicky. 'Something sensitive?' He sounded puzzled.

She merely nodded.

Jane rang the bell and within seconds the butler and the housekeeper appeared, and gathered up the tea things.

Once they were alone, Jane went to sit in the chair next to Edward. 'Vicky was somewhat reluctant to tell you, confide in you, but I persuaded her.'

He nodded. 'Please tell me what this is about?' He had a

peculiar feeling it had something to do with him. He trusted Vicky; she had shown her worth and her friendship to him many times in the past. Whatever was now on her mind had to be important.

Vicky cleared her throat, and said in a low, steady voice, 'It has to do with Elizabeth. I was reluctant to speak to you at first, Ned, because I do loathe getting in the middle of a relationship between two people. Especially a marriage. However, after a lot of reflection, and listening to Jane's advice, I decided it was better that you knew.'

'Please tell me, Vicky. I would appreciate it. And I know you well enough to understand that you're not a meddler.'

'Thank you. It's like this, Ned . . . Apparently Elizabeth said something about Fenella to one of her sisters, who repeated it to Maude Tillotson, and Maude told a friend, who told a friend, and the story spread like wildfire. You know perfectly well what London society is like. Some of these women have nothing better to do than gossip about others.'

Dismay settled in the pit of his stomach and he looked at Vicky keenly. 'I assume the gossip about Fenella has something to do with me?'

'Yes. Elizabeth told her sister that the entire story about Grace Rose being found in a cart in Whitechapel by Amos Finnister was a pack of lies, a fabrication. That in fact Grace Rose was Fenella's illegitimate daughter by you, and that the child had been brought up on Fenella's father's estate in Yorkshire. She added Fenella had been your mistress for years. That she still is, and that the only reason she was marrying Mark Ledbetter was to throw her, that is Elizabeth, off the scent. In other words, Fenella is your mistress as well as Jane.'

Edward was stunned. He sat back, staring at Vicky in total astonishment. 'How preposterous!' he finally exclaimed, as a rush of anger flooded him. 'What on earth can she be thinking of, inventing a story like this? Who on earth would ever believe it, anyway? It's so far-fetched, it's not plausible.' Although he kept tight control of himself, he was shaking inside. And he was enraged.

Vicky said, 'I doubt that anyone believes it, Ned darling. Nevertheless, it's not very nice story to be out there, and in a way it adds another hint of scandal to the name Deravenel. Not to mention to Fenella's name. A woman so blameless and so philanthropic she's thought of as a . . . saint.'

'Elizabeth has to be insane!' he exploded, no longer able to harness his anger.

Jane reached out, put a calming hand on his arm. 'No one believes it, I'm certain, Ned. However, I encouraged Vicky to tell you. Because you *must* know these things, so you can deal with them. And you have to speak to Elizabeth.'

'I certainly do.' He gave Vicky a sharp look. 'Has the gossip reached Fenella's ears?'

'It did, but only recently. She's risen above it, and so has Mark. They are being very wise by ignoring it completely.'

He nodded and stood, reached into the inside pocket of his jacket, took out an envelope. 'Here is the cheque, Vicky. For the recreation centre.' Turning to Jane he added, 'I'm sorry, darling, I have to leave. I must go back to Berkeley Square and deal with this matter immediately.'

TWENTY-SEVEN

'It was so nice of you to come to tea,' Anne Watkins Deravenel said, smiling at her sister Isabel. 'We don't seem to see much of each other these days, and so I'm happy you suggested it.'

Isabel sighed. 'Marriage and children take up a lot of time, don't you think?' She shrugged, made a face, added, 'And as you know, George is very demanding of my time.'

'How is he?' Anne asked politely, not really caring. He was not a favourite of hers. In fact, she detested him.

'Rather burdened down by work at the moment. He's doing such a lot of extra things for Ned, and it keeps him very late at the office. Almost every evening.' As she spoke Isabel poured herself another cup of tea, filled her cup, dropped in a slice of lemon.

That is not true, Anne thought, knowing that Ned was still furious with George after the Scottish deal had fallen through because of him. Richard and Will had had to put it all back together; which they had done, and it had finally closed the other day. George was lying. He was seeing other women. But she couldn't tell her sister this, and so she merely smiled, and changed the subject, saying, 'Mother wants us all to go to Thorpe Manor for Easter, Isabel, and we've said yes. Are you going to accept her invitation?'

'I don't really know. George is somewhat noncommittal about it. You see, he's hoping we might be able to go to the continent by then. He said he'd love to take me to Paris for Easter, and what did I think? And I said it would be lovely, just perfect, which it would, don't you know. Rather like a second honeymoon since we'd be going alone.'

'You're right, it would be very special,' Anne agreed, wondering how her sister could tolerate George. He was good-looking, no question about that, but a bit of a bully, and a liar and cheat as well. Still, perhaps Isabel saw him differently. They had both chosen their Deravenel husband when they were little girls. There had never been anyone else for her but Richard; and everyone had known even then that Isabel had felt the same way about George. These days she was besotted by those good looks of his, and his sex appeal was also a big consideration.

Isabel, who was staring at Anne, felt a sudden rush of jealousy and anger. Her sister appeared to be in blooming health, and she was wearing a very smart outfit, an exceeding expensive outfit, and *pearls*. Furthermore, she was living in the house Isabel craved. As did her husband. 'It's really ours,' he had said the other day. 'You'd better tackle her about it, about moving out.' And that was why she was here today. So far she had not said a word, had not broached the subject, had lost her nerve. However, she knew that soon it would be time to leave, to go home, and she had to accomplish what she had been sent to do. George would punish her if she didn't.

Taking a deep breath, Isabel said, 'I'd love to walk around the house, Anne, can I do that? After all, I grew up here.' She stood up, started to move towards the door, filling with memories for a moment or two.

'Of course you can,' Anne was quick to answer, also rising.

'Come on, let's go to the library first, you know how much Papa loved that room. It was his *haven*, he always said that. Don't you remember?'

Isabel shook her head. 'Actually, I don't. No.' She shrugged again and stared at Anne, filled with a sudden rush of jealousy once more, remembering that Anne had been her father's favourite. Only Anne had existed for Neville Watkins. And Nan, their mother. *She* hadn't mattered.

A delicate-looking young woman, with a peaches and cream complexion and light brown hair streaked with gold, Anne Watkins Deravenel had the most refined looks, and was endearingly pretty, coltish, with a lovely willowy figure and long legs. Her sister Isabel, older by a couple of years, was very similar in appearance, except that she always seemed to look discontented, or worried, and she was frequently gloomy. And she had never been quite as lovely as Anne, and knew it.

Anne thought her sister had appeared troubled since arriving at the Chelsea house a short while ago, and she wondered if her brother-in-law was correct. Ned was forever saying Isabel looked strange and troubled because she was dreadfully unhappy with George, and that he was probably a monster to live with. Anne was quite sure about that. She had stayed with them for a while, at one moment in her life, and he had been mean-spirited, even cruel, and *always* unkind. But to her, not to his wife. On the other hand, she had often heard raised voices from behind closed doors and Isabel sometimes looked as if she had been crying.

'What are you thinking about, you look burdened down?' Isabel said, peering at Anne, then switching on a lamp on a table as they entered the library.

'I'm perfectly all right,' Anne answered, and went around the room, turning on lamps as her sister was doing, thinking of the way George cheated on Isabel with other women. It was dreadful.

For her part, Isabel was drawing on her inner resources,

endeavouring to find a way, and the right words, to open up the conversation on a very serious subject. After a moment of strolling around the library, looking at her late father's possessions, which had been left intact, Isabel swung around in the middle of the floor, and exclaimed, 'You've really no right to be living here, Anne! I am the oldest of Father's heirs, you being the other one, and, as the eldest, this house is supposed to be mine, you know. Mother made a grave error when she gifted it to you and Richard as a wedding present. She had no right to do it. Didn't you know that?'

'She had every right,' Anne answered swiftly, assuming a businesslike voice, suddenly realizing what was coming. Ned had warned her and Richard. He had said something like this might happen.

'No, no,' Isabel contradicted, shaking her head. 'Father merely gave her the right to live in it. She didn't own it.'

'You are absolutely wrong.' Anne walked over to her sister, stood in front of her and stared at her pointedly. 'Father bought this house for Mother, and then he gave it to her outright, gave her the deeds. She was the owner, not our father, and she had every right to do what she wanted with it. At any time.'

'Oh, don't be so silly. You know she didn't! By rights this house is *mine*, since I'm older than you. The eldest.'

'We are co-heiresses of our father's estate, after Mother dies, and don't ever forget that, Isabel. AFTER SHE DIES.'

'You don't have to shout at me,' Isabel muttered in an irritable, complaining tone. 'One of the things I came to talk to you about today was this house. We would like to move in later this year. So you see, you must tell Richard that he has to start looking for a new home for you. A new house. This is *mine* . . . it is *ours*.'

'I think you had better come and sit down over here,' Anne murmured, making her voice softer but keeping it firm. Seating herself on the sofa, she indicated the large wing chair nearby. 'Come along, Isabel, I've something important to tell you.'

Isabel, as slender and elegant as Anne, glided across the carpet and took the chair Anne had suggested. 'And what is it that is so important?'

'The truth,' Anne replied. 'The *painful truth*, perhaps I should say. You see, everything I told you about Mother owning this house is true. It *was* Father's gift to her, an outright gift. He didn't own it from the day he bought it because he bought it in her name and instantly gifted it to Mother. And she sold it before it was given to us.'

'*Sold it!*' Isabel shrieked, her eyes widening. 'She had no right to sell it. I don't believe you. *She had no right.*'

'But she did have the right. I keep telling you, it was hers to do what she wanted with. She could have burned it to the ground if she so desired.'

Isabel gaped at her sister speechlessly.

Anne went on, 'Mother sold the house to Ned, your brother-in-law and mine. He paid good money for it, a lot of money, which Mother Pocketed, because it was hers to pocket. Immediately, Edward drew up new deeds. New deeds in Richard's name. That is why the house is ours. Edward Deravenel bought it for us, and gave it to us, and the deeds are in Richard's name. So there is no way George can take this house, get it from us, or throw us out. And you can't either.'

Isabel was furious, her face extremely pale with fury. She stood up swiftly, and took a step closer to Anne, who was also on her feet. 'We'll see about that,' Isabel threatened in an icy tone, and before Anne could respond she had flounced out of the library.

Hurrying after her, Anne caught up with her in the large entrance hall. 'I told you, Isabel, there is nothing you can do. The house belongs to us. It's all very legal.'

Isabel snorted and went to the closet, took out her coat. 'You'll be hearing from George,' she snapped, going towards the front door. 'Or rather, your husband will.'

Anne nodded. 'I shall inform him,' she answered coldly, and felt a rush of relief the moment her sister had left. And all she could think about was how smart Ned had been to buy the house and give it to them. In Richard's name.

Broadbent was waiting for him in the Rolls-Royce when Edward came hurrying out of Jane's house, and within moments the car was pulling away from the curb, heading towards Mayfair and Berkeley Square.

Leaning back against the seat, Edward tried to still his rage. This time Elizabeth had gone too far, and she had to be stopped. Spreading malign gossip about him was one thing; to involve Fenella was outrageous. Elizabeth was telling a pack of lies about Fenella and himself, and anyone with any sense would know that. Nonetheless, she had to be told a few home truths, and curtailed.

Mallet greeted him in the entrance foyer of the Berkeley Square house. 'Good evening, sir.'

'Evening.' Struggling out of his overcoat and handing it to the butler, Edward went on, 'Where is Mrs Deravenel?'

'In the upstairs sitting room, I believe, sir.'

'Thank you, Mallet.'

Edward took the stairs two at a time, strode across the wide upstairs landing and went down the corridor. He flung open the door of the upstairs sitting room with such force it flew back on its hinges and banged against the brocade-covered wall.

Elizabeth, seated near the fireplace reading a French fashion magazine, jumped in surprise, so startled was she. Instantly, she sat up straighter, staring across the room, and when she saw the rage on Edward's face she shrank back in the chair, her eyes widening with fright.

'What is wrong with you?' he shouted, banging the door shut with his foot, and walking towards her. 'You must be out of your mind, woman! Spreading ugly stories about me. About Fenella Fayne. A woman who has never done you or anyone else one iota of harm, a woman who has never been anything but kind and loving towards you, shown you the utmost respect. Impugning her name, dragging it through the gutter. And what about my name? The Deravenel name, which also happens to be *your* name. Have you no pride? No sense of integrity? Inventing lies like that is utterly contemptible, unconscionable. And I will not have it. Do you hear me, I will not have it.'

'I don't know what –'

'Shut up! And don't try to lie your way out of this like you always do when you've caused undue trouble. You know very well what I'm talking about.'

'Edward, I –'

'I told you to shut up!' he yelled, his face turning bright red as his fury mounted. 'You are monumentally stupid!'

Standing a few yards away from her, he glanced around the room, his eyes sweeping over the priceless Post-Impressionist art, the fine antiques, the rich brocades, silks and velvets everywhere: the utter opulence was staggering. All his doing, he knew that, because she had no real taste. But nonetheless she occupied a house that was renowned for its beauty, grace and elegance.

'You live in total luxury! You wear couture clothes by some of the greatest couturiers in the world. You are bedecked in jewels. I give you anything you want, I deny you nothing. And you *gossip* about me! *You*. My wife,' he cried, almost choking on the words in his spiralling rage. 'It beggars belief. And the gossip is all lies.'

She shrank farther back on the chair, not daring to say a word to defend herself, because she knew she couldn't.

He stepped closer, stood towering over her, looking down at her, an expression of total disgust on his face.

She swallowed, tried to keep calm. She did not fear him physically. He would not strike or hit a woman ever. He was too gentle to do that; too much of a gentleman, as well. Physical violence of any kind appalled him. But his words hurt, they always had. He became more articulate than ever when he was enraged, as he was now; his words pierced her soul. How stupid she was. Why did she say bad things? He was right. She *was* stupid.

Almost as if he had read her mind, Ned leaned down, brought his face closer to hers, and asked in a cold voice, '*Why?* Why have you invented this story about Fenella? Why have you said she is Grace Rose's mother? Why, Elizabeth? In God's name, *why?*'

'I-I-don't know,' she mumbled, her voice shaky.

'It's because you want to hurt me, isn't it?'

She shook her head.

'Oh yes, it is,' he snapped, his voice cold, hard. 'You are so insanely jealous of every woman I know you need to hit back at me, just for smiling at one of them. Or having a long platonic friendship with some of them, such as Fenella whom I have known for donkeys' years. And what about Vicky? Is *she* next? Are you going to malign her? Tell wicked lies about her soon?'

Elizabeth shook her head. She had no defence. Her brother was always telling her she was a fool, and he was correct. Why did she do these stupid things? Was Ned right? Was it jealousy? Looking up at him, looking into that furious face, those cold blue eyes, she began to weep.

'Stop that!' he shouted in her face. 'Stop it, do you hear me! Your tears are meaningless to me. You've caused horrendous damage to our name. More importantly, you have damaged Fenella's name, hurt a woman who has been deathly ill with pneumonia. And all because you can't rule me, make me do your bidding, have things your way. *You disgust me.*'

'I'm sorry –' she began.

'No, you're not, not really. You never are. You're like George. Always creating havoc and not really caring that you have.'

'Don't say I'm like G-G-G-eorge,' she stuttered, losing the last remnants of her composure.

Ignoring this comment, he leaned down, brought his face close to hers once more. 'Listen to me, Madam. And pay attention to my words. Because I will not repeat them. If you ever again dare to say a bad word about me or any of my friends to *anyone*, and that includes your family and mine, I will leave you. Or rather, you will leave me. I will have you removed from this house, and you will go to live in the country, where I shall buy a small cottage for you. You will have a reasonable allowance for your upkeep. And you will stay there permanently, out of London society. You will not live in this house with me ever again, nor in London. You will, very simply, be banished to live the country life. I will give you certain access to our children, not that you actually really care for any of them, except perhaps Young Edward. And that's because he's the heir, and important to your future if you outlive me. Do you understand me? *I will send you away.*'

She merely nodded, shaking, knowing full well that he was capable of doing exactly that. There was a ruthless streak in Ned, and he never ever made idle threats. He always did what he said he was going to do.

Ned swung around without another word, strode towards the door.

'Where are you going?' she whispered.

'Out,' he answered laconically, and left, slamming the door behind him.

He ran downstairs, found Mallet in the pantry, and said, 'Oh, there you are, Mallet. I will not be here for dinner after all. Would you please pack a small valise for me, with the usual items, fresh linen, my shaving tackle. I shall be spending the night at my club.'

'Immediately, sir.'

'Take your time, Mallet, I have an engagement this evening.

I will send Broadbent back, once I arrive at my destination, and he will take the bag from you.'

'I'll have it ready, Mr Deravenel.'

'Thanks, Mallet, and goodnight. You can lock up after Broadbent collects the bag.'

'Yes, sir, and goodnight.'

The butler stood at the open front door, watching him go down the steps to the Rolls-Royce which was parked outside. Edward Deravenel was such a good man, so philanthropic, always helping those in need, those less fortunate. He was very charitable, Mr Deravenel was. Pity he was married to a shrew. A woman who drove him away from her constantly. What a fool she is, he muttered under his breath, filled with dislike for the lady of the house. Some lady, he added to himself, with a stab of disdain as he closed the front door and went off to pack the valise.

TWENTY-EIGHT

'**I** want a divorce,' Edward said quietly, his blue eyes focused on his mother with great intensity.

Cecily Deravenel, startled though she was, remained absolutely silent for a moment. She sat back in the chair and regarded her eldest son. 'So it's come to that has it, Ned? *Finally.*'

'Yes, I'm afraid so. Elizabeth is just . . .' He paused, sought the right word, the right phrase, 'impossible to live with. She's rather dangerous as well, in my opinion. She's liable to say anything about me, invent anything she wants, and about the Deravenels in general, if she sees fit.'

Cecily frowned. Her greyish-blue eyes, so like her son Richard's eyes, became reflective, and a sense of enormous dismay flooded her. 'Something has happened that has genuinely upset you, Ned. I can see that you are not in a very good state of mind. In fact, I thought you looked distraught when you arrived. What is this all about? You'd better tell me, darling. We must talk about this, and perhaps between us we can sort it out to your satisfaction.'

Edward sat back on the sofa, crossed his long legs and took a deep breath. 'She's been spreading a ridiculous story about me, one which impugns Fenella's reputation. She apparently told one of her sisters, more than likely Iris, the dunderhead, who told Maude Tillotson, who told someone else, and it went around like wildfire, to use Vicky's words.'

'You and Fenella,' Cecily murmured, her eyes narrowing. 'But you've only ever been good friends, nothing else. Why would she pick on someone like Fenella, who is so revered by everyone?'

'I don't know. Perhaps that's why, the reason. Fenella is beloved by all of her friends, and even people who don't even know her at all well.'

'Are you saying that Elizabeth has actually accused you of having . . . an affair with Fenella?'

'Yes, and a continuing one.' He leaned forward. 'And it only gets worse.' Edward now told his mother the entire story, as he had heard it earlier that day from Vicky Forth.

'But this is outrageous,' his mother exclaimed when he had finished, looking horrified. 'Elizabeth is clearly determined to make a great deal of trouble for you.' She shook her head in genuine puzzlement. 'How perfectly ridiculous of her, and *vindictive*, to say the least.' Cecily paused, glanced at the fire, her mind working with its usual rapidity and clarity. She said at last, 'What she has done, Ned, is really quite . . . *wicked*.'

'And destructive.'

'When did you find out?' Cecily asked anxiously, disturbed by her daughter-in-law's treacherous behaviour.

'This afternoon. I went to tea with Vicky and my friend. The purpose of the tea was for me to give Vicky a cheque for the recreation centre she and Fenella are starting, for wounded veterans. I told you about it.'

'How generous of you,' his mother answered. 'So you found out earlier today and went home to tackle Elizabeth. Is that the way it was?'

'Yes, yes it was. She tried to deny it, but I wasn't having any of that. I threatened to send her to live in the country, very modestly so. And *alone* . . . if she ever spoke about me or any of my friends in a derogatory way ever again.'

'That was good thinking on your part. She couldn't stand that – living modestly anywhere – but especially in the country, cut off from London society. That's her whole world.'

'I know, but I can't help wondering if she'll toe the line. That's why I thought of getting a divorce, getting rid of her in a legal sense, and so I came to talk to you about it.'

'Do you really want a divorce, Ned? Think of the consequences most carefully, and also do not let us forget that we're Catholic.'

'How much does religion matter these days, Mama?' He suddenly laughed a little hollowly. 'We once had a Catholic king, a few hundred years ago, who broke with the Pope and Rome in order to get a divorce –'

'Yes, and he became a Protestant,' Cecily rejoined, cutting across him.

'Very true, Mother.'

'Let me ask you a particularly sensitive question,' Cecily began cautiously, shifting slightly in the chair, looking across at her son carefully. 'Do you wish to marry Mrs Shaw?'

'I don't know. However, I don't think I count very much in that decision. I am quite certain Jane does not want to marry me, and wouldn't marry me, even if I were suddenly free.'

'Why ever not?' Cecily asked in surprise.

'If she and I married, she would think I had created a job vacancy – for a mistress. And that she couldn't and wouldn't tolerate. At least that's what I believe.'

Cecily smiled at him, then sighed, became very quiet, fell down into herself, thinking hard. After a second or two, she said in an extremely sober and concerned voice, 'What prompted Elizabeth to tell this rather ridiculous story? To hurt you? Or was it more out of jealousy . . . jealousy of Jane Shaw?'

'I think both points are relevant . . . it's not *only* about hurting me, Mother, and it's not *only* about being jealous of Jane. She's jealous of any other female, whatever her age, who comes near me, or whom I seem to favour.'

He stood up, went over to the fireplace, planted himself in front of it in his usual way, and after a moment's silence he continued. 'At Christmas she was even jealous of her own daughter, of a nine-year-old child, for heaven's sake. She was really angry because I had bought Bess that little Victorian brooch. It was actually made for a child, and so small. So insignificant – silver with a few tiny diamond chips. It was not an expensive gift, cost almost nothing. However, Elizabeth took exception to it – just imagine, a gift from me, Bess's father to our own daughter. Outrageous, frankly.'

'Yes, I know, I found it rather strange myself,' Cecily admitted.

'Then there's Grace Rose,' Edward resumed. 'At times, Elizabeth has been very jealous of her, and of my relationship with Grace Rose. And also yours with the girl, actually. Although I'm quite sure Elizabeth has never said anything to you about it. In the last few weeks my wife has been very sarcastic about the girls being bridesmaid for Fenella.' Edward shrugged, lifted his hands helplessly, and shook his head in bewilderment.

'She is obviously extremely jealous by nature, and perhaps envious. I must confess I've noticed it from time to time . . . Elizabeth appears to resent it when you show any kindness to other women or interest in them, however platonic that interest is,' Cecily pointed out. 'Ned, that's rather . . . *sick*. What I mean is that this kind of behaviour is definitely irrational and demonstrates, to me at least, a sick mind. A delusional mind, in my opinion. I wonder what the clever Dr Sigmund Freud would make of your wife?' She raised a brow.

'Is that what you think, Mother? That Elizabeth needs to be treated by a psychiatrist?'

'Perhaps she does. Let us not become sidetracked though. I want you to listen to me, and very carefully. First of all, if you start divorce proceedings, you're going to expose yourself and the family to untold trouble and nasty gossip. Elizabeth will be so angry and outraged she'll go to any lengths to destroy you. She'll hire the best lawyers, extremely tough lawyers, who will have no qualms about crucifying you. They'll put private investigators on you, and they'll dig deep, very, very deep. They'll be into every nook and cranny of your life. She'll have Mrs Shaw hounded. Vicky and Grace Rose will become targets. There will be a monumental scandal, Ned, and we cannot afford that, now can we?'

'No, we can't, Mother, I realize you're right. We don't need a scandal, or our name besmirched any more than it has been by George and his ghastly gambling debts. And thanks again for bailing him out, and especially for making certain he paid me back.'

Cecily nodded, and gave Edward a long look, but made no comment.

Edward was also silent, gazing at her thoughtfully. He hadn't meant to bring George's name into this conversation; it had just slipped out. He knew he had to accept the fact that for some reason his mother had always protected George, ever since his childhood. He supposed she would continue to do so until the day she died. And that was her right; she could do whatever she wanted.

Cecily announced softly, 'I really do think a divorce is the wrong way to go, darling. Under the circumstances. Don't you?'

He nodded, then groaned, answered her in a weary voice. 'What on earth can I do, though? How can I live with her after this? After this terrible act of . . . yes, *wickedness*, as you called it.'

His mother said quietly, but in a very confident and self-assured tone, 'You have probably frightened her to death, really scared her, by saying you'll send her to live in the country. Was that an idle threat, Ned? Or did you really mean it?'

'I did indeed mean it. You see, it would be the only thing I could do. Get her out of my hair that way, rather than divorcing her.'

'I agree. So this is my advice to you. Forget divorce, or a legal separation, and go the other route. Continue to live your life as you have been leading it. However, get away more, to be alone, and I do mean *alone*. Take some trips with Will Hasling, or Richard, and play the game as you've always played it, by being a good, considerate, kind husband, generous to a fault, who has his own private life on the side, like most men of your class do. Be discreet. Especially in regard to Mrs Shaw. Don't create any problems, in other words. Just go about your business in the same way you have all of the years you've been married. And remember, at the back of your mind you know that you can send Elizabeth to live in the country if you so wish. I can assure you *she* won't forget that threat. It will haunt her.'

'It will indeed, and I'll do as you suggest, Mother.'

'There is one other thing,' Cecily ventured. 'Don't be too forgiving too quickly, Ned. Keep her at a distance, as best you can. Also, don't do anything foolish, but remember you are holding all of the cards. It is, after all, your money and power that support her position, and especially in society. She would prefer to die rather than lose that.'

'You're correct there. What about the girls being bridesmaids for Fenella, Mother? How shall I handle that?'

'Good Lord, Ned, need you ask? Surely not. Of course they are going to be Fenella's bridesmaids: she and her father, the Earl of Tanfield, and her siblings, have been lifelong friends of mine. I won't hear a word of complaint from your wife about the girls being attendants at Fenella's marriage. We agreed, and the Deravenels never go back on their word. Onto another matter: where were you going when you passed by Charles Street, and decided to come in to seek my advice?' Cecily asked with a knowing smile, her eyes suddenly twinkling.

'I was on my way to my club, actually.'

'Don't go to White's, darling. Not tonight. A man's club is cold comfort when he has marital problems. Go and see your friend instead. Much better for your well-being, and general state of mind, to have a woman's tender loving care.'

Cecily Deravenel remained seated near the fireplace in her small sitting room long after her son had left, her thoughts on him. She had always known that Elizabeth Wyland was the wrong woman for Ned, from the first moment she had met her.

But it was too late to influence him in any way. He had married her in secret; that marriage, impulsive and regrettable, had been the cause of the trouble between Ned and Neville Watkins, had created a terrible rift in the family which had never truly healed. At least not until Neville and John Watkins had died in that ghastly crash at Ravenscar. Only then had the women of the family come together to comfort each other. And the breach had been healed at last.

Ned was not happy in his marriage, everyone knew that, and it was mainly because of Elizabeth's character and personality. She was an avaricious, ambitious woman, and jealous. Cecily knew only too well that her daughter-in-law was shallow, lacked compassion.

And yet she still somehow managed to lure Ned into her bed, held him through sex, there was no question about that. And their sexual union kept producing these glorious children.

Cecily's thoughts went to her grandchildren – those darling, beautiful girls, and the two little boys, just as handsome and endearing as the girls were pretty. She focused for a moment on her beloved Bess, who at nine years old was quite extraordinary, not only lovely to look at but lovely inside. She cherished them all, of course, but there was something special about Bess, and Cecily expected great things from her. The girl was practical, down to earth, and resourceful, more like her father than her mother.

When Ned had mentioned divorce a short while ago, Cecily had been dumbfounded. It was the first time he had ever brought up the subject, and the mere thought of it frightened her. She believed it was far better for her son to continue living his life the way he had all these years of his marriage, rather than create problems which inevitably would lead to bitterness and resentment.

Elizabeth did not want to be divorced from him, and she would create havoc, Cecily was convinced of that. The scandal would be enormous. And Ned would never be rid of Elizabeth, no matter what, even if they *were* divorced. Nothing really would be accomplished. And then there were the children to consider. They needed their father, who adored them, enjoyed them and spent a great deal of time with them; whereas their mother left them to their own devices, or with Nanny and the new governess, Miss Elliot.

Unexpectedly, Cecily wondered what other mother would have sent her son off to his mistress, as she had done tonight. Many would have done so under similar circumstances, if their son was hurting and despairing, especially if they knew the mistress was a compassionate and loving woman who never made demands.

Years ago she had made it her business to find out everything there was to know about Mrs Shaw and she had been relieved and grateful that it was Jane who was the other woman in his life. He was in safe hands with her. She hoped he had gone to Jane's and not to his club, where he would sit and drink with other men, and become even more morose than he already was. She did not want him to feed his unhappiness and discontent. She wanted him to be comforted by someone who obviously loved him dearly, and who would steady the situation.

TWENTY-NINE

'I'm so sorry to bother you, Jane,' Richard said, 'I'm looking for Ned. Does he happen to be there with you?'

'No, he's not, Richard,' Jane answered, gripping the receiver tighter, all of her senses alerted to trouble. 'Actually, I'm not expecting him tonight. However, he just might come over.'

'I understand. I spoke to Mallet, but you know what butlers are, one never gets a straight answer from them. They're protective by instinct and training. I have also spoken to our mother, and she did say he had been there earlier, but that he had left. Anyway, would you please ask him to telephone me, should he arrive? It's quite important that I speak to him.'

'I certainly will, Richard. Goodnight.'

'Goodnight, and my apologies for disturbing you.'

'You didn't, it's perfectly all right. Goodnight again.' She hung up, and walked across the library, sat down, picked up the book she had been reading, but she was unable to concentrate. Her mind was on Edward Deravenel. The man she loved, and who always seemed to be in the line of fire.

He had been extremely angry when he had left this afternoon, and she knew he had gone home to deal with Elizabeth.

235

As only he could. She was quite certain he would have handled the situation appropriately; he could be really tough; even ruthless when he had to be. It was imperative that he silence his wife, stopped her inventing stories, spreading lies about him, and about Fenella, lies which inevitably led to awful, damaging gossip.

The woman was a troublemaker. Jane had long known this, and yet she herself was not in a position to tell him what to do about her unconscionable behaviour. It was not Jane's place.

He had been to his mother's house in Charles Street tonight, according to his brother, and perhaps Cecily Deravenel had been able to help him, to advise him. She was a wise woman, a worldly woman of great sophistication; she had untold knowledge and she understood people, knew what made them tick.

His marriage to Elizabeth was not ideal, everyone close to him knew this. However, Jane was well aware that Edward Deravenel was not an unhappy man. Far from it, no matter what the world thought.

He had his children, whom he adored, and he relished being with them. And, of course, he had her for companionship, friendship, shared interests, and there was a sexual relationship between them as well.

Edward enjoyed this house, which he had lovingly helped to create and design; also, their somewhat domesticated existence here pleased him enormously. He was able to relax in the tranquil atmosphere she had created, feel truly at home. In a peculiar sort of way it was a kind of marriage they shared; he often teased her and said they were like Darby and Joan, an old married couple.

Their relationship aside, he was extremely happy in his work, completely fulfilled by it. Deravenels meant so much to him, the whole world; in fact, it was his life. He enjoyed going to the office every day, relished the routine of it, the challenges, the triumphs, the problem-solving, and the camaraderie he shared with his top executives, lauded the part they had played and still played in the building of this mighty company.

He never stopped working; he took immense pleasure from it, and he was proud of what he had accomplished since taking over fourteen years before. He had built it into the greatest trading company in the world; there were none bigger, and this was a huge thrill to him.

Ned enjoyed his immense success, his fame, his power, the money, and the privileges that came to him. But unlike a lot of successful people he had time for everybody in his orbit, from the commissionaires who worked at the front door of the building, to the telephonists, typists and secretaries, as well as the top brass.

He was a friend to all. A man of exceptional kindness, Ned was there for everyone who might need him, and nothing was ever too much trouble. He never spoke badly about anyone, nor did he criticize. 'Live and let live,' could easily be his motto.

His close friends knew how loyal he was to them; whenever they had problems or troubles, he was there for them, too, and there was no limit to the effort he would make on their behalf. He was philanthropic as well, very charitable, and generous to a fault when it came to those in need, those less fortunate than he was. Put very simply, he was a genuinely good man.

Those who truly knew him intimately, as she did – Fenella, Vicky, Stephen, and Will – *his lot*, as he called them, recognized all of these qualities and loved him for what he was as a man. Their loyalty to him was staunch and unwavering, and their devotion knew no bounds.

Those people who didn't know him at all thought he was a snob, a womanizer, and a playboy, because they looked at this extremely handsome man, the expensive clothes, the way he was elegantly dressed and turned out, and made a snap decision based on nothing of any consequence. Some saw that unique and extraordinary self-assurance as arrogance, which, again, was not true. But *they* did not matter in the scheme of things. His friends knew he wasn't a snob, a womanizer, a playboy, or arrogant, the last least of all. And anyway, the womanizing had been exaggerated, in her opinion. He had been faithful to Lily Overton, just as he was faithful now to her.

And if there were some who characterized him as an adulterous husband, then so be it. They were usually those people who were uninformed, knew nothing of his private life, or more to the point, had no knowledge of his shrewish and disagreeable wife. A woman most of his intimates despised.

Leaning back in the chair, Jane glanced around the library, still thinking of him. This was Edward's favourite room in the house, along with the blue-and-yellow room. He loved libraries, and what's more loved designing and creating them. Sometimes she thought it was because he loved books as much as she did.

The library here was panelled, but the wood had been painted a peculiar faded green which Ned called French Green; it was clear apple green which had been muddied down with grey paint so that it took on a somewhat smokey hue . . . like a meadow covered in mist, that was the way Jane thought of the colour.

Shelves of books lined the walls, many of them rare first editions, which he had found for her. They were mostly bound in red Moroccan leather; dark red fabrics echoed the bindings, were used to upholster the sofas and chairs, while French Green velvet hung at the windows. It was a comfortable room which a man could feel at home in, but one which was not too overpoweringly masculine.

Earlier, Jane had asked Wells to light the fire, and she was glad he had. Even though it had been a sunny day for March, the weather had changed tonight. It had grown chilly by nightfall and she could hear the wind howling outside.

Picking up her book, Jane tried to become involved with the story, and was eventually absorbed, until she suddenly heard a noise – the front door closing. She leapt up, putting the book on a side table before leaving the room swiftly.

Hurrying out into the front hall, she was relieved and happy to see Ned taking off his overcoat.

'Sorry I didn't let you know I was coming, darling,' he said to her, and threw his coat on a bench, took her in his arms, gave her a tight hug. 'I didn't even want to ring the doorbell for fear of disturbing everyone.'

'Don't be so silly, you could have.' Taking his arm she led him into the library, and continued, 'You look rather pale. Tired, Ned. I hope things weren't too difficult?'

'No. She won't do it again, I feel fairly certain of that.' He shook his head. 'I don't really want to talk about it, if you don't mind, Jane. The less said the better. I'd like to forget about that particular encounter.' He shivered, headed for the fire, as usual, stood in front of it, warming his back. 'I'd love a Scotch, but please don't ring for Wells, I'll get it myself.'

'No, no, I'll do that, and before I forget, Richard telephoned you a short while ago. He said it was important that he spoke to you. Apparently he'd already called Berkeley Square and Charles Street, and no one knew where you were.'

'I see.' He went to the Georgian desk, sat down in the chair and dialled his brother's Chelsea house. Richard answered immediately.

'Were you looking for me, old chap?' Ned asked warmly.

'I was, yes, Ned. Thanks for returning my call. I'm assuming you're at Mrs Shaw's?'

'I am indeed. I just arrived. Jane said you told her it was important you heard from me.'

'It is. Listen, Ned, George has been up to some of his rotten tricks today. Out of the blue, Isabel invited herself to tea this afternoon, and at one moment she told Anne that this house was hers. *Theirs*. And that we had to move out. What about that then?'

Ned threw back his head and laughed uproariously. 'Well, well, well,' he said at last, as the laughter died away. 'And what did Anne say to her sister?'

'She told her that you had bought the house from their mother, paid for it lock, stock and barrel, and that you had then given it outright to us, or rather to *me*. So it was not theirs at all.'

'Bravo to Anne! And I suppose Isabel left, after making threats, and went home to tell the tale to George?'

'She did leave in a big huff, yes. But that's all I know, and will ever know.' Richard chuckled, and finished, 'All I can say is thank God for your foresight, and for doing what you did. It's obvious that George is still on the rampage . . .' He allowed the sentence to drift off, and waited for his brother to respond.

'I hope he isn't, I truly do, Dick. That's all I need. I've just calmed everything down at Deravenels, and you and Will have solved the problems with Ian MacDonald, closed the deal. I was hoping for a bit of peace.'

'Then you shall have it. We'll all see to that! As for George, there is nothing he can do about my house, because that's what it is, thanks to you . . . *My house*.'

'Indeed it is, and now I'll say goodnight, if you don't mind. I just arrived here and have hardly said hello to my friend. I'm being rather rude.'

'Of course, Ned, and goodnight. See you at the office tomorrow.'

'That you will, Dickie. Goodnight.'

Jane had returned carrying two glasses, Scotch for Ned and a glass of champagne for herself. After handing him the crystal glass, the two of them went to sit near the fire.

Ned clinked his glass to hers, sat back in the chair, and said, 'George has been up to his tricks again.'

'Oh no, Ned, I can't stand it!' She looked horrified.

'Ah, but I've bested him.'

'You always do.' She frowned, asked 'What was it about?'

'I suppose I do manage to stop him in his tracks, but this one was a real shocker for him. I'm absolutely sure of it.' He then proceeded to tell her about Isabel's visit to the Chelsea house that afternoon, and the manner in which Anne had put her in her place.

She listened attentively, brought him another drink almost immediately, and then sat patiently, paid great attention as he spoke about business, and things in general. Not once did he mention Elizabeth, and neither did she.

She was well aware that he was truly tired tonight, on the edge of exhaustion, she thought. There was a weariness in his voice, and his face had remained pale, had not become flushed as it sometimes did when he was in the warmth and having a drink. It worried her, that unusual paleness and the weary voice, the sense that he was at the end of his tether. He who was so robust seemed oddly depleted, unusual for him.

Much later he told her he would stay the night with her, and they had gone up to bed together. But as they lay there in the dark, with the firelight making patterns on the walls, luxuri-ating in the peace and quiet of the moment, Ned had started to doze.

Suddenly bestirring himself, shaking himself awake, he said with a faint laugh, 'Sorry, darling, I'm afraid I dozed off.'

Pushing herself up on one elbow, bending over him, Jane said softly, 'And I think you should, you've had such a tiresome day. Let's go to sleep. Both of us. *Right now.*'

'I'm sorry,' he apologized again. 'I don't think I can make love to you. I'm absolutely deadbeat, Jane.' He put an arm over her body, and added, 'Consider yourself well and truly kissed, darling girl.'

'I do,' she answered. 'Now go to sleep.'

Much to her relief, he did so almost immediately. But she lay awake for a long time, worrying about him. He had taken a lot of emotional punishment lately, especially from George, who should be horsewhipped for his bad behaviour. She didn't trust him and never had. He was treacherous and greedy. Nor was she overwhelmed by Richard; Little Fish, Ned had called him since Richard had been a child. There was something wary, secretive and overly cautious in Richard. Those she trusted were his intimate friends. Not his family. Except for his mother who adored him.

Jane herself soon fell asleep, but it was a restless sleep filled with bad dreams about the warring Deravenels and their internal vendettas, death and destruction.

Anthony Wyland was an exceptional man. He was honourable, loyal, totally devoted to Edward, and if needs be he would lay down his life for him. When the Wyland Merchant Bank had run into trouble some years ago, it was Edward who had come to Anthony's aid, offered to help in any way he could. Anthony had been honest, had told Edward not to waste his money trying to bail out the troubled merchant bank. And then he had asked him for a job. Ned had given him one and never regretted it. Neither had Anthony.

He had worked for Edward for a number of years now, and because of his financial knowledge and skill with figures Ned had found him invaluable. Apart from his loyalty, devotion and honesty, Anthony was a cultured man who shared many of Edward's interests, especially books and art, and they had become firm personal friends as well as colleagues, and brothers-in-law.

Now, on this rainy March Thursday afternoon, Anthony sat with his sister in the library of Edward's family home in Berkeley Square. She had welcomed him with a degree of reserve, no doubt because she knew why he had asked himself to tea. However, she had said nothing so far, merely greeted him and asked about their mother.

Thankfully tea had been brought in by Mallet at an awkward moment when their sister Iris's name had come up. Anthony suspected it was Iris to whom Elizabeth had spoken . . . how stupid she was. Iris was the family chatterbox, the gossip, the carrier of tales out of school. An idiot, in his opinion.

Once Mallet had poured tea and departed, Anthony said slowly, 'I hope you won't be doing any talking to Iris in the future, Lizzie. She's a bit of a risk, you know.'

'No, she isn't, she's a sweet girl, and don't call me Lizzie. You know I hate it.'

Her tone made him cringe. He had come here with the best of intentions, and she was prickly and argumentative without any real provocation on his part. He didn't have much time for her these days, and he was sorry for Ned who had to cope with her on a daily basis. She must be a thorn in his side; certainly she was in his. More like a chain of thorns, he thought. Poor Ned.

Sipping his tea, Anthony said, after a moment, 'Don't take an attitude with me, Elizabeth. I'm one of the few friends you have, a *real friend*, I mean.'

'I doubt that: you work for *him*. Where is he, by the way? He hasn't come home for days.'

'I've no idea where Ned is – more than likely he's staying at his club if he's not here.'

She merely stared at him, and sipped her tea.

My God, she is beautiful though, Anthony thought, gazing at his sister for a moment. She was already thirty-eight going on thirty-nine, and looked like a girl of twenty-eight, perhaps even less. The hair was spun gold, piled high on top of her head like a crown; the complexion was milky white, flawless, unlined, without blemish, and the pale blue eyes clear, crystalline almost.

As for her figure, it was superb. She was not tall, but she had never put on weight over the years, and she was slender, her breasts high and taut, and she had lovely legs. No wonder Ned fell into her bed so often. There were few women as beautiful as she, anywhere in the world. But what a harridan she could be. More's the pity, her brother thought.

'You're staring at me,' she snapped.

'No, admiring you, that's all.' Anthony leaned forward, and said in a quiet, conciliatory voice, 'Listen to me, my dear. Ned is a good husband, he lavishes you with everything you could possibly want . . . so give him some slack, leave him alone.'

'I haven't done a thing to him! Why do you say that?'

'You've lied about him and Fenella Fayne, you know you have.'

'The original story was an utter fabrication, the one about the cart, and Finnister finding the girl, and all that rubbish about a woman called Tabitha James. There was no such person. It was Fenella. Always her. He slept with her, has done so for years, and he got her pregnant, and he may well get her pregnant again, since he's still sleeping with her. She's a slut. Just like all the other women in his life.'

Anthony shrank away from her, shrank back into the chair, shrivelling inside. He was appalled at what he was hearing. *Was she crazy?* Was his sister actually *insane?* He didn't even want to think such a thing, but certainly she was ranting at him, and she obviously believed what she was saying.

Clearing his throat, he explained patiently, 'I have seen the evidence, the original evidence Vicky found. I really have. I do think you should let this matter drop. You've caused immeasurable damage, Elizabeth, created a scandal. You and Iris together have actually.'

She stared at him blankly, as if she did not understand.

'I'm ashamed of you both!' he exclaimed suddenly, speaking in an angrier tone. 'The two of you have behaved in the most despicable manner possible. Spreading stories about your own husband.'

'It's my husband who's despicable. Where in God's name is he? That's what I'd like to know.'

Anthony put his cup and saucer down, and stood up. 'I wouldn't talk about your husband in that way or in that tone of voice, if I were you, at least not to anyone else other than me. You might find yourself without a husband, if you do. And here's another piece of advice, my dear. Keep your mouth shut when it comes to Edward Deravenel and the Deravenel family. Otherwise you might find yourself on the outside looking in at them. Good day, Elizabeth. And if you know what's good for you, heed my words.'

'How dare you speak to me like that!' she cried.

But she spoke to an empty room. Her brother had walked out on her, slamming the door behind him.

As was his custom when he returned home late at night, Edward Deravenel always went into the library to settle himself down and have a cognac. Sometimes Mallet was there, sometimes not, and tonight the butler was absent. It was his day off. He always went to see his sister in Maida Vale.

Striding toward the library, Edward pushed open the door, walked in, and stopped in his tracks. His wife was sitting there in a chair, looking nervous and quite ill; her face was deathly pale and there were dark rings under her eyes.

Frowning, he asked, 'Why are you waiting here? For me, I've no doubt, but why *here* and not upstairs?'

'I need to speak to you,' she said in a low, subdued voice.

'We don't really have much to say to each other at the moment, do we? I think you've actually done too much talking already. Wouldn't you agree?'

She nodded her head. 'I'm sorry, Edward, really sorry. Please, please say you forgive me.'

'I'm afraid that is going to take some time . . . forgiving you I mean. I'm still reeling from the backlash of your gossip.'

'I'm so sorry, so very sorry,' she whispered, her voice wobbling.

'Don't start weeping, it won't do you any good.' He went over to the chest, poured himself a small brandy and stood near the fireplace. 'You've damaged our name and hurt a good woman, damaged her name too. Fenella has never done anything to hurt you. Why, she's always been your friend. I just can't understand your behaviour.'

'I don't understand it myself, Ned, I really don't,' Elizabeth whispered, twisting her hands together in her lap. 'I can only think that it was my terrible jealousy. I am jealous of you and other women, I might as well admit that now. I just can't help myself.'

'Fenella has been a friend of the family since she was a young girl, and there has never been any romantic dalliance between us. And there are no other women for you to be jealous of, Elizabeth.'

She opened her mouth to say something and then closed it, suddenly knowing it would be better not to aggravate him. After all, she had waited for him to come home in order to apologize, not accuse.

He said slowly, 'And don't bring up my mistress. She exists, yes. But then men like me do have mistresses. Thankfully, you are one of the luckier wives in these circumstances. My mistress doesn't create trouble in any way, for me or for you, or for this family. She likes the status quo. So do I. And so must you.'

'I know this, I do accept it.' Rising, Elizabeth walked across to him, took hold of his arm. 'Please, Ned, let's put this behind us.'

He stared at her for a long moment and then lifted her hand off his arm. He said in the softest of voices, 'I will do my best,

Elizabeth, for the sake of our children. Now please go up to bed, it's very late.'

'Aren't you coming?'

'I'm afraid not. I have quite a lot of work to do.'

THIRTY

London 1920

It was Wednesday, the thirty-first of March, and it was her birthday. Her twentieth birthday. Grace Rose could hardly believe it, but it was true. And she suddenly, and wonderfully, felt quite grown up. Very grown up, in fact.

Last night her father had called her a lovely young lady, and she had beamed at him, hugged him, and told him she was so happy to have him and Vicky, have them as her parents. There was no one luckier than she was; Grace Rose believed that with all her heart.

It was last night, over dinner, that Vicky and Stephen had told her how proud they were of her and what she had become, and of her accomplishments, and she had experienced an enormous rush of love and gratitude towards them. Stephen had gone on to add that she had a wonderful life ahead of her and she believed him. He always told her the truth.

Her dream of going to Oxford had come true . . . her mother had made it come true, and for the past year she had been living her childhood dream and attending lectures. She enjoyed every moment of living in that glorious ancient city of shining spires, gracious quadrangles and beautiful old architecture. It was an extraordinary experience to be in this place of such great learning, a treasured place in her heart, one which she would remember with love long after she had left.

Grace Rose was reading English and French history, her favourite subjects, and one day she hoped to be a historian, give lectures herself, and write books. She loved writing, and thought that perhaps this was her true *métier*.

When she was not attending lectures she was working and studying in her spacious and comfortable room at Millicent Hanson's lovely old house set in a quiet lane. Her mother's long-time friend had welcomed her warmly, and Grace Rose had felt instantly at home amongst the mellow antiques and many volumes of books. Mrs Hanson made her feel cared about without being possessive or intrusive, and left her to her own devices. They met for occasional meals and the arrangement worked well for both of them. Millicent was a writer herself, and was always working on a book in her upstairs study, and constantly told Grace Rose she had the freedom of the house. It was a quiet place, peaceful and pleasant, a real haven.

'Grace Rose!' Vicky called from the bottom of the stairs. 'Broadbent has come to fetch us. Please hurry, darling.'

'I'll be right there, Mother,' Grace Rose called back, poking her head out of her bedroom door. Then she went and picked up her blue coat, evening purse and gloves, and cast a last look at herself in the mirror.

She loved her dress. It was new, specially designed and made for her by Madame Henriette, of delphinium-blue silk, well-cut, tailored, with a narrow skirt that was the new calf-length. She smiled as her eyes took in her pearls, which were all birthday presents. The strand around her neck was from her parents, the bracelet a present from Amos, and the earrings were from Fenella and Mark. She glanced at her new watch, a gift from Uncle Ned. It was by Cartier, and it told her it was just seven o'clock. She left the room and ran downstairs, excited about her birthday dinner at the Ritz Hotel, which was being given by Uncle Ned. They would be eight: she and her parents, Fenella and Mark, Amos, Uncle Ned and Jane Shaw. It was going to be a lovely evening, she was sure,

After they had left their coats in the cloakroom, Vicky took hold of Grace Rose's arm, and explained, 'We're to meet Uncle Ned upstairs, darling. Maisie and her husband are here from Ireland, and they've invited us to have a glass of champagne with them for your birthday.'

'Oh, how nice,' Grace Rose exclaimed as Vicky led her towards the lift. She glanced back over her shoulder, and asked, 'What's Father doing over there?'

'I think he's asking the young man at the reception desk to announce us. Oh, here he comes now.'

A moment later the three of them were in the lift going up to the fifth floor. 'It's just along this corridor,' Stephen announced, as they stepped out of the lift, leading the way. A second or two later he was knocking on the double doors of a suite.

It was instantly opened by Edward Deravenel, who smiled hugely, took hold of Grace Rose's hand and swiftly brought her into the room where the people gathered there cried in unison, 'Happy Birthday, Grace Rose! Happy Birthday!'

Grace Rose was so taken by surprise, so flabbergasted, she couldn't speak; her throat tightened with emotion and she truly thought she would burst into tears, so touched was she.

Her eyes swept around the room, taking in everyone who was present, the men so smartly dressed in dark suits, the women in lovely frocks ... Fenella was standing with Mark and Jane Shaw, and both women looked superb in their gowns and jewellery, Grace Rose thought.

On the other side of the room, near the fireplace, she spotted

Aunt Cecily, very grand in dark rose-coloured silk and ropes and ropes of pearls, with Bess leaning against the chair. And she saw that Bess was perfectly lovely in a crimson dress, an unusual colour for a redhead but rather striking nonetheless.

Alongside Bess was her dearest, sweetest Amos Finnister, and on his other side, smiling at her very brightly, was Charlie Morran with his new lady friend, Rowena Crawford. Next to Rowena, looking like the beautiful stage star she had once been, was Maisie, Charlie's sister, and her husband Liam, who were actually Lord and Lady Dunleith from Ireland. Maisie was in navy blue, bedecked in sapphires, and utterly glamorous.

Tears sprang into Grace Rose's eyes when she looked up at Uncle Ned, knowing that he had arranged this surprise party and invited everyone. She attempted to give him a smile but it was a rather quavery one, and then, unexpectedly, as he stood there looking down at her with a huge smile on his handsome face, she herself began to smile, and then they were laughing together and hugging each other.

'That's my girl!' Ned exclaimed, and ushered her forward, turned to include Vicky and Stephen, brought the three of them into the room to mingle.

Grace Rose was surrounded.

Bess, eleven now, and very grown up in her appearance these days, was the first to rush over to her. Her half-sister hugged her and announced, 'I've got a lovely present for you, Grace Rose. Papa let me choose it and I'll give it to you later.'

'Thank you so much,' Grace Rose replied, smiling, and then turned to Amos, who gave her a big hug and kissed her cheek. 'Happy birthday, Grace Rose,' he murmured, his eyes full of pride and love. And she showed him her arm, smiling at him, and thanked him for the bracelet.

Fenella came over to her, and wished her many more birthdays and kissed her cheek affectionately, as did Mark, and she thanked them for the earrings; when Jane came to her side, she said, 'Thank you so much for the leather writing case, it's beautiful, Jane.'

She received a loving smile in return from Jane Shaw, who had become her friend in the last two years, and then she swung around as she heard her name and smiled at Charlie, who smiled back and introduced Rowena to her.

Finally she was able to make her way across the room to the fireplace, where Aunt Cecily was sitting.

'Come and let me look at you, my dear,' Aunt Cecily said, smiling at her lovingly. 'My goodness, you are a beauty, aren't you Grace Rose?' And so like your f –' She cut herself off. But Grace Rose knew she had been about to say she looked like her father.

Leaning forward, Grace Rose kissed Cecily's cheek, and Cecily whispered against her ear, 'You are a true Deravenel, Granddaughter, at least in your looks. Happy birthday!'

'Thank you, Aunt Cecily,' Grace Rose answered and swallowed hard. She was overwhelmed by sudden emotion. It was the first time Cecily Deravenel had ever called her that . . . granddaughter. Now she added, 'Thank you for the dressing-table set – the silver brushes and looking glass with my initials are lovely. I'll treasure them always.'

'They come with much love.' Cecily smiled and her eyes were misty. Bess looked like Ned, very much so, but this one, his first-born child, was the spitting image of him.

Excusing herself, Grace Rose went over to Maisie, whom she had met twice before when Charlie's sister had come to visit him, but she had never met Liam, her husband. Maisie introduced them, and then said, 'And it was such a lovely coincidence, Grace Rose, that we had decided to come here for Easter, and Charlie passed on your uncle's invitation to join you for dinner for your birthday.'

'Yes, it is, and isn't Charlie looking wonderful?'

'He is indeed, and I'm delighted he has finally met a nice young lady,' Maisie responded. 'Well, he's met a lot, but this one he really likes.'

There was suddenly a lot of popping noises, and two waiters came in from the adjoining room carrying trays with glasses of champagne and white wine on them, and they moved amongst the guests, offering the drinks.

A moment later, Charlie came over to Grace Rose, and murmured, 'I have a gift, I'll give it to you later.' He cleared his throat, confided, 'Rowena helped me to pick it out.'

'Thank you, Charlie. She looks very nice, your young lady. And very pretty.'

'Thank you.' He grinned. 'I'm glad she has your stamp of approval.'

Grace Rose laughed with him. She and Charlie had become good friends in the last two years, since his return from the front, and they shared a similar sense of humour. She then said, in her usual honest and forthright way, 'Your face looks better than ever, Charlie, and the skin grafts are miraculous, hardly visible. My goodness, the surgeons have done wonders for your face, put it back together again.'

He burst out laughing, as always amused by her blunt manner. 'It's a good thing everybody present here tonight saw me when I was badly scarred, isn't it? Or they wouldn't understand.'

A blush spread across Grace Rose's neck and went up into her face; she was bright pink, and chagrined. 'I'm so sorry, I didn't mean to embarrass you,' she responded sotto voce. 'But I meant what I said, you do look wonderful, and you'll soon be back on the stage. I just know it.'

'I hope so.'

'So do I and I'm really looking forward to seeing you act. I bet Rowena is, too. Are you going to marry her?'

Amused, Charlie lifted his shoulders in a slight shrug and smiled at Grace Rose. 'I'm not sure.' Lowering his voice, he murmured, 'I haven't asked her yet, but when I do you'll be the first to know.'

Grace Rose smiled, and excused herself and went to talk to Jane Shaw. The two of them instantly became engaged in a long and very animated conversation.

As the host, Edward was paying attention to everyone, making certain champagne and wine were poured quickly when glasses were empty; he moved around the sitting room of the large double suite he had taken, wanting his guests to feel comfortable. At one moment his mother caught his eye, and he strode across the room to her. Leaning over her chair, he asked, 'Is everything all right, Mother? Do you need something? More caviare? Another glass of champagne?'

'I'm perfectly fine, Ned,' Cecily replied, and then asked in a low voice, 'I was just wondering where Will and Kathleen were. Are they coming?'

'Yes, they are, but Will was away on business, Deravenel business, of course. They're just a bit late, that's all. I know they wouldn't miss this little party for Grace Rose, not for the world.'

Touching his arm lightly, Cecily said, 'I remembered something this afternoon, do you know, Ned: it came back to me quite unexpectedly, and I thought I ought to tell you. I simply don't know why I forgot all about it.'

Ned frowned. 'You sound serious. What is it?'

'I remembered something Neville said to me years ago, when you were only just married. He made a comment, said that it was a pity you had married secretly, because of his negotiations with Louis Charpentier . . . he was so keen to have you marry Louis's daughter Blanche, as you well know. Anyway, he grumbled to me a little bit, complained that you'd let him down–'

'I know all this, Mama, what are you getting at?'

'Just this . . . he told me that Henry Turner was related to Louis Charpentier, through his mother Margaret Beauchard, something I'd never known. He added that your marriage to

Blanche, had it taken place, would have healed the breach between the Lancashire Deravenel Grants and the Deravenels.'

Ned burst out laughing. 'He can't have been serious, Mother! *Surely not.* I am quite certain Margaret Beauchard and her son are my sworn enemies, our enemies, and were then. After all, Turner is the heir to Henry Grant. Some say it's dubious, but there really isn't anyone else, as you well know. And Turner did inherit Grant's shares in Deravenels. However, I must add, not enough shares to rock the boat in any way whatsoever. And we've always honoured those shares, by the way, ever since I took over. I've had their shares and their holdings in the company checked out very recently, in fact, and everything is proper and in order. And incidentally, Mother, the dividends go to Margaret Beauchard on a regular basis, held in a trust for her son.'

'Well, well, I never knew *that*,' Cecily murmured, looking up at Ned, her expression slightly puzzled. 'You never told me.'

'There was no special reason why I didn't, Mama. I didn't think it was very important, actually. The Grants have held shares in Deravenels for hundreds of years. However, just to reassure you, we are the majority shareholders, and that's all that matters, wouldn't you say? Also, I happen to be in charge, control the company, and run it on a daily basis.'

She smiled at him. 'With an iron hand.'

'Oh, but in a velvet glove,' he shot back, and smiled at her in return. It was his lopsided, boyish smile that turned most women's heads.

At this moment, the door of the suite opened and Will Hasling stood there with his wife Kathleen. She was the sister of the late Neville and Johnny Watkins, and also Cecily Deravenel's niece. She looked very much like a younger version of her aunt, with the Watkins's good looks and dark hair. Her features were fine, well sculpted, similar to her aunt's, and it was easy to see they were closely related.

Edward went over to Will and Kathleen, greeted them affectionately, and then escorted them into the room. Once Will and Kathleen had gone around, saying hello to everyone, and had accepted glasses of the Krug, Ned brought Kathleen to sit with his mother.

After she was settled, he and Will moved away, stepped closer to the window, and stood alone, quietly talking for a moment. 'It's as you thought, Ned,' Will murmured, his tone low, confiding. 'Our old adversary Louis Charpentier was very much in favour of his niece marrying into the Deravenel family – an old story, eh? I understand he's been after Meg to help him for some time. Fortunately, your sister finally had the good sense to discourage such a union. I think she suddenly realized that Louis, the old fox, might eventually try to do you harm, grab the company somehow. You were more important to her than George in the end. So I do believe you've managed to nip something in the bud by talking to Meg. Your sister truly is loyal to you, and also your intervention was brilliant.'

Edward sighed. 'George is such a fool, always after power, thinking he can beat me, do me ill.' He shook his head sadly. 'Isabel's only been dead six months and here he is already looking for another bride.'

'Not *any* bride, though, remember that, Ned. A bride of great wealth is what he seeks so assiduously. The Charpentier heiress was perfect. And that is exactly what Louise now is. After Blanche's death in childbirth, along with the baby, Louis was compelled to name his only brother's only child. Louise has become *it*.'

'Oh, believe me I haven't forgotten that, or anything else. Now what about the other matter? Did you find out anything else . . . regarding Henry Turner?'

'Yes, I did, I'm happy to report. Jean-Paul was very helpful, and I'm relieved he is now running the Paris office of Deravenels. He's turned out to be a damned good executive. Jean-Paul used some extremely well-qualified private investigators. Listen to this! Henry Turner is about to go back to work for Louis Charpentier. He has now been given a bigger position in the company, although it's not yet been announced. Apparently he's a very good businessman. Cautious, wary, tight with money, even a bit parsimonious, shall we say? Dull chap, seemingly, according to the private investigators. No scandal attached to him, no gossip either. It looks to me as if Louis is grooming him for even bigger things.'

'Marriage to Louise?'

'Apparently not. Louis Charpentier is very strict about inter-marriage within a family. Doesn't approve.'

'I see.' Edward nodded, added, 'So we have all of our ducks in a row . . . and we know exactly what's what. But we must keep an eye on Turner, don't you think, Will?'

'Absolutely. He could prove to be very dangerous in the long run.'

Half an hour later, after everyone had consumed lots of cham-pagne and white wine, and sampled the best Beluga caviare, Ned asked his guests to come into the adjoining room. This was another sitting room in the double suite which had been turned into a dining room for the evening.

The doors were thrown open by two of the waiters, and everyone trooped in. The long table covered in a white linen cloth, had been set for sixteen, and there were perfect arrange-ments of white roses lined up the centre; white candles in tall silver candlesticks were interspersed between the silver bowls of roses. The candlelight reflected on the silver and crystal so that the table sparkled, and there were flowers and candles throughout the room. A very festive feeling prevailed.

As he glanced around the table, observing everyone, Ned was

pleased to see that each one of his guests appeared happy to be here tonight. He knew they all loved and admired Grace Rose, and were delighted to celebrate her birthday.

His guests were relaxed, chatting to each other, and enjoying themselves thoroughly. It was a warm, happy group of old friends. At one moment, just before the first course was served, Ned tapped his glass with his fork, and said, 'I would like to propose a toast to Grace Rose on her twentieth birthday.' He raised his crystal flute of champagne, and so did everyone else; in unison they cried, 'Happy birthday, Grace Rose.'

Ned said to the table at large, 'I know there are those who wish to say something, to make a little speech, to honour Grace Rose, and that will be lovely. But I do think we're all very hungry by now. So let's have dinner, and then we can continue to toast Grace Rose afterward, and later she will open her presents.'

As Edward was speaking the white-gloved waiters carried large platters of smoked Scotch salmon and smoked trout around the table, serving everyone, and offering brown bread and butter, the bowl of lemon wedges, and creamy horseradish sauce for the trout from Scotland.

Ned leaned closer to his mother on his right and told her, 'There are two courses to choose from next . . . roast duck with cherry sauce, or, if you prefer, you can have leg of lamb. Spring lamb from the Yorkshire Dales. With all the trimmings, I might add.'

'I think I shall have the latter, even though I do love duck.' Looking at Ned through the corner of her eye, Cecily now said, 'Will's just come back from Paris, hasn't he?'

'Yes. And we've nothing to worry about. Meg has done her duty to the Deravenels. She is no longer encouraging Charpentier in his schemes. The proposition, such as it was, has been nipped in the bud. That was the way Will put it anyway.'

'What a relief,' was Cecily's only comment.

Ned himself was greatly relieved. The last thing he needed

was his newly-widowed brother George marrying the Charpentier heiress. Louis, the old fox as Will called him, still appeared to have designs on Deravenels, he was positive of that. The big grab, that's what George thought he could do. His brother had become a menace. And was behaving worse than ever since Isabel's untimely death. She had died in childbirth some months ago, and after a brief period of mourning it was business as usual. He was getting greedier than ever, discontented and wicked. Ned expected George to create more trouble any day now, that was George's nature. And he was prepared, well armed, so to speak.

But finally he pushed this troubling thought to one side. Tonight was a happy occasion, and especially for Grace Rose. He wanted her to enjoy it, as he planned to do himself.

PART TWO

Ned

Truth & Love

Truth is truth and love is love,
Give us grace to taste thereof;
But if truth offend my sweet,
Then I will have none of it.
Alfred Edgar Coppard

Preserve, within a wild sanctuary,
an inaccessible valley of reveries.
Ellen Glasgow
A Certain Measure

He who knows others is wise;
He who knows himself is enlightened.
Lao Tzu

THIRTY-ONE

Constantinople 1921

Oil. Black, stinking, greasy, sulphurous oil. Black gold. His long-held dream of discovering oil had come true. *At last.*

Edward Deravenel sat on the terrace of a stunning yali on the banks of the Bosphorus. It was a lovely sunny morning in July, and he was sipping a glass of hot mint tea, eating an almond biscuit and thinking about his oil.

Deravco oil. It had happened. He now had an oilfield in Southern Persia, thanks to the vision, endurance, and skill of Jarvis Merson, in whom he had always believed, and Merson's partner, Herb Lipson. And *his* money, of course. He had financed the whole kit and caboodle.

The two men had done what they had promised. They had discovered a vast and rich oilfield in the long Persian valley where they had bought an oil concession from the Shah. Their geology samples, instinct, and nose for oil had told them that this most valuable commodity did exist there. They had chosen to drill in the valley in the summer of 1918, after persuading Edward to go along with their scheme, to back them financially, in essence to become their full partner. Deciding to take a chance on them, he had jumped in with both feet and a lavish cheque-book, and hoped and prayed the two men would succeed.

Their venture had begun in May of 1918. Taking him by surprise, they had arrived in London at that time, en route to Persia to investigate the situation. He had gone to lunch with them at Rules, and over lunch they had convinced him to become their partner. Their enthusiasm, belief in themselves, and the fact that they were two well-proven oilmen had engendered great enthusiasm in him. Also, he trusted them.

Alfredo Oliveri and Will Hasling had been present at the lunch, and both had cast doubts on the whole scheme initially. It was Oliveri who had pointed out that buying the concession and then drilling were only the first steps. 'Let's say you do actually find oil,' Oliveri had said, 'you're going to need tons of money to continue ... money for collecting it, piping it, refining it, shipping it. Yes, you're going to need an enormous cash flow to get underway.' He had looked pointedly at Edward and finished, 'What could it be? A million pounds? Perhaps even a couple of million pounds? Are you prepared to risk all that?'

Now Edward remembered how he had inwardly flinched but managed to keep a smile on his face, and then he made a snap decision based on his gut instinct alone. He had always had faith in Merson, and he had taken a shine to Lipson as well, and so he said, 'Point well taken, Oliveri, but I think I'm going with these two wildcatters. However, I won't use Deravenels' money ... you're more than likely quite correct about it being risky. Indeed it *is* a risky business, oil. But I believe in these two chaps, so I am going to back them. But with my own money. If they don't find oil, then it will be my own personal loss. If they do succeed, then Deravenels can pay me back, and Deravco will then belong to the company. How does that sound?'

Oliveri had nodded, having no alternative, and Will had laughed. 'You've just given our American friends your stamp of approval, and since you've always had that golden touch they're bound to succeed. So – here's to the oil business!'

The five of them had lifted their glasses and drunk to the success of the Persian venture.

Once they had arrived in Southern Persia, and having swiftly acquired the concession they wanted from the Shah, Merson and Lipson had soon put together two teams. They were made up of wildcatters from America, oilmen from England, and from Baku in Azerbaijan, the biggest port in Russia and also the centre of the Russian oil business. In 1918 the Russian Revolution was in the process of winding down to a certain extent; even so, many oilmen had fled from Baku to Persia, where foreign oil companies, mostly American and British, were hiring. And drilling. It was the place to be if you were looking for oil.

Merson and Lipson had also managed to persuade local tribesmen in the area to work alongside them, in a variety of different capacities. The promise of black gold had been an enormous incentive to all.

Every week the two oil men wrote a report for Edward and sent it to London, and they were scrupulous in everything they told him.

There had been, over the next two years, many disappointments and dreadful failures after months upon months of backbreaking toil; heartbreak as well because of accidents, some of which were fatal. And yet the two Americans had never given up hope of finding oil, even in their worst times and after numerous unexpected disasters.

Impressed by their dogged determination, total commitment and a genuine belief that there *was* oil deep under the earth on their concession, Edward had kept the money flowing to his partners, to pay wages, buy food and additional equipment as it was required, along with other supplies.

But at the end of two and a half years of grim struggle, and often joyless toil, Merson and Lipson knew that they must find oil soon or quit. It had become an extremely expensive venture and they had the sense to realize that Edward Deravenel was not going to back them indefinitely. They loathed the idea of leaving in total defeat, yet they accepted that they would have to close the camp in the Valley of Stone, as they had come to calling it, if their third well did not produce oil. The first and second wells they had drilled were dry. The only thing the Mother Hubbard drill bit had hit so far was solid rock.

They were very much aware that everything now depended on their third well. If it came up dry they would have no option but to conclude the whole operation. They had already drilled to two thousand two hundred feet, but with no success; still, they wanted to give it another shot. 'Let's call it one last fling,' Merson had said to Lipson, grinning. 'Let's take it down to three thousand five hundred feet and see what happens.' Yet again, they had written their report and sent it off, explaining to Edward that this was their *final* drilling effort.

It was just after they had hit three thousand two hundred feet that their luck changed. There was an extraordinary rumbling noise, like an earthquake starting, followed by a series of booms. And then it came – a gusher of oil the likes of which none of them had ever seen. Glorious black oil, spurting up in the air at least eighty feet, and it did not stop. It just went on gushing upward.

They were in business. The oil business.

Covered in grime and thick black oil the two Americans and their crews laughed, shouted, and danced around like whirling dervishes. The next day they sent one of the English oilmen down to Abadan to telegraph Edward, announcing their stupendous news.

When he had received the telegram Edward had initially found it hard to take in. After these difficult and disappointing years in Persia, Merson and Lipson had finally done it. Discovered oil. And in a big way. He was staggered; there was great jubilation throughout Deravenels that day. Edward had immediately cabled back his congratulations, promising to come out to see them in July.

And three weeks ago he had finally been able to leave London. He had travelled to Marseilles and from there had taken a ship to Abadan. Alfredo Oliveri and Will Hasling had gone with him, and from Abadan the three of them were taken overland to the oilfield, escorted by Merson, who had come to meet them.

What a wonderful sight it had been to see all of those derricks rising up to touch the pale blue Persian sky. His derricks. Deravco's derricks. His dream of owning an oil company had come true. Edward had been thrilled.

Edward, Will and Alfredo had been given the grand tour of the oilfield by Merson and Lipson, and had met every single one of the crew members. Each night they had listened to amazing stories – many of them rather tall stories – until dawn broke; there had been much celebrating throughout their visit, and a lot of beer, Scotch and Russian vodka consumed.

After four days they had left the valley, still called the Valley of Stone, but with knowing winks these days. Turkey had been their destination, and once again they had gone overland – to Constantinople. The three of them had journeyed there to meet Ismet Bozbeyli, the charming and anglicized Turk, an Oxford graduate who ran their Turkish operation, following in the footsteps of his father and grandfather before him.

It had gone without saying that they would stay at the lovely old yali belonging to Ismet Bozbeyli. This extraordinary villa was situated in the most glorious gardens on the banks of the Bosphorus.

After resting for several days, Alfredo and Will had gone off with Ahmet Hanum, who also worked for Deravenels in Turkey, to visit the marble quarries. Some of these were located on the islands of the Sea of Marmara which flowed into the Bosphorus. Alfredo was looking to buy new quarries for Deravenels.

Edward had not accompanied them because he had caught a

chill in Persia, and, fearing a bout of bronchitis, to which he was prone, he had remained at the yali.

And now, as he glanced around, he was delighted that he had. The villa was luxurious, the servants polite, kind and instantly on hand to be of service, and the food delicious. He had recuperated in this opulent villa, surrounded by flowers, green lawns sloping down to the water and shady trees. It was an idyllic place, soothing to his soul. He had been able to relax here alone, and he had enjoyed his solitude during the day when Ismet was at the Deravenel offices in the central part of the city.

Deravenels had done business in Turkey for several hundred years, mostly importing carpets from Hereke and Canakkale, kilims from Denizil, and carpets and kilims from Konya. Fabrics and silks were another import, along with every kind of spice, Turkish Delight, the jelly-like sweet candy so beloved by the English, and pure Bulgarian rose oil. This was used in the making of perfume, and was also an oil for the body.

The Deravenel Company exported many goods to Turkey, exceptional cloths from their Bradford woollen mills, ready-made clothing from their factories in Leeds, and wine from their French vineyards. Trading between them had always been excellent, and profitable, and Deravenels was a company completely trusted by the Turkish importers and vendors.

Rising, Edward walked down the path that cut between the sloping green lawns, heading in the direction of the long lower terrace overlooking the Bosphorus. When he came to a low wall he opened the small gate set in it, went out onto the terrace itself. There was another low wall which fronted the large body of water, and he sat down on it. As he glanced around, he couldn't help marvelling. What a tremendous waterway this was – a link between the west and the east.

The Bosphorus Straits flowed down from the Dardanelle Straits, and into the Golden Horn, an inlet that created a natural harbour in Constantinople. And beyond was the Black Sea . . . and Russia.

Lifting his eyes, Edward now looked across the Bosphorus to the other shoreline, and there was Asia Minor. How amazing it was, the way the city straddled Europe and Asia.

Just below him, underneath the terrace, was the caiquehouse, where the caiques were housed for sailing up and down the Bosphorus and for going across to Asia Minor. Straight ahead of him was a long jetty where the boats dropped off guests coming to and from the villa.

Edward had enjoyed every moment he had been in Constantinople – it was certainly different from anywhere else he had visited before. This ancient city was both exotic and mysterious, and it fascinated him. For the last two days, in the cool of early morning, Ismet had taken him to see some of the ancient places – the Blue Mosque, a very old church called the Haghia Sophia, and Topkapi Palace, now a museum. It was a city of mosques, minarets and churches, and many palaces as well. They had gone to the Spice Market, where Edward had been pleasantly assailed by the amazing and tantalizing scents and aromas of hundreds of spices. They were all redolent of Asia and Africa floating on the warm air: cumin, curry powder, chili pepper, saffron, paprika, coriander, tumeric, caraway, and cinnamon.

Later this week Ismet planed to escort him around the Grand Bazaar, an excursion he was looking forward to immensely. Everything was sold in this ancient market, from jewellery to carpets. He wanted to find presents for his daughters and sons, and he must seek out gifts for Elizabeth, his mother, Jane, Vicky and Fenella. He mustn't forget them – they would be far too upset if he did.

On his way back to his suite of rooms Edward took the long way around to go back up to the yali. He walked through the many flower gardens ablaze with colourful blooms and fountains shooting water into the air. Ismet had told him that these gardens were at their best in the spring when the tulips bloomed; the tulip had been the favourite flower here for many centuries, and had been cultivated here long before it had been grown in Holland, something he had never known. In fact, the Dutch had discovered the tulip in Constantinople and taken it back home.

This morning it was extremely warm, very sunny, and yet there was a lovely, light breeze coming off the Bosphorus which was cooling, refreshing. Ismet had invited him to return in the spring, when, his host had said, the weather was truly superb, and he now decided to accept the invitation.

Yes, he would come back here, and perhaps bring the family; he knew they would enjoy it. Most especially Grace Rose who was so involved with history. There was much to interest her here. Certainly he had been more relaxed these past few weeks, and had acquired a feeling of genuine well-being; he also felt rejuvenated, as if years had fallen away. There was a youthfulness about him. His face was tanned, his hair golden, and there was a spring in his step.

Turkey was an interesting place, and it would become much more interesting soon, Edward believed. A new and more modern country was being born, according to Ahmet Hunam. Founded in the seventh century B.C., Constantinople had gone through all manner of changes in the past. For sixteen centuries it had been the imperial capital of the Byzantine empire and then of the Ottoman sultans. But now there was a new and important figure on the horizon, a man who would bring change, Ahmet had told him only last night at dinner. His name was Mustafa Kemal Ataturk, and he was a former general in the army who had led the Turks to victory and glory at Gallipoli, when the Allies had attacked the Dardanelle Straits in the Great War.

According to Ahmet, Ataturk was going to pull the country into the present. The young executive from Deravenels predicted that Ataturk would abolish the sultanate by next year, and introduce political and social reform. Ahmet seemed absolutely convinced that Ataturk would be elected president of what would be a republic, and Ismet tended to agree with the younger man.

The only thing that's permanent is change, Edward thought, remembering an old saying of his mother's, one she still uttered occasionally. And as he mounted the white marble steps and entered the cool entrance hall of the yali, it struck him that change was in the air now that things had settled down since the end of the war. New beginnings are obvious everywhere, he added under his breath, climbing the circular staircase to his suite.

There was no way he could know that there would be new beginnings in his own life. And changes . . . drastic changes which would affect them all, engulf them.

The room was quiet, serene, the only noise the faint whirring of the ceiling fan which created a welcome coolness on this hot day.

Edward was dozing on top of the bed, as usual enjoying a siesta after lunch in the garden with Ismet. He had grown accustomed to this afternoon break since arriving at the villa to stay with his Turkish partner and had decided it was a most civilized custom.

The white wooden shutters were closed against the heat and the sun, and only tiny slivers of daylight filtered in through the narrow spaces between the slats. They created golden strips of light in the air, and now he noticed dust motes rising up in them.

Sighing, bestirring himself, Edward came fully awake, and lay there staring at the ceiling, his eyes following the movement of the fan's blades. Then he turned on his side and closed his eyes, trying to recapture the strands of a dream he had just had . . . a dream about a blonde woman . . . a blonde woman stroking his brow, kissing his mouth . . .

Elizabeth? Or Jane? Or the White Russian woman he had met with Ismet and Ahmet at the Pera Palace Hotel? He was not sure. Perhaps it was all three of them rolled into one, to become a composite of all three.

His mind focused on Elizabeth, true beauty that she was. *His wife*. Her looks were incomparable; she was indeed a great beauty . . . the whole world knew that. But, God knows, she could be so difficult at times. Not lately, though, and as he thought of the tranquillity of these last twelve months he mentally crossed his fingers, hoping nothing would change or go wrong. She had become docile and quiet during her pregnancy last year, and they had both been thrilled when she had given birth to a son. He was their third son, and they named him George, although of late Edward was beginning to wonder why.

It was a Deravenel family tradition, of course, to use the same family names for sons and daughters over the generations. Most other families of their ilk followed the same tradition, since it was typical of the English aristocracy.

But George, whom this latest child had been named for, was more than a nuisance these days; wherever he went he dragged disaster in his wake.

Edward sighed under his breath when he contemplated his troublesome brother, and pushed his image away. He focused once again on his wife. They were going to Kent for the month of August, which they had done for several years now. The children loved being on the marshes and they were looking forward to it; so was he. The month at Aldington was a huge treat for him because he got to spend a great deal of time with his offspring.

There were seven of them now. Bess, Mary, Cecily, Young Edward, Richard, Anne and George. And there was Grace Rose also, who had promised to come over every day when she was staying with Vicky and Stephen at Stonehurst Farm.

She danced around in his head all of a sudden ... *Grace Rose*. A lovely young woman of twenty-one, who did everybody proud. She had reached her majority this year, and Vicky and Stephen had given her a supper dance at the Ritz Hotel in March. Elizabeth had been invited, since this was a formal family occasion, and Jane had simply slipped quietly away to Paris for a week, as always thoughtful and discreet. She never intruded.

Ah, Jane, his lovely Jane, so loyal, so constant, the perfect companion and friend. Sometimes he wondered how he would manage without her; she had become such an important part of his life. Elizabeth still captivated him sexually, though, as she had since the first day he met her. At forty-one years of age she was like a woman in her early thirties, not a line on her flawless face or an unsightly bulge on her body. She was svelte and youthful, careful about what she ate and drank.

He was now thirty-six, although he didn't look his age either. Nonetheless, it constantly bothered his wife that she was older than he was by five years. But he didn't care. To his way of thinking, age was merely a number and therefore meant nothing.

His thoughts turned to Natasha Troubetzkoy, the White Russian princess who worked as a hostess in the restaurant and bar of the Pera Palace Hotel. She was blonde, beautiful and aristocratic. But such a tragic figure.

She had fled St Petersburg in 1917, at the beginning of the Revolution, when the Romanov autocracy fell, and after the Bolsheviks had murdered her brother, Prince Igor Troubetzkoy. She was a cousin of the Tsar, as were her sister-in-law Princess Natalie Troubetzkoy and her niece Irina. Natasha had still not managed to trace them, but hoped to be reunited with these missing members of her family. Her plan, she had eventually told him, was to save enough money to move to Paris, where there was a White Russian community similar to the one in

Constantinople, but larger. The Russian network might be able to help her, she believed; she wanted to try at least, she had confided.

Ismet had introduced Edward, Will and Alfredo to Princess Natasha when they had first arrived in the city. He had taken them to the Pera Palace Hotel for dinner; after dinner they had gone to the bar where an orchestra played and hostesses were available to dance with the guests.

Will and Ned danced with the princess, and she had sat with them for a while sipping mint tea. And in the course of the evening she had told them about her missing family, her only relatives left alive, and her longing to find them. They were refugees, like she was, and she was absolutely convinced they were still alive, living *somewhere*. Finding them was the only thing she ever thought about, she had explained in perfect English.

Edward viewed her as a lovely but sorrowful woman who was enveloped in tragedy. Women like her tended to frighten him – he ran from them as fast as he could . . . catastrophe had forever haunted him from his youth. He wanted to keep it at bay; he must.

One evening, when they had visited the hotel again, just before Will and Alfredo had gone off to look at the marble quarries, Will had teased Ned about Natasha. But his words had fallen flat. Edward had shaken his head, explained that he wasn't interested in her sexually, and had added that neither was she, his instinct told him this. And Will had let the matter drop, knowing his best friend was speaking the truth.

However, Natasha and her plight had continued to trouble Edward and now he swung his legs off the bed, went over to the desk, and took out his chequebook. He wrote a cheque made out to Princess Natasha Troubetzkoy, slipped it in an envelope and addressed it. He would give it to her this evening; Ismet had told him over lunch that they would be dining at the Pera Palace Hotel this evening.

Edward closed the desk drawer and walked over to one of

the windows, opened the shutters. In the distance he could hear the plaintive voice of the muezzin summoning the faithful to prayer . . . it was a lonely, melancholy voice floating to him on the warm air, and it reminded him how different this world was and how far away he was from England.

The sun had gone down . . . it would soon be nightfall.

When Edward and Ismet walked into the bar of the Pera Palace later that evening, Edward spotted Princess Natasha at once. She was standing near the bar, sipping a mint tea, as she usually did, and she was talking to the manager, Abaz Gurcan.

When she saw them coming in she nodded in greeting, but remained standing with the bar manager, obviously not wishing to intrude.

'I would like to ask the princess to join us,' Edward murmured.

Ismet nodded his agreement. 'But of course. She enjoys our company, you know that.' He smiled, shook his head. 'Such an intelligent and educated woman, a cultured woman . . . and reduced to *this*. It hurts me, it hurts my heart, Edward, to see this *aristocrat* working as a dance hostess.'

'I know what you mean. On the other hand, she has managed to make a living,' Edward pointed out, raising his hand, beckoning to a waiter, ordering Krug rosé champagne.

'I think *ekes out* a living would be more accurate,' Ismet suggested, his dark brown eyes soulful in his pleasant, humorous face. He was in his late fifties, unmarried, and therefore without any encumbrances, but he did like the ladies. Edward knew he had a mistress, who never came out in public with him, and he loved to come here to dance with the Western women, mostly Russian emigrés.

Rising, Edward said, 'I shall go and ask her to sit with us, Ismet. Is that all right?'

'It will make her happy . . . because once she sits down she will be earning money.' He added, 'I always ask her to join me so that she can make some money.'

Edward walked across the room; he cut a dashing and dazzling figure in his white suit, immaculate white shirt and a blue tie. As he came to a standstill at the bar he said, 'Good evening, Princess Troubetzkoy . . . good evening, Mr Gurcan,' and inclined his head to them courteously.

They both responded, and Edward continued swiftly, barely pausing, 'Would you care to join us, Princess? I have ordered pink champagne, but you can have your mint tea, of course, if you wish.'

Her quick smile brought sudden animation to her somber face, and was instantly gone. She said, without the trace of an accent in a cultured English voice, 'Thank you so much, Mr Deravenel, I can think of nothing better than sharing a glass of champagne with you.' Excusing herself to the manager, she turned to Edward and said, 'Shall we join Mr Bozbeyli?'

'I would like to take a turn around the dance floor with you first, if you don't mind,' he responded.

Putting his hand under her elbow, he led her to the small dance floor at one end of the bar. They moved together in perfect harmony, following the music, not speaking, until Edward said, 'I have brought you a gift, and it *is* a gift, without any strings attached.'

She leaned back slightly and looked at him, her large smokey-grey eyes fastened on his face. She appeared puzzled, and said, after a moment, 'I'm afraid I am not really following you. What do you mean when you say you have brought me a gift?'

'I've written you a cheque. I want you to go to Paris, or wherever you think you should go, to find your family. I can't bear it that they are lost to you, that you have no one. There is nothing more important than family. I have always believed that.'

'A cheque?' She frowned, looked bemused, as she still gazed up at him. 'But I can't possibly take money from you, Mr Deravenel. I can't take anything from you. You see, I don't know you.'

'I know you don't. I'm just an acquaintance, I realize that. Also, I'm aware of your upbringing, your royal background. But I am going to give you the cheque, and you will take it – to please me. As I said, *it is a gift.* I want nothing from you, nothing at all . . .' He looked down at her and started to dance again, moving her around the floor. 'That's not true,' he went on. 'I do want to see a smile on your face, and I want a letter from you when you have found your sister-in-law and niece. When you have found them I shall come and meet them, wherever it is that you all are.'

'I don't know what to say,' she began and abruptly stopped, filled with bewilderment and uncertainty, startled by the generosity of this man.

'Come and sit here alone with me for a moment,' Edward suggested, and promptly led her off the floor to a small table in a corner. Once they were seated, he took the envelope from the inside pocket of his jacket and handed it to her without a word.

She stared down at the envelope in her hands for a long moment, and then reluctantly opened it, took out the cheque. She gasped quite audibly, and exclaimed in a low voice, 'But I can't take this, Mr Deravenel! It's far too much money. Oh, my goodness –' She put it back in the envelope and handed it to him.

He refused to take it, shook his head, glanced at her evening bag on the table. 'Put it in there, in your bag. Cash it tomorrow and make your plans.'

'But I can't take it. *Five thousand pounds*, Mr Deravenel. It is far too much.'

'Think of it like this . . . I haven't properly celebrated my luck since striking oil . . . this is *my* way of celebrating . . . helping *you* to find your family. So please indulge me, celebrate with me, and for me. Now, let us go and join Ismet, toast each other with a glass of pink champagne.'

Natasha put the cheque away, but still with reluctance; they stood up together, and as she turned, she said softly, 'Thank you. Thank you so very much, Mr Deravenel.' And he saw the tears glistening in her smokey eyes. She placed her hand on his arm and continued, 'Thank you is not enough . . . I'll never forget this extraordinary gesture, this enormous kindness you have shown me. Never as long as I live, and I will never forget you for doing this for me. You have been so very generous.'

Later, it pleased Edward when he saw her obvious happiness as the evening progressed. He was not at all accustomed to seeing her smiling and laughing, nor had he ever heard the excitement and sudden energy in her mellifluous voice. There was a sparkle about her that was startling, and gratifying especially to him. He had given her hope.

He had done one small good deed, had perhaps helped to turn a woman's life around, and just because he had given her the money to go and look for those she loved, who had been lost to her since 1917. Now she could go and seek her family whom she yearned for.

Her beauty was very evident tonight. She wore a bluish-grey chiffon dress that was fluid and floated around her gracefully as she danced with Ismet. With her blonde hair, smokey eyes, and refined features she was most arresting. Tall, slender and lissom, there was something special about her. Elegance, culture, breeding, those were the words that sprang to mind, yet there was much more to her than these things. Then it struck Ned most forcibly. She carried herself with an air of immense dignity, and she was regal in her bearing. And why wouldn't she be? She was a Romanov, a former member of the Imperial Royal Family of Russia. Cousin of one of the world's great autocrats, the late Tsar Nicholas, who had been murdered with his family in Ekaterinburg.

And here she was tonight, in Constantinople with them. A princess down on her luck, a victim of catastrophic events – the upheaval of her country and her life, the death of her brother and the mysterious disappearance of his wife and child. Her home gone, a way of life lost forever. And yet to his credit he had not run away from her in fright, because of her catastrophes. Instead he had done her a good turn.

All of a sudden Edward thought, if only everything were this simple, how easy life would be. My life in particular; but usually things are much more complicated.

He was soon to find out exactly how complicated his life truly was.

THIRTY-TWO

Kent

'I don't know whether you realize it, but George is drinking again, and rather a lot these days,' Elizabeth said from the doorway, looking across the room at Edward.

He was seated in a chair near the French windows in the library of their house in Aldington. He put down the book he was reading, took his glasses off and stared at her. 'Yes, I noticed that when I returned from Constantinople. But George has always been given to excesses, you know.' Edward shook his head, and his face hardened slightly. 'However, he does have a rather strong sense of his own self-preservation, don't you think?'

'I suppose he does,' Elizabeth agreed, walking into the room, sitting down opposite Edward. 'But what are you getting at? I don't quite understand you.'

'George overdoes things, and then he stops all of a sudden, pulls himself together. He . . . sort of pulls back, and starts being a good boy, behaving himself. It's as if he has a demon . . . telling him things.'

Elizabeth answered, 'On the contrary, Edward, it is *George* who is *telling* things these days.'

His interest immediately caught, Edward straightened in the

chair and gave his wife a swift glance through narrowed eyes. 'What *exactly* are you getting at?'

'He's gossiping. It was my friend Olivia Davenport who told me,' Elizabeth explained. 'She was at a dinner party the other night, and she said George was muttering something about you not being legitimate, and therefore you were not the rightful heir to Deravenels. That he was the rightful heir. Some such silly nonsense.'

Edward was completely taken aback, and he gaped at her, then spluttered, 'Nonsense it is!' Once again he was irritated with George. And then suddenly very angry. 'That's some old rubbish put about years ago by the Lancashire Grants! Scandal-mongering they were, making digs at my father, wanting to embarrass him, diminish him, making him look like a cuckold. George should know better.'

Edward sprang to his feet, walked across the room, his sudden anger turning into genuine fury. 'George is so stupid. And it is quite scandalous of him to impugn the reputation of a woman like Cecily Deravenel. *His own mother*, for God's sake! What can he be thinking of? If I could get my hands on him right now I'd give him a thrashing he would never forget.'

Edward's fury with his brother had taken complete hold of him, and he was beside himself. How could George make their mother out to be a faithless wife who bore another man's child?

Aware that Ned's temper had got the better of him, Elizabeth stood up, went over to him and took hold of his arm. 'Come and sit down, Ned. I do agree with you. He's being awfully malicious about his mother – your mother – and you have to make him stop.'

'*Obviously.*' Ned allowed himself to be led back to the sofa, where they sat down together.

His wife went on, 'He's trying to diminish *you*, in his usual treacherous way. But he's doing it in an extremely hurtful manner, as far as your mother is concerned. It's hard to think he'd stoop so low.'

Edward nodded, settled back on the sofa, and managed to calm himself. He did not want to spoil the day, or disturb the tranquillity that abounded in this house at the moment. Elizabeth was being sweet, caring, and loving, and there had been no cross words between them for a long time. He was relieved to live in a calm atmosphere, and was enjoying this summer holiday by the sea with the children and his mother.

He glanced at Elizabeth, and said in a low, urgent voice, 'We mustn't say anything to her. I don't want her upset. My mother mustn't know.'

'I understand. But it's quite awful when you think about it – she's always been so protective of George, standing up for him, defending him, all of his life. He's betrayed her as well as you.'

'That's what's so galling about this!' Ned declared.

Elizabeth started to say something then stopped abruptly.

'What were you about to tell me?' he asked, giving her a long, questioning look.

'Well . . . actually, other things were said that evening. Last week actually. By your brother. Olivia said he made some remarks to her husband. You know him, Ned. He's Roland Davenport, the famous barrister.'

'Oh yes, he's a brilliant chap. So, what did brother George say to Roland?'

'He said your children were bastards, too, like you, and that I was not your legal wife. Although Roland was startled and annoyed with George, he decided to laugh it off, since it didn't make sense. He told your brother he'd had too much to drink. He apparently added, and very sternly, that George had better watch himself, watch what he said about you, or he might find himself in serious trouble.'

Elizabeth paused, then finished in a rush of words, 'Seemingly George muttered something about Greenwich, or Norwich, perhaps both places, I'm not sure now. And there was also mention made of a man, Olivia said she couldn't remember the name. She and her husband thought George was really in his cups, behaving in the most dreadful way. Her husband said he was being a reprehensible cad. They also think he was talking rubbish, like many drunks so often do.'

Edward did not utter a word.

He sat absolutely still. He felt the blood draining out of him, and he was so stunned he was unable to think clearly. Shock seemed to freeze him, and he sat there without moving a muscle. For a split second he was floundering; then he told himself to think. *Think. Think.* Questions flew into his mind. What did George actually know? How could he know anything? Who could have told him something? It was so long ago . . .

'What's wrong, Ned?' Elizabeth exclaimed, her voice rising shrilly. She stared at him anxiously. 'You've gone as white as chalk. Are you ill?'

Knowing he must behave in the most normal way, Edward tried to pull himself together. And then a lifetime of self-control, absolute discipline, suddenly kicked in. He forced a smile, and, clearing his throat, he said with a short laugh, 'I don't know what happened, darling, I really don't. I felt a bit dizzy all of a sudden, sort of lightheaded. That's all it was, nothing serious, really.' Relaxing his taut body, smiling at her warmly, he added, 'It may have been anger. Anger with George. That he can speak at dinner parties, in public, about our mother in the way he has makes me livid.'

'Yes, of course, that's it!' She nodded and got up. 'I'm going to go and ask Cook to make tea for us. Would you like something to eat? Perhaps you're also hungry.'

He shook his head, gave her another relaxed smile. 'No, but the tea would be wonderful.'

As Elizabeth hurried out Edward sat back on the sofa and closed his eyes. He had no idea what he was going to do about this matter. However, he did know one thing for certain. His brother

George had gone too far and he had to be stopped. Immediately. He had become far too dangerous. He had to be removed.

The following morning Edward Deravenel went to London. It was not unusual for him to do this, since he went back and forth all the time when the family was staying at the house in Kent, rather than at Ravenscar. As he walked out to the car in the driveway with Elizabeth, he said, 'I must attend the meeting with Oliveri, regarding the marble quarries. I know you understand that. Hopefully, I'll get back in a couple of days. And certainly by Friday.'

'All right. Do try to be here for the weekend, Ned. The children are going to miss you for the next few days.'

The words had hardly left her mouth when Bess came running out into the driveway, followed by Mary and Young Edward.

'Oh, Papa, why are you going up to town?' Bess cried, taking hold of his arm. 'You promised you would stay all week.'

Smiling down at her, smoothing a hand over Young Edward's head, he said to them all, 'Business calls, unfortunately. But just think of this . . . I shall have a chance to visit Harrods. I'm sure I can find those things you have asked me for lately. Something for all of you. How does that sound, children?'

They all three hugged him, and he kissed Elizabeth on the cheek, and stepped into the Rolls. Just before he closed the door, she said softly, 'Do something about George when you're in town, won't you, Ned?'

'I certainly will,' he promised, meaning it.

The moment Edward arrived at Deravenels on the Strand, he sent for his two key executives.

'I have to do something about George,' Edward said, looking from Will Hasling to Alfredo Oliveri. 'He has been spreading vicious rumours, casting aspersions on my mother's character and her virtue, by saying I am illegitimate and not the true heir of my father. Therefore I'm not entitled to run Deravenels. He's talking too much, and he has to be stopped.'

Neither Will nor Alfredo appeared to be surprised by this statement, and Will said, 'I'd heard he was being vicious again. And yes, you must put a stop to it. He's unconscionable, Ned, I just hope the gossip hasn't come to your mother's ears. She would be devastated.'

'So do I. And actually, I think perhaps it hasn't. Elizabeth heard it the other day from Olivia Davenport, the wife of the well-known barrister, and they don't move in our circles. Apparently, George was at a dinner party and spouting this nonsense, but I understand the Davenports just laughed it off. Afterwards, Roland Davenport warned George, cautioned him to be careful what he said.'

'I've always said he's a dangerous drunk,' Alfredo murmured, shaking his head; a grim expression settled on his face. 'In fact, I think he's grown worse since Isabel's death. Too much time on his hands, that's the problem.'

Edward stared at Alfredo. 'But he does come in to the office every day, doesn't he? Because –'

'Oh, you'd have known if he didn't! Because I would have told you,' Will interjected. 'I keep my eye on him all the time. He comes in all right, but he doesn't do very much. He's a lazy bugger, if you ask me, and he's a wastrel in every sense of the word – wasting time, wasting money, wasting people.'

'How do we stop him talking about my mother?'

'Put the bloody fear of God into him, if you ask me. That's how!' Will exclaimed.

'That's easier said than done,' Alfredo remarked, looking directly at Will. 'He doesn't scare easily, and there's something totally dense about him. He doesn't seem to get it, doesn't seem to realize when he's doing wrong. He's very – *nonchalant* about his behaviour.'

Edward sat up straighter in the chair and threw a sharp look at Alfredo. 'It's funny you should say that. There have been times in the past when I've thought George wasn't all there, that he had a screw loose.'

'I keep telling you he's three bricks short of a full load,' Will pointed out, sounding impatient.

'But that just means not very bright. I am going beyond that. I'm beginning to wonder if he's . . . well, if he's actually mentally unbalanced.'

'You could send him away . . . put him in an insane asylum,' Alfredo suggested. 'A few weeks in a straitjacket would do him good, in my opinion.'

Edward had to laugh at this comment and Alfredo's dour expression. 'You're right there, but I am very serious about his mental state. He just seems to be, well, so careless about his behaviour, saying the things he does, acting like a lout, falling down drunk – so I've heard anyway.'

'It's an odd thing,' Will said slowly, in a reflective tone. 'It's as if he isn't aware of the damage he causes. He almost seems quite oblivious to everyone and just bumbles along, wreaking havoc.'

'That's what I'm getting at,' Edward said, nodding in agreement. 'Now tell me, how *do* we shut him up?'

'I don't know that we can . . . how on earth can we muzzle him?' Alfredo asked Ned, then added, 'There's only one solution, you know. He has to be put away, in a mental hospital; or he has to be *sent* away. He can't remain in London, it'll only get worse, because he's eaten up with jealousy and envy of you, and you know only too well that he has betrayed you so many times in the past.'

Edward nodded, but made no comment.

'Think of all the bad things he's done to you over the years,' Will said. 'He sided with Neville Watkins, got involved in the intrigue with Louis Charpentier. Then he ran off with Isabel Watkins without so much as a by your leave. He was hand in glove with Neville for years, conspiring, plotting, and only came crawling back to you when he saw Neville was about to sacrifice him, and move on. All in all, he's not shown much loyalty to you . . . his own brother and his employer. He *is* dangerous, Ned, you were absolutely right when you said that.'

'I would rather deal with a clever enemy than an enemy who's a fool. That spells trouble,' Alfredo announced. 'George is big trouble, and he'll never change. That is the nature of the beast.'

'If we sent him away, exiled him, so to speak, where would we send him?' Will asked, his eyes on Edward. 'And anyway, how do we know he'll go?'

'Oh, he'll go all right, when I've finished with him!' Edward exclaimed. 'As to where he'd go, I don't know. The three of us should analyse that.'

'He would have to be sent out of the country,' Alfredo answered in a firm voice. 'You can't just send him to the provinces. He must be sent out of England.'

'What do you have in mind?' Will asked.

'In order to make sure he went in a peaceful way, he would have to be made to think he was getting a promotion,' Alfredo volunteered. 'You know what I mean . . .' "We need you to go and run the sugar mills in Cuba, George, nobody can bring that company back up to scratch except you." That kind of thing. We need to give him a bag of toffees when we send him away, and lots of praise. Otherwise, he'll put up a fight, he just won't go.'

'Do you *really* mean Cuba?' Edward asked, looking puzzled.

Alfredo grimaced. 'Not especially. I'd like to see him closer to home and on hand, so we can make quick checks on him anytime we wish. He could go to the Paris office, couldn't he?'

287

Alfredo instantly shook his head. 'I can see by your face that that's not feasible.'

'Nowhere's feasible really, because he's useless,' Edward replied. 'I believe we should come up with a reason to send him . . . *somewhere*, though. Anywhere, actually, that's *my* thought. I just can't think of any other way to get rid of him.'

'There's always murder,' Alfredo Oliveri said with a somewhat ghoulish smile.

Staring at Alfredo askance, Edward exclaimed, 'I can't kill my brother!'

'What if someone else did it for you?'

'Do you have some clever idea?' Will asked, his eyes on Oliveri.

'I haven't given it much thought,' was Alfredo's response. But, in fact, he had.

Thirty-Three

Kent

E dward was finding it hard to sleep. He tossed and turned for hours, and then finally got up, put on his dressing gown and slippers and went downstairs.

The house was still; everyone was asleep. He turned on a small lamp in the library and looked at the carriage clock on the mantelpiece. It was two thirty already.

Opening the French doors, he stepped out onto the terrace, and stood for a moment staring up at the sky. It was a black velvet night, with a handful of stars thrown up onto the black velvet. They glittered like diamond chips. The moon was a silver sliver, a half moon that looked as if it had been carefully hung there by one of those Hollywood chaps, it was so perfectly in place.

The air was mild, warm even, and he caught a faint whiff of the sea; salt was coming up off the Romney Marsh. He knew if he walked down the long garden path he would come to the strip of land where the children loved to play; from that vantage point he would see the Dungeness lighthouse, its beams of light making giant silver shafts across the sea. He loved it on the marsh, but he was not in the mood to go there tonight; in fact he was not tempted at all.

He was troubled, burdened down, and his mind kept turning to Natasha Troubetzkoy and *her* terrible plight. Then, she had had no one. He had given her hope by making a gift of money to her, so that she could go and search for her relatives. But she might not find them. They might not even be alive.

In 1917 her life had changed because of the Revolution in her country. Her life had been turned upside down. Her home, all of her possessions, her clothes, her jewels, and her money, had disappeared, had vanished just like that in the blink of an eye. Because she had had to run away to save herself. She had fled, become a homeless refugee seeking shelter and a way to earn a living.

She had said to him one evening in Constantinople, 'My world became topsy turvy. My life as I knew it was savagely taken away from me by the Bolsheviks. I can never get it back, nothing will ever be the same.'

And nothing will ever be the same for me, Edward thought, sitting down on the garden seat, still staring at the dark sky, thinking of the past . . . his past. And of Elinor Burton.

The beautiful, bewitching Ellie. Once his lover. Oh, God, what a stupid fool he had been all those years ago. Why had he made that committment to her? Now his life could so easily be ruined, just as Natasha's had been ruined by a different kind of catastrophe.

That was what it was . . . *catastrophe*. It was hanging over his head like a blade ready to drop. His marriage, his children, his business, all those things he held dear were in jeopardy. *It was his own fault. There was no one else to blame but himself.* Well, there was George, babbling all over the place and being treacherous. His brother should have been taken in hand years ago; that was his fault, too. He had been too lenient, too forgiving.

After George had run off with Isabel, both of them far too young to marry, his mother had begged him to be kind to George, to forgive him. She had also pleaded with him to give George a job at Deravenels when he had finally fallen foul of Neville's plottings.

And, fool that he was, he had done as she asked. He had made many mistakes with George. And with Ellie. He should not have fallen for that calm beauty of hers, that Madonna-like face, become entrapped in her web. But he had and now he would pay for that indulgence with his family and his career. He would lose everything.

The first thing he must do was deal with George. Swiftly, efficiently. Except that brother George was not in England. He was off to France, spending a week with their sister Meg. Richard had told him this yesterday afternoon. When Richard had telephoned Meg to ask if he and Anne could come and stay for a few days in September, she had mentioned that George was currently staying there. After agreeing to Richard's request, and in a warm friendly way, their sister had explained that George was presently at the château, and was 'Having a rest, poor darling.' That was the way she apparently put it to Richard.

Edward had told Richard about George spreading gossip about their mother, his legitimacy and that of his children. His Little Fish had been outraged and had agreed that George should be sent away. But Richard's thought was to pack him off to America.

Was that the best place to exile him? Edward was not sure. Perhaps it was too far away; Oliveri wouldn't like the idea of the States, Edward was positive of that. Will and Alfredo wanted George closer, so that they could check up on him easily. Amos Finnister agreed with them.

Edward had consulted with Finnister later in the afternoon, and then the two of them had gone to White's for dinner. It was quiet in his club in the summer; so many members were on holiday with their families.

Amos had had the best idea, last night over supper. He had suggested that George might be eager to go to the vineyards in France, since he liked wine and was a connoisseur, prided himself on his knowledge of red and white wines and their vintages.

'But he'd be drunk half the time,' Edward had swiftly pointed out.

'Perhaps,' Amos had answered cautiously. 'Then again, perhaps not, Mr Edward. It's a perfect fit, in my opinion. You wouldn't have to persuade him. He'd go of his own free will, and rather speedily I should've thought.'

Amos had sat back in his chair, his eyes trained on Edward very steadily.

Edward stared back. He was the first to blink and look away. And it was as if he had read Amos's mind. They understood each other very well.

Elizabeth knew there was something terribly wrong. Edward was behaving so strangely that she spent hours worrying about him, worrying about his health, his peace of mind, and what was troubling him.

He had gone up to London on Tuesday, using the Turkish marble quarry contracts as an excuse; part of her believed him. He was not a liar, she had learned that a long time ago, but sometimes he arranged things in order to accommodate his private life. However, in this instance, she was absolutely certain he was not going to town to see Jane Shaw or any other woman, for that matter. She was truly convinced he was going to London because of the situation with George, who never learned his lesson; he was treacherous and bore Ned a great deal of ill will.

Sighing, she left her bedroom, went downstairs and crossed the main hall of the house. After taking a straw sun hat out of the hall cupboard, and putting it on, she walked rapidly down the garden path before any of the children saw her. She had the need to be alone. To think.

It was glorious August weather. The sky was a perfect cerulean blue filled with cotton-white clouds puffed up and hardly moving in the stillness of the balmy summer air. There was no breeze this morning yet the salt of the sea was pungent, seemed to hang over everything. She glanced about, pleased with her gardens; they were flower-filled and glorious, the brilliant hues of pinks and reds, yellows and oranges, and varying shades of blue and purple mingling together riotously. She loved it here in Kent; the weather was so much warmer than it was at Ravenscar, which was cold even in the summer months.

Elizabeth enjoyed being near the Romney Marsh. There was something about it that captivated her . . . what that was she wasn't quite sure, could never put her finger on it. Nonetheless, this ancient low-lying marshland held her under its spell.

Her favourite spot was a gazebo which Edward had had built several years ago, and now she hurried inside, sat down in one of the comfortable wicker chairs, and stared out towards the Dungeness lighthouse. At night they often sat here watching the great arcs of light play across the English Channel, sipping a glass of champagne or a lemonade depending on their mood. Now she gazed absently at the sea, her mind still focused on Edward.

Their marriage was better than it had been for a long time; she was trying so hard not to do or say the wrong thing. Also, Ned seemed more at peace with himself, calm, tranquil, and they were at ease with each other in a way they hadn't been since the early days.

And now *this* . . . this situation with George. It had upset Ned much more than she had anticipated it would. He was restless, morose, moody, preoccupied and at times looked worried out of his mind. He would not tell her anything, and this troubled her. Usually he confided, got things off his chest, said what he had to say, used her as a sounding board, and then moved on. She couldn't imagine why he was being so uncommunicative, keeping things to himself.

She knew he was not sleeping well. In all of their homes they had separate bedrooms and those bedrooms always adjoined each other. Often he slept in her bed with her wherever they were; he certainly needed her to be close, wanted to walk in on her whenever he wished, and for whatever reason . . . to talk, to make love, usually the latter. And so because of their close proximity at night, she knew he got up in the early hours, went downstairs and outside, to sit on the terrace, or walk around. This concerned her; it was obvious he could not sleep. It was beginning to show. He had dark rings under his eyes, and he looked drawn; preoccupied all the time, he seemed remote. He had come back from Turkey in radiant health, full of vigour and enthusiasm. All of a sudden he appeared to be carrying mighty burdens on his shoulders.

Ned had returned from London yesterday afternoon, keeping his promise to be back by Friday no matter what. He had been loving with the children, had brought them small presents from Harrods, and he had appeared relaxed at dinner. Elizabeth was aware that he was a consummate actor, and especially when he had to hide his true feelings. And he had been giving a wonderful performance last evening – because his mother was present.

She knew he was still in bed sleeping. He would get up in time for lunch with her and the children, because he always did that; he enjoyed their company. She would say nothing to him about his problem, and this new nocturnal habit of wandering around the garden, or walking down towards the lighthouse and the marshland. Tonight his mother was going to dinner with Vicky, Stephen and Grace Rose at Stonehurst Farm. She and Ned would have a quiet supper alone, just the two of them, and she was determined to make him tell her what was driving him to distraction.

An Englishman's word was his bond. An Englishman's handshake sealed a deal. An Englishman did not lie, cheat, or double deal. Those were a gentleman's code of honour. They were also the rules of the City, the financial world, and the world of business. Everyone lived by those rules; the rules were instinctual: Englishmen had been born with those rules inherent in their genes. At least Edward Deravenel believed that to be so.

He was proud of his record in business. He had not put a foot wrong, never in the seventeen years he had been running Deravenels. He was a champion to his colleagues, those he worked with at Deravenels, and to other businessmen in the City. He was proud of his accomplishments and his fine reputation; it pleased him that other successful men held him in such high regard. His business was his life, his be and end all.

If he lost that world of finance and business, of wheeling and dealing, and the camaraderie of his colleagues, he would be heartbroken. And now there was a possibility that he might indeed lose it. He could lose everything, in fact. His inheritance and his family were in jeopardy. All because of George and his idiotic behaviour, his desire to destroy *him*.

Yesterday, he had driven down to Kent with Will Hasling, who had a country house near Waverley Court, his house, and Will had exploded at one moment in the Rolls, when they were in the middle of a discussion about George. Will had long ago lost patience with his brother, just as he had himself.

Now Edward stood at one end of the dining room at Waverley Court, near the sideboard. He poured himself a glass of white wine, and then walked outside, strolled down to the gazebo. It was a lovely evening, the sky tinged with the red and pink of a setting sun along the rim of the horizon. Red sky at night, shepherd's delight, red sky at morning, shepherd's warning, he muttered to himself. An old saying of his mother's. He backed away from thoughts of her. She was George's defender, protector, and tonight he did not wish to dwell on this fact. Not at all.

He was tired, and worn out from worry. For once in his life he did not want to face reality. Yet he knew he must. Trouble was staring him in the face.

Inside the gazebo, Edward put down the glass of wine, took a box of Swan Vestas out of his pocket and struck a match, lit the candle in the hurricane lamp.

Once settled in the chair, he let himself drift, random thoughts trickling through his head. After a moment, he closed his eyes, again pushing reality away . . .

'Ned, Ned, it's me . . .'

Vaguely, he heard a voice. He roused himself, and saw his wife standing on the steps of the gazebo, staring at him.

He pushed himself up in the chair, blinking in the dim light, and as he pulled himself back into the present he realized that she looked unusually beautiful tonight, ethereal, otherworldly, in a floating white muslin dress.

'I'm afraid I fell asleep,' he murmured, 'I'm so sorry . . . I'd better come in for supper, I suppose. Just us, is it?'

'Yes, and no you can't come in, not yet.' Elizabeth stepped into the gazebo, continued, 'Supper's not ready.' Moving forward, coming closer to him, he noticed that her face was extremely pale, her silvery-blue eyes filled with concern. He knew she was going to tackle him, ask what was amiss. He held himself still, knowing he could no longer hide his problems. But he must stay calm.

When she came to a stop she sat down in the chair at the other side of the table, reached out, touched his arm. 'I know full well you're very upset, truly perturbed, Ned, so please don't deny it, I also know you can't sleep . . . and that you are preoccupied. Please tell me what this is about. Is it George? I feel that it is. Because of the things he's saying about your mother. Isn't that it?'

Edward did not answer her.

After a moment, she exclaimed, 'Listen to me! He's always been jealous of you, everyone knows that, and if he can make trouble for you he will. He's an intriguer, a schemer, full of treachery. Actually, I firmly believe he is . . . wicked. *Bad*, Ned. Really bad.'

Taking a deep breath, using his discipline to keep his voice steady, his demeanour neutral, Edward said, 'There's something I must tell you, Elizabeth. It's something you have a right to know.'

'You sound so serious, so *grave*,' she replied in a low voice, unexpectedly filling with fear, and not sure why. 'Is there something else wrong?'

'I am facing catastrophe,' he announced in his mellifluous voice, managing to keep it steady. But he was despairing inside, his nerves taut, and he suddenly wondered if he actually could tell her, if he dare . . .

'Oh, Ned, it can't be all *that* bad,' Elizabeth was saying, propelling him out of his inner thoughts back to the awful reality of this moment.

He still did not speak. He could not. Then at long last he murmured, 'It's worse.'

'I don't know what you mean. Please tell me what's wrong, Ned.'

Edward took a deep breath and swivelled slightly in the chair, so that he sat facing her. He asked, 'Do you remember how I behaved when we met? That I told you I didn't want to get married? That I was too young?'

'Yes, I do, and I became self-conscious about my age. I thought you didn't want to marry me because I was five years older than you.'

'That wasn't the reason. Age differences have never worried me. They mean nothing.'

'I'm afraid I'm still not following you.' Her puzzlement was evident. 'What are you getting at?'

'I couldn't marry you.'

She frowned, shaking her head. 'I don't understand.'

'I couldn't marry you, because I wasn't free. I was already married.'

Elizabeth sat gaping at him, utterly astounded, her eyes wide and staring. She shook her head in a denying way. 'No, no, that can't be! It can't be. Tell me it's not true, Ned, *please*,' she pleaded, tears in her voice.

'I can't tell you that. It *is* true.'

Her eyes held his, and she whispered in a raspy voice, 'You committed bigamy, is that what you're saying?'

'Yes. It happened so long ago, I'd pushed it out of my mind . . . hadn't thought of it in years . . .' His voice petered out.

'Where is she now?' Elizabeth asked in a voice he could hardly hear.

'She's dead.'

'When did she die?'

'A year after you and I were married. She and I had separated. We weren't together anymore. It was amicable. She had been sick and suddenly wanted to go and live in . . . Norwich. Alone.'

'Who was she?'

'Elinor Burton.'

Elizabeth shook her head; she did not know the woman, and she found herself incapable of speech anyway. She was reeling from his words. He was correct. It *was* a catastrophe.

'She was a widow,' he volunteered. 'The widow of Sir Ellis Nutting. Her father was Lord Kincannon.'

Elizabeth swallowed hard, blinking back her tears. 'Who knows about this?'

He shook his head helplessly. 'I thought no one did. Until you told me the other day about George's conversation with Roland Davenport.'

Elizabeth was shaking and she was unable to keep her voice steady, could barely ask the next question. 'Who married you?' she finally managed to say.

'A priest. In Greenwich. But he would never speak.'

'Then how does George know?' she asked, her voice quavering, tears filling her eyes, trickling down her face unchecked.

'I don't think he does know, at least not the *facts*. Maybe he's heard some sort of rumours.'

'He must know *something*,' she snapped, her voice unexpectedly hardening.

'Perhaps,' he agreed quietly. 'When Elinor died I remember worrying at the time that she might have confessed to her priest, wanting to make atonement for her sins, wanting forgiveness on her deathbed.'

'*George knows!* That's all that concerns *me*.' Elizabeth stared at him coldly, then brushed the tears away from her face with her fingertips.

At a loss for words, Edward was silent. He simply sat there, staring back at her, his face as white as bleached bone, his blue eyes filled with intense distress.

Suddenly, unexpectedly, she sprang up out of the chair, and cried in a furious voice, 'How *could* you? *How could you marry me*? When you were already married? Our marriage is not legal, and you've always known it. Our children are illegitimate. Seven of them. Your heirs are not your heirs. GEORGE IS YOUR HEIR.' Elizabeth swung around, headed for the steps, seemed about to rush out of the gazebo, and then, changing her mind, she swivelled to face him.

He had also jumped up and stepped towards her, saying, 'Elizabeth, please listen to me –' He broke off when he saw the horror on her face.

She stretched out her arms, held them in front of her, her palms towards him, as if she were pushing him away before he even got close to her.

He stopped dead in his tracks. His heart sank.

She shouted in a very loud, clear voice, 'Oh, God! Oh God! What are we going to do? This is disastrous. Our lives are in ruins. *You* are ruined in business. I am ruined and our children, our innocent children, they are all ruined. And all because of you, Edward Deravenel. You lied to me!'

'I did not lie. I never said anything –'

'You lied by omission!' Her face was twisted with grief and rage, and she had turned as white as he was. 'No wonder your brother is calling you names, licking his chops. He's got you – by the balls!' she rasped, filled with the deepest hatred for him.

'I think I have a solution,' Edward began, 'the only solution–' He stopped speaking. She had run down the steps and out of the gazebo, fleeing. He ran after her, fell over a large stone protruding from the rockery; he righted himself, and ran on, crossing the gardens. She was nowhere in sight; he sped up to the house, ran through the rooms, seeking her, calling her name.

She was not there. Ignoring Faxton, the butler, who was

gaping at him, he went back outside, headed in the direction of the marsh which had a view of the Dungeness lighthouse. He called her name, again and again. There was no response. She had vanished.

Edward covered most of the marsh, thankful that it was only eight o'clock and still light. But he knew dusk would start to descend soon, and he was anxious, concerned. Where was Elizabeth?

It suddenly struck him that she may have gone to the strip of land which he had had cleared years ago, and where the children went to play most of the time.

Within minutes he arrived at the area, and he immediately spotted her, sitting on the wooden seat, huddled over. An enormous sense of relief swept through him, and he began to run faster.

She did not look up when he came to a standstill next to her. Curled in a corner of the seat, her legs under her, she was sobbing as if her heart would break. It was broken, he knew that. But he could mend it. He had to do so for all of their sakes, especially his children.

Edward reached out, put a hand on her shoulder. She shrugged it off, mumbled, 'Get away from me. Don't touch me. You'll never touch me again. Just go away. Leave me.'

He pulled away from her, but only slightly. He said softly, 'I'm sorry, Elizabeth, sorry for causing you this pain. It was a stupid thing to do. I just . . . she had become a memory by the time I met you, and I wanted you so much. I loved you.'

'Lusted after me, don't you mean?' she hissed.

'Yes, that's true, I *did* have a raging desire for you physically, more than for any other woman. Believe me, it's true.

And I had to have you . . . I just had to, Elizabeth. And you were the virtuous widow. You wanted marriage, so I married you.'

'And gave me seven children. All bastards.'

'Don't! Don't say that. I can fix it, I can make everything right.'

Something in her broke; she stood up, looked directly at him. Her eyes were full of hatred for him. Before he could move, she rushed at him, began to beat him on his chest with her clenched fists, beating him harder and harder, screaming, 'You have ruined my life, and the lives of our children. I loathe you for what you've done to all of us! I'll never forgive you, Edward Deravenel. *Never.*'

He managed to grab her hands, and held her by her wrists, looking into her face. 'I've been wrong. I'm so very sorry. I can make everything all right, if only you'll listen.'

'Why should I listen to *you!*' she exclaimed, but her energy was sagging slightly; also, something inside her told her to listen to him. She had to, there was no choice. And then she began to cry, the tears rolling down her face. Immediately he pulled her into his arms, wrapping them around her, holding her close. She wept and wept; he consoled her, stroked her hair, kissed her face and her eyelids. Slowly he calmed her; after a while he led her back to the garden seat.

Sitting down next to her, he brought an arm around her shoulders, and said gently, 'I know I've hurt you, and I am so sorry. But if you'll listen, I will tell you what I can do to solve our problem.'

She nodded, not trusting herself to say anything.

'I must marry you, and immediately. Legitimize our union. That is imperative.'

'How can we do that? Someone will find out.'

'They won't.'

'But we'll have to go to a church or a registry office. How

can we, just like that? It's not possible. You're so well known.'

'That's quite true, you're right. However, I married you in secret once, and I must marry you in secret again.'

'Where?'

'In the chapel at Ravenscar.'

'When?'

'As soon as possible. We'll go up there tomorrow on the train, get married at once. It's a perfect time. My mother and the children are here. Once we arrive, I'll see Father O'Connor in the village. He'll marry us, I've no doubt about that.'

'But he'll think it strange, and he'll talk. You know what village priests are like . . . like old women, gossips.'

'No, no, not Father Michael. He's always been devoted to the Deravenels. He is well looked after at Ravenscar, I can assure you of that, and he's been our family priest for over thirty years, ever since he came over from Ireland to take his uncle's place with us. You must believe me, he's extremely trustworthy. And as silent as the grave.'

'But won't he think it's peculiar? Marrying us again, when he believes we are in fact married?'

'I shall tell him that we want to renew our vows, that it's a romantic thing . . . that we are planning another child, and that our stay at Ravenscar is our second honeymoon.'

Drawing away from him, she laughed in his face.

He ignored this sudden spat of anger, and said, 'It's the only solution, believe me. I've wracked my brains. We shall be married in the chapel, and only the three of us shall know. Once we are married, George can say anything he likes. You will be my legal wife.'

She said not one word, made no sound.

They sat there for a long time, until dusk began to fall. And then, when the sky turned colour, he took hold of her hand and pulled her to her feet. Together they walked up to the house in total silence.

She had not given him an answer, but Edward was certain she would do as he suggested. What choice did she have? There was no other way to put things right.

Thirty-Four

Ravenscar

It was a cool evening, even though it was August, but then it was normal weather for the northern coastline. A full moon rose high above Ravenscar, casting its silver glow across the ancient stone house, the trees and the path that led up to the chapel. This stood at the corner of a copse of tall trees, a little way from the main house, and it was just as ancient, had been built at the same time.

Edward caught hold of Elizabeth's hand, guided her into the chapel. It was here that he, his brothers and sisters had been christened, and where the memorial service for his father and brother Edmund had been held . . . so long ago now, seventeen years ago. How time moves along so quickly, he thought. Glancing around, he remembered how much Edmund had loved this little chapel built of pale Yorkshire stone; it had stained glass windows, carved-oak pews, and a beautiful altar.

Father Michael O'Connor, the family priest, was waiting for them, and he hurried forward as they walked down the main aisle.

He was a cheery, convivial man, and there was a warm smile on his face as he greeted them enthusiastically. He said to

Elizabeth, 'It's a lovely thing you're doing tonight, Mrs Deravenel, a lovely thing indeed.'

She smiled back, said in a low voice, 'I thought it would be rather nice to renew our vows, Father. Thank you so much for coming to the chapel at this hour.'

'It's not a problem, no, no, not at all. I am happy to do it, to perform the ceremony,' the priest answered. He drew them to the front of the church and the altar.

They stood before him, and Father O'Connor, in the light of many candles, spoke the marriage vows, and they repeated those vows, and he pronounced them man and wife. 'For a second time,' he added in his lilting Irish voice, when it was done. After blessing them he sent them on their way, watching them from the steps of the chapel.

Edward took Elizabeth down through the hanging gardens to the ruined stronghold, and for a few minutes they stood together in silence, gazing out across the North Sea. It glittered like chainmail in the moonlight, and they both felt a sense of peacefulness here in this ancient spot. They did not speak for along time, simply stood there thinking their own thoughts; both were relieved that they had been married so easily, so swiftly.

Eventually, Edward murmured, 'Now we are truly *legally* married. You are my one true wife, I am your one true husband. From now unto eternity. And our children are our children.'

For the longest moment she remained silent, unable to utter a word. She was still pushing down the anger and resentment which had lingered for days after the dreadful scene at the house in Kent. It was a scene she would never forget. Later, he had tried to cement their relationship again, by trying to make love with her that ghastly Saturday night. But she had declined, had not allowed him into her bed. To give him credit, he had under-stood, and had behaved like the gentleman he was. He had simply gone away, left her alone in her room.

A small sigh escaped her lips, and at last she admitted that he had won. He had won because she had no alternative. She had no choice but to marry him. By doing so she had saved the family; she had saved Ned from the catastrophe he had always dreaded.

If she was honest part of her was glad they were still together, that this marriage had taken place. She did love him; there were few men like him. Apart from his looks and his athletic body, which he was so proud of, and his enormous sexuality, he was also a very kind man. He was generous to a fault, and an extraordinary father. Unfortunately, there was Jane Shaw somewhere in the background of his life; on the other hand, the woman did not create any problems.

And now she took a deep breath, leaned against him. Conscious of this sudden relaxation on her part, he tilted her face, kissed her on the cheek.

She knew he would not make another move, not after last Saturday night, after her rejection of him, and so she put her arms around him, gazed up into his handsome face.

Fully understanding that she had now put their problems away, he bent his head and kissed her on the mouth. She responded with her usual ardour, pressed her body against his, and they stood entwined for a long time, kissing each other with a soaring passion.

After several moments, Edward drew away. 'It will be all right.'

'Do you promise me?'

'I do promise you.'

It was Elizabeth's turn to stand back, and as she looked deeply up into his eyes she shivered with desire. He was such a beautiful man. Tonight his eyes were a very deep blue, almost navy, and full of the desire she herself was feeling.

He said softly, 'Let's go in, let's go to bed.'

She nodded. They moved out of the stronghold, and suddenly she took hold of his arm, and said, 'Ned, there *is* George. What are you going to do about him? He's a danger to us, you know that.'

'I do. And I'll handle the situation, you mustn't worry. It will be dealt with. He will be dealt with.'

'Even though we're now properly married, you've got to stop him talking about you and the children. About us.'

'I will.'

'When?'

'I'll deal with George the moment we get back to London. Now let's go to bed. It's your wedding night, Mrs Deravenel, and we're starting our lives together all over again.'

The house was silent.

Cook had retired long ago, and when they had left earlier for the chapel Edward had told Jessup they were going for a walk and would be back in half an hour.

Now, as they crossed the entrance hall, the butler appeared from his pantry and inclined his head. 'Do you need anything, Mrs Deravenel?' He glanced at Edward. 'Do you, sir?'

'No, but thank you anyway, Jessup. You can lock up. Goodnight.'

'Goodnight, sir, and goodnight to you, Mrs Deravenel.'

'Goodnight, Jessup.'

Once they were in her bedroom, Edward turned her to him, touched her cheek gently with one finger. 'Thank you, Elizabeth, thank you for helping to put things . . . in order.' There was a short pause, and he smiled. 'Can I share your bed tonight?'

'Yes.' There was a moment's hesitation, before she added, in a low voice, 'You know very well you've won, Ned.'

'I know that you put aside our problems finally, when you relaxed down in the stronghold. But I'm not an arrogant man, and you above anyone must know that by now. Kissing me passionately, holding me close to you doesn't necessarily mean you will allow me to make love to you. Or sleep in this bed with you tonight. Which is what I actually meant.'

'You can share my bed,' she answered, her voice lighter, and with sudden nonchalance she walked across the room. She took off her pale-blue chiffon frock, stepped out of her shoes, and slowly removed all of her underclothes. Then she reached for the white satin robe already laid out on a chair.

He watched her avidly, rapidly growing hard, hot with desire for her as she disrobed. He turned on his heels, went into his own room, and came back swiftly, clad in a navy-blue silk dressing gown.

Elizabeth was standing at the window looking out at the inky sea and the dark sky littered with a mere scattering of stars tonight. He went and stood behind her, put his arms around her, nuzzled the back of her neck. She twisted around in his arms, turned to face him, and murmured, 'I capitulated because I had no choice, Ned.'

He made no response. Catching hold of her hand he led her to the bed, where they lay down together, facing each other. After a little while, he said, 'Nonetheless, I think we should consummate our union, don't you? That way we really will be man and wife.' His irresistible smile flashed across his mouth; his eyes were very blue.

Looking into his face, smiling at him, she untied the belt of his dressing gown, then opened her own robe, moved closer to him, reaching for him.

He bent over her, kissed her deeply, stroked her breasts, brought his mouth to one of her nipples. The other hand slid down her thighs, to rest between her legs. After a moment or two, she sighed a long, rapturous sigh, let her hand enfold his erection. Within seconds, he pushed himself up on one elbow, stared down at her very intently. 'But you also capitulated for this . . . for me, for us, for this marvellous sex we have together, and which we have shared for fourteen years. I know I can't do without you . . . for this. And admit it, you can't do without me, for *this* either.'

'No, I can't.' Her eyes spilled her desire. 'It's true.'

He fell quiet, said nothing more, began to stroke her again, touching her everywhere, thinking how lovely she was. And she thought of his enormous potency and masculinity. And eventually they were as they had always been with each other.

'Ah yes,' he breathed softly, as he entered her, drawn by the heat of her body, and her raging desire for him. 'Oh, yes, Elizabeth,' he moaned. 'My wife . . .'

He moved against her and she responded instantly, her body arching up to his. They clung together, moved together, as always in perfect harmony until they came together as one. He lay on top of her and did not move. Nor did she. And they stayed like that for a long time.

He knew at this moment that he would never leave her, and asked himself why he had even contemplated divorce. The mere idea of it was ridiculous. She held him in her sexual thrall. And in her own special way she *did* make him happy.

As if reading his thoughts, she asked a moment later, 'Do I make you happy, Ned?'

His answer was to start kissing her again, and then he lifted his head and looked down to her. 'Ecstatic, that's how I feel when we're together like this. And so are you, aren't you?'

'I am Ned, I am,' she answered, and she meant it.

He enfolded her, brought her close, and they slept in each other's arms all night.

THIRTY-FIVE

London

'I have a strong feeling that Fate is playing right into our hands,' Will Hasling said, walking into Edward's office which adjoined his own and gave them easy access to each other.

Edward looked up swiftly, his expression quickening. 'In what way?'

'I have just received a long letter from Vincent Martell, and seemingly he's ready to retire, wants to do so, in fact. He has volunteered to work for us as a consultant, but he no longer wants to run the Mâcon vineyards anymore.'

'That's a surprise, I always thought he would die in the vineyards. After all, he's worked in them for most of his life.'

'Let's not forget he's over sixty. I have a feeling he's tired, Ned.'

Edward looked thoughtful for a moment, then asked, 'Did he recommend anybody to take his place?'

'Yes, he did. Marcel Arnaud, who's been at the vineyards for about ten years or so. I think we should take Vincent's advice, and use him as a consultant. But I do see an opportunity here, and one we should take advantage of immediately.'

'*George*. You want me to send George to Mâcon, to get him out of my hair, and also because in Burgundy it doesn't matter what claptrap he utters about us because nobody actually cares. Nor do they understand.'

'That's right.'

'What makes you think he'll go?' Edward asked. His expression was sceptical for a moment, and then he laughed quietly. 'Why would he object? He speaks quite good French, he won't have a lot to do, since he knows nothing about wine-growing and making. It'll be an easy, cushy life, and with Vincent retiring we should not have any problems, such as clashes, rows. In fact I think he'll get on quite well with Marcel. And there is the added attraction of sister Meg, not too far away in Dijon. You know she's always adored him.'

'Exactly what I thought. It also occurred to me that it would be a good idea for me to take him down to Burgundy, show him around, show him the château. The last time I was there it looked beautiful, in perfect condition. George could live there and be comfortable. No, I can't think of a reason why he wouldn't jump at the chance,' Will finished.

'He might object, just to be contrary.'

'That's a point,' Will muttered. 'Anyway, do you agree? Agree that it's an opportunity not to be missed?'

'I certainly do! Is he in today?'

'I believe so.'

'Then I'll take him to lunch at the Savoy. I'd like you to join us. After all, you oversee the running of all of our vineyards and you know more about them than anyone.'

'Delighted to oblige. What time?'

'Is one o'clock all right?'

'It's good for me, Ned. Shall I ask Oliveri to come along?'

'Good idea.'

Will nodded, swung around and walked towards the door opening into his office.

Alfredo Oliveri watched George Deravenel walking towards them through the Grill Room of the Savoy Hotel. Once again he was struck by the young man's appearance. Although not as tall or quite as handsome as his brother Edward, George was, nonetheless, very good looking. He had Edward's fair colouring, although his hair was pure blond, rather than red-gold, and his eyes were a peculiar blue-green. Almost turquoise, Alfredo thought, staring at George as he came to a stop at the table.

'Hello, George, thanks for joining us,' Edward said in a cheerful voice.

'Thanks for inviting me,' George answered in a cold tone and sat down opposite his brother.

'What would you like?' Edward asked. 'Champagne?'

'That'll be fine, thanks.' He looked first at Oliveri and then at Will, and inclined his head to both. 'So, what's this pow-wow about?' As he spoke he brushed his blond hair back from his forehead, and stared at Edward. 'You said something about good news, implied that it was good news for *me*. So come on, tell me, Ned.'

'It *is* good news, at least I think so,' Edward answered evenly, keeping tight control of himself. George sounded petulant as usual, and Ned detected that same hostility he'd been displaying recently. It was there, beneath the surface, and it was a hostility towards *him*. Will George never learn, Edward asked himself, then said to his brother, 'Vincent Martell is about to retire. Will heard from him just today. Whilst Marcel Arnaud will be running the Mâcon vineyards, I thought it might be a good opportunity for you. To go to France, to learn as much as you can about the vineyards. Vincent's going to be available as a consultant to us, and you could certainly benefit from being with him. He knows more about wine than anyone else around. I'm sorry he's retiring, but I do understand his reasons. He's tired.'

Although he rather fancied the idea of going to live at the château, and of being in France, George had no intention of letting Edward know this, and he said in a somewhat truculent voice, 'What makes you think I want to go to France? To live there? Actually, I don't.' He made a face just to make a point.

'Please don't dismiss this out of hand,' Edward murmured softly, his voice placating. He wanted George out of England, and he was prepared to be conciliatory, persuasive, in order to achieve his purpose.

'I'm not dismissing it. I just want to know what's in it for me?' George now managed to sound both petulant and grasping, which was typical of him.

Edward contemplated his brother for a long moment. 'There's a lot in it for you, George. A beautiful home, a new start at Deravenels, and close proximity to the woman who has nothing but unconditional love for you – our sister, Margaret. Frankly, I expected you to jump at it.'

'It might very well work for me,' George responded after a few minutes. 'I'm interested in wine, and I do know quite a lot about it. And I would like to know more, in fact. Also, I'm assuming there will be an increase in salary, and that there'll be some good bonuses as well along the way.'

'Oh, yes, George.' Edward was quick to reassure him of this. The money didn't matter, just so long as it did the trick. But he couldn't help thinking how avaricious George was.

George decided not to say anything: he just picked up his wine glass and raised it to Edward. 'Here's to you, brother mine. May you prosper, and Deravenels as well.'

'And here's to you,' Edward answered, lifting his own glass.

'I know you will prosper, George. Certainly I've every intention of making that happen.'

The four men clinked glasses, and it was Will who asked, 'And so what's your answer, George?'

'I'll think about it,' was his quick response, and he offered them a bland smile.

'What's all this about you sending George to run the vineyards in Mâcon?' Richard asked the following afternoon, sitting down in the chair opposite Edward's desk.

'I'm not sending him, Richard. I asked him if he'd like to go and he hasn't answered me yet. He's thinking about it.'

'I don't think he should go,' Richard answered.

'Why not?'

'It's dangerous for him. He'll drink himself to death, you'll see.'

'No, he won't, he's not that stupid. And as I just told you, Dick, it's his choice.'

Richard stared at Edward, shaking his head. 'I can't believe this.' He let out a long sigh. 'Its not like you to be so ... so *obtuse*. Surely you can see the dangers?'

'You might be right. But I can't worry about that. I need to get him out of my hair. He's saying the most terrible things about our mother, saying I'm a bastard. You *know* this. You've surely heard the gossip he's been spreading. And he's been saying my children are bastards as well. I've excused him, forgiven him for so many things, so many transgressions, and so many times, Dick. You know this. He never learns any lessons, and my patience has now worn thin.'

'I know, and I sympathize. George was very disloyal when Neville was plotting against you, and his betrayals have been quite ... well, *staggering*, Ned. On the other hand, offering him a vineyard to play in is like putting a gun in his hand.' Richard grimaced. 'He won't be able to resist tippling.'

'He might drink, yes. On the other hand, *I* think he's wise enough not to over-indulge. Anyway, he may very well refuse to go. After all, I *offered* it to him, I'm not *insisting* that he moves to France.'

Richard stood up. 'I understand,' he murmured in a low voice and walked over to the door. 'Let me know what happens, what George says finally. I'm going to Yorkshire this afternoon. Francis Lowell needs me at the mills in Bradford. We've got a problem.'

'Presumably not too serious?' Edward asked, looking at Richard intently.

'No. And we'll deal with it.'

'You've done well with the northern companies, Dick. I'm proud of you. I want you to know this.'

'Thanks, Ned. Let's face it though, I do have some good men who work with me. Francis Lowell, Robert Clayton, and Alan Ramsey. I'm lucky.'

After Richard had left Edward swivelled his desk chair and sat staring at the large map on the wall behind his desk. His father's map.

At this moment, Edward's gaze was directed at France, and in particular at Burgundy. The Deravenel vineyards produced some great Mâconnaise wines, including a marvellous Pouilly Fuissé, one of their best whites, and some good Beaujolais which was extremely popular. These vineyards had always been profitable, as were their vineyards in Provence.

He wondered suddenly if they had selected the wrong place to send George, and instantly dismissed this thought. Provence would be the worst, dangerous; it was too close to Marseilles and the Riviera. There was no question that Burgundy was the proper spot.

Margaret and Charles were not too far away at their château just outside Dijon. Charles's family had produced Nuits-St-Georges and some other great reds for several hundred years, and George could go and spend time with them. He knew full well Meg would always welcome her favourite, whom she had loved since childhood.

Broadbent was waiting to drive him home to the house in Berkeley Square, and Edward settled back in the Rolls, pondering about his two brothers.

He had no sooner opened the front door with his key and stepped inside when Mallet appeared and murmured in a low voice, 'Good evening, sir. Mrs Deravenel is waiting for you in the library. Your mother, that is, sir.'

Startled though he was, Edward merely nodded. 'Thank you, Mallet. Tell Cook I'll have dinner at the usual time, and I will let you know if my mother will be dining with me.'

'Yes, Mr Deravenel.'

Edward strode across the marble entrance hall and went into the library. 'Good evening, Mother,' he said, walking towards her. 'This is a nice surprise. I didn't know you had come up to town. Will you join me for dinner?'

'No, no, I can't, Edward, but thank you.'

He stood in front of the fireplace, even though there was no fire on this fine August evening. 'Do you wish to talk to me about something, Mama?' he asked softly, reverting to his boyhood name for her.

'Yes, I do, Edward. I wish to talk to you about your brother. *George.*'

'I see.'

'I don't want you to send him to Burgundy. Being at the vineyards in Mâcon means certain death for him. I know this.'

'I think you are underestimating George. I believe he will curb his appetite for drink, and handle himself with a degree of sense. He knows liquor is his downfall, so he won't drink much, please be assured of that.'

Cecily Deravenel stared at her eldest son and shook her head, an expression of disbelief on her face. 'He's an *alcoholic*. He can't help himself. And he's in a poor state in his bereavement. He misses Isabel.'

'It's his choice whether he goes to France or not, Mother, and to my knowledge he has not yet made a decision, so this conversation is a trifle premature, wouldn't you say?'

'No, it isn't. He'll go all right, he won't be able to resist. I'm asking you to revoke this offer you've made to him. Exile him if you must, but don't send him to the vineyards, Edward. *Please.*'

'I told you, it's his choice.'

'You are being very obdurate, I can see that. All I can say is that you are sentencing him to death.' She rose, and walked slowly towards the door. When she reached it, she turned around and gave Edward a long look, and her face was grave, her eyes filled with a terrible sorrow. 'I've never ever asked you for anything, Ned, not once since you took over Deravenels seventeen years ago. All I've ever done is support you, stand behind you. Whatever you did. I am begging you to rescind the offer to your brother. *Begging*, Ned.'

'I just told you, Mother, he doesn't have to go. We'll find another spot for him elsewhere. We have offices all over the world.'

'You don't understand, do you? He won't go anywhere else, not now. He's thrilled about this promotion of yours, as you've called it, to him. I can assure you he *will* accept it. He'll go. He's suddenly proud, full of hope because you've . . . picked him to go to Mâcon.'

'Please, Mother, don't look at me like that, with such disdain. I'll talk to George tomorrow. He *can* go anywhere he wishes, I've told you that, as long as he leaves England.'

'It's that bad, is it?'

'Yes. He's committed far too many betrayals against me for too long, and he's behaved in treacherous ways. George is untrustworthy.'

'I know he's committed quite a few crimes against you, if one can call them that. Nonetheless, he *is* your brother. Can't you forgive him?'

'No, that's not possible. Please wait a moment, Mama,' Edward exclaimed, walking quickly across the library but she had opened the door, had stepped out into the entrance hall.

'Please wait, stay for supper with me,' Edward continued.

'No. Thank you. I'll see myself out.' She opened the door as she spoke and stepped out onto the front steps. 'And don't worry about walking me home. Charles Street is just around the corner. As you well know.'

He stood staring at the front door, which his mother had closed quietly behind her. After letting out a long sigh of weariness, Edward returned to the library and sat down at the desk. He put his elbows on the top and dropped his head into his hands, groaning out loud. If George *did* go to Burgundy and if he *did* revert to his bad drinking habits, his mother would blame him. She had made it perfectly clear that she would hold him responsible for whatever George did. So be it, he thought sadly.

THIRTY-SIX

Mâcon

Will Hasling and Alfredo Oliveri sat together in the small red dining room of the Château de Poret, drinking large cups of *café au lait* and eating freshly made *croissants* on which they had both slathered large amounts of farm butter and raspberry jam. It was a sunny morning in late August, and they had arrived in Burgundy the day before, having travelled down from Paris on the train.

'So do you think George is really going to show up?' Alfredo asked, giving Will a careful look. He sat back in his chair, waiting for an answer, his expression sceptical.

'I know *you* doubt he will come,' Will responded after a moment of reflection, 'But I believe he'll show up and with bells on. Why wouldn't he come? He's nothing to lose, and he does have a choice – he can say yes or no to our proposition. Anyway, in my opinion he probably thinks this place would be . . . well . . . a little fiefdom of his own, actually, and I'm sure he feels he'll be able to lord it over everyone, perhaps even rule the roost.'

'God forbid!' Alfredo exclaimed, shaking his head, looking aghast. 'That's all we need, George attempting to take over these vineyards. We'd really be in trouble if that happened.'

'It won't,' Will replied emphatically. 'George is basically a lazy man, I've told you that before. He wants a cushy life with nothing to do and pots of money. He doesn't like to work, you know.'

Will poured himself another cup of coffee, added the frothy hot milk and sugar. After taking a sip, he continued, 'This is the best coffee I've ever had. It's one of the reasons I enjoy coming here. The coffee, the food, and the château.' He laughed. 'Not sure which comes first.'

Alfredo confided, 'I've always enjoyed this particular château myself, and I must say I do think Vincent Martell has done a wonderful job of keeping it in perfect condition since Madame de Poret died.' He threw Will a questioning look, remarked, 'I never quite understood why he wouldn't live here after her death. I know you did ask him if he wanted to move in, but you never told me why he refused.'

'In his eyes, it was the home of the de Porets, and always had been as long as he could remember. Even though there was no living relative to move in, he did not change his mind. He was born in the village, his father worked in the vineyards before him, and I suspect he thought it would be wrong, that he would be stepping out of place. And don't forget, he had just been widowed. I'm sure he didn't want to leave his house on the estate here, where he had lived with his wife Yvette for years. That was his home and I don't think he liked the thought of making a change. Too many memories in the old place.'

'I can understand that.' Alfredo glanced across at Will, studied him for a moment, knowing what a decent, caring man he was. 'I'm glad you told him he could remain here after his retirement, live in his house. After all he'll be a consultant, working for us.'

'And he's lived in that house for over thirty years,' Will pointed out. 'Knowing him the way I do, I realized he was worrying about where he would live. I picked up on it straight away.'

'What did you think about Marcel Arnaud? Did you like him?'

'He's a bit quiet, somewhat uncommunicative. However, I

trust Vincent's judgement. If he is comfortable with Arnaud taking over, running the vineyards, then I must go along with him. He's the genuine expert around here. Vincent's never been anything but straight with me, honest to the point of bluntness sometimes, ever since we bought this vineyard in 1906.'

'He *is* a quiet man, I agree with you there, and of course you have to take Vincent's advice. By the way, after George arrives and he's been given the tour, are you planning to go to our other vineyards in Mâcon?'

Will nodded, shifted slightly in the chair. 'Yes, I am, but I'm not intending to take George. I want to go to the Côte d'Or, visit our vineyards in Beaune. You know how important our Montrachet white wines are. Good decision on Edward's part, buying those particular vineyards in 1910. They're great money-makers for us.'

'I'd like to come with you, if you don't mind. And then I'll head for Italy afterwards. I want to check on the marble quarries in Carrara.'

There was a small silence, and then Will cleared his throat, murmured quietly, 'I haven't ever been back there since we came to see you, after Richard Deravenel's death . . . seventeen years go now. That was when we first met, remember?'

'It's a hard trip for me to make also,' Alfredo murmured, and let out a sigh. He then pushed back his chair, went on in a brisker tone, 'Shall we go out and find Vincent? Go for a walk around the vineyards?'

'Good idea. And by the way, I'll be glad to have your company on my trip to Beaune.'

They found Vincent Martell in one of the large wine vaults, and when he saw them he came hurrying forward to greet them. He was a stocky man, well-muscled, with a broad chest and a craggy face tanned nut-brown from the sun. This contrasted markedly with his pure white hair. His brown eyes held a bright sparkle and he had great vigour, lots of energy.

'*Bonjour*!' he cried as he came to a stop, thrusting out his hand first to Will and then to Alfredo. 'I hope you both slept well, and that Solange gave you a good breakfast,' he added in slightly accented English.

'Thank you, she did,' Will answered, and glanced around. 'This cellar is very pleasing to my eyes, Vincent. So many casks in here, and that makes me extremely happy.'

'*Ah, oui, et moi aussi!*' Vincent smiled broadly. 'We have had a good year.' He led them down one of the long alleys between the casks; these were laying on their sides, piled on top of each other, from floor to ceiling.

Alfredo followed slowly on their heels, realizing he had not been in this particular vault before; it was huge. The casks were large round barrels made of wood, bound with hoops of wood and metal, and they were stacked extremely high.

He paused, stared hard at one stack, wondering how the casks remained stationary. This row was composed of eight barrels laid out on the floor, with seven on top, then six, five, four, three, two and finally one single cask at the very top of the stack. Each row of barrels was held in place by a wooden wedge; this was pushed underneath the first barrel, and the wedge stopped it from rolling forward and falling onto the floor.

Quite a feat to set this up, Alfredo thought, and threw a last look at the casks before walking on. He noticed, as he went deeper into the vault, that some of the stacks were even higher, and he couldn't help wondering if this stacking process was dangerous. What if a barrel fell? They would all fall, wouldn't they?

Will and Vincent had disappeared from view, and Alfredo now had to hurry to catch up to them. He shivered slightly; it was cold in here. They had turned a corner, and were walking down another alley, chatting animatedly, he could see that.

'Must be difficult to stack all these barrels, I should think,' Alfredo said as he finally joined them. 'Especially since they are stacked on their sides. There's a danger of them rolling around, isn't there?'

Vincent laughed, shook his head. 'No. And it's not too hard when you know how. The Burgundy casks are easy to handle, lighter than the Bordeaux casks which are the ones more commonly used.' He then went on explaining about the stacking process, the making of the casks themselves, as well as the corks, how the bottling and the labelling were done, taking Alfredo through the many steps required to produce a bottle of wine.

Will knew it all by heart, having learned at the knee of this master, and so he strolled ahead, feeling chilled all of a sudden. The vaults here were vast, and cool, with their flagged stone floors, and walls of stone, and the high-flung ceiling made of wood and stone. He wanted to get out into the sunshine as soon as he could, where it was decidedly warmer.

He had visited this château and its vineyards many times, and the others they owned as well. Edward had put him in charge of the entire wine division when he had first started working at Deravenels, and he was proud to be running the division.

Because he was diligent and dedicated, Will had made it a point to learn as much as he could . . . about the growing of the grapes, the vinification of the wine, the bottling and storing. He had wanted to understand the entire process. It was Vincent, of course, who had taught him everything he knew, and over the years they had become good friends as well as colleagues. He came to France six times a year to visit all of the Deravenel-owned vineyards, and it was a country he had come to love.

Will now realized as he walked along that he must have a private talk with Vincent later. He had to explain that George must not be permitted to interfere with the running and management of the vineyards under any circumstance. He must tell Vincent, and also Marcel Arnaud, that George was merely a figurehead, that he should be given respect but no duties whatsoever.

An hour later the three men were sitting in the charming drawing room of the château, toasting each other with a fine Pouilly Fuissé for which this vineyard was renowned, a prelude to lunch.

The room had a certain style about it, a style which Will found charming. A faded floral fabric, a gentle blur of parchment-beige, red, pink, and a hint of blue was used on the walls, as draperies, and on some of the sofas and chairs. Against this soft background there was the mellow gleam of lovely old furniture, the wood polished to a burnished gleam. There was a welcoming warmth in evidence. The old white marble fireplace, high ceiling, tall windows looking out onto the gardens all added to the grace of the overall design.

Will suddenly hoped George wouldn't be critical about the old-world charm of the château, and deep in his heart he begrudged George this fine house which dated back to the seventeenth century.

On the other hand, George *had* to be removed from England, to make Ned totally safe, and this place was the best spot to put him. If only he knew it, he's a lucky sod, Will thought, and then looked across at the door as it burst open.

Standing in the entrance was George Deravenel himself. He was well dressed and well groomed, and, of course, as handsome as usual.

Will jumped up at once, hurried across the room to greet him. 'There you are, George!' he exclaimed. 'We were just wondering where you'd got to.'

'I had a terrible journey,' George began, the petulant look instantly in place. 'And I thought –'

'Come and meet Vincent Martell,' Will said in a firm voice,

cutting him off. 'He's lived here all his life, and he'll certainly be able to teach you a lot about wine if you decide to move here.'

George nodded. 'I wouldn't mind a glass of that stuff you're all drinking. I need it after my foul trip.'

'It's a fine Pouilly Fuissé, made in this very vineyard, Mr Deravenel,' Vincent announced, coming forward to greet the new arrival. And he couldn't help thinking what a wonderful looking young man George Deravenel was; he bore a strong resemblance to his brother Edward. No doubt some of the local ladies would find this recent widower quite a catch, not to mention an attractive one.

After Will and Oliveri had left the vineyard to go back to London, George decided to take off himself. He told Vincent he had to go to the Riviera on business for forty-eight hours, and took the train to Monte Carlo.

From the moment he checked into the Hôtel de Paris near the casino he felt his spirits lifting. Monte Carlo was his favourite spot on the Côte d'Azur. Even though he knew all of the other towns and their casinos ... Cannes, Nice, and Beaulieu-sur-Mer, and had enjoyed them over the years, he always gravitated to Monte.

The evening he arrived, he dressed carefully in his Savile Row dinner jacket, well cut and elegant, a crisp white shirt and black bowtie. After glancing at himself in the mirror in the hall of his suite, he went downstairs to the lobby of this most magnificent hotel. He walked over to the cashier's desk, glancing around. He was well known at the hotel, as was the entire Deravenel family, and by chance he happened to be acquainted with the cashier on duty. Greeting the man cordially in perfect French, he cashed a cheque for two thousand pounds, pocketed the money, left the hotel and strolled across the square to the renowned casino.

He savoured the moment when he walked into the Grand Salon: it was always a magic moment for him. He stood perfectly still, taking in his surroundings . . . the great crystal chandeliers dropping from ceiling, the plush red carpet, the magnificent cream-coloured panelling on the walls highlighted with gold-leaf, and those wonderful gambling tables. Here he could play roulette, chemin de fer, and baccarat: he knew he would enjoy himself.

George had always loved the fragrant, mingled perfumes of the women, the masculine haze of cigar and cigarette smoke, and the spicy hint of the aftershave lotions of the men in their impeccably-cut evening jackets. The sounds were also magical to him – the ball whizzing around the roulette wheel and clatter-ing into a slot after the croupier had spun it, the sharp slap of chips against each other on the tables, the shuffle of the cards from the shoe. He was in his element here.

Throwing back his shoulders, George sauntered through the Grand Salon, heading in the direction of the cashier. Here he used the money he had brought with him from London, plus the two thousand he had just cashed at the hotel, and purchased four thousand pounds worth of gambling chips.

A passing waiter stopped at his side as he turned away from the *Caisse*; George smiled, nodded, and took a crystal goblet of champagne. He cut quite a swathe as he sauntered on, this tall, handsome young man with striking features and blond hair, and many of the beautiful women turned to stare at him.

He noticed this, but pretended not to, and smiled inwardly. After his fun gambling, and drinking more of this delicious champagne, he would attempt to find two women who were alone at the casino tonight, and invite one of them, or both, into his bed.

After three quick glasses of champagne George felt absolutely wonderful. Excited yet controlled and full of confidence. Immediately, he made for one of the roulette tables, arrived just as the croupier was shouting, '*Rien ne va plus*,' . . . no more bets. And so he had to wait for the ball to fly around the wheel, come to a rest, and to be spun again. Only then could he participate.

At the next throw George was in, and he placed some of his chips on the numbers nine, eleven and thirteen. To his great delight, he won. He won again and again, and tripled his money.

And that was how it was for several hours. Eventually, he moved on to play baccarat, and slowly lost. Next, he went over to the chemin de fer table, where he lost once more. But he wasn't going to give up, or give in. He started all over, using his last thousand pounds, and, to his enormous chagrin, he lost everything. Four thousand gone, just like that!

Never mind, he thought, as he headed back to the *Caisse* window. I'll change my luck, I know I will. He produced his passport again and signed a marker for five thousand pounds. The name Deravenel was well known here at the casino, just as it was at the Hôtel de Paris, and he was a welcome guest, one to whom every courtesy was given.

It ended up being an unlucky night for George Deravenel in the end. At two in the morning, a little bit worse for wear, George headed back to the Hôtel de Paris. And he was alone. He felt a stab of dismay as he crossed the square . . . He had lost all of the cash he had come to the casino with and had signed markers for another five thousand pounds . . . He now owed money to the casino. Not only that, he had not managed to find a woman, and he had not eaten dinner. But those things didn't matter. What mattered were his gambling debts. His brother Edward would be furious with him, and he certainly wouldn't help him. Neither would Richard; he wasn't even sure he could go to his mother yet again. His heart sank.

Then a brainwave hit him. His sister lived in Dijon. He would phone Meg tomorrow and she would come and rescue him. He hoped and prayed she would, but he wasn't even sure of *her* at the moment. As he entered the hotel, he felt sudden depression envelop him, and deep down within himself he knew he was doomed. He always had been doomed, hadn't he?

THIRTY-SEVEN

Kent

'What a huge bonfire you've made, Amos,' Grace Rose said, walking around it, followed by Bess. They were both eyeing the enormous pile of wood, branches and sticks piled high in the centre of the cobblestone yard at the back of Waverley Court. 'There'll be a terrific blaze when we light it later.'

Amos laughed, explained, 'I can't take credit for it, I'm afraid, my dear. It was Joby, and his under-gardener Stew, plus the boot-boy, who built it up into this veritable pyre. I just stood and watched them working.'

'This is going to be the best bonfire night we've ever had,' Bess said, adjusting her woollen scarf. 'Nanny says everyone can come, except for Baby George, because he's only one year old, and too young. Oh, did you remember to bring the fireworks, Amos?'

'I did indeed, Bess. Catherine Wheels, starbursts and lots of sparklers, which I know are your favourites.'

'Thank you. We've been helping Cook,' Bess now confided. 'We've made parkin, gingerbread boys, and Cook has baked potatoes. She says we can warm them up at the edge of the fire later, and there'll be roast chestnuts as well.'

'My goodness, we're going to have quite a feast!'

On hearing Edward's voice, Bess swung around and raced across the courtyard to her father. He hugged her tightly, put his arm around her shoulders, walked with her to the bonfire.

'Afternoon, Mr Deravenel,' Amos said, thrusting out his hand.

'Hello, Amos, old chap,' Edward responded, shaking his hand. 'I'm glad you're here. When did you arrive?'

'About an hour ago, sir. I drove down with Broadbent.'

'I hope you've been looked after, had some sort of refreshment.'

'Oh yes, sir, I have. Cook saw to that. Most obliging she was, and kind. She made me a brawn sandwich and a very nice cup of tea.'

Edward nodded, and turned to Grace Rose, offering her a warm and loving smile. She came to his side at once, and he gave her a hug and then said, 'I hope your parents are coming over later. They did say they would.'

'Oh yes, Uncle Ned, they're looking forward to it, they wouldn't miss it for anything.'

It was early evening on Saturday, November the fifth, Guy Fawkes Night, which was mostly known as Bonfire Night throughout England. Bonfires were lit all over the land, and effigies of Guy Fawkes burned. After the fireworks display everyone ate the baked potatoes, roast chestnuts, and gingerbread boys and the parkin. The origin of Bonfire Night went back to the year 1605 when a conspiracy to blow up the Houses of Parliament was concocted by Guy Fawkes and his followers.

Edward said, 'I can't imagine how Guy Fawkes thought he would succeed. From what I remember from my history books, he didn't have enough gunpowder, did he?'

Amos shook his head. 'I don't think he did. It was hidden in the cellars of Parliament, and if I remember correctly some of it got damp. At least that's what I recall from *my* history lessons.'

'He wanted to blow up King James as well,' Bess interjected.

'He was hoping to incite the Catholics to riot because they were upset by the new severe laws against their religion.'

'Well done, Bess,' her father exclaimed, and smiled with a degree of pride.

'I like history, Father,' she told him, and went on, 'I'm following in Grace Rose's footsteps.'

He laughed, and so did Amos and Grace Rose, and then he continued, 'I shall go inside for a short while. I have to talk to Amos about a few things.' He glanced up at the sky, saw that the sun had set, that twilight was beginning to descend. 'It's going to be dark in about half an hour, and then we shall come out and enjoy the bonfire.'

Edward led Amos through the back of the house, to the library on the other side. He closed the library door behind them, and went over to the fireplace as usual. 'Take a seat here, near the fireside,' he said to Amos. 'You know I like to stand and to prowl about a room.'

Amos nodded. 'I do indeed, Mr Edward.'

Bending down, Edward threw a couple of logs onto the fire, and then said in a low voice, 'When did you get back from Mâcon?'

'This morning. I travelled overnight to Paris and took the morning boat train. I didn't get in touch because I knew I'd be seeing you tonight.

'That's all right, Amos, no problem. How did you find things at the vineyards?' he asked, giving Finnister a keen look.

'Everything seems to be very calm, sir. Mr George was quite cordial, and when Oliveri and I arrived with the children and the nanny he was delighted, happy to see them. And later in the day your sister came down from Dijon, and she was equally pleased to see them all, especially her namesake, little Margaret.

Solange made a proper English afternoon tea and it was very jolly, we enjoyed it.'

'I'm glad Meg is there for a few days,' Edward murmured, and looked off into the distance for a split second and then turning to Finnister again, asked, 'Is he drinking?'

'I'm afraid so, Mr Edward. He's dropped off the wagon . . . he doesn't seem to be overdoing it though.'

'I suppose he *would* be careful with you and Oliveri present. What did Vincent Martell have to say about the vineyards? Anything special?'

'Not a lot, and everything seems to be on an even keel. Mr George hasn't been causing trouble.'

'So far,' Edward interrupted with a wry smile. 'But you never know with George, he can erupt unexpectedly. What about Marcel Arnaud? Does he get on with my brother?'

'I'm not sure about that, sir. Mr Arnaud appears to be a quiet man, introspective, so I thought. Oliveri said I should tell you that he is quite certain your brother doesn't like him. We were there for only three days, of course – nonetheless, we picked up quite a lot in the time. According to Solange, Mr George has become a bit of a Casanova in the area: there seem to be quite a few women hovering around him. He's also made several trips to Nice. That worried Oliveri, because of the casinos. He said I should alert you to this. He's concerned that Mr George might have started gambling again.'

Edward nodded. 'Did Vincent have anything to say about my brother's work habits? Has he been learning about the vineyards, do you know?'

'In the first few weeks he was apparently very diligent, but according to Vincent Martell he's slacked off quite a lot lately.'

'So he's doing nothing much . . . as usual. Well, what can you expect? He's lazy, Amos, and he always has been.'

Edward walked across to the windows, looked out, thinking of George. He was a wastrel, no two ways about it.

Turning around, he looked across at Amos, and said, 'So what it boils down to is that he's womanizing, drinking again, and he's more than likely making trips to the Riviera to gamble in the casinos of Nice. And also in Cannes and Monte Carlo, I've no doubt.' Edward paused, his eyes narrowing as he asked, 'But has he done any talking? Is he spreading bad stories about me and mine?'

Amos stared at Edward, remained absolutely silent for a moment or two. He had not wanted to say anything about George Deravenel's nasty talk about his brother, at least not until tomorrow. This was a night for the children to enjoy, and he had not wished to upset Edward. But his great loyalty and devotion to him made it impossible for Amos to lie, and so he said quietly, 'He's up to his old tricks, yes, sir.'

'Who's he been talking to, Amos?'

'Vincent Martell, certainly. But I doubt that he has said anything to anyone else. It wouldn't mean a thing to Solange, and I don't believe Mr Arnaud would understand, or care. He's a bit of a loner, that chap, and not one to fraternize. Keeps himself to himself, seemingly. I realized that Vincent was very annoyed, put out that your brother would speak ill of you, and in such a terrible way. He was flabbergasted, and disgusted, and mentioned it to us, because he thought we ought to know. He's very loyal to you, sir.'

'I know he is.'

'In our opinion, mine and Oliveri's – well, we think Mr George has done himself a disservice, done himself in with Vincent Martell. Before Oliveri left for Turkey he asked me to make a point of informing you about Mr George and his tittle-tattling. He says your brother is besmirching you, and it worries him quite a lot I think.'

'I'm certain Oliveri is correct about Vincent. We've enjoyed an excellent relationship for years. He was very happy when I rescued the vineyard, all those years ago, when Madame de

Poret was widowed and didn't know how to cope alone. He was truly grateful, actually.' Edward shrugged, added, 'We'll talk again tomorrow, Amos, but now we'd better turn to happier things, go and join the children.'

At this moment there was a tap on the door, and Edward called, 'Come in.'

The door opened, and Faxton, the butler, put his head around it and said, 'Sorry to disturb, sir, but Mr and Mrs Forth have arrived with Lady Fenella and Mr Ledbetter, and Mrs Deravenel just came down.'

'Thank you, Faxton, we'll be right out.'

Edward squeezed Elizabeth's arm, then went over to greet Vicky, Fenella, Stephen and Mark. Once he had welcomed his closest friends, he glanced around, spotted Joby, the gardener, the under-gardener Stew, and Elias, the bootboy. They were all amply armed with large boxes of Swan Vesta matches and were waiting for his order to light the bonfire.

His eyes scanned the rest of the group, which included Cook, some of the other domestic staff, and Faxton, who had just hurried out of the house to join the others. Then they settled on the row of youngsters standing near him.

Edward was enormously proud of his children. Bess, such a beautiful girl, and tall for twelve; next to her was Young Edward, a handsome boy of eight, and his little brother Ritchie, now five. Mary, who was eleven years old, was clutching Cecily's hand. A golden-haired child like her brothers, she was a little timid, even though she was nine. Nanny was holding three-year-old Anne in her arms; next to her was his darling Grace Rose. A rare beauty at twenty-one and everyone's favourite. Even Elizabeth treated her kindly these days, and was obviously quite fond of her.

His family. His large family, whom he loved, adored and treasured. They were safe, thank God. He and Elizabeth had made them safe through their secret marriage this past August. He would always be thankful that she had married him again without too much fuss; but then, she had not had any alternative really.

Thoughts of George intruded, and then he pushed them to one side. He had hopefully foiled his brother and his treacherous intentions. If he hadn't put a stop to the gossip, what did it matter, actually? He could deny it and in all truth insist he was well and truly married to Elizabeth because now he was.

Suddenly, Bess was standing in front of him and her words brought him out of his reverie. 'Father, you must give the order, tell Joby and the others to light the bonfire.'

'Yes, I must, Bess.' He stepped forward and cried, 'All right, lads, do it. Get the bonfire going.'

Within seconds the twigs and branches caught light, and once the flames were flaring up into the sky and the effigy of Guy Fawkes was burning, Bess gathered her brothers and sisters together, and holding hands, dancing around the roaring bonfire, they began to sing the old song:

> *'Remember, remember, the fifth of November,*
> *The gunpowder, treason and plot,*
> *I see no reason why gunpowder treason*
> *Should ever be forgot.*
> *Guy Fawkes, Guy, 'twas his intent*
> *To blow up the King and the Parliament.*
> *Three score barrels of powder below,*
> *To prove old England's overthrow.'*

When the children had finished singing, the adults applauded them and shouted their hoorahs; Cook and several of the young maids passed around plates of gingerbread men, the parkin and other sweet cakes, while Faxton brought out a tray holding tall glasses of lemonade. And Elias, armed with a pair of long tongs, ran around the edge of the bonfire, pulling out the hot baked potatoes which had been placed there earlier to warm. After everyone had tasted the special treats and drunk the lemonade, Amos distributed the sparklers. The other men went around and lighted them for the children.

The children ran through the yard, waving the sparklers in the air, laughing with glee and enjoying themselves.

Edward stood with Elizabeth and the other adults, the men drinking Scotch and water, the women sipping glasses of sherry, chatting together in the glow of the fire.

Finally it was time for the fireworks. This was carefully managed by Stephen Forth, Mark Ledbetter, Amos Finnister and Edward. There was a fantastic display of Catherine wheels, star-bursts, rainbows, and falling stars, as well as many other unique fireworks. The women stood back and watched the children, and exchanged glances of pleasure. It was wonderful to see the happiness and delight on the young faces.

THIRTY-EIGHT

London

Will stood in the library of Edward's house in Berkeley Square, staring at the Renoir painting of the two redheaded young women. It hung above the fireplace, and Will understood why it took pride of place in this room. It was beautiful, a masterpiece, and he understood why it reminded Edward of Bess and Grace Rose.

He had told Edward he needed to speak to him privately, and they had arranged to meet here. Elizabeth was at Waverley Court in Kent with the children. The house was empty, very quiet and still this afternoon.

Mallet came in and, clearing his throat, asked, 'Would you like something, sir? Perhaps a cup of tea?'

'No, thank you, Mallet,' Will answered. The butler nodded and left.

Will continued to study the marvellous Renoir, and then suddenly Edward was striding into the room, apologizing for keeping him waiting.

'What's this all about, Will? You look serious, even a bit grim,' Edward said.

338

Will was silent. He went and sat on a chair near the fireplace, leaned back, crossed his legs.

Edward took the other chair, staring at him intently, and picking up on his sober mood at once. 'Is there something wrong?'

'Vincent Martell telephoned me just before I was leaving for the lunch, Ned. He had apparently attempted to get hold of you here, but the line was busy. He in fact tried several times with no success. Which was why he finally got in touch with me.'

'Is there a problem at the vineyards? Oh, no, wait. A problem with George! Is that it? Has my brother been up to his old tricks again?'

Will took a deep breath, spoke in a low tone. 'George is dead, Ned.'

Edward recoiled, sat back in the chair, gaping at Will. He was stunned. Frowning, he shook his head. '*George* . . . he's dead?'

'I'm afraid so. Vincent found him this morning. He noticed the door of one of the large wine vaults swinging in the wind, and went to see what was going on.'

Edward had turned pale, and now he asked in a low, gruff voice, 'How did he die? Was he sick? What happened, Will?'

'It seems there was a terrible accident some time last night. Apparently George had made it a habit to go to the largest wine vault if he ran out of wine at the château. There was a tasting table and racks of wine were kept at the far end of the vault. Vincent thinks that George may have been drunk when he went in there. He found him on the floor this morning, laying in a pool of red wine, face down, surrounded by a slew of broken barrels. Vincent believes that George, very likely inebriated, stumbled against a stack of barrels, and stumbled very hard, so that they came tumbling down on him. Vincent explained that one of the casks obviously hit him on the head and killed him because George had very severe head injuries. The entire pyramid of barrels is decimated, some smashed, others lying on the stone floor.'

'Oh my God . . . how ghastly.' Edward brought a hand to his face. 'I can't believe this.'

'I know, it's all so . . . sudden, so unexpected.' Will shook his head slowly. 'But perhaps not really all that surprising, not if you think about it. It seems to me that George was *fated* . . . somehow he always managed to get into trouble . . .' Will's voice trailed off; he was at a loss for words.

The two old friends sat for a while in silence, lost in their own thoughts.

It was Edward who finally spoke. 'I assume Vincent called for a doctor? Got medical help?'

'Yes, he did. But George had apparently been dead for some hours. Rigor mortis had set in. The police were also informed and came to the château. However, as Vincent said, it was pretty obvious what had happened because of all the broken wine casks and his head injuries.'

'They'll blame me. My mother will say it's my fault George is dead . . . and so will Richard. They both asked me not to send him to the vineyards in France. They believed he would die there, and they were right. My mother *begged* me, Will –' Edward broke off, his voice suddenly hoarse, almost a whisper.

'No, they can't blame *you*. Listen to me, Ned, it wasn't your fault. Believe me it wasn't. And I've never quite understood why your mother has always taken George's side . . . I know one shouldn't speak ill of the dead, but your brother was most unbrotherly towards you for his entire life.'

'Yes, that's true, he was.'

Edward rose, went over to the tray of drinks on a table near the window, and poured himself a cognac. 'Do you want one, Will?'

'Yes, thanks,' he answered.

A moment later, when Edward handed Will the brandy balloon, he murmured, 'I shall have to telephone them. My mother is at Ravenscar – oh, and so is Richard, come to think of it. And I shall have to let Meg know.'

'Do it tomorrow,' Will suggested.

'No, I must do it now. At least I must get in touch with my mother.' Edward went to his desk, sat down, and dialled Ravenscar. It was Jessup who answered, and a moment later Edward heard his mother's voice saying, 'Yes, Ned?'

'Mama, something quite terrible has happened. There's been an accident. In France. At the vineyards.'

'What kind of accident?' Cecily Deravenel asked, her voice trembling slightly.

He told her about George going into the wine vault, perhaps stumbling, and unseating the stack of wine casks. Before he had even finished, she interrupted him.

'He's dead. George is dead, isn't he?'

'Yes.'

'I knew he would die there,' she said and hung up the phone on him.

Fog. Outside the window. Suddenly in the room. It surrounded him. Trapped him. He sat up in bed. Struggled to see. Blinking in the fog. How had it floated into the room? The window was closed. He threw back the bed clothes. Put his feet on the floor. Moved slowly across the room. He banged into a chest of drawers. Stubbed his toe. Winced. Who had put the chest there?

He went into the bathroom. Fumbled for the light switch. It was then he realized he was not at Ravenscar. He was in London. At his house in Berkeley Square. The bright lights hurt his eyes.

Edward peered at himself in the mirror, and blinked again, saw his face in a blur. He leaned against the sink, slightly dizzy, feeling nauseous. His head throbbed. He filled a glass with cold water, drank it down quickly. Then he splashed cold water on his face, wet a small towel and held it to his eyes. There. That was better. The fog had disappeared. He could see.

His headache was blinding. And he had a hangover. He went back to the bedroom and crawled into bed, lay still, nursing his hangover. And thinking.

Slowly everything came back to him. He remembered that he and Will had sat drinking cognac for several hours. *Talking*. Talking about George. About his death. About bringing the body back to England. About burying him in Yorkshire. At Ravenscar. They spoke about others. His mother. Richard. Neville Watkins and his beloved Johnny Watkins, and they relived the past. And they discussed George's children, who had to come back to England as soon as possible. Maybe Meg could escort them.

Will had finally left, had been driven by Broadbent to his house behind Marble Arch. Near Jane's house. Jane. He must telephone her. No, he couldn't, it was the middle of the night.

George. His brother. George was dead. What a beautiful child he had been, and he had become a beautiful young man. Blond. Turquoise-blue eyes. Skin-deep, that beauty. *George*. A mystery to him at times. So uncertain inside . . . needy. He had always run to their mother, wanting her protection. As a child, as a boy, as a man.

Edward had loved him once. That love had changed slowly. To concern, to mistrust, and finally to disbelief. How blatant George's betrayals and treacheries had been. It was as if he hadn't cared that *he* knew. His love for George had changed to wariness, had eventually curdled into total dislike.

Edward sat up in bed with a jerk, staring out into the darkened room. And he asked himself the question he had posed to Will Hasling last night when he had been drinking himself into a stupor.

Had it been an accident? Or murder?

Will had said he didn't know. Neither did he. But now he focused on it, wondering. He had no answer for himself.

He lay awake until dawn broke and light seeped in through the curtains, wrestling with that question which still hovered in his mind.

Later that morning Edward had just finished dressing when Mallet knocked on the door. He knew it was the butler. There was no one else in the house except for Cook and a couple of maids.

'Come in, Mallet,' he called.

The butler opened the door. 'Good morning, Mr Deravenel. Mr Hasling is here. In the morning room.'

Frowning, Edward slipped on his jacket, buttoned it, and replied, 'I'll be right down, Mallet. And a cup of coffee would be most welcome.'

'Yes, sir. Right away.' The butler quietly closed the door.

Striding over to the wardrobe mirror, Edward looked at himself and nodded his head. Certainly there were no telltale signs of a hangover. He looked exactly the same as he had yesterday. And yet . . . he felt different inside. There was an emptiness, a terrible aching void, and something more intangible . . . Then he realized it was a strange aloneness. He *was* alone now. And he always would be . . . for the rest of his life. His mother would never treat him the same way ever again. Neither would Richard. Because they would blame him for George's death.

And so I stand alone. As I always have.

Will was sitting at the round table in the morning room, drinking a cup of coffee, *The Times* next to him, but still folded and unread.

'Good morning,' Edward said from the doorway and walked in, forcing a smile.

Will nodded. 'Morning, Ned. You'd forgotten, hadn't you? That we said we would lunch together today, and make plans for me to leave for France tomorrow morning. With Oliveri. To bring George's body back. I made a reservation at the Ritz Restaurant. Is that all right?'

'Yes. I had forgotten,' Edward admitted, sat down and reached for the silver pot of coffee. As he poured a cup, he went on, 'But that doesn't present a problem. I had no other plans for lunch.'

They sat together drinking their black coffee and talking about all the arrangements which had to be made; after their second cup of coffee they left the house, walked slowly across the square, up Berkeley Street in the direction of Piccadilly.

It was a sunny morning, with a bright blue sky and a light breeze, pleasant for November and not at all cold. They walked in silence, until Edward suddenly said, 'I remember the wedges, Will. And I kept thinking about them in the middle of the night. I woke up and couldn't get back to sleep. I started thinking about George, wondering whether he was murdered or not. And the wedges came into my mind.'

'I know what you're getting at, Ned. If someone moved the wedges holding the casks in place then the pyramid would tumble.'

Edward said nothing, simply nodded.

'But who would move the wedges? And how could anyone be certain George would go into that particular wine vault?' Will wondered aloud.

'Everyone knew his habits. And there are a number of people who *could* have loosened the wedges, Will. If someone *did* do that, then all he had to do was sit back and wait. Inevitably some-thing would happen. Because George had to walk down that particular alley to get to the bottles of wine at the other end.'

344

It was Will's turn to be silent.

Edward said at last, 'Perhaps someone thought they were doing me a favour, ridding me of George. God knows, he's caused me enough heartache and anguish over the years.'

'I'm sure it was an accident,' Will was quick to answer, although he was not sure at all. Like Edward, he, too, wondered if George *had* been murdered. But they would never discover who was responsible, if this were the case. There was one thing he *was* absolutely certain of – finding a culprit was only the beginning. Proof was needed. Absolute proof. He thought then of Vincent Martell, and of Amos Finnister, and finally of Alfredo Oliveri. Possible suspects, certainly. The three of them were utterly devoted to Ned, and capable of doing it. But had they?

THIRTY-NINE

Paris

P aris was her favourite city at any time of year, in
any kind of weather, but Jane Shaw particularly loved
it in May. And now as she walked through the
Tuileries she felt a wonderful surge of happiness at being
there today.

It was lovely weather, sunny and balmy, with a pale blue
sky and sunlight filling the branches of the trees with shimmering light. But Paris and the beautiful weather aside, there
were other reasons for her carefree spirit and lightearted-
ness. She and Edward were in Paris for five days, and in a
short while she would be meeting Grace Rose at the Louvre
Museum.

Grace Rose had been studying at the Sorbonne for a couple
of years now, and Jane couldn't wait to see her. They had
become close in recent years, shared a love of French history
and a number of other things French, and, in fact, they told
everyone they were a couple of genuine Francophiles. After
their visit to the Louvre, they were going to lunch at the
Grand Véfour with Edward, a restaurant he and she enjoyed.
At this moment he was attending a meeting at the Paris

office of Deravenels, and would rendezvous with them at the restaurant in the Palais-Royal.

As she walked through the beautiful gardens, originally designed by Louis XIV's famous gardener André Le Nôtre, her mind focused on Ned. Last month he had celebrated his fortieth birthday; not that he looked it. He was as boyish as ever, and she hoped her age was not showing either. She was now in her fiftieth year; she and Ned had been together for eighteen years, since 1907, and she considered herself truly blessed to still be with him.

It was the year 1925, and Jane was dressed in the most popular style of the moment, and looked as chic and as beautiful as she had ever looked. Her suit was by Chanel, the French designer who had become all the rage since the end of the war in 1918. Jane's outfit was made of navy-blue light wool tweed, and was composed of a skirt with pleats at the front and back, and a cardigan-style boxy, edge-to-edge jacket with no buttons.

These days Jane was wearing only Chanel. She found the designer's beautifully-made haute couture clothes elegant without being at all structured, and they had ease, comfort and practicality. It was Coco Chanel who had first designed trousers for women, and Jane had purchased several pairs yesterday – one of grey flannel, the other of butter-coloured wool Jersey, both worn with man-tailored white silk shirts. Edward had been with her at the Chanel boutique on rue Cambon, and he had been so entranced with her in the grey trousers and white silk shirt that he had persuaded her to buy the second set.

He had been happy yesterday, more relaxed, and this had pleased her. Ever since his brother George had died in Mâcon he had been given to sudden and unexpected bouts of moroseness, that was the only word she could use to describe the way he was. He was not depressed, not at all; just melancholy, and preoccupied, as if he were thinking of the past, lost in his thoughts about his brother's rather peculiar death. Although George had died of his head wounds, which had been most severe, Ned had once muttered that George had 'drowned in Beaujolais'. But when she had asked him what he meant he had simply shaken his head and remained silent, looking faintly puzzled.

Jane was pleased about one thing, and that was the thawing of the ice in the family. His mother had been remote and cold with Ned since George's death, four years ago now, but lately she had been civil to her son, at least, even cordial. As for Richard, he had come around much sooner, and was certainly friendly, on good terms with his brother again. Yet he kept himself in Yorkshire, running the companies, factories and mills, as well as the coal mines in the North. Ned relied on Richard to do this, and she was thankful there was a degree of ease between them these days.

It had appalled her when his mother, Richard, and also his sister Meg in Burgundy, had taken umbrage, had blamed him. She knew full well that George had brought everything on himself . . . The man had tempted Providence for years, and had been a most treacherous and faithless wretch all of his life. George Deravenel had never had any time or thought for anyone else because he was too consumed with himself.

Whether or not George had been murdered was something else altogether. Nobody would ever be able to prove anything, and there was no one to pin the blame on. But certainly she had her own ideas . . . and those wedges that had so troubled Ned *had* been partially pulled out . . . the gendarmes from Mâcon had told Edward that. They had found loose wedges on several other pyramids of wine casks. And nobody could explain why they were loosened.

Jane realized that she was already at the Louvre, one of Paris's gems she thought, a magnificent museum filled with some of the greatest and finest paintings in the world. She knew Grace Rose would be waiting inside and she increased her pace, hurried along the path, walking faster. She could hardly wait to see Ned's daughter, whom she had grown to love as if she were her own child.

Grace Rose was waiting inside the museum, and she hurried forward to greet Jane when she saw her walking inside. After the two of them had embraced affectionately, Jane held the young woman way from her, staring hard. 'Grace Rose, you look perfectly wonderful! And what an air of Gallic chic you have acquired. That's a wonderful outfit.'

Grace Rose began to laugh, pleased by the praise for her somewhat unorthodox get-up. 'It's not really an outfit, Jane, just bits and pieces which I bought here and there in Paris. At odd little shops, the flea market, and several boutiques which were having summer sales. The ensemble, if I can call it that, cost me hardly anything. I had fun doing it, and it's amusing, I think.'

Jane laughed with her, eyeing the short red silk jacket, the narrow ankle-length beige wool skirt, the huge blue rose pinned onto the jacket, the yellow beret with red and blue feathers attached, and set on one side of her auburn head in a jaunty way. She looked adorable.

Tucking her arm through Grace Rose's, Jane said, 'Come along, let's go and feast our eyes. How much do you know about the Louvre?'

'Not a lot, actually. I've only visited it once before and I wasn't able to stay long. But what I saw impressed me.'

'Let me tell you a little bit about some of the paintings: by Leonardo – the *Mona Lisa*, the *Virgin of the Rocks* – works by

Raphael Titian and Veronese, as well as Goya, and one of *my* favourites, Delacroix.'

Jane talked about the art as the two women meandered around the Louvre gazing at these masterpieces.

'My goodness, I'm overwhelmed.' Grace Rose said, looking at some of the most beautiful paintings in the world. She was awed and touched by the beauty of the works, transported by them. 'Thank you for insisting I come with you today. I'll keep coming back as long as I'm in Paris, and whenever I return.'

'I think you will,' Jane agreed. 'I know I do.'

Edward was waiting for them at Le Grand Véfour, and he stood up when the two women came into the restaurant, a warm smile lighting up his face.

Once they had greeted each other, and the women were seated, the waiter poured glasses of pink champagne.

Raising his glass, Edward said, 'To the two of you, my beauties.'

Smiling, they did the same, clinked their glasses to his, and they both said in unison, 'And to you.'

He looked across at them, nodded, then said, 'Rather an interesting costume, Grace Rose, there's no other word for it.'

Grace Rose smiled and told him how she had created it, and Jane added, '*I think she looks très chic!*'

'Agreed.' Glancing around the restaurant, Edward addressed Grace Rose when he explained, 'I believe Le Grand Véfour is the most beautiful restaurant in Paris, I always enjoy coming here. I hope you'll enjoy it as much as we do.'

'I know I will. It's very old, dating back to before the French

Revolution. Napoleon used to bring Josephine here, I think.'
She turned to Jane, asked, 'I'm correct, aren't I?'

'Yes, they did come here, a lot of famous people did. I believe
it was opened in 1784, when it was called the Café de Chartes,'
Jane answered. 'I love the décor, especially the antique mirrors
on the walls and ceiling.'

Grace Rose agreed with her, and confided, 'I have an addic-
tion to the Palais-Royal, enjoy walking through the arches.'

'Lots of boutiques for you to browse in,' Edward murmured
with a wink, and then asked, 'When do you finish at the university here?'

'Next month, Uncle Ned, and then I shall return to London,
and hopefully I'll get a job teaching.'

'I thought you wanted to write books,' he remarked, sounding
surprised. 'You don't have to worry about getting a job, you
know, not if you don't want to, Grace Rose. You perhaps ought
to concentrate on a book.'

'Oh, I do know that, about a job, I mean, and thank you
again for my Trust, and everything else you've done for me,
Uncle Ned. You know I'm very grateful.'

He merely smiled, asked Jane about their morning at the
Louvre and then summoned the waiter, asked him to bring
them the menus.

Once they had ordered lunch, Edward, Jane and Grace
Rose talked about their plans for the next few days in Paris;
it was not until after they had finished the first course that
Grace Rose brought up a matter which had lately concerned
her.

'Uncle Ned,' she began softly, and then hesitated, before finally
continued, 'I need to speak to you about Amos.'

Edward stared at her alertly, and asked, 'What about him?'

'I'm a little worried about him. He hasn't seemed quite
himself of late, and he seems terribly preoccupied. Haven't
you noticed it?'

Edward sat back in his chair, regarded her for a moment. Then he nodded. 'I have, actually, and I've wondered myself if something was wrong. Do you think he's ill?'

'No, I don't actually, because he seems so fit, *extremely* healthy, in fact.'

'He's in his sixties, but I agree with you, he's as fit as a fiddle. And actually I've asked him several times if he wants to retire, but he always declines. Do you want me to talk to him again?'

Grace Rose answered quickly, 'Yes, if you would, but I don't want him to think you're trying to push him out. Deravenels, and you, are his whole life, you know. I think he'd die if he had to leave you.'

'I know that, my dear,' Edward answered, smiling at her gently, understanding fully her deep affection for Amos. 'Don't you worry about it, I'll be most careful.'

'Thank you so much, Uncle Ned, and I know my mother will be happy I've talked to you about Amos. She agrees with me that he seems burdened down ... *by something*.'

Edward and Jane were staying at the Plaza Athénée Hotel on the Avenue Montaigne, and the moment they returned to their suite Edward slipped out of his jacket and loosened his tie, and went to sit in a chair near the window.

Jane stared at him, frowning. 'Are you all right, darling?'

'Yes, of course I am. Why do you ask?'

'You seemed somewhat quiet this evening over dinner. I thought that perhaps you were worrying about Amos.'

'No, I wasn't. Actually I was thinking about something else entirely. As for Amos, I have a feeling I know what's troubling him, and I'll talk to him the moment we get back to London.'

'So what was preoccupying you?' she asked, seating herself opposite him.

'I was mentally reviewing the meeting I had in the office today, that's all.'

'Was it a good meeting?'

'*I* think it was, yes.' He shook his head. 'I met with . . . an interesting man . . . Henry Turner, in fact.'

Jane gaped at him. 'The heir of Henry Grant?'

'Yes.'

'But why? He's the enemy!'

'I wouldn't say that. In fact, he's rather a mild-mannered young man, and actually very intelligent. Even a little serious-minded, I would go so far as to say.'

'But why did you meet with him?'

'He actually had written to me, and requested a meeting several weeks ago, and that was one of the reasons I wanted to come to Paris,' Edward explained, rising, walking over to the drinks' tray. He picked up the bottle of Napoleon brandy and poured himself a measure in a balloon, and asked, 'Would you like some of this, Jane?'

'No, thanks. Oh, why not . . . yes, I will, please,' she said.

A moment later he strode back to the chairs, handed her the brandy balloon and sat down.

'He wanted to meet because he wants a job. With Deravenels in Paris. He was working with Louis Charpentier, but seemingly they have had a number of quarrels and disagreements. Also, Henry feels the way I did years ago. He doesn't want to have his bride chosen for him. And Charpentier was endeavouring to get Henry married off to his niece Louise.'

'But you once told me Charpentier's niece was his heir.'

'That's perfectly true, darling, you're right. But Henry is not interested in marrying her, heiress or not. So he left Louis Charpentier's employ, and decided I might take pity on him and take him in.'

'Why do you say *take pity*? Doesn't he have any money?'

'He's not too badly off, but he strikes me as the sort of man who *wants* to work, needs to work. And since he and his mother Margaret Beauchard hold a lot of Deravenel stock he decided he wanted to work for the company that he has a stake in . . . the family company.'

'Is he related to you? Is he a Deravenel, Ned?' Jane asked. 'I thought he was from Grant's side.'

'That's true, he is, but don't forget Grant's full name was Henry Deravenel Grant of the Lancashire Deravenel Grants, and he was descended from the original founder of the dynasty, Guy de Ravenel. As am I. He and I were cousins.'

'So where *exactly* does Henry Turner fit in?'

'Henry Turner's father, the late Edmund Turner, was the half-brother of Henry Grant – they had the same mother, but different fathers. Edmund Turner was not a Deravenel, but Margaret Beauchard Turner, Edmund's wife and Henry Turner's mother, can trace her line right back to Guy de Ravenel, and that's the other family connection. It is Grant's shares they hold, because Henry Turner is the last heir of Grant. All the others are now dead.'

'*Have* you given him a job?' Jane asked quietly, a worried expression crossing her face.

'I have, yes, here at the Paris office. He's going to be doing general things at first. I haven't placed him in a division as such.'

'But *why?* Isn't this a dangerous move?'

'No, it isn't, trust me, darling. Henry Turner knows there is no way he can challenge me for Deravenels. It's mine and he knows it. He doesn't have the experience, enough shares or clout to mount any kind of takeover ever, or *coup,* if you want to call it that. He just wants a job.'

'Well, of course, you know best, Ned,' Jane said finally. Although she meant this, trusted Ned's business judgement and acumen, she was wary of Henry Turner and this move. And she was to remember this conversation in the not-too-distant future, and be filled with regret for not exercising more influence on Edward. And for not being more forceful with him about her concerns. But by then it was too late.

PART THREE

Bess

Loyalty Binds Me

The human heart has hidden treasures,
In secret kept, in silence sealed.
Charlotte Brontë
Evening Solace

I slept and dreamed that life was beauty.
I woke – and found that life was duty.
Ellen Sturgis Hooper
Beauty and Duty

I lingered round them, under that benign sky: watched the moths flutter among the heath and harebells; listened to the soft wind breathing through the grass; and wondered how anyone could ever imagine unquiet slumbers for the sleepers in that quiet earth.

Emily Brontë
Wuthering Heights

FORTY

Kent

'What's wrong with your father, Bess?' Will Hasling asked, after greeting her, embracing her with affection. Stepping back, Will peered into her face. It was pale and filled with worry. 'He merely had a head cold a few days ago. What happened?'

'His cold turned into bronchitis, as it so often does with him. I think it's a family weakness . . . a weak chest, I mean. That's why I telephoned you, Uncle Will, he seems so poorly.'

'I'm glad you did, and I'm certainly glad I decided to come down to Kent last night.'

As they walked across the entrance foyer of Waverley Court, heading towards the staircase, Bess went on, 'I think you know that my mother went to Rome for Easter. She took Cecily and the two boys with her. I didn't want to go with them, and now I'm relieved I stayed here, so that I can look after my father.'

'I'm assuming you've telephoned the doctor?'

'Yes, he'll be here very soon. Faxton and I have been treating Father the best we can. He's been inhaling Friars' Balsam, and taking his cough mixture. I do think that's helped.'

As the two of them came up the last few stairs and onto the landing, they saw Faxton emerging from Edward's bedroom.

Will asked, 'How is Mr Deravenel, Faxton?'

'He's about the same, sir.'

'As soon as the doctor arrives, please send him up.'

'Yes, of course, Mr Hasling.'

Bess went into her father's room first, exclaiming, 'Papa, here is Uncle Will!'

Edward, who was propped up in bed against piles of white linen pillows, gave Will a faint smile, and half raised a hand. 'I can't believe this,' he said in a low, hoarse voice. 'I had to cancel Rome. I wasn't well enough, and I was so looking forward to it.'

'I know you were,' Will replied, pulling up a chair to the side of the bed and sitting down, scrutinizing Ned intently. 'But you're better off here, getting yourself well, rather than traipsing around Rome. Your health is important. And by the way, who's gone with Elizabeth and the children?'

'Anthony took my place. He doesn't mind travelling with his sister. And the girls' new governess, Miss Coleman, has gone along as well as Elizabeth's maid . . .' He stopped, found a handkerchief in his pajama pocket, began to cough into it. After several minutes the hacking cough finally subsided and he leaned back, looking exhausted.

Eventually, when Ned seemed more settled, Will said, 'Do you need a glass of water, Ned?'

'Hot tea with lemon,' he answered. He looked across at Bess, asked in a whisper, 'Can you get it, darling?'

'Of course, Father, and do you want something, Uncle Will?'

'Yes, please, Bess, the same. Thank you.'

She nodded, then hurried across the room.

Once they were alone, Will said, 'You're awfully pale, Ned. I wish there was something I could do. I feel helpless.'

'Dr Lessing's a good chap,' Ned responded quietly. 'He'll fix me up in no time at all. But I do feel wretched. I took my boys fishing at Ravenscar last weekend, and caught a cold then. It was chilly out on the North Sea, and very windy, and it poured with rain. We got drenched. But still, they enjoyed it, so it was worth it.' He took a deep breath, added, 'I'll have to get better before I can come to work, Will.'

'Don't worry about Deravenels, for goodness sake. It runs like clockwork, you've set it up that way. Everything is in good order . . . you have made it so streamlined and efficient, and we do have the best executives in the world.'

'I know we do . . .' Edward closed his eyes for a moment or two. He felt weary, and yet there were so many different thoughts running through his head. Urgent things to do.

Will sat perfectly still, watching him, almost guarding over him; he was extremely worried, alerted to trouble. He had never seen Edward Deravenel look as ill as this. He had told Ned his face was white, but to Will it seemed almost grey, and he was very feverish. Reaching out, Will placed his hand on Ned's, which lay on top of the sheet.

Edward immediately opened his eyes and looked straight at Will, stared into his eyes. 'You've been my dearest friend always, Will. My very best friend and ally –' His voice petered out weakly.

Will did not like the sound of this statement; to him it smacked of a farewell, or some such thing, and he frowned. 'I still *am* your dearest friend, as you are mine, and we'll be friends for a long time.' He suddenly pushed a grin onto his face. 'We're only in our forties, Ned, we've a good stretch ahead of us yet.'

Edward smiled at him. 'We do, indeed, and I for one still have a lot of damage to do.'

At this moment the door opened and Bess came in, followed by one of the maids, and behind the maid was Dr Ernest Lessing. He was the local country doctor the family used when they were at the house in Kent.

Will stood up, turned to the doctor, whom he knew, and greeted him cordially. 'How are you, Dr Lessing?'

'Very well, thank you, Mr Hasling,' he answered, and then he stepped up to the bed, put his black bag on a chair, took out his stethoscope. He looked at Edward for a long moment, and then said quietly, 'Good morning, Mr Deravenel. Bronchitis again, eh?'

'Afraid so, Lessing. I'm prone to it, so it seems to me.'

Nodding, drawing closer to the bed, the doctor put the stethoscope in his ears and listened to Edward's chest. After a moment or two, he said, 'I'm afraid I'll have to get you up on the edge of the bed. I need to check your lungs.'

'No problem.' Edward struggled to sit straighter, and Will and the doctor helped to get him totally upright. Will unbuttoned Ned's pyjama top for him and slipped it off his broad shoulders.

While the doctor examined Edward, Will walked over to the seating area at the far end of the bedroom, where the maid had deposited the tray. Bess was sitting watching the doctor, but brought her eyes to Will's, and whispered, 'He'll be all right, Uncle Will. Father has the constitution of an ox and always shakes off these bouts of bronchitis, pulls through them quickly.'

'Yes, I know that.' Will now reached for the cup of lemon tea, dropped in a lump of sugar and stirred it; he sat drinking it for a few moments. Quite unexpectedly he felt *unusually* worried all of a sudden and he asked himself why he was feeling so . . . *fearful* for Ned. Bess had spoken the truth, her father did have a good constitution, was rarely ill, and Ned had been vigorous, energetic and strong for as long as he had known him. Yet Will was inordinately troubled, and was unable to explain this acute sense of foreboding to himself. It was an odd kind of unease.

Will came out of his reverie when he heard Dr Lessing saying to Ned, 'It's as you thought, Mr Deravenel, you've got a bad case of bronchitis, which is why you've been having trouble breathing. Your air passages are infected. But you'll be all right. Just continue inhaling the Friars' Balsam, and take the cough suppressant. I'll send more over to you later today. You need rest and lots of liquids.'

Ned eyed the doctor and murmured, 'Then nothing's changed, Dr Lessing.' He tried to force a smile, wanting to make light of it.

'That's true, it hasn't. I'll come to see you tomorrow, Mr Deravenel. Rest comfortably in the meantime.' The doctor left, after saying goodbye to Will and Bess, adding that he would see himself out.

Bess brought the cup of lemon tea to her father, and Edward sipped some of it then placed the cup on his bedside table. 'I feel quite tired, Will. I think I'd like to have a nap.'

'Then that's what you must do. I'll be off, but if you need me I can be back in ten minutes, Ned.'

'I'll be fine.'

'I'll go downstairs with you.' Bess looked at her father and said in a soft voice, 'I'll look in on you later, Papa. Rest now.'

Edward gave her a faint smile and closed his eyes.

As they went down the staircase together, Will suddenly stopped, took hold of Bess's arm. 'You must promise to phone me, day or night, if he becomes worse, or if you need me for anything at all.'

'I promise, Uncle Will. But I know the doctor's right. And anyway, Father does recoup quickly, soon gets over bronchitis if he sticks to the regime.'

'Who's here in the house, Bess? Other than Faxton?' Will asked as they continued down the stairs. 'Cook, I assume, and the maids. But where are your little sisters, the ones who haven't gone to Rome?'

'Here with Nanny in the nursery at this moment. Anne *was* invited to go with Mother and the others, because she's eight, but not Katharine and Bridget, Mother says they're too little. But Anne didn't want to go, Uncle Will: she likes to mother her sisters. She misses Little Georgie, she's never stopped grieving for him. Or for Mary.'

Will nodded. Ned's third son, Little Georgie, had died in 1922, four years ago now, when he was just two years old. He was another child they had lost in infancy, like baby Margaret who had passed on several years earlier. But then Ned and Elizabeth had been fortunate to have two more children after these deaths, Katharine in 1922, who had helped them to get over the sad loss of Little Georgie, and then Bridget in 1923, who was now three years old. Mary, their second-born daughter, had died last year, quite prematurely of rheumatic fever, much to their immense sorrow. She had been fifteen.

Will sighed, shook his head as they walked across the entrance hall towards the front door.

Bess, looking at him quickly, asked, 'What is it, Uncle Will?'

'I was just thinking what a lucky couple your parents are, in so many ways. Just think how many children they've been fortunate to have – ten altogether and only two of them died in infancy, and then Mary of course. That's quite a remarkable achievement, in my opinion.'

'Yes, it is.' A hint of sadness crept into her voice when she said softly, 'I miss Mary very much. She was close to me, and we were close in age.'

'I know you miss her. We all do. Although it doesn't make it any easier for me to say this to you, because you'll grieve for Mary for a long time, you must take consolation in your other brothers and sisters.'

'I do, and they're all rather beautiful to look at too, just like Mary was, and sweet. Really good children.'

'I think this brood is quite a remarkable achievement for your parents, and obviously the Deravenels are a fertile family. I expect you'll have a big family when you grow up and get married,' Will told her.

'*I* certainly don't want ten children!' she exclaimed, sounding horrified at the idea, and grinned when she saw the look of amusement on his face. 'And I *am* grown up, Uncle Will. Have you forgotten I'm now seventeen?'

'And in charge,' he added succinctly. 'That's what you forever announced when you were a little girl. "I'm in charge", you used to say to me. And you know what, Bess? *I* believed you.'

Bess found Nanny on the nursery floor of Waverley Court, where there was a parlour, bathrooms, a baby nursery, and bedrooms for the children, as well as for Nanny, and Madge, the assistant nanny.

Going into the comfortable, cosy parlour, Bess found Nanny sitting at the table holding a cup of tea, whilst her three little sisters were drinking glasses of milk. There was a plate of sliced fruit on the table, Nanny's antidote to sweet biscuits and chocolate fingers, which they all adored and Nanny frowned upon. 'Too much sugar,' she was forever saying, wagging a finger.

'There you are, Bess,' Nanny said, putting her cup down. 'How is your father?'

'He's not too badly, Nanny, and it's bronchitis, as we all thought. The doctor just left.'

'I saw his car through the window, and Mr Hasling's as well.'

'Uncle Will went home, but he'll come back if we need him for anything.'

'Will Dr Lessing make a visit to your father tomorrow, Bess?'

'Yes, Nanny, he said he would. In the meantime, we must look after Father the way we always do when he gets bronchitis.'

Nanny nodded sagely. 'Yes, we'll do our best. It seems to run in the family,' she murmured, thinking of Young Edward, who was prone to it, just as his father was.

'I want to see Papa,' Anne announced, giving Bess an imploring look. 'Can I? *Please*. I want to give him a kiss – he likes my kisses, he told me.'

'A little later, darling,' Bess said in her most authoritative voice. 'Father is resting now . . . you know he's not well.'

'But he promised me a threepenny bit for Good Friday. That's today,' the eight-year-old pointed out.

'If he promised, he'll keep his promise, Anne, but later.' She glanced at Katharine, who was four, and Bridget, who was a year younger, and added, 'Everyone will get a threepenny bit for Good Friday. From Papa. I promise.'

Her three younger siblings beamed at her, and she broke into a smile as she studied them for a moment. They were all blondes, and beautiful, just like their brothers and their other sister Cecily.

Katharine now looked at her through those alluring turquoise eyes of hers, and announced, 'We're having hot cross buns for tea, Nanny says so.'

'I shall come and join you,' Bess promised.

'And Papa?' Katharine asked eagerly.

'We'll see.' As she spoke Bess looked across at Nanny and shook her head.

FORTY-ONE

London

Bess was sitting by the side of her father's bed, in the bedroom of his house in Berkeley Square. Yesterday, Easter Sunday, he had insisted on returning to London. His health having improved since Good Friday, he had explained that he much preferred to be in town, and so Broadbent had driven them up in the late afternoon.

Now, as she glanced at him, Bess had to admit that he did look a bit better; his colour was more normal, his eyes were less glazed, and the feverishness was diminishing, for which she was most thankful.

Looking at her thoughtfully, Edward said, 'Thank you for reading *The Times* to me, Bess. Now, there's something I wish to explain to you.'

Sitting up straighter in her chair, his eldest daughter was immediately alert. 'What is that, Father?' Her curiosity was aroused because he sounded serious.

Pulling open the drawer in the bedside table, he took out a piece of paper and handed it to her. 'First, I would like you to read this.'

She did as he asked, and then focused her clear blue eyes on him. 'The numbers here, they're a combination ... for your safe, aren't they?'

'Good girl! For the safe in my dressing room here, and for the one at Ravenscar. Those numbers open *both* safes, it was so much easier to make one sequence. I want you to open the safe here and take out the manila envelopes on the top shelf.'

Jumping up, she hurried across her father's bedroom, taking the piece of paper with her. A moment later she was back, carrying the large envelope. After handing it to him, she returned to the chair.

Edward held the envelope for a moment, then placed it on the bed, and said, 'These papers are for you, Bess. To keep. They are the rules of the company, of Deravenels, updated by me in 1918. You must remember when I had that fall on the terrace at Ravenscar that year ... at Christmas?'

'Of course I do, Father.'

'I was very lucky that day, you know. I could have been rather seriously injured, broken my back or my neck. I could even have been killed. Fortunately, I wasn't. What that fall did was alert me to the truth ... that I am vulnerable, just like anyone else. I started to think about the rules of Deravenels, and I decided I must have them changed. I was delighted when the board went along with me. And what the new rules in the envelope explain is that a woman who is *born* a Deravenel can inherit the company, run it as managing director. Understand?'

'Yes, I do. But what about the male heir? Doesn't he come first?'

'*Absolutely*. But what if something happened to me and your brothers at the same time? What if we had some kind of accident and died? Or what if both boys were together, had an accident and were killed? One never knows what life is going to bring, Bess. And so I got to thinking, as I said, and I realized that after your brothers, you would be the heir to Deravenels. And so I studied the old rules, drafted some new ones, and took them to the board at our annual board meeting in January of 1919. They were immediately approved by my fellow board members, and registered.'

'The rest of the board agreed that *a woman* could run Deravenels?' Bess exclaimed. 'I can hardly believe that!'

'Well, we are living in modern times now, you know. It's already 1926. Anyway, if I should die, or if your brothers die, or are in any way incapacitated, then you immediately become my heir. In other words, if you are the only one left standing, Bess, *you*, as my eldest child, are the next in line and will inherit *everything*, including Deravenels. Apart from the trusts I have created for your sisters, and your mother, of course. Grace Rose also has her own trust. And you do, too, and that remains intact no matter what.'

For a moment Bess was flabbergasted, and then as the implications set in, she exclaimed tremulously, 'But you're not going to die, Papa! And the boys are not going to die! Please don't talk about you all dying. It upsets me.'

'I know it does, but we must be practical, businesslike, there's too much at stake. I want to safeguard the company. I must. I built it into everything it has become today. *I must protect Deravenels for future Deravenels.* That is what this conversation is about.'

He now handed his daughter the manila envelope, and explained, 'Along with the company rules, there is my cheque made out to you, Bess, for five thousand pounds. I want you to telephone Aunt Vicky, when she gets back from Kent later this week. She will take you to her bank, where you will open an account and rent a safety deposit box. The cheque –'

'Father, it's too *much*. A fortune.'

'The cheque will enable you to open an account, and it will be there for you for any emergencies you might have one day. Explain you want it to be in an interest-earning account, all right?'

Bess, at a loss for words, simply nodded.

'And no doubt you realize the safety deposit box is for the papers in the envelope?'

'Yes, Father, of course.'

'Please read them later.'

'I will.'

'Another point. Endeavour to commit the sequence of numbers to memory if you can, and then destroy the piece of paper.'

'Yes, I will.'

He smiled at her. 'Don't look so worried, darling, nothing's going to happen to me for a very long time, or to your brothers. I'm merely being my usual efficient self, that's all.'

Bess nodded, not trusting herself to speak. Her father's talk of accidents and death and dying troubled her tremendously. A little silence fell between them for a moment, but she finally said, 'You did improve quickly, Father, but you must still take care. I hope you're not thinking of going to Deravenels on Tuesday. You're not, are you?'

'Not even I am that foolish. No, I'll do as Dr Lessing says, and remain in bed with my cough mixture and my Friars' Balsam handy.' Edward sat back against the pile of pillows; he always felt better sitting upright when he had bronchitis. He seemed to cough much less in that position.

Bess rose, and picking up the envelope she glided across the room, heading for her father's safe, saying as she did, 'I'd better lock these away until I can take them to the bank later this week.'

'That's a good idea.'

She came back and stood next to the bed, looking down at Edward; all of a sudden a smile appeared on her face, dislodging her grave expression. 'I think I'll go downstairs and talk to Cook, Father. I want to know what she is making for your dinner. Do you fancy anything special?'

'I'm not all that hungry, Bess. Something light. He leaned his head on the pillows. 'I feel tired. Would you wake me in an hour, my dear?'

'Yes, I will.' She hurried out of the room, heading for the kitchen.

Edward watched her go, thinking what a unique young woman she had become. She was beautiful as a child, but now a new loveliness had settled over her. She seemed to him to have an inner light, a radiance that frequently took his breath away. Bess still had his vivid colouring, the red-gold hair, the startlingly blue eyes. But her face was now much more like her mother's; she had Elizabeth's elegant bone structure, delicate features, her classical beauty. He was very proud of Bess, and in so many different ways. He trusted her implicitly; she had always been more his child than her mother's. In fact, it seemed to him that Bess had been instinctively wary of her mother for years.

As she shut the door behind her, Edward closed his eyes, fell down into himself, his thoughts running on. He did not sleep. All manner of things rushed through his mind . . . George, his brother, was suddenly there, clear as day inside his head. Beautiful boy, handsome man. Too young to die . . . there was Neville now, his cousin and mentor whom he had revered . . . he also had died too soon. That ghastly accident at Ravenscar . . . so long ago now . . . twelve years. His beloved Johnny, Neville's brother, dying there with Neville on the beach at Ravenscar . . . he remembered their youth together, growing up in Yorkshire, riding across the moors. They had loved the moors best in August and September; it was then the heather bloomed, a sea of purple . . . wave upon wave of brilliant colour undulating under the light breeze . . . the moors . . . implacable . . . wild, empty spaces filled with silence and solitude . . . he had never felt lonely there . . . the moors flung up against the uncertain northern sky were home to him . . .

Unexpectedly, his thoughts swung to Amos Finnister. Last year, in Paris, Grace Rose had been worried about him, and so

371

he had spoken to Amos when he returned to London. There had been no hesitation when he asked Amos if something was troubling him. He had unburdened himself at once. Edward could hear his voice now, low and sorrowful. 'It's about your brother, Mr George,' Amos had confided. 'Oliveri and I, well, we feel it's our fault he's dead, sir. You see, we told Vincent Martell about that old saying, you know, the one referring to Thomas à Becket . . . when King Henry said something like, "Who will rid me of this turbulent priest?" and how some of the king's henchmen had gone off and murdered Thomas in the cathedral on behalf of the king. Oliveri and I have always believed, ever since then, that Vincent loosened the wedges that held the barrels in place. He sort of . . . well, he kind of indicated that he had. And we've felt responsible since that time, and guilty. We never meant harm, but perhaps he thought we were giving him a hint.'

Edward recalled now how he had reassured Amos that day, explained that it was not his fault, nor Oliveri's, and that George had brought everything on himself. Later, Amos had confided that Vincent Martell had grown to genuinely hate George, in the most virulent way, because his brother was saying such dreadful things about him. Nothing could ever be proved, of course, nor did he want to prove it. In any case, Vincent had cancer and was very ill at this moment, more than likely dying.

My fault . . . If anyone's to blame, I am. I left it too long . . . should have reined George in years before, held him responsible for his actions, not been so quick to forgive . . . not taken him back . . . perhaps if I'd controlled him, handled it better, he would be alive today . . . Mama always got to me, convinced me to be kind, begged me to help George, to let bygones be bygones. His mother had not forgiven him yet, he knew that . . . she thought he was a murderer, had said that to him one day . . . 'you killed my son' . . . she had thrown those words at him . . . at the time he had thought, 'But I'm your son also'. He had not said this to her . . . sometimes, like now . . . he wished that he had . . .

Downstairs in the library, Bess was seated at her father's desk, speaking on the telephone to Will Hasling. 'Father is better, honestly, Uncle Will, please do believe me. I'm telling you the truth.'

Listening carefully, paying attention to every word, Will now said, 'I'm just checking to be sure that all is well, and I also wanted you to know that we are coming back up to town tonight. So if you do need to get in touch with me, you'll find me at the house in London.'

'Thanks for letting me know, Uncle Will.'

'Oh, and Bess, there is one other thing . . . have you told your mother that your father is ill, that he has bronchitis again?'

Bess gripped the phone a little harder, frowning to herself. 'No, I haven't. Father didn't ask me to telephone her. Do you think I should have?'

'No, no, I'm sure it's not necessary,' Will said swiftly. 'If you say your father is a little better tonight, perhaps there's no point.' As he said these words, Will experienced that odd feeling once again; he had that peculiar flash of foreboding he'd had on Friday, and he made up his mind to get in touch with Anthony Wyland, who was in Rome with his sister Elizabeth. In his bones he knew they should be told.

'Uncle Will, are you there?' Bess was saying.

'Yes, yes, I am, Bess. Give your father my best love, and tell him I'll come and see him tomorrow.'

Bess hung up the telephone and sat staring at it for the longest moment, still frowning. Was her father not as well as he seemed?

She couldn't help wondering that . . . because why had Will Hasling asked her if she had talked to her mother in Rome? Did Will know more than she did? Was there something really wrong with her father? If not, why his concern? Well, he was her father's best friend, his colleague in business.

Bess went out of the library and ran upstairs; she flew down the corridor to her father's bedroom, tapped on the door and hurried in. To her surprise, he was sitting up in bed.

'I came to wake you up, Father,' she said, suddenly filled with relief, 'and here you are, already awake.'

A smile flickered. 'What has Cook got in store for me tonight?'

'Hot chicken broth with noodles, grilled sole with parsley sauce and mashed potatoes. It sounds delicious.'

'Hardly. More like a menu for a sick man.'

'I shall have supper with you, Papa, up here on a tray. Is that all right?'

'Perfect.'

Edward awakened suddenly in the middle of the night. He felt as if he had steel bands fastened around his chest. The pain was excruciating. He tried to move, to sit up, and found he could not. Rolling, he managed to turn himself on his side, and that felt a bit better. He realized then that his right side was hurting him. And then there it was again, that terrible searing pain across his chest. Congested, he thought, I'm congested, it's the bronchitis.

A small voice in his head told him it wasn't the bronchitis, that it was something else, something worse. He wondered if he was having a heart attack; he couldn't be sure.

Edward lay very still, trying to breathe evenly, and eventually the chest pains abated, and finally they ceased altogether. His right side still hurt him, but as he remained in one position in the bed this, too, began to lessen. When he felt more comfortable at last he dozed, drifted off, soon fell fast asleep.

In his dreams he was with Lily Overton, his darling Lily, the woman he had loved so much when he was a very young man . . .

FORTY-TWO

Bess sat waiting in the library for her father's London physician, Dr Avery Ince. He was upstairs with her father, and had been there for quite a while, and now she was beginning to worry more than usual. Why was the visit lasting so long?

A moment or two later she heard his footsteps crossing the marble hall and hurried out of the library. 'What do you think, Dr Ince?' she asked, her concern reflected in her dour expression.

'Let's go into the library for a moment, Bess,' he said, guiding her into the room. He had known her since she was a child, and in the last two or three years had come to admire her; she did her father proud.

'Is Papa any better?' Bess asked as she seated herself on the edge of a chair.

'No, about the same,' the doctor answered, also sitting down. 'But he seems rather tired this morning.'

'Father wanted to see some of his friends yesterday afternoon, and they came over for tea,' Bess explained. 'Perhaps it was a bit exhausting for him.' She sat back in the chair, not daring to tell the doctor about the evening. Her father had invited Alfredo

Oliveri and Amos Finnister to come over last night with Uncle Will, and they had stayed a long time.

'From now on no more visitors, Bess,' the doctor admonished. 'I want your father to have complete and total rest. And please make sure he takes the expectorant I brought with me today. He has a lot of mucus in his chest, and I want to clear that up as fast as I can.' The doctor rose, picked up his bag and went towards the door.

Bess followed him, asking, 'Are you going to come and see Father tomorrow, Dr Ince?'

'I shall stop by in the late morning. Oh, and by the way, when is your mother returning from Rome?'

'Tomorrow. Uncle Will telephoned Uncle Anthony who is with her, and he's made all the travel arrangements.'

'Excellent.' He smiled at her warmly, and added in a reassuring way, 'Don't look so worried, Bess, we'll soon have your father up and about. He'll be his old self in a few days. Make sure he drinks plenty of liquids, won't you?'

'Yes, Dr Ince,' she said, seeing him out. Locking the front door, she raced across the large entrance hall and went into the morning room. Will was sitting there with Grace Rose and Jane Shaw. Jane's presence in the house had been made possible by the absence of Mallet. Today was Wednesday, the butler's day off.

'What did Dr Ince say?' Jane asked anxiously as Bess came in. She looked weary, and was obviously worried.

'That father's about the same, but very *tired*.' Bess shook her head. 'That's no doubt because he had visitors yesterday, but Vicky and Fenella did cheer him up.'

Will said, 'This is the worst I've seen your father, Bess. He's never been quite this sick with bronchitis. He has to rest, and you must keep him in bed. He was talking to me about coming back to the office next week. However, I don't think that's wise.'

'Neither do I,' Jane said, and stood up, looking even more anxious. 'May I go and see him now?' She gave Bess a smile, and added, 'I'm sure you realize that I feel a trifle . . . awkward . . . being here in this house.'

'I understand. And of course you can see him. Come on!' Bess led the way upstairs.

Within minutes she returned to the library and sat down next to her half sister. 'Father says he'd like you to go up in fifteen minutes, Grace Rose. He's looking forward to a visit from you.'

'And I can't wait to see him.' Clearing her throat, Grace Rose now ventured, 'Shouldn't Uncle Ned be in a hospital?' She looked from Will to Bess, her eyes full of questions.

'We've both suggested it, and discussed it with Dr Ince,' Will answered. 'Ned won't hear of it, won't budge from this house, and the doctor seems to think it's better to cater to him rather than put him in a private clinic, which I suggested.'

'I understand.' Grace Rose sighed. 'Dr Ince is very good; he's our doctor, too. I suppose he does know best.' Nonetheless she still believed her natural father *should* be in a hospital, no matter what Edward himself wanted. He was stubborn, and used to getting his own way; his condition troubled her.

'The doctor asked me when Mother is coming home, and I told him tomorrow. That's correct, isn't it, Uncle Will?'

'According to your uncle, Bess, they'll arrive Thursday afternoon.'

Bess gave Will a pointed look and said in a low voice, 'I hope she's not going to upset him, make him feel worse. She always brushes Papa up the wrong way.'

Will was silent, knowing that Ned's daughter spoke the truth.

Grace Rose did not say a word either, having witnessed at first hand Elizabeth's remarkably bad temper being directed at Uncle Ned. She simply stood, said softly, 'I'll go up and see him now.'

Finally the house was quiet. Silent. All was peaceful again.

Bess's mother had arrived home this afternoon, a day earlier than expected, and for a short while chaos had reigned. She had stepped into the house haughtily, looking coolly beautiful and controlled, the Ice Queen, followed by Cecily, Young Edward, Little Ritchie, Miss Coleman, the new governess, and her maid, Elsie. In the rear guard, managing the luggage, were Uncle Anthony, Flon, the bootboy, and three of the household maids, as well as the new under-butler, Jackson.

Without so much as a word of greeting, her mother had swept passed her, gone up the stairs and into her father's room, closing the door behind her very firmly.

Bess was annoyed that her mother had not even acknowledged her. She had been left to organize the other children, and give Uncle Anthony all of the details of her father's illness, plus a report of his progress so far.

As she had poured her uncle a cup of tea, and made sure her two brothers and sister had glasses of milk and arrowroot biscuits, she had silently thanked God they had not arrived two hours earlier.

If that had happened they would have all been caught red-handed – she and her father, Uncle Will and Grace Rose – entertaining Jane Shaw, her father's mistress, to a lunch of smoked salmon sandwiches and white wine. That would have caused a genuine full-blown war . . . the war to end all wars and their marriage. But Jane, always so proper, so careful and extremely well-mannered, had been somewhat nervous and ill at ease about being in the Berkeley Square house, and had made it a short lunch. How lucky that had been.

After half an hour her mother had come downstairs to the drawing room looking extremely put out, but she had finally greeted her, and kissed her on the cheek. What had seemed strange to Bess was that she had made no reference to her sick husband on the floor above. It was only when her brother Anthony had begun to question her that Elizabeth had thrown him an angry look and muttered, 'We'll talk shortly, but not *now*.'

Fourteen-year-old Cecily had spoken out then, had insisted on going up to their father, and Young Edward and Little Ritchie had exclaimed that they, too, wished to see their father as well. And she had been told to take them to their father's bedroom at once.

Now, as she thought back to the afternoon, Bess realized what a supreme effort it had been for Papa to appear cheerful for his two sons, his male heirs, and for her and Cecily, also.

Usually the boys were rambunctious, liked to jump all over him and hug him, but this afternoon they had been suitably well behaved, and chastened, perhaps a little frightened even to see their father prone in bed and not looking all that robust either.

Both boys had been sweet and loving as had Cecily, and when her father had asked where the other girls were, she had thought that perhaps they should be here with the family, now that their mother had come home.

'They're down in Kent with Nanny,' she had reminded him, and he had nodded, told her to have them brought up to London the next morning. And then he had smiled that irresistible smile of his – a smile like no other smile in the whole world.

Bess suddenly awakened with a start.

She sat up, looking around, and realized that she had fallen asleep in her father's chair behind the desk in the library. She glanced at the carriage clock on the mantelpiece and saw that it was already ten. Unexpectedly, she felt a rush of sudden fear, a strange uneasiness, and she left the library, flew upstairs and stood outside her father's bedroom door. All was quiet. After a moment, she opened it, and went in, crossed the floor. The bedside light was on, and he turned his head, becoming aware of her, looked directly at her. And she couldn't help thinking how very blue his eyes were tonight, bluer than she had ever seen them.

'Hello, sweetheart.'

'Papa, do you need anything?'

'Will . . . get Will.'

'Now, Papa?'

'Yes.'

Bess went to the telephone in her father's dressing room, dialled the number of Will Hasling. When he himself answered, she said in a low voice, 'Uncle Will, it's Bess. My father wants you to come. Now. Can you?'

'I'll be there as fast as I can. Is something wrong?'

'I – I don't know. I'll go downstairs and wait at the front door, so we don't . . . wake anybody up.'

'I understand.

After she had replaced the receiver, she went back to her father's bed. 'He's coming, Papa.'

Edward nodded his head, and then said, 'Lock the door.' As he spoke he pointed to the dressing room.

'To the adjoining bedroom?'

'Yes.'

Bess ran into the dressing room and very quietly turned the key in the door which opened onto her mother's bedroom.

'It's locked. I'm going downstairs, Father,' she said as she returned to his bedside. 'To wait for Uncle Will at the front door. I don't want him to ring the doorbell, disturb the house.'

'Good.'

FORTY-THREE

Jackson, the under-butler, had already locked up for the night, and Bess immediately set to work pulling back the bolts and unlocking the door. She then stood waiting, listening for the sound of Will Hasling.

She did not have to wait long.

Within fifteen minutes she heard a car drawing up, the sound of one of its doors closing, and muted voices, followed by footsteps.

Opening the door a crack, she came face to face with Will. He slipped inside, then closed and locked the door behind him.

'The whole house is fast asleep. Father didn't want anyone to be disturbed. The boys and Cecily were especially tired after travelling so long,' Bess explained.

Will nodded. 'Is he all right?'

'He seems about the same, but very quiet. Mother and I sat with him for a short while after supper, and he was . . . withdrawn. I think he is worn out. At least then he was. When I looked in on him a short while ago he was more like himself, and he asked me to telephone you to come over.'

'I'm assuming that everything is all right between your parents?

Nothing untoward happened when your mother got back, did it?'

'Not that I know of, Uncle Will. Mother went to see father immediately she arrived. She didn't say anything to me when she came down for tea, but we did eventually talk later. She asked me a lot of questions and wanted to know everything. She was very upset about Father, and she was weeping. I made her go and take a rest before dinner, and she seemed a bit better when she joined us at seven.'

Will said nothing; he took hold of Bess's arm and the two of them crossed the hall, hurried up the grand staircase, and went into Edward's bedroom.

'Here I am, Ned!' Will went over to the bed, looking for tell-tale evidence of a worsening condition, or signs of emotional upset. But there was nothing visible, nothing unusual about Ned's appearance tonight, much to Will's profound relief. Elizabeth could easily have upset Edward when she had arrived from Rome today.

'Thanks for coming, Will,' Ned said. 'Can you help me to sit up, do you think?'

Will did as he asked, propped him against the pillows, and then sat down in one of the chairs near the bed.

Bess, hovering near the doorway, cleared her throat. 'I'll leave you to yourselves, Papa, and –'

'No, no, you don't have to go, Bess.' Ned gestured to the seating area at the other side of the bedroom. 'You can sit there if you wish, whilst I talk to Will.'

Bess did as her father suggested.

The room was quiet for several minutes, until Will broke the silence, saying, 'Anthony let me know everyone was back safely from Rome, a day early.'

A faint smile touched Edward's mouth but only fleetingly. 'Yes, and *we* almost got caught red-handed, didn't we? At least that was the way my Bess put it.'

Will laughed. 'Only too true.'

'Elizabeth has been very upset since she got back,' Edward confided. 'And she has made a suggestion to me, which I would like to pass by you. She wants me to take three months off from Deravenels and go on one of the big ships to New York. She believes the trip will do me an enormous amount of good – sea air and all that. And to make the idea more palatable and appealing to me, she pointed out that we have offices in New York and the oil fields in Louisiana. What do you think?'

'She's right for once, Ned. It's a splendid idea. You should do it.'

'Will you run Deravenels for me whilst I'm away?'

'Of course I will, you surely know that.'

'When is Richard returning from Persia?'

'Not until next week. Before he left he told me he was taking your advice and going on to Constantinople, after visiting the oil fields. As you know, he took Anne with him. He wanted her to have a holiday. She's not been at all well.'

Edward sighed. 'She's never been a strong person. Like her late sister Isabel, Anne has a poor constitution. Strange, isn't it, that Neville's daughters would be such delicate little creatures, when their father was so robust and strong.'

'It is, yes.'

'I can't wait for tomorrow.' Edward's eyes lit up. 'The girls are coming back from Kent with Nanny. I'm really looking forward to seeing my little beauties.' Edward looked across at Bess, sitting on the sofa near the fireplace. Turning to his best friend, he said softly, 'My daughter has been wonderful. She hasn't stopped running after me, doing things for me, and for days now. I do think I have to take Ince's advice and let him hire a nurse. It's all too much for Bess, don't you think?'

Will looked at Edward alertly, searchingly, and asked, 'You think you need a nurse, do you, Ned?'

'Not in the sense you mean, no. I'm not feeling any worse,

Will. But I can't have my daughter acting as one, now can I?'

'I suppose not. Do you want me to get in touch with Ince tomorrow morning, ask him to send someone to the house?'

'If you would, please. There's something else –' Edward stopped, hesitated, lay staring at Will intently but saying nothing.

'What is it?'

'It's a question, actually. I never told you this, but last year I spoke to Finnister . . . about George's death. Grace Rose had alerted me to the fact that he was worried. She didn't know why. When I questioned him he said he and Oliveri were concerned, and felt guilty about George's death. He explained that they had told Vincent Martell about that old saying and Amos then confided that he and Oliveri thought that perhaps Martell had loosened those wedges under the barrels in the wine vault himself.'

'He was suggesting that Martell created a situation to injure George?'

'Yes, he did indeed suggest that.'

'But Ned, that's murder!'

'I know . . . and murder is something I've always worried about. I've asked myself a thousand times if George *was* murdered. It haunts me these nights when I can't sleep. Tell me, Will, what is your opinion? Was my brother murdered?'

Will thought that Finnister was more than likely correct, that Martell had indeed taken matters into his own hands, because of the foul things George had been saying about his brother. On the other hand, he had no proof and he did not want to upset Edward further. He wanted to squash the idea. And so he lied, when he said, 'I don't believe it's true, no, not at all. For one thing, why would Martell murder George? Yes, your brother slandered you in the worst way, constantly. But you know, Martell is pragmatic, he wouldn't pay much attention to George's words. He would simply ignore him, go about his own business.'

'I'm not so sure . . .'

Will leaned closer to Edward and murmured sotto voce, 'Believe *this*, Ned, hear my words. Martell would not risk wasting hundreds of barrels of fine Beaujolais wine. As I just said, he is very practical, and he loves the vineyard and everything about it.'

A faint smile struck Edward's mouth, and he nodded. After a moment, he said, 'But enormous hatred can cloud a man's judgement.'

'That's true. However, forget Martell. You must put George's death out of your mind, stop dwelling on it. Please, forget about Amos's suspicions for your own peace of mind, Ned.'

'As always, you're right . . . You have never told me anything but the truth. I don't know what I would have done without you all these years, Will. I really don't.'

For the first time in days Edward Deravenel slept a dreamless sleep that night. No ghosts came to torment him; they left him alone. He rested peacefully.

The following morning he appeared to be much better, and even Dr Ince commented on his improved health. After examining him, the doctor said, 'A nurse is waiting downstairs. Her name is Margery Arkright, and I've hired her to look after you at the request of Mr Hasling. May I now bring her upstairs to meet you, Mr Deravenel?'

'Yes, and thank you, Ince. I'm sure Hasling explained that I've been relying on Bess far too much. It's not fair to her.'

'He did explain, and you are correct: better to have a professional. Why burden your daughter? Excuse me for a moment.'

Within minutes the doctor had returned with Nurse Arkright, a pleasant-looking woman in her thirties. After they had been introduced, Edward said, 'Perhaps you should make yourself at home in my adjoining dressing room, Nurse Arkright. There are chairs and a sofa in the room, and a desk. You'll be perfectly comfortable, and nearby if I need you.'

'Thank you, Mr Deravenel,' she said, and followed the doctor who was walking towards the dressing room, beckoning her to follow.

That night Bess was unable to sleep. Several times she got up and went down to her father's bedroom on the floor below. Each time she looked in on him he appeared to be sleeping soundly, and Nurse Arkright would look up, put a finger to her lips, then mouthed silently, 'All is well.'

Around three o'clock Bess ventured downstairs again, and once more the nurse reassured her that her father was sleeping soundly. Returning to her bedroom, she finally dozed off. Some time later, just as dawn was breaking and daylight was seeping in through the curtains, Bess awakened with a start. She sat up and turned on the bedside lamp, saw from the clock that it was almost five in the morning. As she struggled into her dressing gown and stepped into her slippers, she felt that strange but now familiar sense of unease invading her. Her father needed her, she was quite positive of that.

Rushing down the stairs, she saw Nurse Arkright coming out of her father's room, and she hissed, 'Nurse! Is something wrong?'

The nurse beckoned to her, stood waiting next to Edward's door.

'I was on my way to your room. Your father has been calling for you, Miss Bess. And for Lily. He suddenly woke up about fifteen minutes ago. He was feverish. I believe he's had a heart attack. A bad one. Come with me.'

Bess was terribly frightened when she saw her father's face. He had black smudges under his eyes and he was extremely pale, paler than she had ever seen him. How gaunt he was, and drawn around the mouth. Then she noticed the tremor in his hands resting on the sheet. She was stunned, and more afraid than ever.

Kneeling down at his bedside, she took hold of his hand and whispered, 'Papa, it's me, Bess. I am here.'

He did not respond for a while and then he suddenly opened his eyes. She saw how sunken they were, as if they had been pushed back into his head, and they were red-rimmed. He did not speak, but he tightened his grasp on her hand.

Bess said again, 'Papa, it's me. I am here to help you. It's Bess.'

'I'm so sorry, so very, very sorry, Bess.'

Whatever had happened to him in the last few hours he was, nonetheless, lucid, and she knew he had recognized her. 'There's no reason for you to be sorry, Papa,' she whispered, staring into his tired face. 'We'll have you better very soon.'

'Forgive me . . . I don't want to leave you . . .'

'Please, Father, don't say that. There is nothing to forgive. And you can't leave us, we love you so much.' Tears were seeping out of her eyes and rolling down her face, splashing onto their hands clasped together. 'Oh, Papa, please try, fight.'

'I'm tired . . . the pain in my chest . . .'

'Papa, oh Papa, whatever will we do without you?'

Suddenly he seemed to revive. He opened his eyes wider and looked into hers . . . brilliant blue impaling brilliant blue. And he said in a calm voice, very clearly, 'You'll be fine, my Bess . . . look after them all for me . . .' He smiled at her, and it was that irresistible smile of his, like no other in the world, the smile she would never forget as long as she lived.

Bess laid her head on his chest, wrapped her arms around him, and held him close. Her grief knew no bounds.

A few minutes later she heard a faint noise and lifted her head. Her mother was standing at the entrance of the dressing room, staring at her. 'Bess,' Elizabeth said in a trembling voice. And then again, 'Bess . . .'

'He's dead,' Bess whispered in a hoarse voice full of tears. 'My father is dead.'

Elizabeth stepped forward, walking unsteadily towards the bed. Her face was frozen with fear, her eyes filled with tears.

It was Friday the ninth of April, 1926. Edward Deravenel had died of a massive heart attack just nineteen days before his forty-first birthday on April twenty-eighth.

Three sons she had buried here at Ravenscar. First Edmund, then George, and now Edward.

It was Tuesday the thirteenth day of April in the year of Our Lord 1926, and as she watched his coffin being lowered into his grave Cecily Deravenel felt as though her heart was breaking yet again. Tears ran down her cheecks unchecked as she stood there engulfed by sorrow.

Her darling Ned was gone from her forever. She had only one son left, her youngest child, Richard. He was absent today, delayed on the Continent by his wife's sudden illness. How devastated Richard must be. He had so adored his eldest brother.

Now Cecily wished, and with all her heart, that she had spoken to Ned more openly, had made sure he truly understood that she did not blame him for George's death. No one was to blame, except perhaps George himself. Regrettably she had said nothing to Ned, and so he had gone to his grave without knowing how she truly felt.

Cecily lifted her head, her eyes settling on Ned's widow, Elizabeth: pale as death, her great beauty dimmed by her pain and sadness. Bright sunlight broke through the leaden clouds and suddenly the children's red-gold curls were like burnished halos around their innocent young faces. Cecily, Anne, Katharine,

Bridget, Young Edward and Little Ritchie were clustered together looking bewildered, and next to them were Bess and Grace Rose, standing guard over them like sentinels, endeavouring to control their own grief.

Cecily heard a muffled sob, turned to Will Hasling, took hold of his arm affectionately; she had always thought of him as another son, and wished to comfort him. He, too, was burdened down with sorrow. Close to him were Mr Finnister and Mr Oliveri; and like Will's, their faces were wet with tears. When grown men wept so openly and without a hint of shame, the depth of their love showed, and she knew how much they had cared for her son.

'Ashes to ashes, dust to dust,' Father O'Connor was intoning, and as handfuls of earth clattered down onto Ned's coffin she felt her heart tightening; she swayed slightly, and then Will's arm went around her, supported her. Looking up at him, Cecily whispered, 'The chldren, those little children – they will be lost without Ned.'

'I shall look after them,' Will promised softly, bending his head to hers. And Cecily was comforted, knowing that indeed he would. She had always trusted Will. Yes, everything would eventually be alright.

But she was wrong. Trouble, the likes of which the Deravenels had never known before, was about to begin.

FORTY-FOUR

'What in God's name do you think you're doing, Richard?' Will Hasling asked, keeping his voice steady, controlled, even though he was furious. He stared at Edward's brother, now the new head of the company.

Richard, sitting behind Edward's old desk in his late brother's office, looked up and returned Will's stare. 'I'm not sure what you're referring to, Will.'

Will stood in the doorway which linked his office to Richard's, put in twenty-one years ago by Edward Deravenel, so that he and Will had easy access to each other.

Now stepping forward, walking towards Richard's desk, Will said, 'I just heard you've sacked Anthony Wyland, that he's actually already gone.' His eyes narrowed, and he asked, '*Why*?'

'As the head of this company I don't owe anyone an explanation, not even *you*. However, you've heard the old saying, haven't you? A new broom sweeps clean.'

'And that's what you're doing, is it? Sweeping clean, getting rid of a talented executive who's a decent, honest and loyal man, who's worked for this company for years, and done a lot of good things for it. I must admit I'm startled, to say the least.'

'Don't be startled, Will,' Richard shot back in a cold voice. 'Instead, get used to changes. There are going to be a lot around here, and sooner than you might think.'

'Don't start tampering with Deravenels, Richard!' Will exclaimed. 'Your brother set it up in an extraordinary way. It runs smoothly, efficiently and very successfully the way it is. Ned made sure of that. Leave things the way they are, otherwise you might regret it.'

'Are you threatening me?' Richard straightened in his chair, his face tense.

Recoiling slightly, taken aback by the icy stare, imperious tone and the question itself, Will shook his head. 'Don't be ridiculous, Dick. Of course I'm not threatening you. I'm simply advising you.'

'I don't need your advice. I know what I'm doing. I've worked for this company for years, or have you forgotten that?'

'No, I certainly haven't. Nor have I forgotten that you have always run the Northern division of Deravenels. You haven't been running it worldwide, and that's a different thing entirely.'

'Are you suggesting I'm not capable of being the chief executive worldwide?'

'Certainly not! Ned always trusted you, spoke highly of you, and your abilities. That's why he named you to run Deravenels until his eldest son is old enough to take over and take charge. Ned added that codicil to his Last Will and Testament, and that's good enough for me. Look, let's get back to Anthony . . . I just don't understand why you have let such an important executive go.'

'I let him go because he's a Wyland, and I've never trusted them. In fact, I never understood why my brother gave him a job in the first place.' Richard let out a short, dry laugh. 'I shouldn't say that. I *do* know. He was forced to give Wyland a job because of that bitch of a wife of his. Elizabeth pushed Ned into it. There's no other explanation.'

'I don't really know anything about that. I only know that Wyland has been running the financial and banking divisions of the company brilliantly. Won't you reconsider your decision?'

'No, I won't, why should I? Just because you want me to reinstate him. Good God, I'm surprised at you, Will. I thought you hated the Wylands as much as we all have all these years. Gone over to their side, have you?'

'I didn't know they had a side, actually,' Will answered, holding himself in check. 'As for Anthony, he's a bloody good chap, truly reliable and honourable. You should trust him. Ned did.'

'More fool he. No, I won't change my mind.'

Will shook his head, worry settling on his face. 'I don't know who you'll find to replace him, I really don't.'

'I already have,' Richard announced, a small smile flashing.

Taken aback though he was, Will nevertheless kept his face neutral and still. 'Who are you going to appoint?'

'Alan Ramsey – and he's already been appointed. Actually, Will, he's sitting in Wyland's old office at this very moment. I move quickly, once I've made up my mind.'

'So I see.' Will nodded, and added, 'Ramsey's a good man.'

'You don't have to tell me that. He's been one of my best friends since childhood. I'd trust him with my life.'

Will half turned, took several steps towards the door.

Richard said, 'There's one other thing, Will.'

'Yes?' Will halted, turned, stared at Richard.

'I would like to know why you arranged Ned's funeral before I got back from Constantinople? My God, my brother was dead and buried within only a few days. I think it should have been delayed until I was here in England.'

'It had nothing to do with me, I can assure you of that.' Will came back into the room, stood in front of the desk, and continued quietly, 'I suggest you speak to your mother about Ned's funeral. In fact, it would *behove* you to do so, and she will probably tell you that she was annoyed with you because you didn't make it back sooner. She couldn't understand why it took you so long. That is what she said to Kathleen. My wife also told me that your mother was extremely put out with all of us, Ned's wife included, because no one saw fit to make sure Ned was given Extreme Unction. She thought it was appalling that no one had thought to bring a priest to Ned's bedside.'

'And I'd like to know why one wasn't brought to him as well?'

'Because none of us knew he was dying, that's why! Can you imagine how enraged Edward Deravenel would have been if one of us had done that? Especially since Dr Ince was not alarmed, and thought he was on the mend. Only Ned knew the true state of his health, and he kept the truth from us all.'

'I'm glad at least that he's buried in the family cemetery at Ravenscar.'

'Where else would he be buried? But as I said, Richard, your mother took over, she was in charge of everything. If you have any bones to pick about Ned's burial, then I think you ought to go to her.'

'Thanks for that tip,' Richard responded, sounding sarcastic.

Will decided to make no other comments, glanced at his watch, and exclaimed, 'I'm running late. I'd best be off. And I'll be happy to meet Alan Ramsey whenever you wish.'

'I'll arrange it.'

Will nodded, went back into his own office and closed the door.

He stood leaning against it, letting out a deep breath. He was angry and shaking. Jumped-up young pup, he thought. Richard is exactly the way Finnister said he is: arrogant, self-satisfied, and a know-it-all to boot. He's hungry for power, ambitious beyond belief. Will shivered, even though it was a warm June day. Someone just walked over my grave, he thought, and felt the hackles rise on the back of his neck.

Walking across to his desk, Will picked up the phone and dialled Oliveri's extension. When Oliveri answered, Will said softly, 'If you have a lunch date you must cancel it immediately. I have to see you, and also Finnister. I'll step by his office, and then I'll leave the building with him. You leave ten minutes later.'

'What's wrong?' Alfredo asked worriedly.

'I will have to tell you when I see you.'

'Shall I book us a table at the Savoy? Or do you prefer Rules?'

'Neither. And don't suggest the Ritz either.'

'How about White's, Will?'

'Good idea. I'll book a table for one o'clock.' Will hung up and sat back in his chair. Richard was not a member of White's and therefore was unable to go there. He could only be taken and that was most unlikely. Even Ned had never taken him there. Richard hated White's.

Will's eyes swept across his desk: no urgent papers, nothing to deal with that was pressing. He left, went down the corridor to Finnister's office, knocked and walked in.

'Amos, I want you to come with me immediately. I'm taking you to White's for lunch with Oliveri, and if you have a lunch appointment you must cancel it.'

'*Trouble*,' Finnister stated and stood up, adding, 'And I don't have a lunch date.'

'Come on then, let's go.'

The two men left the building and went out into the Strand. It was truly hot, especially for June in England, and Will said, 'Let's get a taxi,' and hailed one passing by.

When they were settled and heading towards Will's club, Will turned to Amos, and asked, 'Why did you suspect trouble the moment I asked you to lunch?'

'Because I've been expecting it: your manner, the sudden urgency. I also heard about Anthony Wyland being sacked. And I know our new boss very well, since his childhood. I have him pegged, always have. He's not the man his brother was . . . not by a long shot. You know what they say . . . still waters run deep and the devil's at the bottom.'

Anthony Wyland sat with his sister Elizabeth in the drawing room of the Berkeley Square house. He put his hand out, let it rest on her arm, said gently, 'Don't be angry, and don't be upset. I can fend for myself, Lizzie.'

'But what he's done is humiliating, Anthony. I'm just startled that *you* are not angrier than you are.'

'I was enraged, of course I was. But there was nothing I could do. He chucked me out, politely, coldly, and told me to leave the building at once. So I packed up my desk and left by the end of the afternoon. Yesterday.'

'What will you do?' she asked, frowning, her eyes filled with worry.

'Get another job. Or perhaps not. I don't have to rush into something I don't like. I've made a lot of money –'

'I don't understand. I thought you were a director of Deravenels.'

'I am, or rather I *was*. I had to resign as a director. He demanded it.'

'I'm so sorry . . . Ned would turn in his grave if he knew.'

'He would that.'

'What shall I do about the summer problem?'

Anthony shook his head. 'I honestly don't know. Perhaps Will can advise you about that.'

'I can't go to Will . . . We've never liked each other.'

'Perhaps you ought to let Bess explain the situation. She's always been very close to Will. And he loves her like an uncle, as I love her.'

'What a good idea! I knew you'd have a solution to my

dilemma.' The tension in her face eased a little, and her eyes cleared. She sat back in the chair. 'Thank you for coming to lunch. I do get lonely.'

'You don't have to be . . .' He grinned at her, assuming a demeanour that did not reflect his true feelings. 'I'm probably going to have lots of time on my hands.'

FORTY-FIVE

'It's June the third today and Ned has been dead only seven weeks,' Alfredo exclaimed, looking from Will to Amos. 'He's hardly cold in the ground and Richard is sacking people. His brother would turn in his grave if he knew. It's bloody outrageous if you ask me.'

'*People*?' Will repeated, staring hard at Alfredo. 'I was talking about Anthony Wyland. Has someone else gone? Someone I don't know about?'

'I thought you *did* know,' Alfredo answered swiftly, frowning. 'Edgar Phillips has been let go. I know he's only been with us for eight years, but Ned thought very highly of him, and he was very good in the oil division. A great manager.'

'Nobody told me,' Will muttered. 'But then I wasn't informed about Wyland, either. I had to hear it on the grapevine . . . this morning.'

'Richard dismissed Anthony Wyland yesterday afternoon, and you were out of the office, Will. You went to St Alban's, didn't you?' Oliveri reminded him. 'Edgar Phillips went late on Tuesday, the day before Wyland. Who's next, do you think?'

Amos announced, 'More than likely it'll be me. He's never

liked me, merely tolerated me. And frankly, I'm sure he thinks I don't serve a purpose now, with Mr Edward dead and gone –'

'I'll fight him tooth and nail about that, Amos, believe you me,' Will cut in. 'Mr Edward was inordinately fond of you, and respected you, and anyway, you've been with Deravenels for fourteen years, for God's sake!'

'Things like that don't matter to Richard Deravenel,' Amos replied. 'I know him inside out. Quiet he might be, and clever and cultured, but there's much more to him than that.'

'I know,' Will said, and picked up his glass of white wine. 'Are you sure you won't join us in a drink, Amos?'

Finnister shook his head. 'The soda water is fine, thank you, Mr Will.'

The three men were seated in the dining room of White's, the oldest gentlemen's club in London. The large, well-appointed room was half empty on this lunch time in June. Many of the members left on Thursday afternoons to go to their country homes, and there was a tranquillity about the place today.

The silence at the table was compatible. The three old friends and colleagues were lost in their own thoughts at this moment. Will was thinking of Ned and how much he missed him; Oliveri was wondering if *he* was about to get the axe; Finnister's mind was on Grace Rose. He had seen her for tea yesterday, and she had told him that Jane Shaw was not well, that she was worried about her. The two women had become good friends over the last few years, and close. Grace Rose had explained that Jane was grieving terribly for Ned, weeping every day and was often felled by terrible depression.

The waiter arrived with the menus, and handed them out, then left. Each man studied one, and Will said, 'It's too warm today for soup. I shall have Morecambe Bay potted shrimps, I think, followed by grilled plaice. Keep it light, that's my motto these days.'

'I'll have the potted shrimps, too,' Oliveri muttered. 'And the lamb chops.'

'That sounds good to me,' Finnister said and put his menu down on the table. He then told Will and Oliveri about his tea with Grace Rose, and what she had confided about Jane Shaw, how troubled and unhappy Mrs Shaw was.

'My sister did mention Jane's unhappiness to me,' Will said. 'But Vicky didn't make it sound quite as bad as this, Amos. I think perhaps I'd better go and see Mrs Shaw, suggest she joins us on holiday. My wife and I are going to Cap Martin later in the summer, my sister and her husband are joining us, along with Grace Rose. Mrs Shaw just might enjoy it, you know.'

'That's an excellent suggestion.' Amos nodded. 'I hope she accepts your invitation.'

The waiter returned, the orders were taken, and he hurried off. When they were alone again, Will moved on to another subject. 'I must confess I was very startled by Richard's attitude towards me today. His manner was at times cold, abrupt, and, now that I think about it, he was somewhat *hostile*. He's going to be a problem.'

Oliveri stared at Will, his expression one of total surprise, then he said in a low voice, 'I have a feeling he's going to get very tough with us all.'

'Why do you say that?' Will asked.

'He wants Deravenels for himself. For his *own* son and heir, Little Eddie, as his grandmother calls him. You'll see, he'll go for the big grab in no time at all. He'll grab Deravenels lock, stock and barrel.'

'But that's hardly possible,' Will declared. 'In the codicil attached to Ned's will he made Richard head of Deravenels, *until his heir was old enough to take over, at the age of eighteen.* Then he would be guided by Richard until he was twenty-one. Ned also made Richard guardian of his two boys.'

'Not the rest of the children?' Oliveri sat back, obviously puzzled, gazing at Ned, frowning.

'No, just the two male heirs,' Will replied. 'I'm an executor, and obviously I know.'

Finnister's voice was perturbed when he confided, 'That's something that troubles Grace Rose no end. She says it's making Mrs Edward crazy, that she's really put out about that part of the codicil. She says she's the children's guardian, that she doesn't need their uncle interfering.'

Will was silent, staring into the middle of the dining room, his expression troubled, a faraway look in his eyes. He was experiencing that sudden feeling of unease yet again, almost a sense of foreboding, of onrushing doom. Edward Deravenel had handed immense power on a plate to his youngest brother. And Will couldn't help wondering now if Richard Deravenel was going to let ambition and his lust for power get in the way of brotherly love and duty. This unexpected and frightening thought made Will feel queasy. He would not be able to stomach it if Richard shoved Ned's sons to one side, somehow managed to get Deravenels for himself and his own heir.

Pushing back in his chair, Will stood up. 'Excuse me for a moment.' He hurried out, went to the men's cloakroom. The attendant murmured a greeting; Will nodded, walked over to the three washbasins set along one wall.

He stared at himself in the mirror, saw what a ghastly white he was; perspiration speckled his face and he felt clammy. He took a few deep breaths, pushing back the nausea, washed his hands, then slapped cold water on his face.

The attendant came over, and asked in a low voice, 'Are you not feeling well, Mr Hasling? Can I help you?'

'I'm fine, Boroughs, thank you very much. Heat got to me a bit today, that's all it is.'

'I understand, sir.' The man stepped away politely.

Will dropped some coins in the silver bowl and left the cloak-room.

Finnister and Oliveri had been worried about Will, and looked relieved when he sat down at the table. 'Sorry, chaps,' he apologized. 'I suddenly felt a little queasy but I'm all right now.'

'Amos and I have been talking whilst you were gone,' Oliveri began. 'We've decided we must watch each other's backs, because we both think that Richard Deravenel has got the knives out, and we three may well be the next to go because we were so very close to his brother.'

'I couldn't agree more. The Little Fish, as Ned called him, might well turn out to be the shark.'

FORTY-SIX

Kent

'I'm so relieved you're here, Will,' his sister said, walking with him through the entrance hall of Stonehurst Farm. 'Bess is rather upset, actually perhaps agitated would be a better word to use, and she really does need to speak to you.'

'Did she say what it's about?'

Vicky shook her head. 'Not exactly, but Grace Rose did confide in me the other day. Seemingly, Elizabeth is upset that Ned made Richard guardian of the boys.' Vicky gave her brother a keen look, and added, 'I have a terrible feeling Richard might be trying to . . . impose his will about something, shall we say?'

'It wouldn't surprise me,' Will answered, his heart sinking. Richard apparently throwing his weight around. 'Where *is* Bess?' Will asked.

'She's outside in the garden, with Grace Rose. I'll take you to them and bring you some lemonade. Or would you prefer a cup of tea?'

'The lemonade would be nice, it's rather hot.'

It was a glorious June Saturday. The sky was a perfect blue, without cloud, and there was a light breeze that rustled through the many trees surrounding the manicured lawns. Full-blown

June roses filled the air with their scent: the garden was aflame with colour and beauty: it was Vicky's pride and joy. She had worked hard for many years to turn it into the flower-filled haven it had become, with wonderful exotic plants and flowering bushes and fountains spraying jets of water into the air.

Bess and Grace Rose were sitting at a table on the terrace, shaded from the sun by a large green-and-white striped umbrella. Both waved when they saw Will coming towards them with Vicky.

'Hello, you two beauties,' Will said as he came to a stop, smiling at them broadly, thinking how pretty they both looked today in their light summer dresses.

'Hello, Uncle Will,' they exclaimed in unison, and Vicky said, 'Would you like lemonade, girls? Or something else?'

'Lemonade please,' Grace Rose murmured, smiling at her mother.

'The same for me please, Aunt Vicky.' Bess then turned to Will, who had seated himself at the table. 'Thank you for coming. I really do need to talk to you, Uncle Will.'

'I understand, and I'm happy to listen, to be of help if I can. What's this all about, Bess?'

Bess sat back in her chair, looking across at the man who had been constantly in her life since the day she was born – her father's dearest and longest friend.

Suddenly realizing she was staring at him, Bess cleared her throat and said, 'It's about Uncle Richard. He's upset my mother because he's interfering with the boys.'

'In what way?' Will asked, sitting up, his attention on Ned's eldest child, his senses alerted to problems.

'He's insisting they must go to Ravenscar for the whole summer, and then be tutored there in the autumn and winter. My mother's troubled by this because she thinks they should be with her. Our father has just died and we are full of grief. She says the boys need her comfort and love, that all her children do. Also, she has planned to spend the summer here with us, then she was going to take us to the south of France in late August or early September. Mother doesn't understand why Uncle Richard wants to tear the boys away from her and us, his siblings, when we all want to be together at this sorrowful time.' Bess shook her head. 'It's a mystery to me, too, it's not like Uncle Richard to be unkind. I'd just like you to know that I agree with my mother about this. The boys should be with us.'

'You're correct, and Richard is quite wrong. Of course, your father did make him the guardian of the boys. But as I remember the codicil, your mother is their guardian as well. I don't think he can force anything on your mother as long as she's not incapacitated in any way. And I know she isn't unwell.'

'I need your advice, Uncle Will. Shall I talk to Uncle Richard? You see, my mother thinks he won't listen to her.'

'She's probably right about that. Look here, Bess, would you like me to have a word with him? I'll be seeing him next week at Deravenels.'

'Oh, would you, please? I'd be happy to explain everything myself, but I have a feeling you might be more successful than me.'

'Let me have a word first, and if he's unbending about it, then you can see Richard yourself. I know he loves you, Bess, and that you're his favourite.'

'Yes. He's always been lovely to me.'

'How *are* the boys?' Will asked, a brow lifting. 'I know they're still grieving, but are they all right otherwise?'

'Oh, yes, and they enjoy being with me and their other sisters, especially down here in Kent. To be honest with you, I believe they find Ravenscar a bit daunting.'

Will couldn't help laughing. 'I can understand that! But your father loved Ravenscar, you know. He couldn't get enough of it.'

'I love it, too. So does little Cecily, but my mother doesn't like it. Nor do Edward and Ritchie. To be truly honest they much prefer to be here at Waverley Court.'

'I can't say I blame them. It's a lovely house, and the gardens are beautiful. And of course the weather's warmer.' Will smiled at her. 'Try not to worry, we'll sort it out.'

Grace Rose interjected as she said, 'Bess, you haven't mentioned what reason Richard has given, about having the boys at Ravenscar during the summer, and then presumably living there in the autumn and winter.'

'He wasn't very forthcoming, my mother said. However, Grandmother is going to be living at Ravenscar for the next six months or so, and I have a feeling Uncle Richard and Aunt Anne will be, too, at least at weekends.'

'With their boy Little Eddie?' Grace Rose asked, curious as usual.

'I suppose so.' Bess fixed her eyes on Will again, and said slowly, 'Perhaps he's looking for companions for his son, our cousin?'

'I don't know what it's all about, and I'm not going to hazard a guess,' Will replied, reaching out to her, patting her arm. 'Don't worry in the meantime. I'll get to the bottom of it, I promise you that,' he went on in a warm, comforting voice.

At this moment Vicky arrived with the tray of glasses and the lemonade, and Will made sure the subject matter was changed to more general conversation. He did not want Bess to be worrying or dwelling on Richard and his motives. It was bad enough that he himself was filled with alarm. Warning signals were going off in his head.

At twelve years of age, Young Edward Deravenel, the heir, was capable, practical and highly intelligent, extremely clever for his age. Apart from these attributes, he was well-mannered with a charming personality, one that was most endearing. As were his looks. Quite simply, he was a most gorgeous-looking boy. Blond, blue-eyed and tall for his age, he was his father's son, there were no doubts about *his* lineage.

Unfortunately, Young Edward had a diseased jaw for which he was undergoing treatment when he was in London. He constantly fought the pain, and also toothache.

It was bothering him on this sunny June day, and he was sitting in the kitchen with Cook, whose favourite he was, and who had given him a small cheesecloth bag she had made and filled with cloves.

'That should do it, me lovey,' Aida Collet said, smoothing a work-worn red hand over his blond curls. 'Just keep yer finger on the bag, press it down on yer tooth. An old-fashioned remedy, but it helps.'

'Thank you, Mrs Collet, you are very kind.' Shifting on the stool, he now asked, 'Could you please tell me that story again? About your brave husband, Private First Class Percy Collet of the Seaforth Highlanders, how he prevented himself and the other soldiers from sinking into the mud in the trenches, when he fought in the Battle of the Somme.'

Cook's face lit up. She loved this boy, who was so beautiful and polite; he was a little darling, that he was. 'It was like this ... the Fray Bentos tins of corned beef were his remarkable solution. My Percy, well, he started ter line the bottom of his trench with 'em, and –'

The door opened and Bess walked in. 'I have good news! Uncle Will is going to talk to Uncle Richard, and I know Will can make everything all right!'

Edward took the cheesecloth bag out of his mouth, and shook his head. 'I don't think he will, Bess. No, I have a dreadful feeling Little Ritchie and I will be at Ravenscar next week at this time.'

He made a face, and his voice was grave as he continued,

407

'We'll just have to be brave about it, but I'll miss you, Bess. And Cecily and Anne and the Little Dumplings. Katherine and Bridget are very precious to me.'

Bess went and put her arms around him, held him close. She loved him so much, she couldn't bear the thought of being parted from him. Neither could their mother. She closed her eyes and said a silent prayer, begging God to let her younger brothers stay with them in Kent.

FORTY-SEVEN

London

Amos Finnister tapped on Alfredo Oliveri's office door and then walked into his office without waiting for a response.

Oliveri, who had been expecting him, looked up and said, 'Sit down, Amos. Please tell me everything you know.'

It was Tuesday the eighth of June. The day before, the rumours had been rampant throughout the company. The gossip was that more of the top executives were going to be axed on the explicit orders of Richard Deravenel. But nobody knew who would be sacked, so most people were alarmed, extremely worried about losing their jobs. An atmosphere of fear reigned for the first time in over thirty years, and there was a sense of gloom on every floor of the building.

Amos had all the information, as he had just told Oliveri on the phone, a short while before; now he leaned closer and confided, 'I understand Frank Lane was given his walking orders late on Friday afternoon. And this week we'll see the departure of John Lawrence and Peter Stokes, two good men also.'

'My God, Frank Lane! This is terrible news, Amos, he's been with the company for donkeys' years. About as long as I have.

He was one of Mr Edward's big supporters when he was trying to get the company back from the Grants. Frank stood by our lot, he was a real trooper.' Oliveri was truly shocked and it showed. He felt a sudden rush of sadness. The company had changed the moment Richard Deravenel had taken control, and it genuinely concerned him.

'I know how much Frank was respected. Mr Edward used to call him True Blue,' Amos said. 'He took it on the chin apparently, simply cleaned out his desk on Saturday morning and left. We won't ever see *him* again. More's the pity, he was a nice chap.'

'There's something radically wrong here, Amos. What's going on? Do you know?'

'I can only agree with what you said the other day at White's Club. Our new boss is making way for his own men . . . those childhood friends mean a lot to him. I think we'll be seeing Francis Lowell around here anytime soon, and also Robert Clayton and Robin Sterling. They're as thick as thieves and have been for ever. It has to be that. You know what I mean . . . birds of a feather . . .'

'How do you know the names? Who told you?' Oliveri threw him a quizzical look.

Amos held up a warning finger. 'Don't ask any questions, my friend. That way you'll remain as clean as a whistle. The less you know the better off you are. Let me just say this . . . I have my ways of finding things out.'

Alfredo merely nodded, knowing Finnister's reputation for breaking and entering. Edward Deravenel had often boasted about it.

'Can I come in?' Will Hasling asked as he opened the door and walked inside. 'I hear Frank Lane was pushed out on Friday. I wasn't here, I'd gone to Kent. What do we know?' Will came and sat down next to Amos, and looked at him intently and then turned to face Oliveri.

Alfredo said swiftly, 'Amos will fill you in, and, by the way, the new boss was looking for you a short while ago.'

'Was he now? I also need to see *him*. Now, Amos, give me the bad news quickly.'

Amos repeated the things he had just told Oliveri, and Will listened, his face grave, then he said succinctly, 'He's on the bloody rampage.'

After discussing the terminations with Amos and Alfredo for a few minutes, Will Hasling returned to his own office, and buzzed his secretary. When she came in he gave her a pile of letters to file and then stood up. Striding across the room, he paused at the door which Edward had put in all those years go. It had been usual for the two of them to move in and out of each other's offices in the most casual way, but Will had quickly come to understand that Richard would not tolerate this kind of intimacy. And so the door had remained closed since Ned's death.

Lifting his hand, he knocked and waited.

After a moment he heard, 'Come in.'

Smiling broadly, Will said, 'Good morning, Richard. Did you have a good weekend?'

'Yes, I did. I was actually looking for you on Monday. But you weren't here yesterday afternoon.' Richard gave him a cold look.

Why the animosity? Will asked himself, but said in an amiable tone, 'That's right, I left before lunch. I had a meeting in the afternoon with Rice and Hepple, regarding the Montecristo vineyards in Italy. It dragged on, so I didn't come back. It was too late in the afternoon.'

'Ah, yes, you're dealing with them. How did it go?'

'Matters are moving along quite well. I'll let you know what happens. In the meantime, you said you were looking for me yesterday. Did you need something?'

'I wanted to let you know that Francis Lowell will be coming

411

to work alongside me here. Either next week or the week after.'

Although Will already knew this from Finnister, he feigned surprise 'That's good to know! He's done a wonderful job at the factories in Yorkshire, and I look forward to meeting him again, getting to know him better.'

'He's invaluable,' Richard murmured, and dropped his eyes to the papers on his desk, shuffled them, then glanced up when Will remained standing there. 'That's all I had to say, Will.'

'I realize that. However, I wish to ask you something, Richard.' Stepping closer to the desk, Will went on, 'Bess is upset that you plan to move her brothers to Yorkshire this summer. I can't help wondering why you're interfering with Ned's children.'

'That's none of your bloody business,' Richard snapped, glaring at him.

'It *is* my business when Bess comes to me, asks me to speak to you about it. When she's almost in tears.'

'Why did she come to you and not me? I'm her uncle, am I not?'

'It was, in a sense, quite by accident,' Will said carefully, wary now, and cautious. 'She was at Stonehurst last Saturday, visiting Grace Rose, and I had gone over to see Vicky about some family matters. Bess just happened to mention it in passing.'

'What a bloody cheek she has. Bess could have come to me herself. You're not family.'

'That's not exactly correct, Dick, now is it? My wife is your mother's niece, and your first cousin.'

'So what, I said, *you're* not family, I wasn't talking about Kathleen.'

Will recoiled, taken aback by this insulting remark. Gathering himself together, he said quietly, wanting to be conciliatory,

'Elizabeth is their guardian along with you, don't forget that, Dick.'

'No! Ned wanted *me* to be in charge of them. Fully in charge, I might add.'

'I think he wished you to be in charge of his sons *if* their mother was incapacitated, not able to look after them, or dead. I honestly don't believe he meant you to . . . control their lives.'

'You're overstepping the mark, just watch what you say!'

'Richard, why are you being so antagonistic towards *me*, your brother's oldest and dearest friend? This is so silly, we're discussing two little boys, your brother's children. They're grief-stricken for their father, they need to be with their mother at this particular time, this truly sad time in their lives. They should be with their sisters as well. Those children mustn't be separated this summer. Please let this ridiculous matter drop.'

'They are going to go to Ravenscar and they will live there this summer with their grandmother and my son. Anne and I will be going to join them for weekends. Ravenscar is the family seat of the Deravenels, centuries old. They must be there to learn what it means to be a Deravenel, learn the history of our family, and learn to understand their responsibilities.'

'Dick, they're just little boys. Have a heart, for God's sake.'

Ignoring this remark, Richard cried, 'Stop calling me Dick, for Christ's sake, I can't stand it.'

Will held himself in check, and said as mildly as possible, 'Please, Richard, for Ned's sake, leave the boys alone, especially this year. They're heartbroken, they need their mother.'

'Don't be maudlin with me. They have to learn to stand up and be men.'

Appalled, Will stared at him, his respect for Richard dwindling. 'Is that your last word on it?'

'Yes.'

'Then I shall tell Bess that you are adamant about her brothers going to Ravenscar, and then it's up to Elizabeth. As their mother, and their guardian, she has –'

'Why can't you get it through your head? *I am their guardian.*'

'*One* of their guardians, Richard, not the sole guardian. I am an executor of Ned's will, and so I know this is the way the codicil is worded. Elizabeth can discuss the matter with Ned's solicitors, if she so wishes.'

'Are you threatening me again?' he shouted, his face congested with anger.

'I have not threatened you at all,' Will answered. 'Stop being so daft. I've known you since you were a little lad in short pants.'

Losing his temper completely, Richard jumped up, took hold of Will's arm and tried to strong-arm him out of his office.

Startled, and taken unawares, Will struggled hard, tried to extricate himself. Richard let go of him; a moment later he rushed at him even harder. Raising both hands Richard pushed Will hard, hitting him on the chest. Not expecting such a violent shove, Will lost his balance, and went down hard, hitting his head on the edge of the open door.

Out of breath and panting, Richard stood over Will, staring down at him. 'Come on, get up, and let's get on with the day's business,' Richard exclaimed.

When Will did not move or say anything, he frowned, bent over him. It was then he noticed the trickle of blood on the carpet, under Will's head. Alarmed, Richard felt for a pulse and found one. Faint though it was, it told him Will Hasling was alive, but he was obviously unconscious. He took hold of Will's feet and pulled him away from the door. Then, Richard stepped behind his desk, turned on the intercom. 'Eileen?'

'Yes, Mr Deravenel?' his secretary asked.

'Mr Hasling just passed out. He wasn't feeling very well when he came into my office. Would you please call an ambulance. He appears to be unconscious. We must get him to a hospital.

Fourteen years ago, when Amos Finnister had come to work at Deravenels, 'to watch my back,' as Edward had said to him, he was given the title of Chief of Security. That had been his actual job, as well as looking after Edward Deravenel's security and welfare.

He was well liked, was, in fact, rather popular with everyone, and he had created his own little network of spies and informants throughout the entire company. And so within minutes he was surreptitiously informed that Will Hasling had collapsed in Richard Deravenel's office and was unconscious. The informant added that an ambulance was on its way.

Amos was not only nonplussed, but highly suspicious. Twenty minutes earlier, Will Hasling had been fit and well, talking to him and Oliveri in the latter's office.

What had happened in that short elapse of time? He did not know, but he certainly aimed to find out. After stopping to inform Alfredo that Will had been 'taken ill', these words uttered in an acerbic tone, he went to the room he still referred to as 'Mr Edward's office'.

The door was wide open; Richard was hovering; Eileen, his secretary, was looking upset, and two ambulance men were carefully lifting Will onto a stretcher.

Edging his way into the office, Amos immediately went over to Richard and asked, 'What happened to Mr Hasling, Mr Deravenel?'

Richard stared at him, looking annoyed. 'I don't actually know.'

'But he collapsed in your office, so I heard,' Finnister retorted.

'He did indeed. He came in to discuss something, then began complaining that he hadn't been feeling well, and he suddenly fell down on the floor. He collapsed, just like that. It was most peculiar, Finnister, most peculiar.'

You can bet your bottom dollar on that, Finnister thought, but said, 'I see. Well, he's in good hands. These lads will look after him. I'll see them out.'

Richard looked as if he was about to object, but obviously changed his mind. 'As you wish, Finnister, as you wish.'

'Shall I telephone Mrs Hasling? Or will you, sir?'

'Oh, don't worry about that, I'll take care of it,' Richard said irritably, ushering Amos out after the ambulance men.

Oliveri was waiting for Amos in the lobby of Deravenels, by pre-arrangement, and they accompanied Will to the hospital. On the way he slowly came round, and when he saw Amos and Alfredo sitting with him he attempted to smile.

'How do you feel, sir?' Amos asked, bending over him in concern.

'I've got a headache,' Will muttered. 'Where are we going?'

'The hospital, Mr Hasling. Guy's. It's the nearest,' Alfredo explained.

'I see.' He looked at Amos and said, 'My wife, Amos . . . phone her, please.'

'I will sir, and now you rest easy. You'll be all right once we get you to the hospital. I'll call Mrs H. from there.'

Will closed his eyes and passed out again.

Amos Finnister and Alfredo Oliveri were shown to a waiting room at Guy's Hospital, and as they sat waiting to hear about Will Hasling's condition they talked about the way he had so suddenly and unexpectedly become ill enough to collapse.

'Collapsed – all my eye and Betty Martin,' Finnister muttered, giving Alfredo a pointed look. 'There was blood on the carpet in Mr Edward's office, and falling onto a good Axminster is hardly going to make him bleed. He was either hit with something, or fell against a piece of furniture and then moved.'

Alfredo nodded, knowing better than to argue. It was Finnister who had been the policeman, and a good one, not he. 'What are you suggesting, Amos? That our new boss is responsible?'

'I am that. I just hope that Mr Will is going to be all right.'

An hour later one of the doctors finally emerged, came to report that Mr Hasling had suffered a head injury and concussion. He told them it had been decided to keep him in the hospital overnight for observation.

Oliveri looked at the doctor and asked, 'May we see him?'

'Not at the moment, I'm afraid. We are still doing tests.'

'I believe Mr Hasling suffered a head wound, didn't he?' Finnister said. 'I mean a wound that bled, correct?'

'That's true, sir, yes. We've been wondering about that. We think when he fell he struck his head on something hard. That's the only explanation.'

'Yes, I understand,' Finnister told the doctor, and then he and Oliveri left the hospital.

As it turned out, Will Hasling made a quick recovery, and several days after being taken to Guy's he was getting ready to go home. On Saturday, June the twelfth, the day he was leaving, he complained of feeling ill. An hour later he suffered a massive cerebral haemorrhage which proved fatal.

Amos Finnister, as heartbroken as everyone else, was never able to find out *exactly* what happened between Will Hasling and Richard Deravenel that day in the office. But, forever after, he blamed Richard for Will Hasling's untimely death. And so did everyone else. It was a black mark against Richard, and it was to haunt him.

FORTY-EIGHT

Ravenscar

The two boys walked down the steps cut into the cliff face, which led from the moorland to the shingled beach at Ravenscar, carrying their fishing rods. They were heading for their favourite spot on the beach, the Cormorant Rock.

The very first time they had gone fishing with their father, he had told them that this was the best place to fish, and to prove it to them he had caught several cod that day. Ever since then they had loved coming here to try their luck.

Young Edward was carrying the fishing basket, and he hoped it was going to be full by the time they returned to the house. He had promised Cook he would bring her a good catch, and she, in turn, had promised to make them fried fish for their dinner. He liked Mrs Latham, just as much as his father had. She was getting on now in years, so his grandmother kept saying, but his father had not wanted to send her off into retirement. 'She's only fifty-nine and in wonderful health,' his father had kept saying recently, just before he had died, and when Grandmother had continued to murmur about replacing Cook, his father simply walked away, refusing to listen. Mrs Latham was there for life, according to Papa. He understood why his father had so liked Cook; she was motherly and warm, and very kind to everyone, and she made special things for them that were delicious. And, like Mrs Collet at the house in Kent, she helped him when he had toothache, which was very often these days.

Young Edward pushed the strap of the fishing basket back on his shoulder, and trudged along with Little Ritchie, glancing around as they headed down towards the big outcropping of rocks where the famous Cormorant was located. The beach was totally deserted today, but there were a number of fishing boats out at sea, and in the distance he could see the fishermen casting their lines.

Even though it was a sunny August morning, it was as cool as it always was at Ravenscar even in the height of summer. There was a constant wind blowing off the North Sea, and for that reason Nanny had bundled them up in warm fisherman's wool jerseys over their flannel shirts, with their trousers tucked into their Wellington boots. As a precaution, in case it rained, she had made them put on their dark-green, rainproof jackets.

Little Ritchie, gazing up at him, said, 'Can we look for fossils, seaweed and seashells later, Ed? I promised the Little Dumplings I'd bring them back some treasures.'

'Of course we can, Ritch,' he answered, smiling lovingly, looking down at his little brother, who was now ten. 'I'll help you, in fact.'

'I wish Nanny had let them come with us, I don't know why she thinks it's wrong for girls to go fishing, do you?'

'I suppose she thinks it's not proper, not dignified,' Young Edward answered. 'You know what Nanny's like –'

'Not suitable,' Little Ritchie interrupted, doing a high-pitched imitation of Nanny, using her favourite phrase, and laughing with glee as he did.

Young Edward smiled at him indulgently, and put an arm

round his brother's shoulders. 'She also thinks it's dangerous because of the way we scramble over the rocks. She thinks Bridget and Katharine might hurt themselves.'

'We should have never let Nanny come to the beach with us last week, then she would have never known about our rock-climbing.'

'That's true.' Young Edward fell silent; the two brothers walked on, not needing to chatter, quite happy and compatible in each other's company. They were very similar in appearance, with their blond curls and blue eyes, but at twelve, going on thirteen, Young Edward was the taller of the two. They had inherited their mother's classically beautiful features, and had a strong look of their sister Bess.

As they drew closer to the Cormorant Rock, Little Ritchie suddenly announced, 'I'm hungry. Shall we have something to eat before we go fishing?'

'Why not?' Young Edward put down the fishing basket, and opened the lid, took out the package of hot sausage rolls Cook had given them a short while before. As he unwrapped the greaseproof paper he exclaimed, 'Golly, they're still warm!'

The two boys sat down on the shingle near the rocks and leaned back against them, munching on the warm sausage rolls which they loved.

'We could've brought Little Eddie fishing with us, if he hadn't gone to Ripon with his mother, to see his grandmother. He's been longing to stand on the Cormorant, he told me so.'

'He can come with us next week . . . when he gets back from Thorpe Manor, if you want. I know he'll enjoy it . . . He's a nice little chap, don't you think? Ritch?'

His brother nodded, and then frowned, shaking his head. 'Why do they have to call us Little Ritchie and Little Eddie, and you Young Edward? I think it's daft.'

Young Edward burst out laughing, more at the disdainful tone than the words. A moment later, he explained, 'It's because *you* are named for Uncle Richard; and to differentiate between you, Grandmother added Little to your name, so everyone would understand. Now, Little Eddie is named for our father, as I am, so I get to be Young Edward, and he's stuck with Little Eddie. To identify us properly. It's a bit confusing, especially for other people outside the family.'

'I understand. But when I grow up I'm going to get rid of the word *little*, and very quickly. I shall just call myself Ritchie, and you can be Edward, without the young part, because father is dead –' Little Ritchie broke off and turned to his brother, and asked in a quavery voice, 'Why did Father have to die? He was young, Ed. I heard Mother saying that to Uncle Anthony . . . "He was too young to die," she said. So *why* did he?'

Young Edward felt a rush of overwhelming sadness and his throat tightened with emotion. He couldn't speak for a moment, and then he said softly, 'He was ill with bronchitis, then he had a heart attack . . . but I told you that before, Ritch.' Staring down at his younger brother, he saw the tears in his eyes, and he put his arms around him, held him close. 'Don't cry, Ritch. We have to be strong, brave boys, Bess told us. And remember, she's coming to Ravenscar this afternoon to stay with us for a week. We'll have a good time with her.'

'Oh, I know! That makes me happy,' Little Ritchie exclaimed, rubbing his damp eyes with his knuckles and visibly cheering up.

Once they had each finished their sausage rolls, the two boys walked on, making for the fishing hut, which their father had built on a concrete ledge on top of a small stretch of moorland slightly above sea level. They walked up the narrow path from the beach, and Young Edward took the key for the hut out of his jacket pocket, once they got there. When the door was open both boys went inside, and looked around at the various boats. Young Edward began to pull out one of the larger rowing boats.

'What are you doing, Ed?' Little Ritchie asked, his eyes wide. 'Are we going fishing . . . on the North Sea?'

'That's where the haddock are, Father told us that.'

'He also told us not to go out there without him,' Little Ritchie pointed out.

'I know, but it's a sunny day, the weather's good, and especially for haddock. I bet there's a lot of fish out there.'

'Probably not,' Little Ritchie answered, suddenly glum, but he helped his brother to carry the boat down to the beach. 'Do you really want to go out?' he asked after a moment.

Young Edward hesitated, murmured, 'Well, I'd better think about it, at least for a little bit, watch the sky, see if the weather changes, it's so uncertain here in Yorkshire. I must be careful.'

'That's a very *good* idea! Now, Ed, let's go to the Cormorant.'

'I'll race you!' Young Edward cried.

The two of them ran down the beach, carrying their rods, and shouting, 'Whooppee! Whooppee!', their voices carried by the wind.

The Cormorant Rock was large and wide, certainly big enough for the two boys to stand on together, and they did so, casting their lines, their bright young faces shining with optimism.

The man rowed in, moving smoothly across the steel-grey sea, helped by the wind behind his back. He would reach the beach quicker than he had previously thought. Not a bad day to be out at sea, he decided, a good day for fishing certainly. Clear sky, no sign of bad weather. And a sunny day to boot. I wonder if I'll catch any fish? Perhaps a couple of little ones at least.

His fishing boat, called the Gay Marie, was quite large and strongly-made and could hold half a dozen fishermen, as it sometimes had. It really required two men to row, but he was well-built, with a broad chest and massive arms. He was managing the boat well, and within ten minutes he was drawing close to the shoreline. The man rowed on determinedly, filled with powerful energy. The moment he spotted the edge of the beach he placed the oars in the boat, jumped out into the shallows, glad he was wearing wellington boots. First he pushed the boat up onto the sand, then he dragged it across the shingle and finally positioned it under the outcropping of rocks.

Sitting down near the boat, he took out his cigarettes, brought a match to one and began to smoke, the morning sun warm on his face.

Not far away was the Cormorant Rock where Young Edward and Little Ritchie were standing, angling for cod. Little Ritchie was excited when he finally caught one, and a moment later his brother was also lucky. 'Whooppee!' they shouted again, filled with happiness and pride at their success.

After another hour Young Edward was convinced they had caught the only fish in the water today, and he also noticed that his little brother was getting tired. Afraid that Ritch might easily fall into the water or, worse, onto the rocks, and hurt himself, he said, 'We'd better go, Ritch. This is pointless. All the villagers come to the Cormorant, and the waters here are probably depleted.'

Little Ritchie nodded. 'But I don't think we should go out there,' he said, indicating the vast expanse of the North Sea. 'Papa would be angry.'

'Yes, I know he would. So we won't go out for haddock. Come on, let's get down off the Cormorant –'

'What have we got here? A couple of spry young fishermen, I see,' the man declared, staring at the two handsome blond boys and grinning.

'Hello!' Young Edward said, smiling back. 'We've caught two fish, haven't we, Ritch?'

Little Ritchie nodded, his innocent young face as bright as a button. 'We *have*! Two nice cod.'

'That's what I hope to do. Catch two nice little fish. Do you think I will?'

'I don't know,' Young Edward answered, jumping down from the rock and then helping his brother, holding his hand.

'Probably not,' Little Ritchie added, and also dropped down onto the beach.

'We'll just have to see, won't we?' the man murmured, and smiled at them again.

FORTY-NINE

'I'm so glad you're here, Bess,' Nanny exclaimed, hurrying out of the butler's pantry and into the grand entrance foyer of Ravenscar. Her voice was strained and she was obviously alarmed.

Bess had only just arrived from London, having taken the train to York, and she was standing in the hall with her luggage. But she spotted Nanny's anxiety immediately, and hurried across to her, saying, 'Nanny, whatever is it? What's the matter?'

'It's the boys,' Nanny answered, her desperation echoing. 'We can't find them. They're missing.' She was on the verge of tears.

'*Missing*,' Bess repeated, sounding puzzled. 'I'm not following you, Nanny.'

Jessup had come out of the butler's pantry, and now he joined them, explaining, 'They went fishing this morning, Miss Bess. Down on Ravenscar beach. They like to go to the Cormorant Rock. Their father, er– er– Mr Deravenel, used to take them there all the time. Cook made them a picnic lunch, which Young Edward took in the fishing basket, and off they went. They haven't been seen since –'

'But aren't they down on the beach?' Bess cut in, giving Jessup a sharp look, her puzzlement apparent.

Nanny said, 'No, they're not. I told them when they left at eleven to come back to the house around two o'clock, two-thirty at the latest. You know Young Edward is very responsible, Bess, and so is Little Ritchie. They return when they're supposed to, they're never late. It's now four. Half an hour ago, I became worried. I asked that nice under-gardener, Jeremy, to run down to the beach to fetch them for me. He came back rather upset, and said they weren't there. In fact, there was no trace of them, and no fishing rods, no fishing basket, nothing. The beach was deserted.'

'How very strange,' Bess muttered. 'Could they be somewhere in the house, Nanny?'

'No, Bess, they're not here.' Nanny shook her head emphatically. 'I've looked everywhere. Anyway, you know as well as I do that they have always been very obedient boys, and no trouble to me at all. Or to anyone else, for that matter.'

'Could they have wandered off somewhere, gone down into the village?' Bess posed this question to Nanny, and then looked across at the butler. 'What do you think, Jessup?'

'It's too far to the village, Miss Bess. Anyway, it's not like them to disobey Nanny. But I'll ask one of the stable boys to saddle one of the horses and ride down to the village to make inquiries, if you wish, Miss Bess?'

'Yes, do it, Jessup, thank you, and now I'll go and have a word with my grandmother. I'll come up to see the girls in a minute or two, Nanny.'

The three of them dispersed, and Bess rushed down the Long Hall and into the library, the room where everyone sat, in the afternoon most especially.

Cecily Deravenel had broken her leg two weeks earlier, and it was now encased in a plaster of Paris cast. She was seated in a wheelchair near the window, looking out towards the sea. She turned the chair at the sound of footsteps, and her tired face lit up when she saw her granddaughter. 'Bess! There you are, my darling. I'm so glad you've come to stay with us.'

Bess hurried across the floor. The library was so filled with memories of her father that she could hardly bear it. This room was his, and it would always be his. His presence was everywhere. And the marvellous painting of him, completed just before his fortieth birthday, hung above the fireplace, dominating the room.

Pushing a smile onto her face, Bess went to her grandmother and kissed her on the cheek. 'I'm happy to be here, Grandmother,' she said and perched on the edge of a chair. In a controlled, very steady voice she said, 'Grandmother, there seems to be a problem.'

Cecily gave her a questioning look. 'What kind of problem.'

'The boys are missing. Young Edward and Little Ritchie seem to have disappeared. Vanished . . . into thin air.'

A graveness settled over Cecily at once; she was suddenly alarmed. 'How can they have disappeared? I don't understand. They told me they were going fishing on the beach, where Ned always took him. They even said they were looking forward to having tea with me, and you, and the Little Dumplings, as they call the girls. I told them not to be late, to get back in time. Where could they be?'

'They're not on the beach, and they're not in the house. Nanny is in a terrible state of upset, but I must say she did send the under-gardener down to look for them, and he reported back very quickly. There's no sign of them and their things are not on the beach either.'

Cecily sat back in the wheelchair; a shadow crossed her face. 'I wish Richard were here,' she said at last, rubbing a hand over her mouth. 'He would know what to do.'

'Where *is* Uncle Richard?'

'He spent a couple of days in Ripon, at Thorpe Manor, with

Anne and Little Eddie. The weekend actually. He went to London yesterday.'

'And Anne and her boy are still at Thorpe Manor with Nan Watkins?'

'That's right.'

There was a short silence; neither woman spoke.

'Excuse me, Grandmother, I'm going to telephone the police –'

'But you should talk to Richard first,' Cecily interjected.

'Why? He's in London. I'm here on the spot. And the sooner we move the better.' Bess hurried out, went into her father's old office and sat down at the desk. She thought for a moment, and then telephoned Lady Fenella in London. The butler at the Curzon Street house answered and a moment later Lady Fenella herself was saying, 'Hello, Bess, how are you?'

'Hello, Aunt Fenella. I'm phoning you because I have a dreadful problem and I need your advice. I just arrived at Ravenscar. My brothers are missing.' Talking rapidly, Bess filled her in, and repeated everything she had learned, then finished, 'I thought of phoning the local police, and then decided to speak to you first. I would really appreciate it if you could ask Mark what he thinks, what I should do.'

'This is shocking news, Bess,' Fenella replied. 'Could it be a kidnapping, do you think? For a ransom? Everyone knows that the Deravenels are an important family, and wealthy.'

'It's a possibility . . . I just don't know what to think at this moment.'

'Is Richard there?'

'No, he's apparently in London. Anne is with her mother in Ripon, and I'm here with my grandmother, who's stuck in a wheelchair with a broken leg.'

'I'm sorry to hear it. Give her my best. Your mother went to Monaco, didn't she?'

'Yes, with Cecily and Anne. I don't want to start worrying her, not yet.'

'That's not necessary at the moment. Let me speak to Mark and he or I will phone you back very soon.'

Bess sat back in the chair, staring into space, waiting for Mark Ledbetter to phone. She knew he would insist on doing so when Fenella explained the situation.

And she was right. Ten minutes later the phone rang and she grabbed the receiver at once, before Jessup could pick it up.

'It's Mark, Bess. I'm sorry about this.'

'Hello, Mark.'

'Tell me everything you know.'

She did so, and then asked, 'Should I get in touch with the police?'

'No, I'll do it for you. It'll be easier all round and much faster if I make the calls. Scarborough is your local constabulary, but I'm going to phone York as well: it's a bigger force.'

'Thank you, Mark.'

'Listen to me, Bess, and very carefully. If the boys are not found by tonight, I want you to contract me immediately whatever the time. And if there's a call or a note about a ransom you must also phone. I shall come up there at once. Not as the head of Scotland Yard, but as a friend of the family. I don't want to step on any local toes. I'm sure you understand. Try not to worry. We'll find them.'

Bess remained seated at her father's desk, her mind racing. After a few moments she came to a conclusion: the boys had disappeared without a trace, so they had either been taken off that beach by someone, perhaps for ransom, or they had gone out in a boat and had some kind of accident. Had they lost an oar and were drifting? Had the boat overturned for some reason? Or sunk? If that were the case her brothers had more than likely drowned. She trembled at this possibility. It was too much even to contemplate.

Suddenly a thought struck her and she jumped up, ran down the Long Hall, took the stairs two at a time, and rushed into her bedroom. She took off her lightweight travelling suit, put on a tweed skirt and blouse, found a warm cardigan and changed into walking shoes. Only then did she go to the nursery.

Nanny looked up when she came in, and asked worriedly, 'Any news, Bess?'

'Not at the moment. But I did speak to Lady Fenella and Mark Ledbetter phoned back. He's getting in touch with the local police . . . York as well as Scarborough. And I'm going down to the beach to look around for myself.'

Nanny nodded and glanced at Katharine and Bridget, the two youngest children, dubbed the Little Dumplings by their brothers.

Bess picked up on Nanny's worried glance and went over to the two girls, who were sitting at the nursery parlour table having their milk and sliced fruit.

Four-year-old Katharine lifted her face to be kissed, and clung to Bess's arm as she bent over her. 'Where are the boys?' she whispered.

'Not far away, darling, I'm sure of that,' Bess answered, and held the child close.

Moving around the table a moment later, she hugged three-year-old Bridget and kissed her cheek, murmured, 'I'll be back in a few minutes, all right?'

'Yes, Bess,' Bridget said.

Downstairs again, Bess decided she must telephone her uncle at Deravenels, and she returned to her father's office and did so. It was his secretary who answered, and when Bess asked for him, Eileen told her he was out at a meeting in the City.

Bess thought for a second, wondering if she should explain the reason for her call, decided not to. 'Please ask him to telephone me, Eileen. I'm at Ravenscar and I need to speak to him. Urgently.'

The beach was empty.

Bess could see that as she hurried down the flight of steps cut into the cliff face. Once her feet touched the shingle she ran to the outcropping of rocks which sheltered the Cormorant Rock from her line of vision. She was a little out of breath and slowed to a walk as she rounded the outcropping and finally stood in front of the famous rock. Below it, the dark sea lapped around its base, swirling and frothing as it usually did all year round.

Dropping her eyes to the shingle, Bess covered the area, searching for *what*? She did not know . . . something that might give her a clue to what had happened. But there was nothing. It was only when she lifted her head and glanced up that she saw the fishing hut on the higher moorland. Its door was swinging back and forth in the wind. Why was it open? Or course, Young Edward. He had obviously unlocked it earlier.

Climbing up the path, Bess reached the hut, went inside and looked around. There were always four fishing boats stored here. Two large and two small. Now there were only three . . . one large and two small. Obviously her brothers had taken one of the larger boats. She looked at the names of the boats still there . . . *Sea Dog*, *Meg O' My Heart* and *Macbeth*. It was the *Lady Bess* which was missing, the boat named for her by her father. She stood very still, her heart tightening in her chest. If they had gone out in it, on the North Sea, they could easily have had an accident. And drowned.

The rest of her energy seeped out of her at the mere idea of this. She leaned against the door jamb for several minutes, trying to calm herself. Then she turned, went outside, closed the door of the hut and locked it. She put the key back in her pocket, continuing down the path, filled with dismay.

Once she stepped onto the shingled beach she looked everywhere again. There was no boat; nor any signs of one being dragged. But then there never was any sign of that . . . because of the shingle.

Deflated and troubled, Bess climbed the steps to the moorland and headed home to Ravenscar, praying that her little brothers had gone off somewhere, and that they would soon return. Or be found.

'I've been down to the beach, Grandmother,' Bess explained, sitting down in the library. 'There's nothing . . . no clues as to what might have happened.'

'I see.' Cecily Deravenel's tense white face and the hint of fear in her blue-grey eyes signalled her apprehension.

Afternoon tea had been brought in as usual, but her cup was still full, had not been touched, and her plate was empty. She had found it impossible to drink or eat. 'Richard telephoned you, Bess. I told him the boys were missing. If the boys are not found by tonight, he said he will come to Ravenscar at once.'

'I'm glad of that, Grandmother. I did speak with Aunt Fenella, and she had Mark Ledbetter phone me. He is sending the Scarborough police, who have the local jurisdiction. But he explained he wanted the York police here as well, because they have a much larger force . . . more men.'

Cecily brought her hand to her eyes for a split second. She said in a low, trembling voice, 'Where can they be, Bess? Oh, where can they be?'

By six o'clock that evening the house, grounds and beach at Ravenscar were filled with the local police searching everywhere.

Inspector Wallis from the Scarborough police station had arrived later and talked to Bess and everyone else, and so had Chief Inspector Allison from York. Like Bess and her grandmother, and the entire staff at Ravenscar, these two senior detectives were baffled.

The disappearance of the two little boys was a mystery. The biggest mystery they had ever encountered.

FIFTY

A mos Finnister had driven all night from London, and now as he headed up the driveway and into the stable block at Ravenscar he felt a great sense of relief that he had finally arrived.

He parked his car in the cobbled stable yard, and walked over to the back door of the house, following the instructions Bess had given him the night before.

He raised his hand to grasp the brass door knocker, but the door instantly opened and Bess was standing there. 'Good morning, Amos,' she said, opening the door wider.

'Morning, Bess,' he replied, and stepped into the corridor, closing the door behind him. 'Any news?'

She shook her head. 'Sadly, no. Come and have some breakfast. Jessup is waiting for us, and Cook has everything ready.'

'That's very nice, thank you.'

'You must be tired and hungry after your long journey.'

'A bit,' he said as they crossed the Long Hall and went down towards the morning room.

Jessup was standing in the doorway, and he stepped forward to meet them, his face cheering up considerably at the sight of

Amos Finnister. 'Good morning, Mr Finnister,' he exclaimed, and ushered them inside the room. 'Miss Bess has been waiting anxiously for you, as we all have. And you must be exhausted, it's a long way from London.'

He smiled at the butler, whom he had always liked, and said, 'It's nice to see you, Jessup, and to tell the truth, it's not bad driving at night. The roads are empty, and I made good time.'

The butler led Amos to the sideboard where, as usual, there was a selection of hot dishes as well as cold. 'What can I help you to, sir?' Jessup asked, lifting the lids of various silver serving dishes. 'Here we have sausages and bacon, in this dish kidneys, here are tomatoes, and there are kippers, if that's your preference. And we do have scrambled eggs as well, but Cook will make fried eggs for you, if you wish.'

'Sausages and bacon, and perhaps a grilled tomato, Jessup, thanks. That will be fine.'

Amos went back to the table and sat down opposite Bess, whilst Jessup put the food he had chosen on a plate and took it to Amos, who thanked him.

'Your usual, Miss Bess?' the butler asked, and when she nodded he hurried to the sideboard, returned a moment later with grilled tomatoes. Within minutes he had brought hot toast and butter to the table, along with a selection of jams, and poured breakfast tea for them.

When they were alone, Bess said, 'The two local detectives said this is the biggest mystery they've ever had to confront, Amos.'

'It is indeed a mystery, Bess, and a very worrying one. Tell me again about the fishing hut. You said the door was swinging open.'

'Yes, it was, that's why I noticed it. Because the door was banging in the wind. I knew at once that Young Edward must have left it open. I went up, looked around the hut, and realized that a large fishing boat was missing.'

'The *Lady Bess*, you said?'

'Yes. Father named it for me.'

'It's good to have a name –' Amos stopped abruptly, annoyed with himself. He could have bitten his tongue off.

Bess said, 'In case of wreckage, that's what you mean, isn't it, Amos? A name helps to identify a boat that's gone down.'

He nodded, looking regretful. 'I'm afraid so.'

'Don't be upset . . . I've thought of that myself.' She shook her head and suddenly her vivid blue eyes, so like her father's, filled with tears. She tried to blink them away; her throat was choked up, and her heart ached.

'Oh, Bess, my dear,' Amos said, his heart going out to her. He stood up, made a move towards her.

She shook her head. 'No, no, it's all right, I'm all right. Tears don't help.' She took a handkerchief out of her pocket and patted her eyes. As she put the handkerchief back in her cardigan pocket her fingers touched the key. 'Oh, and Amos, the key was in the lock, so I locked the door of the hut. And look, I still have the key on me.' She held it up, showed it to him.

'I brought my fingerprinting kit, so I will try and lift any prints off it later, Bess. In the meantime, take me through every-thing again, the way you told me on the telephone last night.'

'Cook, there's a reeght queer looking man in t'yard,' Polly said, peering out of the window in the kitchen.

Cook swung around, a wooden spoon in her hand, frowning at the new kitchen maid. 'Wot's that, lass? Wot are you saying?'

'T'man, outside. Come on, 'ave a look.'

Mrs Latham stepped over to the window and saw at once what Polly meant. There was indeed an odd-looking man in the stable yard, and he was now heading towards the back door.

Putting down the wooden spoon, wiping her hands on a

kitchen towel, Cook straightened her white cap and hurried out of the kitchen and down the corridor. She had opened the door and was on the doorstep as the man approached.

When he came to a standstill in front of her, she knew at once what he did. There was such a strong smell of fish on him she recoiled, and immediately realized he was probably one of the local fishermen, either from the village of Ravenscar, or perhaps from Scarborough nearby.

He touched his cap politely with one hand, and said, 'Mornin', mum, is t'maister at 'ome?'

'No, afraid not. What can I be doin' for yer?' Cook asked, immediately dropping into the local dialect.

The man pursed his lips together, and then grimaced. 'T'was maister I wus 'oping ter see. I've summat ter tell 'im.'

Cook shook her head. 'I can't be pullin' him out of an hat, like a Jack rabbit, now can I? The master is away. Best be telling me, get it off yer chest right quick. I've got work ter do.'

'It's abart t'little lads, Deravenel lads, them that's got lost.'

On hearing this Mrs Latham stiffened at once, and stared harder at the fishermen. Her eyes narrowed. 'If yer knows summat yer'd best be telling me . . . come on, then, let's have it.'

'T'was like this . . . I saw 'em fishin' at Cormorant Rock. Then I spotted a fishin' boat goin' in ter that bit of shingled beach. I sees t'man in boat pullin' it up, draggin' it across beach.'

'And then what?'

'Nuthin', I was fishin' . . . I rowed out, seekin' fish, scarce they wus yesterday. Lookin' fer haddock I wus.'

'Wait here . . . don't go away. I'll be back in half a tick.'

The man nodded, and Cook moved off down the corridor at great speed, seeking Jessup. When she found him in the butler's pantry, she told him quietly about the fisherman, passed on the information he had given her, finishing, 'I must give him a shilling, or summat like that, Jessup, for his trouble. It is helpful information I hopes?'

'Perhaps. Please go and keep the fisherman talking, Cook. Don't let him go away. I'm going to ask Mr Finnister to speak to him.' So saying, Jessup disappeared; Cook went hurrying off to the back door.

'Hang on a minute, please. The butler's gone fetch a person . . . of authority. Yer from round here then?'

'. . . Bin livin' 'ere all me life. Tom Roebottom's me name.'

'Just call me Cook, everyone does.'

Jessup came back with Finnister and Bess. Swiftly, Cook stepped to one side to allow Finnister to come outside onto the step to talk to the man.

'My name's Finnister,' Amos said. 'And I understand you have some information about the two little boys who disappeared from the beach at Ravenscar yesterday afternoon. Can you tell me what you know please? It's vitally important.'

The fisherman told the same story he had recounted to Cook. When he had finished, Amos said, 'Did you see him speaking to the little boys? Or with them?'

'No.'

'But you did see the man land on the beach, saw him pull his boat up?'

'Aye. Pulled it over t'shingle, he did, left it near them big rocks.' Tom paused. 'Then he sat down.'

'And that's all you saw?'

'Aye. I rowed out. Went ter deeper waters. I wus seeking haddock.'

'Can you describe the man? Were you close enough to get a good look at him?'

The fisherman shook his head. 'I wus too far out fer a close look. A big man, aye. Broad, strong. T'was a big fishin' boat.'

'How many fishermen could it hold?'

Tom Roebottom shrugged. 'Five, mebbe six.'

'I understand. Here's a very important question. Did you see the man *leave* the beach in his fishing boat?'

'No. I wus out in t'deep waters. Far out.'

'I see. Tell me something . . .' Finnister paused and asked, 'What's your name, by the way?'

'Tom . . . Roebottom, sir.'

Finnister thrust out his hand. 'Nice to meet you, Tom, and thanks for coming up to the house with this information.'

They shook hands; Tom nodded respectfully.

Amos studied him for a moment, then asked, 'What made you come here, Tom? You must have thought that seeing the man was important, did you?'

'Aye. It wus me wife, Betty, she saw t'police all over yesterday, and she told me them boys wus missin'. When I come ter thinkin', I told Betty. It wus me wife, she tells me to come up ter see t'maister.'

'Well, thank you very much, I'm grateful,' Amos said, and pulled out some coins.

Tom said, 'No, I don't want nuthin'. I wus just doin' me duty. Mr Deravenel, Mr Edward, that is, he allus been good ter us in t'village. Died too young.' He shook his head. 'Mebbe it's naught, seein' that man. Thought I'd best tell Mr Richard, like me wife said.'

Bess stepped forward. 'I'm Mr Edward's daughter, Tom, and it's my brothers who have vanished. Thank you for coming to the house. I'm grateful . . . we all are.'

Amos knew almost at once that they would find nothing on the beach, no clues, no traces of the boys, or anyone else for that matter. It was the shingle that was the problem, and also the incoming and the outgoing tides. The beach, composed of pebbles, shells and fossils, was washed several times a day by the sea . . . it was therefore pristine.

Once they had tramped down to the Cormorant Rock, and

looked around there, Bess led him up to the fishing hut on the ledge. She had given him the key earlier, and he had attempted to life off fingerprints but without much success. Too many people had handled the key lately.

Standing in the doorway together, Bess pointed out the three remaining fishing boats ... *Meg O' My Heart*, *Sea Dog* and *Macbeth*, explaining, 'Father only kept four boats here, but lots of extra oars.'

'So I see,' Amos answered, and poked around in the hut for a few minutes. Again, he found nothing at all helpful – or suspicious. Turning to her, he now said, 'Tom, the fisherman, told us that he had seen a man dragging a boat across the shingle, who had then placed it near the outcropping of rocks. Let's go and look there, shall we?'

Bess quickly agreed, and minutes later they were back on the shingle beach, heading to the giant rocks that sheltered one side of the Cormorant Rock.

It was a blue-sky day, sunny and without any breeze ... a pretty day. Neither of them really noticed the weather, however, so intent were they on their quest. The piercing cries of the gulls made Amos lift his head at one moment, and he saw, high in the sky, the most elegant birds swooping and soaring against the pale sky. 'What are those white birds?' he asked, turning to Bess.

'Kittiwakes,' she answered. 'There are hundreds of them here – they live in the cliffs, they actually nest there. Aren't they beautiful with their black wing tips and yellow bills?'

Amos nodded. 'They're beautiful, yes indeed.' He stopped abruptly, and pointed down at the shingle where they were now standing. 'Look at this, Bess. I believed Tom when he said the man he'd seen landing then dragged the boat across the beach ... look how this shingle is scuffed. And you can see the indentations the boat's rim made as it was dragged.'

'Yes, I do see it. Tom Roebottom was very observant.'

'Yes.' Straightening up, Amos suddenly let out a long heavy sigh, and Bess glanced at him swiftly, but did not say a word.

It was Amos who eventually murmured, 'I know we won't find a thing here . . . even if we look forever. I might as well confess to you, Bess, I believe your brothers *were* taken off this beach yesterday. By whom, and for what reason, I don't know.'

Bess stood staring at him, her eyes clouded with pain, her mouth trembling slightly. 'I have to agree with you . . . do you think it was the fellow Tom saw landing here?' She tried to hold herself still, wanting to keep her self-control intact.

'I'm afraid I do. Also, Tom said the boat could hold *five fishermen*. Your brothers are just two little boys. It was big enough to hold them and the man.'

'But who would *want* to take them?' she asked, her voice wobbling.

'I don't know. I can't explain it. I wish I could. When is your uncle arriving?'

'In time for lunch, so he told me last night. He is very keen on aeroplanes, and he has chartered one to bring him here with Mark. A lot of people are starting up charter companies, he told me, and explained he found one he liked the sound of, because the owners are two former pilots from the Great War. They actually can land their plane at a new airfield near Scarborough.'

'Wonderful things, aeroplanes. They're going to be the future of travel.'

'Do you really think so? Grandmother says they are terribly dangerous, that they can fall out of the sky. And usually she's very much into modern inventions.'

'My money's on air travel,' Amos said.

The two of them walked on, heading for the steps cut into the cliff wall, silent for a while. Suddenly, Amos said, 'Didn't you have a dog called Macbeth? The same as the boat?'

'Yes, a West Highland terrier. Little Macbeth died last year, and Young Edward was so upset he said he couldn't bear to have another dog for a while. And my father named the boat after Mac, as we called him.'

'I understand.' Amos and Bess headed up the steps, climbing up in single file. It was Amos who stopped, at one moment, and took hold of Bess's arm. 'When are you going to tell your mother that the boys went missing yesterday?'

'Today, I think, after Uncle Richard arrives, and we've all had a chance to talk about the situation.'

Richard Deravenel and Mark Ledbetter arrived at twelve-thirty, and joined Cecily Deravenel, Bess and Amos in the library. It was a worried and subdued little group gathered there.

Richard Deravenel opened the discussion about the boys, when he turned to his mother and said, 'I'm making the assumption there are no new employees at the house or in the grounds, Mama? You haven't hired anyone without mentioning it, have you?'

'No, I haven't, Richard. Oh, there is Polly the new kitchen maid, but her mother worked here for years. She's from the village.'

'No new work people on the estate?'

Cecily Deravenel shook her head, giving him a rather disapproving look. 'Anyway, I would never engage dubious or questionable people.'

Richard noticed her edgy tone at once, and said, 'I had to ask, Mother.'

'I know.'

Mark Ledbetter now joined the conversation, explaining, 'I talked to the two detectives who were here yesterday, and they are utterly baffled. As indeed we all are.'

'I do have *some* information, for what it's worth,' Amos

announced quietly and told them about the fisherman, Tom Roebottom, who had appeared at the back door earlier that morning.

Richard's face changed slightly as he listened, and when Amos had finished he asked swiftly, in an urgent tone, 'Do you think this chap who landed on the beach *took* the boys?'

'I'm afraid so,' Amos admitted, his tone regretful.

'*Why?*' Mark asked. He had known Amos for years and trusted him, and his skills as a former policeman. But he felt compelled to pose this question on behalf of the family. He wanted them to hear Amos give a reason for his conclusion.

'Because there's no other explanation,' Amos answered immediately. 'Unless they took a boat out into the North Sea. Bess told me that the boat the *Lady Bess* is missing, in fact.'

'So what you're saying is that they could have rowed into the North Sea, hit a squall, had an accident and been drowned? Or they could have been taken,' Mark asserted. 'Taken by force.'

'Why would anyone want to take my brothers?' Bess asked shakily, on the verge of tears again and filled with anxiety.

Richard threw her a warm, sympathetic look and said gently, 'There are ruthless people in this world, Bess dear. People who . . . well, trade in human beings . . . *steal children* . . . for ransom, for those who want a child and can't have one, or for . . . prostitution.'

'Oh, God, no, don't say that!' Cecily exclaimed, covering her mouth with her hand. 'Not *that*, Richard.' She stared at her youngest son, appalled.

'There are a lot of wicked people out there, Mrs Deravenel,' Amos interjected. 'Ruthless, heartless, money-grubbing people who are less than human, in my opinion.'

Cecily nodded. 'What do *you* think, Mark?'

'I would have opted for an accident at sea, Mrs Deravenel, if it were not for the local fisherman seeing a man landing on the beach. Now . . . well, I'm a bit ambivalent, I must admit.

The boys are very beautiful children, and –' He broke off when he saw Bess and Cecily gaping at him, horror flooding their eyes.

'Oh, God, no, not *that*. I can't bear it,' Cecily whispered, and closed her eyes. Bess went to her grandmother and put an arm around her, endeavoured to calm her.

Richard said, in a concerned voice, 'Mark, can you think of anything we can do? And what about you, Amos?'

Amos shook his head. 'I've covered the beach, found no clues at all, except for deep ridges in the shingle that go from the shoreline to the outcropping of rocks, ridges made when the boat was probably dragged up there. Nothing else. I've talked at length to Jessup this morning, and I've questioned most of the estate workers, the gardeners, the stable lads. Nobody has seen any strangers hanging around the estate, and apparently, there have been no strangers in the village. I've hit a brick wall. As did the police yesterday. The place was teeming with them and they came up with nothing.'

Richard looked across at Mark and asked, 'If somebody had kidnapped the boys for ransom, would we have heard from the kidnappers by now?'

'Absolutely! They don't lose much time contacting the family of the victim, or in this case, victims. They want things to move fast, hoping to get the child off their hands and their hands on the money. And talking of the police, Inspector Wallis from Scarborough, and Chief Inspector Allison from York both tend to think the boys were grabbed.'

'What has made them come to that conclusion?' Richard asked.

'Gut instinct, that's what they said last night. A shared gut instinct.'

'We're helpless, Mark,' Richard pointed out. 'What in God's name can we do?'

'I have a suggestion.' Amos looked from Richard to Mark.

445

'Why don't we go to the people? The people of England. What I mean is this – why don't we call in the press? Have a . . . well, a press conference, tell the story, ask them to run photographs of the two boys. Ask for their help in solving this crime?'

'Brilliant!' Mark exclaimed. 'And you must offer a reward, Richard. A handsome reward for the return of the boys, and smaller rewards for information which might lead us in the right direction, lead us to Young Edward and Little Ritchie.'

'Yes, let's do it!' Richard said enthusiastically, feeling a surge of relief. 'I think it *is* the only thing we *can* do. Whoever took the boys can't keep them in hiding forever, now can they? Somebody, somewhere, will spot them, of that I feel certain, and bring them back to us.'

But he was wrong. And not too much later he would be blamed for the disappearance of his nephews, and castigated for the deed.

FIFTY-ONE

London

Elizabeth Deravenel stood at the window of her bedroom in the Berkeley Square house. It was snowing outside and had been for several hours on this icy December afternoon.

The public garden in the middle of the square was already covered in a coating of snow, and flakes had settled on the bare branches of the trees . . . the bereft trees.

Bereft. That was how she herself felt. Bereft and heartbroken. Almost five months ago now her boys had gone missing, had vanished into thin air was the way Bess put it.

They had never been found.

She leaned her head against the window, staring out at the snowflakes falling . . . falling like her tears. She had wept every day since August. At one moment, she had thought there were no tears left in her, but there were; she still cried herself to sleep at night.

During the day she tried to be strong and brave for her girls, her five daughters – Bess, Cecily, Anne, Katharine and Bridget. They were a family of women now, without Ned, and with the boys gone – God knows where.

447

She closed her eyes, seeing them in her mind's eye. Where were her sons? She dreaded to think that they were alive and living in some kind of terrible hell . . . somewhere in the world, wondering why she had never come to rescue them. But wasn't believing them to be dead so much worse?

Her little boys . . . Edward and Ritchie . . . such beautiful children, and so sweet and endearing . . . *innocents* who had never harmed anyone. Her heart had broken months ago when she had first heard from Bess, on Wednesday the eighteenth of August, a date she would never forget. She had rushed home immediately, had arrived in Yorkshire on Friday, two days later, to face bleakness, pain and a terrible despair that was never ending. It was a sorrow she could not endure.

Her darling, darling boys . . . Tears filled her eyes. Elizabeth brushed them away, taking deep breaths. She must try not to give in, to be more stoic, but it was hard.

1926. A year engraved on her heart. On April the ninth Ned had died. In June Will Hasling had passed away. She and he had never been friends, but within herself she knew that Will would always have been there for her, if she needed him. For Ned's sake, and for her brother's. He had been a good friend to Anthony.

Her heart tightened. Her brother had dropped dead in September, felled by a stroke. She no longer had anyone to turn to really. Well, that was not actually true. Amos Finnister was at the ready if she needed him, and Alfredo Oliveri. They were loyal to her because of their enduring love for Ned, and the many years they had worked with him. And then there was Grace Rose, of course. She had proved to be a kind and loving young woman, who had come to her after the boys had disappeared, and told her she was willing to help her any way she could. This gesture, she knew, had been prompted by Grace Rose's love for Ned and for Bess, but she was also a sincere and caring person. Elizabeth had always recognized this.

There was a knock on the bedroom door, and as Elizabeth called 'Come in,' Mallet's face appeared around the door.

'Excuse me, Mrs Deravenel, but Mrs Turner has arrived. She is in the drawing room, waiting for you.'

'Thank you, Mallet. I'll be down in a moment.'

'Yes, madam.'

Elizabeth looked at the clock on the mantelpiece. It was exactly four o'clock on the dot. Well, at least she's prompt, Elizabeth thought, and went to powder her nose, wondering exactly why Margaret Beauchard Turner had made this appointment to see her.

Although Margaret Beauchard Turner was an aristocratic woman of great breeding, who enjoyed a prominent social standing in London, Elizabeth Deravenel had never met her. And so when she walked into her drawing room a few minutes after four she was surprised to see how petite Mrs Turner was; she was also good looking and extremely chic, dressed in the height of fashion.

Her black-and-white suit was by Coco Chanel, and she wore Chanel's signature jewellery – several strands of long pearls, a Maltese cross on a gold chain, and pearl earrings.

Elizabeth decided, as she walked towards her, that she must be in her mid-forties, probably about forty-five years old.

'Good afternoon, Mrs Turner,' Elizabeth said, extending her hand.

Margaret Turner had risen when Elizabeth entered the room, and she stepped forward, took her hand, said in a distinctive voice, 'I'm very pleased to meet you, Mrs Deravenel. Thank you for agreeing to see me.'

Elizabeth inclined her head, motioned to the sofa, and said, 'Please do sit down, won't you.'

The two women were facing each other, weighing each other up; Elizabeth was still wondering what this was all about; Margaret Beauchard Turner was wondering how to begin.

Clearing her throat, smiling, Margaret finally took the initiative when she said, 'I know you must be curious why I wrote to you, asking to see you, and I will come to that in a moment. I would just like to say first how much I sympathize with you. As a mother myself I can well imagine how you must be feeling. I was once separated from my only child for many years, through no fault of my own, and it was extremely painful. You must suffer agonies of mind and heart every day.'

Elizabeth was touched by this woman's sympathetic words and kind voice, and she said, 'I do, Mrs Turner. I feel sometimes as if I've no tears left, but I do, I'm afraid. We are all suffering in the family, especially my daughters. Thank you for your kindness. I appreciate your sentiments.'

'I followed the press stories most carefully, and I must say, I have to praise the English newspapers, the way they tried to help you. They certainly devoted a great deal of space to your plight, all those banner headlines, the continuous ongoing stories, the photographs of your sons. The campaign went on for several months, didn't it?'

'Yes, it did, and the newspapers were very helpful to us, as was the BBC. There was a great deal of radio coverage.' Elizabeth shook her head, and a sorrowful shadow crossed her face. 'The reward is still sitting there . . .' Her words trailed off helplessly, and she sat, pushing back tears.

At this moment Mallet knocked on the door, opened it and came into the drawing room pushing the tea trolley.

'Thank you, Mallet,' Elizabeth said, regaining her composure. 'Just leave it here near my chair. I will serve tea later.'

'Yes, madam.' He nodded and disappeared.

Deciding to get the ritual of afternoon tea over swiftly, Elizabeth stood up, walked over to the trolley and, looking at Margaret Turner, asked, 'Do you like milk? Or perhaps you would prefer lemon, Mrs Turner?'

'Lemon, thank you,' Margaret answered, regarding Elizabeth

intently, thinking what a beautiful woman she truly was. A little on the thin side at the moment perhaps, and her face *was* drawn, but then she was truly suffering because of her missing boys. How sad she is, Margaret thought, her heart going out to her. This woman's life has been ruined.

Elizabeth brought the cup of tea to her guest, then carried her own to her chair and sat down. 'I didn't offer you anything to eat, Mrs Turner. Do you care for something?'

'No, no, thank you very much.'

They sat in silence for a moment or two, sipping their tea. Elizabeth was trying to keep herself calm, while Margaret was still thinking about her hostess.

Margaret Beauchard Turner was a wise, understanding, and experienced woman, and now she sat back, drinking her tea, saying nothing, giving Elizabeth Deravenel a chance to steady herself. She couldn't help wondering how much of the gossip Elizabeth had heard, and especially the gossip about her brother-in-law, Richard Deravenel. At this moment, Margaret had no way of knowing if anyone had told her how disliked he was at Deravenels, and how so many people believed he had had a hand in the disappearance of his nephews.

After a while, Elizabeth put down the teacup, and murmured, 'I appreciate your kind words, Mrs Turner, as I said before. However, in your letter to me you indicated you had something important to discuss with me.' Elizabeth looked at her pointedly.

'I do.' Margaret put her cup on a side table, and said, 'May I ask you one question first, Mrs Deravenel?'

Elizabeth nodded.

'After almost six months without a word about your sons, what are your conclusions? And those of your family?'

Taken aback, Elizabeth gaped at her, amazed that a woman of breeding like Margaret Turner would ask such a personal question. She did not answer, sat clasping her hands together to stop them trembling.

In her soft, cultured voice, Margaret went on slowly, 'I realize you think this is an impertinent question, from a woman whom you don't know at all, a stranger who has, in a sense, invaded your privacy. But I do have a reason for asking. It will be painful for you to face. But I must proceed . . . if your sons are not found in the next few months, I think you can make an assumption that they will never be found. As unpalatable as that is, I do believe that to be the truth, Mrs Deravenel. At that point your eldest daughter, Bess, will be your husband's heir. Am I not correct?'

'Yes, that is true,' Elizabeth answered, her voice almost inaudible.

'There is a great deal of gossip in London about *your* plight, and about your *family*. And I am sure you know that.'

'Chinese whispers,' Elizabeth muttered, relaxing, suddenly liking this woman's total honesty and directness. She was obviously not one to dissemble.

'To continue, your eldest daughter is the rightful heir to your husband's legacy, and she can become managing director of Deravenels. This I know to be true. You see, everyone at Deravenels knows that Edward Deravenel changed the centuries-old rules in 1919. My son Henry works at Deravenels in Paris. In fact, he has lately become head of the Paris operation. That is how *I* know about the rules being changed: my son told me. It was your husband who gave my son his present job, took him into the company. He has done very well there.'

'I knew, of course, that my husband had changed the rules, but I didn't know that your son worked at Deravenels in Paris.'

'He is well liked, and well thought of at the Paris office. Henry is a brilliant businessman and a very nice young man. He will certainly make some woman a good husband one day.'

Elizabeth stared at her, and suddenly everything clicked into place. And she understood why Margaret Turner was sitting here in her drawing room. Taking a deep breath, Elizabeth said, 'You are thinking of a marriage between my daughter and your son. That is the reason you came to see me, isn't it?'

'Indeed it is. Let me explain about his credentials. He is not a Deravenel through his father, the late Edmund Turner, but he does have Deravenel blood in him through me. I am sure you know that I am a Beauchard, and that I am directly descended from John Grant Deravenel, the fourth son of Guy de Ravenel, the founding father of the Deravenel dynasty. Also, my son is the late Henry Grant's heir, and he inherited all of Grant's shares in the company.'

'So are you saying your son has a claim to the company?'

'No, I'm not saying that exactly . . . but I will tell you this, he might well succeed in claiming the company if he were married to Edward Deravenel's heiress.' Margaret leaned forward urgently, pinning her dark eyes on Elizabeth. 'Just imagine this, Mrs Deravenel . . . your daughter and my son could create a new dynasty – *the Turners*. And their children would have Deravenel blood in them as well as Turner blood. Worth contemplating, isn't it?'

Elizabeth nodded, and a small smile struck her mouth. Her sorrow for her missing sons did not lessen, but she saw a flicker of hope for Bess.

Margaret Beauchard Turner, one of the cleverest women alive, smiled also. 'Let us talk frankly, shall we?'

And this they did for several hours, and they began to plan a wedding.

FIFTY-TWO

London 1927

Bess sat at the bedside of her aunt, Anne Deravenel, holding her hand, trying to comfort her. Anne had been ill for some weeks now, ever since their child Little Eddie had died, suddenly and unexpectedly of an appendicitis. Anne and Richard had been demented, out of their minds with grief, and inconsolable. And Anne had fallen apart, taken to her bed. Richard, too, was grief-stricken, but he was now managing to cope. Deravenels kept him busy.

Suddenly Anne turned her head and looked directly into Bess's eyes, said in a low voice, 'I can't stop thinking about April the ninth, the day Little Eddie died at Ravenscar. Why did God take him from us on that day? The same day Ned died a year ago? To the very day, Bess. Was God punishing Richard?'

Bess leaned closer, staring at her aunt, her bright-blue eyes widening in surprise. 'What do you mean, Aunt Anne? Why would God be punishing Uncle Richard?'

Anne lay there on the pillows, pale and wan, and remained silent, now regretting those words, aware of the shock and surprise on her niece's face. Bess had probably misunderstood her.

454

'What did you mean?' Bess pressed, baffled and frightened by the statement of a moment ago.

Anne looked up at Bess, and smiled faintly. 'Richard did *insist* the boys come to Ravenscar to be with us and Little Eddie. That weekend when we went to my mother's house, we left them alone, and later Richard went to London. They were left unattended, Bess, except for Nanny and the staff. People are saying bad things about Richard, saying that he was negligent, and therefore he is responsible for their disappearance . . . but he wasn't. He loved the boys. And who could possible imagine that they would not be safe at Ravenscar, and that a bad person would come and take them from the beach?'

Anne began to weep, and Bess bent over her, gave her a clean handkerchief, murmuring gently, 'Please don't cry, Anne, don't upset yourself so. You must try and get better. Uncle Richard needs you, he's grieving just as you are, for Little Eddie. Let me go downstairs and ask Cook to make us a pot of tea. Do you think you could eat something?'

Anne wiped her eyes, and shook her head. 'I'm not hungry, I'm really not.' Her eyes focused on the clock on the bedside table, and she went on softly, 'Goodness, look at the time. It's already six o'clock. Richard will soon come home from Deravenels.'

'Why don't you try to get up, Anne, to have dinner with Richard tonight. It would cheer him up.'

'I don't think I can . . . maybe I will feel better tomorrow.'

Bess, looking at her, couldn't help thinking she was wasting away. Anne hardly ever ate, and because she barely ever got out of bed she was suffering from weakness in her legs. Atrophy, Bess thought, and pushed away that ghastly thought.

At this moment the door flew open and her uncle was suddenly standing in the doorway. He appeared tired and drained, but he pushed a smile onto his face as he walked across the room. 'Bess, it's lovely to see you here. Thank you for coming to be with Anne, you're so good to her.'

'I've been here all afternoon,' Bess replied, smiling at him. They had always been close and she was genuinely fond of him. 'I've been trying to persuade Aunt Anne to get up for dinner.'

'And why not?' He came to the side of the bed, and bent down, moved Anne's pale blonde hair away from her face tenderly, kissed her cheek. Looking down at her, he continued, 'Do come downstairs, my love. You don't have to dress, and I'll carry you. It would be so nice to dine with you tonight.'

Anne's eyes were full of adoration for him when she answered, 'I will take a cat nap. I promise I'll come down later.' Her eyes moved to Bess, and she smiled at her niece. 'Stay for supper, darling Bess. You can help me dress later perhaps.'

'Of course I'll help you, Aunt Anne,' Bess answered, and turning to her uncle she added, 'I'll go downstairs now, leave the two of you alone together.'

Bess went outside into the garden of her uncle's Chelsea house, walked across the wide terrace and down to the wall that fronted onto the River Thames.

Resting her elbows on the wall, she looked down the river. For years Amos had entertained her and Grace Rose with the lore of the Thames; she had grown to love it as much as he did, and so did Grace Rose. There were a few small boats on it, on this late afternoon in May, and she couldn't help thinking of the *Lady Bess*.

What had happened to that fishing boat? It was obvious that her brothers had taken it to the beach. But had they actually taken it out onto the water? Had they got into trouble and drowned? Or had the man Tom Roebottom had seen simply tied their fishing boat to his own when he had taken the boys with him?

Not so long ago she had asked Amos this question, and he

had nodded, and explained, 'If I were abducting two boys, of course I would take their boat with me . . . The missing boat, the *Lady Bess*, has created doubts in people's minds. They think the boys may well have drowned at sea.' Then she had asked Amos what *he* believed, and he had said he thought her brothers had been taken, but had no idea what their fate had been.

Bess sighed as she thought of that conversation with Amos. She tended to agree with him . . . no one knew what had happened to her brothers. That was the cruellest thing of all, not knowing. They had been missing almost a year. Today was the last day of May in 1927. She was eighteen, having celebrated her birthday in March . . . and Grace Rose was already twenty-seven. They were good friends and spent a great deal of time together; Grace Rose had been a true sister to her and like another daughter to Elizabeth, and Bess appreciated this.

'I've been looking all over for you,' Richard was saying, coming down the garden path towards her.

Bess swung around, a smile striking her mouth, and she answered, 'I'm hiding in plain sight, Uncle Richard.'

'Thank you again, Bess darling,' he said as he came to her, and leaned an arm on the wall, looking at her intently. 'You do help to cheer Anne up. She seems so weak, very listless, but the doctor can't find anything wrong with her.' He shook his head, his face strained.

'She's sick from grief,' Bess murmured.

He was silent for a long moment, and then he said in a voice that was a whisper, 'Dying of a broken heart, perhaps.'

'Perhaps,' Bess agreed, and took hold of his hand, squeezed it. 'I know how you fret about Anne, you worry yourself sick, but I'll come as much as I can to see her.'

Richard placed his hand over hers. 'Thank God for *you*. You do her good. And you do me good, too. Whatever would I do without you, dearest Bess.' He brought her hand to his mouth and kissed her fingers. 'You are our treasure.'

Leaning forward, Bess kissed him on the cheek. 'I want to help you both as much as I can. I love you both, Richard. And what is a family for otherwise?'

He gave her a curious look, and said, 'Sometimes I wonder, and most especially about ours.'

He stared off into the distance, as if seeing something she could not see. His eyes were a pale, bluish grey at this moment, and with his dark hair and sculpted face she realized yet again how much he looked liked her grandmother, his mother. Richard Deravenel had inherited the looks of the Watkins's side of the family. He was not as tall and staggeringly handsome as her father, and his colouring was totally different. Yet he was a good-looking man, and there were times when he reminded her of her father.

It really was a peculiar thing that his seven-year-old son Little Eddie had died on the same day her father had died one year earlier. She thought of Anne's words; they puzzled her.

She suddenly blurted out, 'Uncle Richard, why do people say such terrible things about you?'

He swung his head away from the river, and gaped at her, startled. His face was changing before her eyes. His mouth became taut, his eyes, pale blue a moment ago, now turned darker, became slate grey in colour.

'I don't know, Bess,' he said at last in a puzzled voice. 'I really don't . . . I'm as baffled as you are. I didn't take your brothers. Why would I? Anyway, I was in London, as you well know. But I suppose there are those who think I arranged for them to be kidnapped . . . killed? But I'm not responsible for this crime, Bess, if there has been one. You must believe that.'

'I do. I know you loved the boys, and I know how loyal you always were to my father . . . I can't imagine you touching a hair on their heads . . . they looked so much like him.'

Tears came into Richard's eyes and he took hold of her hand again. 'Look at me, Bess, please. Please look at me. I swear to

God I did not harm Edward and Ritchie. *You must believe me.*'

Bess, gazing into his eyes, saw the sincerity reflected there, heard the truth ringing in his voice and she knew he was not lying. She believed him even though there were those who were saying scurrilous things about him. She had known him all of her life and she trusted him absolutely. He was her father's brother, her father's favourite, and her father had truly loved Richard.

'I do believe you,' she said finally. 'I trust you with my life, and my sisters' lives.'

'Thank you, Bess. Thank you for having faith in me.' He turned to look at the river, and so did she, and he put his arm around her shoulders and they watched the Thames flowing by, lost in their own thoughts. But both of them were thinking of the future.

Amos Finnister stood in the library of the house in Berkeley Square. As everyone else did when they came into this beautiful room, he was staring up at the painting by Renoir hanging above the fireplace. It reminded him of Bess and Grace Rose. And that was why Mr Edward had bought it in the first place, he was quite sure of that.

'Hello, Mr Finnister,' Elizabeth said.

He swung around to face her. 'Good evening, Mrs Deravenel.'

Elizabeth glided forward into the room, and shook his outstretched hand, and they walked together towards the chairs near the fireplace.

'Thank you for coming,' Elizabeth said, as she sat down. 'I wanted to talk to you about Deravenels.'

'I thought that was probably why you'd asked me to come. But I don't have a lot to report, Mrs Deravenel. If I had I'd have been in touch.'

'I know, you've been very good, Mr Finnister, very helpful this past year. And Mr Oliveri as well. Is he coming, by the way?'

'Yes, he is. He was delayed at Deravenels, but he should arrive within the next few minutes or so.'

'I'm glad. I wondered how things were at the Paris office.'

'Very well, as I understand it. But, of course, Oliveri can fill you in better about that, since he deals with them on a constant basis.'

She nodded, clasping her hands together. And what is happening here in London?' She raised an arched blond brow, and asked, 'Have there been any more sackings?'

'Several, yes, I'm afraid. And Mr Richard has made a few other changes.'

'But the company is all right, isn't it?' she asked, worry suddenly clouding her pale-blue eyes. She brought a hand to her neck nervously. 'He's not ruining it, is he?'

'That would be hard to do, Mrs Deravenel. Mr Edward – well, he made it *very safe*.'

'Madam, excuse me, Mr Oliveri has arrived,' Mallet said from the doorway of the library.

'Oh, thank you, please show him in, Mallet.'

Elizabeth rose to greet Alfredo as he came hurrying in, apologizing profusely for being late. 'Oh, that's all right,' she reassured him, shaking his hand. 'Please sit down here with us. Oh, and do excuse me, I'm being rather rude not offering you anything. Would you like a drink, Mr Finnister? And what about you, Mr Oliveri.'

Both men declined politely, and Elizabeth leaned back in the chair, and said, 'I was just discussing Deravenels with Mr Finnister, and he was assuring me that whatever my brother-in-law does, the company will always be safe because of the way my husband set it up.'

'That's correct, Mrs Deravenel. Mr Edward, well, he was a

genius. His brother is not of the same caliber, I'm sorry to say, but, nonetheless, he's not a stupid man. He might get rid of a few people now and then, but he's not going to rock any boats, believe me,' Oliveri told her confidently.

'I was mentioning the Paris office to Mr Finnister. Things are all right there, aren't they?

'Yes. Couldn't be better. Henry Turner has been running it very well for quite a while now,' Oliveri responded. 'He's proving to be an asset. We were all a bit perplexed when Mr Edward hired him, several years ago, but he's done well by the company.'

'I should hope so, since he's a shareholder. I'm sure you both know he is the late Henry Grant's heir, and he inherited all of Grant's shares in the company.'

'Mr Deravenel, er, Mr Edward that is, did mention it to me,' Oliveri said. 'He seemed to have a lot of faith in young Henry's business acumen, actually.'

'So I understand. I want to ask you both something, and I want you to feel at ease in answering me with honesty. It will be in strict confidence, whatever you say.'

Both men nodded.

Elizabeth confided, 'I hear a great deal of gossip these days about my brother-in-law. It strikes me that Richard Deravenel is not very popular within the company . . . is that *true*?'

'Yes, it is. In fact, I would go so far as to say that he's disliked. Intensely disliked,' Oliveri replied.

'Except for the men he grew up with, and who he brought in after Mr Edward's death last April,' Amos pointed out. 'They kowtow to him.'

'But surely that's a handful only?' Elizabeth interjected.

'Oh, yes, Mrs Deravenel, that's correct,' Oliveri was quick to say.

'Do people believe he was responsible for the disappearance of my sons?' She finally brought the most important question to the forefront.

'A lot do, yes,' Finnister responded swiftly. He was hell bent on telling her the truth. She deserved to know how grave the gossip was these days. 'I would say that eighty per cent of the employees at Deravenels think that your brother-in-law had a hand in their disappearance. Don't ask me why, but they do.'

'They probably think he got rid of them in order to grab the company for himself, and for his son,' Oliveri asserted, following Finnister's lead.

'Now dead,' Elizabeth murmured. 'Odd isn't it, that his son died on the same day my husband died, exactly one year later.'

Neither man spoke; they both agreed with her. It was the strangest thing to most people. Like Divine Judgement, some thought and said.

Elizabeth looked from Finnister to Oliveri. 'My daughter, Bess, is actually the heir, you know, not her uncle. I'm sure you also know that my husband changed those ancient rules in 1919, and made certain that a woman born a Deravenel could become managing director when she was old enough.'

'Yes, we did know,' Alfredo said, answering for them both.

Elizabeth sat looking reflective for a moment, and then she said, 'She's a little bit young to enter the business. At the moment.'

'But she could come and work at Deravenels and be trained,' Alfredo exclaimed, excited by the prospect, and eager.

'In a couple of years she *could* join the company, yes. Do you think she would be made welcome?' Elizabeth asked.

'Very much so,' Alfredo asserted, and then wondered if he was correct. A lot of the men would resent her.

Finnister said, 'She's very mature and grown up for her age, Mrs Deravenel, and extremely intelligent, clever like her father. I've known her all of her life and she has all of his qualities: and she's very practical.'

'That is true, yes. Changing the subject, for a moment, what do you think about Henry Turner joining the London office?

Would he also be made welcome?' Elizabeth looked from Oliveri to Finnister.

Alfredo stared at Amos, exchanging a look with him, and they both nodded their heads. Amos said, 'I think so, yes. Certainly by the employees, because after all, he is sort of, well, part Deravenel, isn't he? At least that's what we've heard.'

'Yes, through his mother Margaret Beauchard Turner he is, and as I mentioned earlier, he is a major shareholder.'

Amos Finnister now said, in a somber voice, 'He wouldn't be welcomed by Mr Richard, not by a long shot.'

'He wouldn't allow him to cross the threshold,' Alfredo announced, grimacing.

'I realize that,' Elizabeth said.

Staring at her, weighing her expression and her tone of voice, Amos now murmured very softly, in a conspiratorial way, 'Are you thinking of an . . . *alliance*, shall we call it, Mrs Deravenel? An alliance between Bess and Henry Turner?'

Elizabeth merely smiled.

Amos smiled back.

After a short silence, Elizabeth rose, went over to the fireplace and stood with her back to it as Edward had always done. Her eyes swept over them, two of Edward's most trusted and devoted employees, two men who had somehow managed to escape Richard's rampage and were still at Deravenels.

Straightening her back, standing tall, she said, 'Change. The only thing that's permanent *is* change. And things do change often, we all know that. People don't live forever, now do they?'

FIFTY-THREE

Ravenscar

Catastrophe. That was something his brother Ned had always feared, and he had done everything in his power to sidestep it, to avoid it at all costs, because he believed it would be his undoing. And Ned had succeeded. He had died too young, this was true, but he had died peacefully in his own bed at the height of his success.

But *he* had not managed to avoid catastrophe. He was engulfed by it. And he was undone. His personal life was shattered; his business life was holding its own but only just. Things had gone wrong at Deravenels, and in a sense he had only himself to blame. He had trusted the wrong people, listened to the wrong people, made mistakes . . . They had been a golden family; but they were cursed.

Richard Deravenel stood in the library at Ravenscar, staring out at the North Sea, his blue-grey eyes taking in the magnificent view. It was the month of August in 1928 and he was thirty-three years old. And a widower. His wife had died this past March, after contracting tuberculosis. But Richard believed she had really died of a broken heart, grieving for their seven-year-old son, Little Eddie.

Richard sighed, thinking of his darling child. He had not only lost his most beloved little boy, but his heir. All the Deravenel men were dead and gone, except for himself, and George's little son who lived in Dijon with his aunt, Richard's sister Meg. An unlikely successor.

No Deravenel man to take over the company if anything happened to him. The only adult heir left was his niece Bess, Ned's lovely eldest daughter and first-born child. Ned had made it legally possible for a woman to run Deravenels, but how could Bess do that? It just wasn't feasible: she had no experience of business and was still far too young at nineteen. The men would not feel comfortable about her presence in the company – no, not at all.

Bess. He loved her because she was his brother's child, and because she was a true Deravenel. But he did not love her in the lustful way some people thought. There were stories told about them these days, stories that were scurrilous and untrue ... His enemies blackened his name and hers, said that they were lovers, that he had poisoned Anne in order to marry his niece, that together they would rule Deravenels. None of it was true. How did you stop the gossip? How did one wipe the mud off one's face? It stuck. And that was the truth of it.

Turning away from the window, Richard stepped to the centre of the library, stood gazing up at the portrait of his brother Ned, known as the great Edward Deravenel these days. And that was accurate, he *had* been great, and there would never be another man like him. They had thrown the mould away when they'd made Ned. He was unique.

The portrait of Ned was lifesize, and showed him standing in front of this very fireplace, wearing jodhpurs, highly-polished brown riding boots, and a blue shirt that echoed the colour of his eyes. The shirt was open at the neck, Ned's medallion just visible, with the enamelled white rose of York showing.

Richard touched his chest, feeling *his* gold medallion underneath his shirt; he always wore the rose next to his skin – the other side, showing the sun in splendour, turned outward. Ned had had the medallions made when he had taken over Deravenels in 1904, had them inscribed with the Deravenel family motto: *Fidelity Unto Eternity.*

The portrait had been painted when Ned was thirty-nine, and finished just before his fortieth birthday. It was striking, dominated this room, which was Ned's creation, had been his favourite. It was so life-like, Richard felt that Ned was standing there, smiling down at him . . .

He had the sudden need to talk to his brother.

'I didn't do it, Ned,' Richard said, sotto voce, 'I didn't take your children or have them murdered. I loved them, Ned, just as we loved each other. I swear to God I didn't harm your blood . . . they were my blood too . . . Deravenels.'

Richard brushed his eyes with his fingers, swallowed hard, not wanting to break down this morning. Bess was staying here at Ravenscar with Grace Rose, and he did not wish to show weakness in front of these two young women. He felt a sudden tightness in his chest, as he so often did these days when he thought of his little nephews. They had been missing now for two years . . . gone without a trace. A terrible mystery, still unsolved . . . and the world blamed him.

He heard footsteps and swung around quickly, saw Bess walking into the library with Grace Rose.

'I was just admiring the portrait of your father,' he said, his voice sounding strange to him, full of tears.

Bess picked up on this at once, knowing him as well as she did, and she hurried forward, took hold of his arm affectionately. 'Uncle Richard, are you all right?' She peered into his face.

'I'm fine, Bess, why do you ask?'

'You sounded a bit odd, that's all.' She smiled at him. 'I thought you'd already gone for your walk on the beach.'

'I'm afraid I was sidetracked by your father's handsome, smiling face,' he replied, then beckoned to Grace Rose. 'And why are *you* hanging back? No greeting for your old uncle today?'

Grace Rose went to join them. Like her half-sister, Bess, she loved Richard, and believed in him; never for one moment had she thought that Richard Deravenel was responsible for the disappearance of Young Edward and Little Ritchie. The mere idea of it was inconceivable to her. She loathed the revolting gossips in London who besmirched his name.

'Wasn't he just the most marvellous looking man?' Grace Rose murmured, also gazing up at the portrait of Edward.

Richard turned to her. 'I was just thinking the same thing a few moments ago.'

'Father was simply the best. True Blue.' Bess looked from Richard to Grace Rose, and added, 'Just as we three are.'

'Indeed.' Richard turned away from the portrait, and walked across the library. He stopped when he had gone halfway, turned around, 'Oh, by the way, Bess and Grace Rose, I heard from your grandmother this morning. She telephoned me, and she sends her love to you both.'

'Is she all right?' Grace Rose asked.

'Very well. She's enjoying being at the retreat in Hampshire.'

'I'm glad,' Grace Rose said, meaning it. Cecily Deravenel had treated her as part of the family since they first met, and she loved her.

Bess said, 'When is she coming out? Or is she staying there? My mother said something about Grandmother wanting to become a nun?'

Richard chuckled. 'I doubt that. I'm sure she was joking. Now I'm off for my walk. I'll see you both at one for lunch.'

His nieces watched him go. Bess went and sat down on the sofa. Looking across at Grace Rose she said, 'It was so nice of you to come up here to spend this week with me, to keep me company, and Richard. Thank you.'

'Don't be so silly, Bess, I enjoy coming here. It's certainly no hardship.' Grace Rose waved the notebook she was holding and went on, 'I've managed to do quite a lot of work on my book here, it's so quiet and peaceful. I'm the one who should be thanking you.'

'You're always welcome. I just wanted to come up to Yorkshire to keep Richard company. He's so lonely these days and troubled.'

Grace Rose nodded, took the other chair, and gave Bess a look. 'I don't think things are too good at Deravenels, from what Amos said.'

'What did he say?' Bess asked swiftly, her curiosity aroused.

'That most people don't like Richard. They don't warm to him. He's not as skilful at making friends as our father was.'

Bess answered, succinctly, 'Unfortunately, he's much better at making enemies.'

Richard was almost at the Cormorant Rock when he saw the two men walking towards him. At first he thought they were local fishermen heading his way, but as he drew closer he recognized one of them, and waved. The man waved back. Richard wondered who the other fellow was; he had no idea, had never seen him before.

'Going out fishing?' Richard asked, as he drew to a standstill in front of them.

'Thinking about it,' the man he knew answered, taking several steps closer to him.

Richard was startled, and was just about to step back when he felt a sharp pain in his side, and then another in his chest. His eyes widened as he stared at the other man and saw the knife in his hand. He looked down at the blood on his cardigan.

'Why did you do that to *me*, Jack?' Richard cried, and staggered back as the man stabbed him again and again. His legs crumpled under him and he hit the beach with a thud, felled by the blade.

'Let's get out of here,' the man with the knife said, and turned to flee. When he saw Richard's cap on the beach he gave it a swift kick. It sailed up into the air and fell on the lower portion of moorland, where it landed under a gorse bush.

The assassin and his companion ran down the beach. They dragged their boat from underneath the outcropping of rocks, took it to the shallows, got in and rowed away. It was Wednesday August the twenty-second, 1928, and Richard Deravenel was dead.

'Has Mr Deravenel returned yet, Miss Bess?' Jessup asked from the doorway of her father's office, where she was working on papers.

Bess looked up, frowning. 'I'm not sure, Jessup, have you looked in the library?'

'Yes, miss, and he's not there. Nor is Miss Grace Rose. I'll tell Cook to hold lunch for a few minutes, and I'll go and look for them both.'

'Thanks, Jessup,' Bess answered, and stood up, glancing at the clock, noting that it was already fifteen minutes past one. She followed the butler out into the Long Hall, and saw Grace Rose coming down the stairs. 'Have you seen Uncle Richard?' Bess called, going to meet her.

'No, I haven't,' Grace Rose responded, coming into the entrance hall. 'Actually, I don't think he's returned from his walk. I've been sitting in the library, checking my notes for ages, almost since he left. I only went upstairs to find a pencil a few minutes ago. No, he's not back, I would've seen him.'

'He's always so punctual,' Bess muttered almost to herself, and felt a sudden uneasiness. It was settling in the pit of her stomach. 'I think perhaps I'll go down to the beach, bustle him along a bit.'

'I'll come with you,' Grace Rose volunteered.

Jessup was hurrying out of the butler's pantry and Bess said to him, 'We'll go down to the beach and get him. My uncle has probably forgotten the time.'

'He's always very *punctual*, Miss Bess,' the butler answered. 'It's not like Mr Richard to be late.'

'I know,' Bess replied and she and Grace Rose hurried out, went across the terrace and down through the hanging gardens. They were making for the steps cut in the cliff face, located at the far end of the property, well beyond the gardens and lawns.

Grace Rose saw him first from the top of the steps, and she cried, 'Bess, look! There he is, on the beach. He must have tripped and fallen . . . I hope it's nothing worse, like a heart attack.'

'Oh, my God!' Bess exclaimed. Together the two young women ran down the steps and flew across the shingle, pieces of it flying around their shoes as they raced ahead.

Bess was athletic and swift, and she reached her uncle's body first. He was on his back; she spotted the blood on his cardigan at once, and she brought a hand to her mouth to stop the scream that was rising in her throat. Kneeling down, Bess took hold of his wrist, fumbled for his pulse. There wasn't one, and she instantly knew why she had felt that sudden unease, that rush of panic earlier. He was dead; somehow, she had always known that Richard would die before he should.

Grace Rose bent down next to her, and looked at Richard's white face, and she said softly, 'His eyes, Bess, look, they're so blue, bluer than I've ever seen them.'

Bess did as her half-sister asked. Richard's eyes were very blue, and this seemed so odd to her. But what struck her most forcibly was the startled expression on his face. He had been taken by surprise when he had been attacked, she was certain of that.

Finally, a sob broke through, and tears were rolling down Bess's face as she gently closed his eyelids. She kissed his cheek, and so did Grace Rose, and then she whispered, 'Safe journey, Richard. My father's waiting for you.'

The two of them hurried back to the steps, and began to climb. At one moment, Bess tilted her eyes to the sky. It was a vivid blue, and the sun was shining. And for once the weather at Ravenscar was warm. Such a beautiful day, Bess thought, such a beautiful day to leave behind. And the tears came again, trickling down her cheeks.

When they reached the terrace, Jessup was waiting for them. His face was white, and his apprehension visible. 'What has happened, Miss Bess?' he asked, suddenly sounding old.

'My uncle is dead . . . there's blood all over his chest.' Her voice broke on the last few words; she took a deep breath and continued, in a steadier voice, 'Please have the gardeners go down to the beach to retrieve his body, Jessup. They'll need sheets to wrap around him. Meanwhile, I shall go and telephone the police.'

Grace Rose and Bess went to the office and the butler rushed off to send the gardeners to fetch the body. Grace Rose said quietly, taking hold of Bess's arm, 'The police will come but they'll find nothing. Someone came in by boat, stabbed Richard and left. It's Wednesday, and everyone in the village is working. The beach has been deserted all morning: in fact, I've not seen one person on it since I arrived here on Friday.'

'I know,' Bess agreed and dialled the number of the Scarborough constabulary. When she got through she asked for Inspector Wallis. He came on the line immediately and she told him what had happened.

There was a sudden silence at his end of the phone for a moment, before he said in a sympathetic tone, 'I'll be there as quickly as possible. I'm so very sorry you're having to cope with yet another problem at Ravenscar, Miss Deravenel. My condolences about your uncle.'

After thanking him, Bess hung up, turned to Grace Rose, and murmured, 'I don't think I can go down to that beach every again.'

'I can't say I blame you.' Grace Rose shook her head. 'Now we're going to have two unsolved mysteries: please believe that.'

Bess was alone at Ravenscar.

Everyone had come for Richard's funeral, and his burial in the family cemetery. Then everyone had left. She had elected to stay on, needing to be alone, to think about her life, and her future, and the things she and her mother had discussed.

Now, as she sat in the library thinking, it was already the middle of September. Her mind settled on the last few years. So much had happened . . . Uncle George had died in the strangest of circumstances at the vineyard in Mâcon; then her father had passed away very unexpectedly. Her brothers had vanished and had never been found. And last month Uncle Richard had been stabbed to death by an unknown assailant. The police had found nothing, just as Grace Rose had predicted. It was another unsolved murder on the books, so Inspector Wallis had told her. They all now believed Richard had been killed by a business enemy, or a disgruntled friend of her father.

Her family had been decimated. All the men dead. Only women left. Richard had said there was a curse on the family. Perhaps there was.

Rising, she went and stood at the window, looking out towards the sea. How her life had changed . . . Not so long ago she had been so very happy, carefree. Now she felt as though she were surrounded by death . . . and enveloped in unhappiness.

Her thoughts swung to her mother. Elizabeth had come to the funeral, bringing her four sisters, accompanied by her grandmother. Cecily Deravenel had looked careworn and exhausted to Bess, and she still worried about her. Cecily had gone back to London, insisting she had doctors to see, appointments to keep. Bess had the feeling that her grandmother could not bear to be here at Ravenscar . . . certainly not at this moment.

Bess loved this house. Perhaps because her father had loved it so much. However, she had not been down to the beach; she did go to the gardens and often visited the ruined stronghold which had been so meaningful to her father.

On a sudden impulse, Bess jumped up, and went outside, running down to the stronghold, swift on her feet, anxious to get there.

Once she was there she leaned against the wall, and looked out, thinking about her father, wondering what he would want her to do. She had two choices. She could remain as she was, a single woman. Or she could marry, have a husband and children, a life of her own as a wife and mother, creating and nurturing her own family.

Her mother had spoken to her at length before going back to London, had broached the subject of Henry Turner yet again. Her mother had been pushing him at her ever since the boys had disappeared; it had actually started in December, two years ago. She had told her mother then that she wasn't interested in marriage with anyone.

Last month her mother had pointed out that this was a chance for them to keep Deravenels steady and on course. Richard Deravenel was dead. She was the heiress. Obviously she could not run the family company, become what her father and Richard had been. She was too young, a woman, who would be alien in the company, resented. Her mother, however, believed that Henry Turner *could* handle it, with her by his side to add credibility and the name Deravenel. She had not met him, and she was not sure if she would like him. Could she grow to love him? After all, this was an arranged marriage, if it took place. But what other choice was there?

Glancing at her watch, she realized Elizabeth and Henry would be arriving very soon. No sooner had this thought entered her mind when she heard her mother calling her name.

'Bess! Bess darling! Are you down in the stronghold?'

'Yes, mother, I am,' she answered dutifully, turning around.

'May we come down? I have Henry with me.'

For a moment she could not speak. 'All right,' she said eventually, holding onto the crenellated edge of the wall. Her legs were weak under her, and she was trembling, feeling nervous, even afraid.

Her mother was standing there, dressed in a beige travelling suit, looking elegant. Next to her was a tall, slender young man, with light brown hair, hazel eyes, and a pleasant face. He was dressed in a dark grey suit, and a grey silk tie.

Her mother brought him forward, and said, 'Bess, this is Henry Turner. Henry, my daughter, Bess.'

He stretched out his hand, took hold of hers, and smiled at her. She saw that his eyes were soft and full of understanding. He said, 'I'm happy to finally meet you.'

'I'm happy to meet you too,' she mumbled, and extricated her hand quickly, took a step backward.

'I'll leave you together for a while,' Elizabeth announced. 'I need to change. I'll see you both for tea.'

Left alone the two of them stood and stared at each other for a long time; neither had the courage to speak. Finally, Henry said, in a gentle voice, 'I know you've been reluctant to marry me, and I do understand why. But I'm not too bad a chap, so I've been told. And certainly I will be very happy if you accept me. And I promise I will cherish you. Also, I feel sure I will probably grow to love you.'

Unexpectedly, and unable to stop herself, Bess started to laugh.

Henry Turner stared at her nonplussed and completely puzzled.

Catching her breath, swallowing her laughter, Bess said, 'I like you for saying that, Henry Turner. I really do.'

'For saying what?'

'For being so honest, for saying that you'll *probably grow to love me*. That's how I feel about you – slightly uncertain, awkward, not sure if we will love each other . . .'

He nodded. 'I do want to marry you, as I said before. Well, you knew that anyway, from our plotting mothers.' He grinned at her. 'I want to make you happy . . . Bess. I think I can. I'll do my damnedest.'

She was silent. She discovered she quite liked him. He wasn't the most handsome man, but he wasn't ugly either, and he seemed to have a pleasant, warm personality. Certainly he was honest, to the point of bluntness. That was important to her. Taking a deep breath, she reached out, took hold of his hand. 'Now that we've finally met each other, I would like to be alone, to be by myself a while. Would you mind?'

'No, of course I don't. I understand. I'll wait for you inside.' He left without another word.

Bess leaned her head against the stone wall, staring out across the North Sea. Who would help her if she married him? There was no one. Not even her mother. She was alone. Totally alone.

I'll fend for myself, she thought. And I'll manage.

We'll have children . . . And at least one of them will be a boy . . . *I must have a boy.* I must have a male heir for Deravenels. And I will help him. I will encourage his ambition, Show him the way.

She smiled, thinking of her handsome father. My son will be like the great Edward Deravenel . . . and there will always be Deravenel blood sitting in Papa's chair, running the company. And I will help to run the business through my husband and my son.

Turning around, Bess Deravenel walked back up to the house, her mind made up.

She found Henry Turner standing in the library, gazing at the portrait of her father.

'He was the handsomest, nicest, cleverest man I ever met,' Henry told her.

'I know,' Bess replied. 'And we will have a son exactly like him: just you wait and see.'

PART FOUR

The Turners

Harry's Women

Exceeding wise, fair spoken, and persuading;
Lofty and sour to them that lov'd him not;
But to those men that sought him sweet as summer.
William Shakespeare:
Henry VIII
Act IV, scene iii

I often have this strange and moving dream
Of an unknown woman, whom I love and who loves me.
Paul Verlaine
Poèmes Saturniens
'Mon Rêve Familier'

I'll not listen to reason ... Reason always means
what someone else has got to say.
Elizabeth Gaskell

Ill luck, you know, never comes alone.
Cervantes

FIFTY-FOUR

Ravenscar 1970

He stood in the library at Ravenscar, staring up at the painting above the fireplace, admiring it. What an extraordinary portrait it was, of a handsome man in the prime of his life.

The great Edward Deravenel. His grandfather.

His mother, Edward's eldest daughter Bess, had always told him that he would grow up to look like her father, and she had been proven right.

This painting had been finished just a short time before Edward's fortieth birthday, and in a few days' time he himself would be forty years old. And he was the spitting image of his grandfather: six foot four, broad of chest, with red-gold hair and blue eyes. He knew that if Edward Deravenel could step out of the portrait, come to stand next to him, they would look like twins, so close was their resemblance.

Harry Turner finally turned away and walked out onto the terrace, headed through the hanging gardens, making for the ruined stronghold. His mother Bess had constantly taken him down there as a child, explaining that it had been her father's favourite spot at Ravenscar, and therefore hers. And now his, of course.

She had brought him up on Deravenel lore, and most of it had been about his grandfather. How she had adored her father; just as he had loved his mother most especially. He had loved his father, too, but the somewhat taciturn Henry Turner had not been quite as warm, outgoing and loving as his mother. And, in fact, he had been a somewhat dull man, boring. Bess Deravenel had been a unique woman. It was from her that he had inherited his fair colouring, and also her indomitability, her strength of will, her ambition, and her positive personality. Her glass was always half full, never half empty, and he felt exactly the same. Tomorrow would always be a better day, as far as he was concerned.

Odd, though, that there were things in his life which so closely echoed Edward Deravenel's life. He, too, had married a woman five years older than himself, just as Edward had. And he dreaded the idea of catastrophe dragging him down, in the same way his grandfather had. Edward, somehow, had managed to side-step it.

He wasn't doing quite so well with that aspect of his life. At this moment, on June twenty-third of 1970, he felt as though he was about to plunge down into a bottomless pit of catastrophe. And, if not quite that, he was, nonetheless, swimming in a sea of problems, in his personal life and in business. Deravenels he could handle. He was not quite sure about his private life.

He had to get a divorce . . . had to get a new wife . . . had to get an heir. But his wife wouldn't budge. Nothing would convince her or persuade her to release him from his torment. No divorce, that was her eternal cry.

He was haunted by his father's last words. On his deathbed his father had told him he must get a male heir for Deravenels. Over and over again, he had said it.

But Harry had only had a daughter, and he knew full well that a woman could never be the boss. Catherine and he had been married for over twenty years and sadly Mary was their only offspring. So many dead babies, so many miscarriages.

Time was running out on him. On June twenty-eight, in four days' time, he would be forty years old and Catherine was already forty-five. How could *they* make another baby? She was too old, that was certain. Yes, it was an impossibility. Besides which, he did not desire her anymore. It was Anne he longed for, ached for, yearned to have, to hold and to possess forever. She was holding out for marriage and would not become his acknowledged mistress. In the past seven years she had thwarted him, would not move in with him ... it had been that long, their dalliance. He was at times driven to the edge.

He knew full well he was caught between the iron wills of two very obdurate women. They were squeezing the life out of him.

Harry rested his forehead against the stone parapet and closed his eyes, wondering what to do ... the words repeated themselves in his head: get a divorce, get married, get an heir, get a big new deal for Deravenels ... get it all before it's too late.

'Harry! Harry! Are you down there?' Charles Brandt shouted, running down the last of the steps that led into the ruined stronghold.

Harry roused himself from his dire thoughts, and straightened. He focused his eyes on Charles, his best friend from childhood, and as he did he suddenly thought, Charles is *my* Will Hasling.

Harry knew all about his grandfather's best friend and closest colleague, a man his mother had loved and held in such great regard. She had constantly told him Will had died in mysterious circumstances ...

So many suspicious deaths in his family's past ... it made

481

one think, didn't it? His mother's Uncle George, struck by wine casks and drowned in Beaujolais at their vineyards at Mâcon. Her Uncle Richard, stabbed by an unknown assailant on the beach here at Ravenscar. And all those other people who had died in peculiar ways years before her birth. The Deravenels seemed to be dogged by weird deaths. Had they been murders? And had some Deravenels been murderers? Yes indeed, it did make you think . . .

Charles Brandt walked across the flagged floor of the stronghold, once a circular tower, now roofless and open to the winds and the weather of this northern coastline. It was sunny on this Tuesday morning late in June, and Charles felt its warming rays on his face. He realized he couldn't wait to get to his house in the south of France next week. He needed a rest from everything.

Standing in front of Harry, staring hard at him, Charles felt an unexpected rush of exasperation. 'Come on, my lad, buck up!' Charles exclaimed. 'You look bloody miserable. What is it now?' Charles smiled faintly and shook his head. 'As if I didn't know . . . you're thinking about the two women in your life who've got you by your short hairs.'

'You've hit the nail on the head.'

'Ouch!' Charles shot back, laughing. 'Unfortunate choice of expression, Harry, under the circumstances.'

Harry laughed hollowly. 'You're right, Charles, I mean about the women. But it's also about *me*. I know I can't go on much longer. I've been thinking a lot whilst we've been up here this weekend, and in four days I'll be forty. Jesus, Charles, forty! I'm nowhere in my personal life. Absolutely bloody nowhere. I'm at the end of my tether with both of them, you know.'

'I don't bloody blame you. Those two are ball-breakers. Catherine's been playing the pious, dedicated, saintly wife for donkey's years, and has become a martyr – in her own eyes, at least. As for Anne Bowles, she's nothing but a pricktease, and you know it. No wonder you're desperate. I think you ought to dump them both, and move on, *tout de suite*. You know that old saying, there's more fish in the sea than ever came out.'

Harry leaned against the parapet, staring back at Charles. They had met when they were youngsters. Charles's grandfather had worked for his father at Deravenels, and he had been killed in a mining accident in India. After Charles's grandfather had died Charles had become an orphan because his parents were already dead. And so Henry Turner, feeling a sense of responsibility, had brought him into their family. Charles and Harry had grown up together.

Charles was six years older, as handsome, as tall and as well built as Harry was, and he was not only his best friend but his brother-in-law. Charles Brandt was married to Harry's favourite sister, Mary. And he was the only person who would and could talk straight to Harry Turner, could tell him the absolute truth without Harry being offended.

Taking a deep breath, Harry now said, 'It's not quite as easy as you make it sound.' He felt around in the pocket of his jacket, and looked at Charles. 'Do you have any cigarettes on you?'

Charles nodded and pulled out a packet, offered it to Harry, then took one himself.

The two men stood in silence, smoking together, and staring out at the North Sea, lost in their own thoughts.

Charles was focused on the ridiculousness of the situation which Harry Turner was now trapped in. Here was one of the greatest tycoons in British business, if not indeed in world business, and he was caught in a complicated triangle, because of the wiles and manipulations of two women and his own weakness.

Harry was thinking similar thoughts, and cursing himself under his breath, and also wondering why Anne had such a terrible hold on him. The truth was she had a sexual attraction for him the likes of which he had never known before.

Charles said suddenly, 'It just goes to show how two really clever women can control a man ... a foolish man, I might add.'

Harry turned to him swiftly, a sudden flash of anger in his bright blue eyes. He was proud, frequently arrogant and imperious by nature; he resented being called foolish, even by someone as close as Charles Brandt.

'Don't call me foolish. I hate it, and you know that,' Harry snapped.

'Sorry, old chap.' Charles held Harry's eyes, and continued in a milder voice, 'You're the smartest, cleverest, most brilliant man I know, have ever known. Unfortunately, you are a fool when it comes to these two women. Why don't you just tell them both to go to hell? I'll find you another woman, a beautiful, pliable, adoring woman who will satisfy all of your needs and not play you for an idiot.'

'That's not strictly true,' Harry protested, shaking his head. 'I mean about being an idiot.'

'I know. And I know what you're going to say, so don't. It's all a lot of bloody bullshit between the two of you. *Jesus*! It beggars belief in this day and age. It's 1970, Harry, not the dark ages. Anne should live with you. I don't know what her problem is.'

Harry nodded, looking chagrined. 'She won't take that final step.'

'Too bad.' Charles took hold of his arm. 'Let's go. Bradley has your bags packed, and mine, and they're already in the Roller. We'll discuss this on the way to town. All right?'

'Good idea. We'd better get going.'

The two friends walked back to the house, crossed the terrace, and went into the library. Charles paused in front of Edward Deravenel's portrait and held Harry back.

'*Look at him*. Look at your grandfather. He wouldn't have put up with a situation like this, and he lived in the 1920s, when manners and mores were entirely different than they are today. Edward Deravenel made his own rules, and so should you. You've got to solve this once and for all, Harry, or they'll take you away in a straitjacket, and in the not-too-distant future.'

Harry remained silent, stood gazing at the portrait for a long moment, and then he allowed Charles to propel him out into the Long Hall, towards the front door.

Bradley, the butler, was standing on the front steps, and he swung around at the sound of footsteps. 'There you are, Mr Turner Everything's stowed in the boot, sir.'

'Thanks, Bradley. I won't be in Yorkshire this coming weekend. I'll see you in a couple of weeks.'

'Right you are, sir.' Smiling, nodding, the butler went out to the discreet black Rolls Royce and stood waiting for them, then opened the doors.

As he got in, Charles took charge. 'I'll drive.'

Harry merely nodded, and got into the car on the passenger side, relieved that Charles was behind the wheel. He felt suddenly tired, from worry, he had no doubt.

Once they were settled, their seat belts fastened, Charles turned on the ignition and the Rolls slid smoothly down the long drive.

At one moment Charles murmured, 'Sit back and relax, and I'll tell you what you're going to do, how you're going to handle those two . . . shall we call them *ladies* for want of a better word?' Charles chuckled. 'Although I could think of a few other colourful nouns that would describe them more accurately.'

Harry laughed for the first time in days.

FIFTY-FIVE

London

'I'm not sure why you persist in living here, Catherine,' Mary Turner Brandt said, eyeing her sister-in-law curiously. 'Harry would have bought you a much nicer house, I feel certain of that.'

Catherine nodded, was swift to say, 'Oh, I know he would, Mary. In fact, he never stops offering to buy me one – a mansion if I want – but I like my little house. It's cosy. And it's mine.'

'I know you bought it yourself,' Mary answered, smiling. 'And that's important to you.' She had always liked her sister-in-law, cared for her quite deeply, in fact. But she also understood her brother Harry only too well, was fully aware what motivated him, and she certainly sympathized with him. Also, she had never been able to understand why a woman would want to hang on to a man who no longer wanted her. That is why Catherine puzzled her so much. But she came to tea on a regular basis, because she knew how lonely Catherine was.

Now, taking a deep breath, Mary asked, 'Why don't you divorce Harry? You've been separated for well over seven years now, Catherine, and surely you know he's not coming back to you. I'm sorry to say that, but I know it's the truth.'

'It probably is. But I'm a Roman Catholic, as indeed you are. Surely you, of all people, understand me, understand what I'm about.'

'I do, yes . . . but then, I don't.' Mary frowned, her light blue eyes filled with puzzlement. 'And I must admit, I don't really quite understand why you would want to cling to a man who obviously doesn't wish to be married to you anymore. I think my pride would get in the way. Doesn't yours?' she finished softly.

'My religion comes before my pride,' Catherine answered in a cool voice.

How self-satisfied, how pious she sounds, Mary thought. Charles was right. Last night, when he had returned from Yorkshire, he had told her that Catherine was turning herself into a martyr. She must explain to her husband that her sister-in-law was becoming a self-satisfied martyr, and she was apparently enjoying the role.

'Harry needs an heir,' Mary murmured, staring across the coffee table at Catherine, then taking a sip of her tea. 'He's desperate for an heir, you know that. He's thinking of Deravenels, and that's something I don't believe even you need to be reminded about.'

'No, I don't, of course not. But he has an heir already. He has our daughter Mary. Your namesake. She can work at Deravenels, any time he'll let her. She'll soon be old enough, she's already seventeen going on eighteen. And don't tell me a woman can't take over and run the company, because your grandfather Edward Deravenel made that possible.'

'I can't deny that.' Mary felt a sudden sense of utter defeat. Catherine was like a stone wall. And *she* was wasting her breath. She sat back on the sofa and glanced around the sitting room of the mews house. It was charming, beautifully decorated and not as small as it looked from the outside. Mary knew why Catherine liked it. This was a perfect house for two people.

Thinking of her niece, she asked, 'How is Mary, by the way? It seems ages since we've seen her.'

'She's very well, but she misses her father.' Catherine leaned forward, her face eager, 'Do you think Harry will come over for tea with us this weekend, Mary? He usually does pay a visit when it's his birthday. Oh, and is he having a party? It *is* his fortieth.'

Taken by surprise, Mary moved her position on the sofa, and thought quickly. 'I haven't heard mention of a party,' she said, 'and I don't know if he will come over to see you, darling. Harry's not one to be confiding his plans to his little sister.' She forced a laugh. 'He's like our father, and our grandfather, Edward Deravenel, he puts business first.'

'You're on his side, aren't you?' Catherine said suddenly, her voice hard.

Mary gaped at her, taken by surprise yet again, and at once she decided to be honest. 'To a certain extent, yes, I am on his side. I do think you ought to release him, so that he can get married and try to have a male heir.'

'And you approve of that bitch Anne Bowles, do you?'

'Whether I approve of her or not is beside the point, Catherine. I just believe my brother should have his freedom after all these years of separation.'

'I just can't go against my religion.' Harry Turner's wife shook her head, and added even more emphatically, 'Never. I'll never divorce him.'

As she walked across Eaton Square, Mary Brandt thied to shake off her sense of dismay and frustration. No one could make headway with Catherine; she was incredibly stubborn and old-fashioned. She was also Spanish by birth, and even though she had lived in England from the age of sixteen she was still very foreign in many ways. She was also deeply religious and this was a great issue, her reason for not granting Harry a divorce.

Mary fully realized how her brother must be feeling. Catherine wouldn't budge and her attitude was more than frustrating, it was downright infuriating. No wonder Harry was at his wits' end. He wanted a male heir so badly, and their father's dying words to him had made such an impression on him, and on his mind. She sometimes thought he had been traumatized by their father banging on at him about a male heir even before his deathbed.

Charles had talked him into coming to dinner last night, when they had finally got back from Ravenscar. Apparently the A1 had been a nightmare, the cars bumper to bumper. She had soon detected her brother's despair, and her heart had gone out to him. Harry was such a generous, giving, loving man, and nothing was ever too much trouble for him. He was extremely thoughtful, also kind to everyone.

After he had gone home to the house in Berkeley Square, where they had spent part of their childhood, and where he now lived alone, Charles had carefully explained Harry's current state of mind.

It wasn't very good, she had decided, once Charles had finished speaking.

And so today, of her own accord, she had gone to see Catherine, hoping to break through that stone wall, but she had not succeeded. She wondered now if anyone ever would.

Deep down, she tended to agree that Anne Bowles, who had her hooks into Harry, was a bit of a bitch. But knowing that did not solve anything. Harry wanted Anne. He was in her thrall, absolutely mesmerized by her, so Charles said. He just wasn't going to give her up, as far as she could ascertain.

Seemingly, on their drive to London, Charles had told him to dump both women and move on, but had Harry listened? And would he do it? She did not know.

Mary loved her brother. And there was nothing worse than

being in a bad marriage, one that was unhappy, with a partner who was intolerable. She knew that only too well.

Her first marriage had been ghastly. Antoine had been too old for her, and a difficult man, and then he had fallen sick. And she had fallen in love. Deeply, truly in love. With Charles Brandt, when he had come to Paris on Deravenel business. The funny thing was, she had known Charles all of her life, because he had been Harry's friend since childhood. It was only when he had arrived in Paris and had taken her to lunch at the Ritz in the Place Vendôme that she had found herself shaking all over and limp with desire for him.

Rather fortuitously, Antoine Delacroix, her first husband, had suddenly died, and she was suddenly free – happily, crazily free. Free to marry the man she had known forever yet had not known at all: Charles Brandt, with whom she was sleeping before her husband's very convenient death, the man she was utterly and completely rapturous about. She had been lucky, very lucky indeed. They had two daughters, and they were the happiest couple she knew.

After leaving Catherine's mews house, just behind Eaton Square, Mary had intended to go to Harvey Nichols to buy summer clothes for their trip to France. Now she changed her mind, and stood on the edge of the pavement in the square, hailing a cab. One came to a standstill within a moment, and she jumped in, gave the cabbie her address in Chelsea. To hell with shopping, she wanted to get home, to be there when Charles arrived. He disliked coming back to an empty house.

'I want a divorce, and I want it now,' Harry Turner said, looking across the desk at his solicitor, Thomas Wolsen. Harry's eyes were blue ice and his mouth was tightly set, almost in a grimace, and an air of acute impatience surrounded him.

For twenty-three years, Thomas Wolsen had been Harry's solicitor, advising him on all matters, some of which were not even to do with the law, and over the years he had come to look upon Harry as a son. Steepling his fingers, gazing over them at Harry, Thomas finally said in a gentle tone, 'I would do anything in this world for you, and I think you know that. I'd even lay down my life for you, Harry. But not even for you can I change the law, or the rules of the Roman Catholic Church.'

Harry sat back in his chair glowering, saying nothing.

Thomas did the same, but his expression remained concerned and genial.

The two men were in Thomas's law offices in Upper Grosvenor Street, and for the last twenty minutes they had been discussing various legal matters. The atmosphere had been warm, cordial as it usually was. But now that Harry had broached divorce the atmosphere instantly changed, became considerably cooler. Thomas knew that Harry was batting his head against a brick wall; however, Harry would not admit that. Not for one moment.

Harry suddenly said swiftly, his voice rising an octave, 'There must be *something* we can do. Can't we pay somebody? Bribe somebody?'

'There is no one, Harry.'

'Why can't *I* get a divorce from Catherine? We've been separated for years.'

'Because *you* deserted *her*, not vice versa. Now, *she* could divorce *you*, on the grounds of desertion, but she doesn't want to do so. Therefore, we are at an impasse.'

'Perhaps I could talk her into it.'

'Harry, be sensible. The Catholic Church doesn't recognize divorce, and if she becomes a divorced woman she will be excommunicated, unable to take Holy Communion. Since she is extremely devout, she won't put herself in this position. I can tell you that quite categorically. I've known her for years, and she will not in any way compromise her faith.'

491

'She can have anything of mine, Thomas, anything at all she wants. *Money*. As much as her heart desires. She can even have Waverley Court. Not the Berkeley Square house, but the one in Kent, yes. A *divorce* . . . that's what I must have, and *at any price*. Just help me to get it.'

'*Divorce at any price*. Quite a phrase, Harry.' Thomas shook his head. 'And one some solicitors would be gratified to hear . . . especially those on the other side. But I think I must be a little more *cagey*, shall we say? I can't use it indiscriminately, especially when in discussion with Catherine's lawyers.'

'Do what you can. Come up with something, Thomas!' Harry exclaimed and rose, crossed the room. He turned around when he reached the door. 'Time is running out for me . . .' He gave Thomas a pointed look, added, 'I must have a divorce . . . for my own sanity. *NOW*. I want it now, Thomas. Do you hear me?'

Harry didn't wait for a response nor did he even say goodbye; he stormed out, slamming the door behind him.

Thomas Wolsen stared at it, shaking his head. Then he sat back, ruminating for a few moments, wondering what on earth he could do. In his opinion he would have to produce a miracle – and with Catherine to deal with, that was an impossibility.

After a few moments, Thomas pressed the intercom and summoned one of his junior partners.

John Upstone walked in immediately and asked, 'Do you need me, sir?'

Thomas nodded emphatically.

'I saw Harry Turner leaving, so I've no doubt there is something to discuss . . . about him.' John's expression was keen, anticipatory.

'Indeed there is. Harry is harping on about his divorce from Catherine again. He says he wants it now. I emphasize the NOW.'

'He has no grounds for divorce, it's not going to happen,' John stated flatly.

'We've got to try and make it happen. I think we're on the line, John, seriously on the line. The firm is on the line. If we don't pull something out of the hat we may lose him as a client.'

John Upstone was taken aback. 'After all these years? And in view of your very close relationship?'

'Close relationships, I've discovered, don't much matter to our old friend Harry. Only Harry matters to Harry.'

'Well, I'll endeavour to come up with something. Somehow.'

'I'm glad to hear it,' Thomas murmured. Leaning forward he added, 'Do anything. Anything at all in order to get him a divorce. Short of murder, of course.'

FIFTY-SIX

Sir Tommy Morle, journalist, author, philosopher and barrister, was sitting with Harry Turner at a corner table in Rule's, enjoying an apéritif before dinner on this lovely Wednesday evening in June.

Having paid close attention to his old friend for the last half an hour, he said slowly, 'Harry, please listen to me, and listen very carefully. This is a pipe dream, wishful thinking on your part. You cannot get an annulment. It's out of the question.'

'That's what Wolsen told me, but some people who have been married a long time have been able to do so –'

'Let me explain,' Tommy cut in peremptorily. 'Under Canon Law, the grounds for an annulment are either an impediment to the union, including non-consummation of the marriage, or bigamy. Or cases of forced unions, or emotional or mental incapacity. Now, I know you and Catherine were in your right minds when you married, and that no one forced you, and you've certainly consummated it – you have a grown daughter to prove it.'

Henry nodded, sighed, 'I know,' he muttered. 'Actually, I know everything. I've studied it upside down and inside out. I'm bloody stuck.'

'You are indeed.'

'I must have an heir, Tommy, you know that better than anyone else. You knew my father and how he was. That aside, though, I love Anne, and she loves me, and I want to be with her. I want her to have my child. My heir.'

Tommy sat back, a reflective look settling in his eyes, and then a shadow crossed his face. 'You've asked me time and again for my advice, Harry, but unfortunately I've none to give. Not before, not now. You're married to a Roman Catholic, and one who is extremely devout.'

'I've about as much chance of getting a divorce as a snow-ball in hell. I shall just have to live with Anne, and if she gets pregnant she gets pregnant. So the heir will be illegitimate.' He lifted his hands in a gesture of helplessness. He had surprised himself, and he suddenly grinned at Tommy and added, 'There! I've finally said it. This is the only solution. We'll live together.'

'No, it's not really the only solution. You could give Anne up, and accept the fact that you do actually have an heir,' Tommy retorted, but his tone was mild.

'You mean Mary?'

'Yes, I do. She is your legitimate heir.'

'But she's a girl. I want –'

'Better not let today's emancipated females hear you say that quite so scathingly. They'll have your guts for garters. This is 1970, not 1907. We're living in a new age . . . an age of modernity. And a lot of women are taking the reins of power in companies. And also in politics. I'm certainly keeping an eye on that young cabinet minister, Margaret Thatcher.'

'Those in the know say she's going places,' Harry murmured. 'I agree with you about keeping an eye on her.'

Tommy suddenly smiled. 'She's going to the top, I'd say. She might even be Prime Minister one day, and in the not-too-distant future.'

'A woman as Prime Minister?' Harry shook his head, looking

sceptical. 'I'm not too sure of that, not too sure at all.' He laughed.

Tommy laughed with him. 'Everything is possible in this world.'

'Except a divorce from a Catholic.'

'Too true.' Tommy picked up his glass of whisky and took a sip, and went on, 'The world is moving at a rapid pace these days, Harry. You never know what might happen. Catherine might say yes. Who would have ever thought that we'd put a man on the moon, two men to be exact . . . Neil Armstrong and Buzz Aldrin. But it happened, the Americans did it last year . . . such a remarkable feat. So in my opinion, anything's possible.'

'Did you know that the maiden name of Buzz Aldrin's mother was Moon?'

'I certainly didn't! What an extraordinary coincidence,' Tommy said, and raised his glass. 'Here's to Miss Moon, whose son walked on the moon. Now, getting back to women in business, what *about* Mary?'

'My daughter hasn't shown any interest in the business, Tommy. Look, I'll grant you that Edward Deravenel made it possible to place a Deravenel woman in the top job at Deravenels, but I don't think Mary would want it, actually. She's more interested in art and music.'

'Most young women are interested in art, music and the like, but she may well have a head for business. Have you ever asked her about joining the company?'

'No, I haven't, and anyway, I believe that a woman must *want* to go into business in order to be a success, don't you agree? And there *would* be opposition.'

Tommy nodded. 'And a woman ought to be ambitious as well, if she's going to succeed.'

Wishing to move away from the subject of Mary, not really wanting to continue it, Harry now said, 'Anne is ambitious.'

Don't I know that, Tommy thought, but did not say. He

merely sipped his whisky and looked contemplative. Anne Bowles was the most ambitious, tough, scheming, determined, clever woman he had ever known. He did not like her, and deep down he did not approve of Harry's liaison with her; he much preferred the sweeter, quieter Catherine. But he was Harry's friend, and he remained true and loyal to him, and he hoped he would be able to influence his friend, steer Harry in the proper direction whenever he deemed it necessary.

Harry touched Tommy's arm, and said, 'Come back, Tom, you're drifting. Anne has a very good business head, as I was saying. The antique shop in Paris has been doing extremely well lately, and so has the one here in London. She has quite the most extraordinary taste. And a superb eye. She's very talented, even though I do say so myself.'

Tommy was saved the problem of thinking up an appropriate response when two waiters arrived with the first course: smoked trout, fresh from the highland streams of Scotland, to be served with creamed horseradish sauce and thin slices of brown bread and butter.

'Now doesn't that look appealing, rather tasty, I must say,' Tommy murmured, glancing at Harry, hoping Anne Bowles would not continue to be the topic of conversation over dinner. It was the most boring subject he could think of and Harry was relentless when he got going.

Having said the words aloud to Tommy over dinner, Harry Turner felt more confident with the idea of living with Anne. Actually, he had never been diffident about this; it was Anne who was the problem. She seemed to find this step a difficult one to take. But he could persuade her, he felt quite certain of that.

It was Charles Brandt who had helped him to sort things out

in his own head on the drive from Yorkshire. And it was Charles who had listed the inducements he could use to tempt Anne, convince her that he would never abandon her, no matter what.

When he went to Paris on Sunday to join Anne and celebrate his fortieth birthday, he would present everything to her. How could she resist what he had to offer her . . . so many material benefits as well as himself. It was a *fait accompli*. He truly believed that.

And he could say to Anne, in all truth, that he had made a last-ditch effort, had talked to Thomas Wolsen yet again, and had dinner with him to discuss the great matter of the divorce. On Saturday, before he went to Paris, he would swallow his pride, take a deep breath and go to have a birthday tea with Catherine. But that would not be the real purpose; once more, and for the last time, he would ask his wife to set him free. If she refused, then he would take matters into his own hands, and set up house with Anne. But, at least by seeing Catherine, he could inform Anne truthfully that he had done his damnedest to get a divorce.

Rising, Harry walked across the library to the drinks' table in the corner, poured himself a cognac. Carrying it back to the sofa, he sat down, sipping it, drifting with his thoughts.

Eventually, his eyes moved up to regard the painting over the fireplace . . . the famous Renoir of the two auburn-haired sisters. It had been hanging here in the Berkeley Square house for many years, ever since Edward Deravenel had bought it because it reminded him of his daughters Bess and Grace Rose.

At the thought of Grace Rose Harry smiled to himself. She was his favourite aunt . . . still alive, seventy years old now and acting half her age, a remarkable writer of best-selling historical books. And her husband Charles Morran was fit and strong, and something of a living legend now in his eighties. What a wonderful actor he had been, a star of the London stage, and on Broadway.

His mother had told him all about Charlie, and his ruined face, badly burned in the First World War, and the work done on it by plastic surgeons; how Grace Rose had befriended him after the untimely death of his wife Rowena, of cancer. Eventually Charlie and Grace Rose had married, much to the delight of the famous Amos Finnister. It was not long after their marriage that Amos had died, and his mother had explained, 'Because he could let go at last, Harry. You see, he knew his beloved Grace Rose would always be safe with Charlie.'

Yes, Bess Deravenel Turner, his extraordinary mother, had been the most amazing storyteller, filling his head with fascinating tales of the Deravenels, instilling in him the history of the family. She never stopped reminding him that he was half Deravenel, half Turner, and that there must always be Deravenel blood in their great trading company.

She and his father had founded a new dynasty, the Turners, but his mother had kept the Deravenels alive in his head. Bess had been the one who had brought him up with his younger sister Mary, and she had been by far the greatest influence on him.

Harry had loved his father but they had not been all that close. Henry Turner had been struggling to keep Deravenels on an even keel and safe, during the years of his growing up. His father had carefully steered the company through the problems of the great Wall Street crash, the Depression in America and Great Britain, and the troubled times in the thirties, not to mention the Second World War. Because of his many business burdens Henry had very frequently been an absentee father, dealing with pressing matters, leaving the rearing of his four children to Bess.

Shifting on the sofa, taking a sip of the cognac, Harry thought now about his parents' marriage. It had been happy, even though it had been an arranged union, cobbled together by his two grandmothers, Elizabeth Deravenel and Margaret Beauchard Turner.

There had never been a hint of infidelity on either of their parts, and when his elder brother Arthur had died unexpectedly his parents' shared grief and sorrow had united them even more. He and his sisters Margaret and Mary had rallied around them as they had all mourned this terrible loss. And that was when he had become the heir apparent, and the one designated to take over Deravenels after his father.

When his mother had died at the age of thirty-seven, in childbirth, his father had been inconsolable, as they all had. For Bess to die so young was the biggest tragedy in the family; he had never ceased to miss his mother, and her golden visage, her lovely laugh, her positive attitude about life. It had been Grace Rose who had comforted him the most. Like his mother, Grace Rose had worshipped her father Edward Deravenel, and so she had become the keeper of the flame once his mother was gone.

What extraordinary dramas they had all lived through, these Deravenels . . . Jane Shaw, his grandfather's mistress, grieving herself to death, leaving all of her money and possessions to Bess and Grace Rose when she had passed away not long after Edward. And then there had been the trauma his mother had experienced after the mysterious murder of her uncle. Richard seemingly had meant a lot to her. And there was the peculiar and even more mysterious disappearance of her brothers, who had never been found dead or alive. How strange that was. Another unsolved crime.

Elizabeth Deravenel's lonely life after her husband's death had haunted his mother. He had never liked her actually; nor had he liked his other grandmother, Margaret Beauchard Turner. *She* had tried to control and manipulate him when he was growing up, but he had managed to slip out of her clutches. Ever since then he had disliked strong, powerful, conniving women.

On the other hand, he had genuinely liked his other aunts, his mother's late sisters Cecily, Anne, Katharine and Bridget, whom his mother had taken care of as best she could. His father had not always been kind enough to the Deravenel women in his opinion, and he had always resented his father's attitude because it had hurt his mother.

His mind went back to his mother's brothers, and after a moment, remembering something, he put the brandy balloon on the coffee table, hurried out of the library and up the grand staircase.

Once he was in his dressing room, Harry opened the safe, found the black leather box, opened it and lifted out the gold medallion. It had belonged to his grandfather; his mother had held it in safekeeping for her brother Edward, because it was his by rights. But Young Edward had never worn it . . . because he had disappeared at the age of twelve. It was his now. His mother had given it to him, and told him its history and why it was made.

Harry turned it in his hands . . . There was the sun in splendour on one side, an enamelled White Rose of York on the other, and inscribed around the edge was the Deravenel family motto: *Fidelity Unto Eternity.*

He held it for a long time, thinking of his mother, the power of the Deravenels and the immense power that Edward Deravenel had wielded. And he made a promise to himself at that moment. Once he had settled matters with Anne he would find a way to make Deravenels even greater . . . *He* would be the true inheritor, in the image of his grandfather.

FIFTY-SEVEN

From the moment he arrived at Catherine's mews house off Eaton Square, Harry wished he had not come. The house, although of good size, somehow made him feel claustrophobic, and he had the terrible urge to flee immediately.

But he knew he could not. He had to stick it out, stay at least for a couple of hours. The thought of this made him shrivel inside; he had nothing whatsoever to say to her anymore.

He had not seen Catherine for almost eight months, and now he found it hard to accept the change in her appearance. She was forty-five, five years older than him, but she looked like a woman in her sixties. The red-gold hair of her youth had turned to a dull blondeness shot through with grey, and her once luminous light-blue eyes, always so expressive, seemed faded and without lustre. She was also far too thin, even scrawny.

As she led him into the drawing room he could hardly believe she was the beautiful young woman he had married over twenty years ago. Spanish by birth and of parentage, she had inherited the English rose complexion and colouring of her mother's great-grandmother, who had been an Englishwoman from the aristocracy, but the Englishness of Catherine's vivid looks had faded away altogether. She had become . . . drab.

'You're staring at me, Harry,' she said as she seated herself in the chair opposite him. 'Do I have a dirty smudge on my face?'

'No, no, not at all,' he exclaimed, caught short, and went on swiftly, improvising, 'You look much thinner, that's all, and I wondered if you'd been dieting again?' He made this last remark sound like a question. 'You shouldn't, you know.'

Catherine shook her head. 'I'm *not* dieting, Harry.' She wanted to add she was simply missing him, fretting over him, but she could not. She was not going to demean herself before him.

As if he could read her mind, he felt a surge of kindness, of tenderness flood him, and he smiled at her. 'You must tell me if there's anything you need, Catherine, and let me help you. I don't want you to feel neglected.'

She gaped at him, utterly astounded by this comment, and before she could stop herself, she exclaimed, 'Of course I feel neglected, Harry! I never see you, nor does Mary. We both feel neglected, actually.'

Realizing his mistake, knowing he had only himself to blame for opening up this aspect of her life, he had the good grace to look chagrined. 'I'm sorry. It's business. You know full well how I become so terribly embroiled with my projects.' He sighed, feeling guilty.

'Yes, I do,' she said, and then glanced over her shoulder as the housekeeper came in carrying a large tea tray. 'You can put it here on the coffee table, please, Mrs Aldford,' Catherine said, and added, 'Thank you very much.'

The housekeeper smiled at her, nodded to Harry, deposited the tray and hurried out.

Catherine looked across at Harry, continued, 'Yes, I do know that business has always been your first love, Harry. You never let anything or anyone get in the way of it. And since you ask, I think it would be nice if Mary and I had somewhere to go in the summer months ... perhaps a cottage by the sea?' She focused her eyes on him, her face taking on a sudden hardness as she stared at him intently.

'You can have Waverley Court, if you want. I'll sign the deeds over to you immediately.'

Her face lit up for a moment, and then it fell. 'At what price?'

'A divorce, Catherine. Surely you know the answer to that.'

'I do. And you know my response. It is not possible. However, I do have all of the jewellery you gave me when we were married, some of your family heirlooms, some of your mother's jewels, and I'm planning to put them up for auction. Or perhaps I'll sell privately. In that way I will be able to buy a country place for your daughter – and myself.'

His chest tightened, and he felt a sudden sense of guilt ... about *her*. He had once been madly in love with Catherine, and she with him; she had been his brother's widow, married only a few months to Arthur, and then Arthur had gone and died on her. Eventually, his father had suggested he marry Catherine, the widow. He hadn't minded that at all. He had been in love with her since he had been a boy and had walked behind her down the aisle where his brother stood waiting to marry her. And so they had married, had a happy life together; it *had* been happy, there was no denying that. He and Catherine had shared so much, had held the world in their arms for quite a while; after the miscarriage of a son, one that had been so longed for, they had finally had their baby girl, Mary, and had been full of joy.

But no other children had come along . . . In fact, they had been dogged by stillbirths and miscarriages. It had broken Catherine, to a certain extent, he knew that. Because it had also affected him. Sadly, her inability to provide a son had eventually turned him away from her. Harry Deravenel Turner needed and wanted a male heir, most desperately, and apparently his wife could not give him what he longed for.

In the most calculated way, he had moved on. And one day his eye had been caught by a darkly beautiful young woman, a woman sixteen years his junior, whose enticing smile and come-hither looks had ensnared him. And once he had tasted her charms he was lost forever. There was only her, his Anne . . .

Harry leaned back on the sofa, watching Catherine pouring the tea, as always graceful, genteel; she was, without question, also a cultured and educated woman, one from whom he had learned much during their marriage. They had always been compatible, at ease with each other, and there had never been any major rows or quarrels. Their shared interests had given them great pleasure. But slowly Harry's life had eroded, as had his love for his wife.

Deep within himself he had known the inevitable would happen and it did. He fell so deeply in love with the alluring sloe-eyed beauty, Anne Bowles, he could not let her go. Her sexuality lured him. She exuded sex, in fact; He was under her spell. Catherine had had no chance, no chance at all, once he had been inveigled into Anne's possessive arms, suffused in her sexuality, thrilled by her desire for him, a willing partner in bed, a great companion out of it.

As all of these thoughts were running through his head, Catherine was thinking about the man who sat opposite. Her beloved husband. He had put on weight, and although he could carry it with his height, he looked much better when he was trimmer, in her opinion. But, despite the added weight, he had not lost his looks: he was still the handsomest man she had ever seen, with his red-gold hair and blue eyes, his height, his broad chest and long legs. He was powerful, charismatic.

She looked at him surreptitiously, and remembered how their colouring had once been the same. She wondered now why Mary had turned out to be just the opposite of them, with her dark hair and eyes? A throwback to *her* Spanish forebears, perhaps.

Harry Turner was a tycoon, one of the world's great entrepreneurs, but she hadn't read much about him lately in the newspaper. Now, as she handed him the cup of tea across the coffee table, she asked, 'How's business at Deravenels, Harry? No big deals in the offing?'

Taking the tea from her, he made a face, looked regretful. 'No, there's nothing much happening, Catherine, but you know me, I'll *make* it happen. And soon. I've got my eye on a couple of companies.'

'Looking to take them over, are you?' she said, and sipped her tea, then gestured to the small almond cakes. 'Those are your favourites, Harry.'

'I know. Macaroons. Did you make them yourself?'

'Yes, just for you, for your birthday.' There was a pause, and she went on, 'You're good when you take companies over, you know. You're not an asset-stripper, thank God. You make them work.'

He stared at her, his eyes narrowing sharply. He had forgotten how she had enjoyed talking about his business with him, and what a good understanding she had had of it. He thought of his daughter then, and remembered Tommy's words. He said, 'Where's Mary, by the way? I thought she would be here for my birthday tea.'

'She'll be down in a moment. She wanted to give us a little while to be alone together. A chance to talk.'

'I see.' After eating two macaroons, and swallowing the cup of tea, he said, 'I've been wondering . . . what do you think she wants to do? Has she any thoughts about a career?'

'She's interested in art, as you well know, Harry, but at the moment she hasn't settled on anything in particular. Perhaps you should talk to her.'

He nodded. 'I will, when I get back from Paris.'

'When are you leaving?'

'Tomorrow.'

'To celebrate your birthday, I presume.' She threw him an icy stare.

Automatically, he shook his head. Why wave a red rag in front of a bull, he thought and said, with a light smile, 'No, no, not at all. I'm going to Paris on business. Rather pressing business, in fact.'

Catherine merely nodded, and then she glanced over at the door swiftly, a smile bringing a sudden radiance to her face.

Harry followed the direction of her gaze, and there was his daughter Mary – slender, tall, and quite beautiful. She walked into the room, carrying several gift-wrapped packages, and her smile was wide, her eyes sparkling with happiness.

He smiled back at her, discovered he was pleased to see her.

She said, 'Hello, Father, I'm so glad you're here. Happy Birthday for tomorrow!'

'Come here, sweetheart, and give your father a kiss.' As he spoke he stood up, opened his arms to her.

Putting the birthday presents on a chair, Mary ran into her father's welcoming arms and clung to him for a moment, filled with love for him.

Harry stayed on for several hours, enjoying Mary, and even Catherine at times. She had always managed to entertain him; and frequently she made him laugh this afternoon. At one moment he could not help thinking that if Catherine had been able to give him a son and heir he would have never left her. They would have been a happy family, and his life would have been very different. And so would hers. They would have all bypassed tragedy.

FIFTY-EIGHT

Paris

Anne Bowles walked swiftly down the avenue Montaigne, looking for a taxi. Although she was not aware of it, preoccupied as she was by business, she cut quite a swathe, and people glanced at her admiringly as she swept past them. She was simply dressed in tight black jeans, a white cotton shirt, high-heeled black sandals and large pearl earrings. On her shoulder was slung a wide black cloth satchel and she carried a white-leather quilted Chanel bag.

Simply dressed though she was, she had, nonetheless, a certain unique style and an undeniable Gallic chic, quite aside from her unusual and striking looks. Her dark hair was long, falling almost to her waist, and she had coal-black eyes in an arresting finely chiselled face. Women found her elegant and wanted to emulate her, copy her style; men found her sexy and alluring and wanted to get her into their beds.

When a taxi came to a screeching stop next to her she jumped in and gave him the address of her destination in perfect French.

Whatever else she was, Anne Bowles was a genuine Francophile. She had lived in Paris, on and off, ever since she was a very small child. Taken there by her parents when she was a baby, along with her older sister, she became bilingual; certainly French was her preferred language and Paris her ultimate place to live.

When her father, a British diplomat, had been posted back to England, the family had returned to London, a city where she had immediately felt somewhat out of place, uneasy even. Within a few years she was back in the City of Light studying art history at the Sorbonne; later, after graduating, she had opened an antiques shop on the Left Bank, and within two years another one in London. Now she commuted between the two cities, relying on her brilliant assistants, one in London, the other in Paris. In the last year she had branched out, become an interior designer by popular demand.

Today she was on her way to the seventh arrondissement, which was the area of the city she loved the most. So much so, she was hoping one day to have an apartment in the seventh. For the moment she lived in a relatively modern building on the avenue Montaigne, a choice made because Harry liked to stay at the Plaza Athénée Hotel. Since this was located on the avenue, it was easy for him to move between the hotel and her flat, which is what he liked to do.

Her mind settled on her newest client, a charming American woman called Jill Handelsman, who had recently bought a beautiful flat in the rue de Babylone. Jill had hired her to do the design and decoration, and she was thoroughly involved in it at the moment. Her client had good taste and a genuine love of French antiques, and they had taken to each other at once, were enjoying working together. Jill's husband was in the fashion business in New York, and because he was spending a great deal of time in France these days the couple had decided to buy a place in Paris.

This afternoon she was going to go over fabric samples with Jill, and also walk her through the floor plans. The placement of furniture was vitally important to Anne, and she wanted the pieces Jill had bought from her to be shown off properly, to the greatest advantage.

The taxi pushed its way through the busy Paris traffic, and frequently came to a standstill, and as they moved at a snail's pace across the city Anne's thoughts eventually, and inevitably, turned to Harry Turner. He was arriving tomorrow to celebrate his birthday with her; now she made up her mind to have a serious talk with him before he returned to London on Monday.

She needed to talk to him about their relationship, which had come to a standstill. That had happened slowly, of course; in a sense, it was inevitable, because, very simply, it was going absolutely nowhere. There was nowhere for it to go.

Harry was a married man – separated, that was true, but unable to free himself. She was his girlfriend because she refused to move in with him, to become his mistress. Anne had always been somewhat nervous about making that move, knowing very well that her family, and most especially her rather old-fashioned diplomat father, would disapprove of such a serious step. She was almost twenty-six, and at the end of her tether. She wanted a good life with a man she loved, and one with whom she could have children.

Last night her brother Greg and she had dinner together at his apartment, and he had tackled her about Harry. Almost at once he had made it quite clear that she ought to be 'moving on or moving out'. Greg had lectured her sternly about her involvement with Harry, a man almost sixteen years her senior. And he had pointed out, for the umpteenth time, that he was bound by steel bands to his wife, whom he characterized as a 'religious maniac'. Which she wasn't, of course, Anne knew that. Catherine was simply a woman who was a devout Roman Catholic, one who would never divorce because she couldn't forfeit her religion.

Anne sighed to herself. With Greg now living in Paris she knew she could expect a lot more stern lectures from him, that was inevitable.

The taxi finally came to a stop at an old nineteenth-century building with a huge *porte-cochère*, and after paying the driver she went through the small side door into the cobbled courtyard. She put her head inside the concierge's little office, and greeted him with a bright smile, then hurried along the corridor to Jill Handelsman's flat, inserting the key in the door, and going inside.

She was the first to arrive, and she hurried through the foyer into the drawing room which faced onto a lovely garden. Although of medium size, it did have a hedge, several trees and a lawn, with a fountain in one corner. There was even a small terrace immediately in front of the French windows, and it was here that Anne envisaged putting a small table and chairs, so that the terrace could be used for drinks or simple meals in the warm weather.

Walking through into the dining room, Anne emptied her satchel, spread out the many fabric samples, and then glanced over her shoulder as she heard a key in the door.

A moment later Jill was hurrying forward through the entrance hall, smiling hugely when she spotted Anne in the dining room.

Smiling in return, Anne walked out to greet her, and, after a quick hug, she said, 'I brought you all of the samples so that we can see how the colours look in the drawing room. I still think my idea of a play of different creams and pinks will be the perfect combination, Jill.'

'I agree,' Jill answered, following Anne into the dining room, where the fabrics were scattered on the table for her inspection.

'There's going to be a few different woods in the room,' Anne explained, 'and also some of the parquet floor will be visible. It struck me that lots of cream fabrics, of different textures, and a hint of green with the rose pink, would be light and airy, perfect for the room looking onto the garden.'

'I think you're right.' Jill sat down at the table, as did Anne, and together the two women went through the fabrics. After choices were made Anne showed her the floor plans, explaining where everything would be placed.

'I'd like us to go to each room,' Anne said, standing up. 'So that I can show you where I envision each piece, and we can discuss it. You and Marty must feel comfortable here, and at ease. It's my job to give you all the alternatives, all the possibilities.'

'I'm glad I have you, Anne,' Jill murmured, glancing at the young Englishwoman. She had taken to Anne immediately they met in the antiques shop, and when she had discovered that Anne was also an interior designer she had hired her at once. There was something very special about this talented young woman, Jill thought, a young woman with a great deal of style, chic and flair, who had such a fantastic eye for furniture, paintings, tapestries and objects of art. Jill thought she was an extraordinary find, and was even thinking of asking her to redesign their home in New York. A perceptive person, she had also detected a certain sadness in Anne, a loneliness even, and wondered about her personal life, but had never asked one question. She was far too polite to do so, and would never infringe on a person's privacy.

They walked on through the apartment and were now standing in the bedroom. Anne said, 'I think the bed should go on this wall, Jill, don't you?'

Immediately rousing herself from her thoughts, Jill nodded. 'It's really the only useable wall, actually. And it's wonderful to have a fireplace in a bedroom. It'll be very cosy in winter, don't you think?'

Nodding her head, Anne walked over to the far wall and explained, 'The fruitwood armoire you liked so much at the shop would be perfect here, and, incidentally, I've found two night tables, and two crystal lamps. We're almost done, you know,' she finished with a light laugh.

'I hope that doesn't mean I won't see you ever again,' Jill murmured, meaning this. She had grown fond of Anne Bowles over the last few months.

'I'm almost always in Paris part of the week, Jill. But you know that, and we can have lunch, or meet up in the evening any time you want. And I would like you to meet my younger brother, Greg. He's living here now, working at the Paris office of a British bank.'

'That would be lovely,' Jill exclaimed. 'And how nice for you to have your brother here now.'

'It is. Unfortunately, he tends to lecture me about my life –' Anne broke off, and shrugged, not wanting to say another word, afraid she might confide her troubles in this very nice American woman who was so sympathetic towards her.

No one would understand how complicated it was to love Harry Turner.

FIFTY-NINE

Anne stood near the window in her living room which looked out onto the avenue Montaigne, hoping to catch sight of Harry as he crossed the street from the hotel. He was due to pick her up at seven o'clock, but he was nowhere in sight.

She glanced at her watch, saw that it was five minutes to seven, and smiled to herself, thinking how old-fashioned he was in certain ways, and gallant.

On the phone early that morning, long before he had left London, he had said he would come and collect her to escort her back to the Plaza Athénée. They were to have dinner in the garden of the hotel, where he was staying. She could have easily walked across the street, met him in the restaurant, but he wouldn't hear of it.

A split second later she heard his key in the lock, and swung around, made for the entrance hall.

He came in, closed the door behind him and stood smiling at her, then began to walk towards her.

As always when she saw him after an absence, her heart jumped and she felt a wonderful rush of excitement, something she had never experienced with any other man. How marvellous he looked in his impeccably-tailored dark-blue silk suit, a precise bit of Savile Row tailoring at its ultimate best. The crisp, white shirt enhanced his light tan and the blue silk tie reflected the colour of his eyes. He was perfectly dressed and groomed right down to his highly-polished black loafers.

They met in the middle of the room, and he looked down at her, his face suddenly turning serious, and then he wrapped his arms around her and held her tightly without saying a word.

Anne clung to him, and she knew at that moment that she could never leave him, certainly not of her own free will. As he kissed the top of her head, and pressed her even closer into his body, all of her worries and troubles, which had been lodged like a stone in the middle of her chest for weeks, just dissolved in that instant. It seemed to her that a great burden had been lifted and she felt herself relaxing against him.

Still holding her tightly, he murmured in a quiet but emphatic voice, 'God, I've missed you, Anne, truly, truly missed you. My life's not worth living without you. I want you to know that.'

'I've missed you, too, Harry. I've been very stressed, but I'm all right now that you're here.'

He tilted her face to his, studied it for a moment, and then bent down and kissed her deeply on the mouth.

It was a prolonged kiss, one which she returned ardently, her passion, as always, matching his. And then he gently moved away, his eyes full of sudden laughter as he said, 'If we don't leave now, *immediately*, for dinner, I'm afraid we won't be leaving at all.'

She laughed with him, nodded, and then went over to the chest in a corner of the room, returned with her black silk evening purse that matched her high-heeled black silk shoes, a striking contrast to her white silk dress and which picked up the colour of the wide black patent leather belt around her slender waist.

'I'm ready,' she said, tucking her arm in his.

They walked to the door, but she held him back before they left the flat, and whispered, 'Happy birthday, darling.'

Every eye was on them as they crossed the lobby of the hotel making for the restaurant in the inner courtyard, which was surrounded by the four walls of the hotel. They made a striking couple, both of them elegantly dressed and good looking, and so obviously in love.

The *maître d'* hurried to greet them as they stood poised in the entrance. 'Good evening, Monsieur Turner, I have your usual table over here in the corner.'

Harry nodded, smiled, followed him, led Anne over to his preferred table near one of the ivy-clad walls. '*Merci beaucoup,*' he murmured, and looked pleased when he saw the bottle of Dom Perignon already in the silver bucket filled with ice. 'I think we'll have a drop of that now,' he murmured to the *maître d'*.

'*Oui, monsieur,*' he answered and beckoned to the wine waiter.

Once the sparkling wine was served, they clinked glasses and Anne said, 'I have a little gift for you, darling. It's in my bag, but if you wish I'll give it to you later.'

He shook his head, grinning at her. 'I'd like it now, if you don't mind. You know I'm like a child when it comes to presents.'

Opening her black silk purse, she took out a small red box from Cartier, and as she handed it to him she explained, 'I didn't think you would want to be unwrapping something in public. So here it is, without benefit of paper and ribbon.'

Harry, still smiling beatifically, opened the box and stared at the pair of gold cufflinks set on the black velvet, his eyes widening slightly. One had an enamelled white rose surrounded by small diamonds, the other an enamelled red rose also edged in diamonds. 'Anne, they're beautiful! Unique. Thank you, sweetheart.' He reached for her hand resting on the table and kissed it; still smiling at her, he went on softly, 'And I have something for you . . . a little gift. But I'd prefer to give it to you later.'

'What is it?' she asked, her dark eyes glowing, her curiosity aroused.

'If I tell you it won't be a surprise, now will it?'

'No, you're correct. And I'm so glad you like the cufflinks. I thought they would be quite meaningful to you . . . The white rose of York and the red rose of Lancaster . . . Deravenel and Turner finally joined as one dynasty, by your mother and father.'

'I love them,' he murmured, and took another sip of his champagne. 'I've a lot to talk to you about, Anne,' he continued. 'But let's relax for the moment and enjoy being together, and we can look at the menu and order.'

'You sound serious,' Anne remarked, frowning. 'Is everything all right . . . at Deravenels?'

'Couldn't be better. As a matter of fact, on Saturday night Charles gave me the best birthday present in the world –' He paused, grinned, and added, 'After yours, of course, my little sweetie.' He took hold of her hand again and explained. 'He has found two companies we can probably take over. Both of them fit very well into Deravenels, and I shall start working on them next week.'

'Both? Or just one?'

'I think I shall work on both of them, since we can afford to buy both. We've got plenty of cash, as we always do. One's a food chain, which would fit perfectly into our wine, liquor and food division, and the other is something I've yearned for for a long time –'

'*Oil*,' she said, cutting in. 'Charles found you an oil company.'

'Right on the button, yes, he did. He has a nose for sniffing things out. The only problem is that I've got two competitors to cope with, and they're both top-notch. Buccaneering tycoons like me.'

'Jimmy Hanson and Gordie White,' Anne said, and sat back in the chair, staring at him. 'I *am* right, aren't I?'

'Almost, but not quite. Good old James Hanson, yes, and with him I include his partner, my old pal Gordon White. But I consider them to be one entity, since they own their company together. The other financier who is after both these companies is Jimmy Goldsmith.'

'He's brilliant! Unbeatable they say.'

'All three of them are, but I shall have a go at it, Anne. As you well know, I've made my mind to take Deravenels to another stage. My father kept everything steady, kept the company on an even keel, but he didn't do anything at all daring, he was too careful, never wanted to take risks. And he was very parsimonious. I spoke to John Dudley about that the other day, and he agreed with me. His father Edmund worked for Father for years; there have always been Dudleys at Deravenels. Anyway, both our fathers were parsimonious by nature. They never wanted to take chances.'

'But you do, I know that, Harry, and you should. Greg always says money must make more money, and it should be used, not just left to sit gathering dust.'

Harry burst out laughing. 'That's a nice turn of phrase. How is your brother?'

'He's fine, he sends his best. He likes living in Paris, and he's doing well at the bank.'

'Good to know. Now, shall we look at the menu?'

'Let's do that, and I think we should start with caviare, because it's your birthday.'

'You *do* have such good ideas, Anne.'

At the end of the dinner, after the waiter had served coffee, Harry felt around in his pocket, saying, 'Here you are, Anne, this is for you. Give me your hand, darling.'

She stared at him nonplussed, and then offered him her right hand.

'No, no, not that one. Your left hand, please.'

Still staring at him perplexed, her black eyes wide with curiosity, she did as he asked, then gasped in surprise when he slipped the extraordinary twenty-carat diamond ring on her engagement finger.

'Harry, my God! It's fantastic.' Anne stared down at the perfectly beautiful pear-shaped diamond ring, and then looked up into his eyes. 'Does this mean you're asking me to marry you?' she asked, sounding a little breathless and excited.

'You know I would if I could, Anne darling, but I'm afraid I can't.'

'So nothing has changed then,' she whispered, her voice suddenly saddened; a cloud crossed her face. 'If you're still not able to marry me, how can I possibly wear this ring? On my engagement finger, I mean.'

He leaned across the table, his handsome face very serious and intent. 'Listen to me, I can't go on any longer, not like this. I really do want you to live with me quite openly. And perhaps if you do, Catherine might be embarrassed into granting me a divorce. I doubt it, though, and I must be honest with you about that. However, no matter, I do believe we should make our relationship much more permanent. We can be so happy together.'

'My family will have a fit, especially my father. He'll be apoplectic.' Anne's dark eyes filled with worry, and she shook her head. 'I'm a bit nervous about taking such a step.'

'I know that and I do have some thoughts to share with you, sweetheart. First of all, I don't expect you to come and set up house with me in Berkeley Square, because I know you will never do that, that you'd abhor the idea. However, I will buy you a larger flat, or even a house. I've already made inquiries and there seem to be quite a few really nice properties available near me in Mayfair. Once you have your own residence, I will live there with you ... most of the time. We'll work out a proper routine, no one need be any the wiser. I will also take care of your future, in case anything should happen to me. I'll create a trust for you, and give you anything else you feel you need to protect your future.'

'I – I – just don't know, Harry,' she answered in a low voice. Even though it was 1970, and things were a lot easier after the Swinging Sixties, she knew there were still codes of behaviour to consider. And certain rules and regulations. No matter how she and Harry might do it, her father would be dismayed, and furious with her. Also, there was her own self-respect to consider. How could she bring herself to live with a man already married to someone else? He would never really belong to her if he had a *wife*.

'Don't you want to spend the rest of your life with me, Anne?'

'Yes, I do, I really do, darling. When I saw you tonight, coming into the flat after two weeks apart, I suddenly realized I can never leave you. But I want a proper life, children, Harry. And you want – no need – an heir. And I know I wouldn't be comfortable if I had an illegitimate child, and anyway, an illegitimate son would not be your legal heir –'

'I can make him legal by adopting him, giving him my name, and making him my heir in my will. I just know you'll give me a son, Anne, and I want a son now, whilst I'm young, so that I can watch him grow, enjoy him. Oh, let's do it, Anne.'

'But my family –'

'I don't really want to hear about them,' he announced, interrupting her. 'It's your life, not theirs, and *my* life, too. And there's a lot at stake.'

'You're right, actually, I should think about myself, and you. But it might be easier, I think, if we lived in Paris. I wouldn't be – well, throwing it in their faces ...' She paused, realising, suddenly, she had started to compromise.

'Paris! That sounds like a grand idea!' he cried, seizing on this. 'I bet you anything I can find us a perfect place in the seventh arrondissement, your favourite spot here.' He beamed at her, and added, 'And we'll also have a home in London. Say yes, Anne, please say yes.'

'Yes,' she murmured in a low, shaky voice, sounding slightly hesitant.

Immediately, he realized she was reluctant, and he squeezed her hand. 'Trust me, it's going to be all right. We'll have two comfortable homes together, and I will protect you in every way. Legally and financially, so that you are always safe, no matter what. Now let's go back to your flat. I want to be with you, to hold you in my arms. Rather urgently, actually.'

The minute they entered her flat, Harry began to kiss her passionately, and he did not stop as they moved across the floor entwined in each other's arms. When they went into the bedroom he finally drew to a standstill, and held her away from him, looking into her face intently, his expression serous.

'I want *you*, Anne, and only *you*, and for the rest of my life. You are my life, if the truth be known.'

'Oh, Harry,' she said, moving closer to him, taking hold of his arm, burying her head against his chest. 'Oh, darling.'

'I love you,' he said against her hair.

'I love *you*,' she responded, her voice muffled.

He stepped away once more, began to unbuckle her belt, let it fall to the floor; a moment later, her white silk dress followed, pooled around her feet. She stepped over it, began to unfasten his tie.

Swiftly, he threw off his jacket, and within seconds they were both undressed and stretched out on her bed. He held her close in his arms, gathering her to him, murmuring her name softly, and then he lifted a handful of dark hair to his lips and kissed it. Leaning over her, he kissed her forehead, her eyelids, her neck, her breasts, and between the kisses he was whispering to her what he was going to do to her, and she to him. Stroking her, easing his hands over her, he caressed her body and the very core of her until she began to quiver, her desire for him rampant, her breathing excited, rasping.

As she always was, Anne felt overpowered by Harry, by the sheer physical beauty of him. More than any other man she had known he had enormous sexual magnetism, and he was a potent and experienced lover. She trembled under his touch; he was making her feel weak with longing.

It was mutual, this aching desire to be together, to be joined physically. They both knew they wanted to become one entity, become, in a sense, each other.

Now Harry kissed her with such sudden fierceness his teeth grazed hers. He pushed his hands under her body and lifted her towards him, crushed her to his chest, groaning against her hair, wanting her so much. Yet he also needed to savour her, enjoy her, and give her pleasure, bring her to ecstasy once more. He lowered her onto the pillows and told her, 'I want our child. I do, oh, I do, Anne.'

She reached out, touched his cheek, let her fingers gently trail down onto his neck; her eyes did not leave his. 'I do, too.' Her voice dropped to a whisper; she urged him, 'Let's do it now, let's make our baby, Harry. I love you, I love you so much.'

He could not resist her any longer, and he slid onto her body, took her to him expertly; he moved against her, staring down into her face and she opened her eyes, looked up at him. He could not help but see her love for him reflected in her eyes and on her face, and he experienced an enormous rush of happiness and joy in her.

Anne began to move under him, her hips thrusting up. He responded to her at once, and they found their own rhythm. At one moment he gripped her tightly, roughly, thrusting forward, taking her harder, thrusting deeper and deeper. He was loving her with more fervour and excitement than he had ever felt with those other women who had gone before her. None of them had been like her, none so exciting, demanding, and sensual. Her legs went up and around him, and her small hands tightened on the small of his back. And he understood he was loving her more thoroughly and with all of himself like he never had before.

As if from a long distance Harry heard her calling his name; as she began to spasm uncontrollably he held her closer. He came into her, a great shudder rippling through him, and he cried out to her, saying her name over and over, telling her that she was his, and he was hers. And much later, when they lay entwined, breathless, he finally murmured against her neck, 'That was a son we just made, sweetheart. My heir. I know it in my bones.'

SIXTY

New York 1971

Charles Brandt sat in the board room of TexMax Oil on Fifth Avenue, talking to the three most important members of the board of the Texas oil company. It was a medium-sized but successful company based in Midland, which Deravco was taking over.

Mostly, Charles was answering questions about Deravco, founded by Edward Deravenel in the 1920s, and giving them a run-down on its current management team. But suddenly the conversation had turned to Harry Turner.

'You've carried the ball all this way, Charles,' Peter Proctor, the president of the oil company, said, 'And a darn good job you've done. We're very satisfied with the way the negotiations have gone, and we're certain the company is going to go from strength to strength.' He eyed Charles appraisingly, and added, 'But the three of us are mighty curious about our new owner . . . Harry Turner.'

Charles looked from Peter Proctor, a man he had grown to like and admire, to Max Nolan, the chairman of the board of TexMax Oil, and Tony Nolan, Max's son, who, along with his father, was a majority stockholder in the Texas company.

'You'll be meeting him very shortly,' Charles said, leaning forward slightly, his façade of immense charm in place, a friendly smile on his face. 'He's only been delayed because his wife is pregnant, and he's on the phone to London.'

'I hope everything's all right,' Max Nolan said, sounding genuinely concerned. 'I'm a father and a grandfather, and I've been there, and then some, I can tell you. My daughter, Kathy Sue, just had another baby and it was tough going for a time. But she made it okay, I'm happy to say.' A white brow lifted. 'Is Mrs Turner having a hard time?'

'No, no, not at all. And there's basically no problem,' Charles now felt bound to explain. 'It's Anne's first child and she had a fall yesterday, but thankfully no damage has been done.'

'Good news,' Max said, and probed. 'Tell us about Harry Turner. He has something of a reputation on Wall Street these days. So what's he really like?'

Laughing, Charles answered, 'Yes, he has gained a bit of a reputation lately, but he's not quite the wild man, the ruthless asset-stripper some journalists like to make out. Actually, you'll find him calm, self-contained, courteous, and extremely practical. I feel quite positive you're going to like him.'

'He's been highly successful this past year, taking over a huge food chain and supermarkets in Britain, those other liquor companies in the Netherlands. And buying us out, of course. So what's he all about? What's the secret of his success?'

'I would say he's a financial genius,' Charles answered. 'He inherited Deravenels from his father Henry Turner, who had kept it on a steady course for many years. It was always highly profitable, but there was no more innovation at Deravenels. That had come in his grandfather's time. After he took over, Harry did the same thing his father had done. He kept it safe. And then slowly he started to make medium acquisitions. He took over a number of small companies that blended in well with Deravenels. Then last summer, to be exact in late June of

1970, he decided to forge ahead, throw in his hat alongside those of the big boys.'

'Such as Goldsmith and Hanson?' Tony Nolan asserted.

'That's correct.'

'Those two Englishmen are real buccaneering tycoons,' Tony announced.

Charles grinned. 'They are indeed! But actually, Jimmy Goldsmith is half French, you know.'

'No, I didn't,' Tony replied. 'So give us a bit more on Harry Turner before he arrives.'

'I would say the secret of his success is his eye for a deal, plus his extraordinary ability to read a balance sheet. He sees things others don't,' Charles explained. 'For example, he can look at a company, spot that its stock is undervalued, pinpoint its real assets, which are frequently undervalued also, and he creates a plan. He makes a bid for the company, buying up the ordinary stock, as much as he can, and goes to the board to make a deal. Once he owns the company he puts it in the hands of truly professional managers from Deravenels. He makes it work. As I said, he's immensely practical, and he's certainly not out to strip a company down and then abandon it. Quite the contrary.'

At this moment the door opened, and Harry Turner came striding into the board room.

As he closed the door behind him, and walked towards the long mahogany conference table, he said, 'Good morning, gentlemen. I apologize for being late. My wife had a fall. I was worried about her, since she's pregnant.'

'Charles filled us in,' Max Nolan said, rising, and shaking hands with Harry, as did the other two men.

Harry seated himself next to Charles, who looked worried, turned to him and explained. 'Everything's all right, no problems. Anne and the baby are not in any way affected by the fall.'

Charles nodded, finally relaxing after a rather bumpy morning with Harry on the phone to London and having to come here without him.

Harry glanced at the three men from TexMax, and said in his quiet, rather understated way, 'I also apologize for not being here during the many negotiations over the last seven months. I know Charles has done an excellent job, and has carried the deal forward on my behalf, and in the most admirable way. I also know you are well and truly satisfied. I simply wanted to explain that my absence did not signify lack of interest in the deal, on my part. It was unavoidable, mainly because I had my hands full with several rather tricky and difficult acquisitions in Europe, especially in Holland.'

'We understand,' Max Nolan said, and turned to Peter Proctor. 'I think you have a few questions, don't you, Peter? Why don't we get everything out on the table, settle things before we go to lunch?'

Harry said, 'Yes, I agree. Let's do that now, tie up all the loose ends. I prefer that myself.'

Peter Proctor nodded, pulled a manila folder towards him, and opened it. 'There are a few points I want to clarify,' he said, and took over the meeting.

Later that night, Harry and Charles sat at a corner table in the Bemelmans bar of the Carlyle Hotel, where they always stayed when they were in New York.

Charles, savouring a cognac, put the balloon down, and said, 'You must feel gratified, don't you, Harry? Now that you own TexMax Oil. It's a big deal, and it was a master stroke on your part to go after it.'

Harry turned to his brother-in-law. 'I do feel good. It's a terrific acquisition for Deravco. It makes our oil company a lot safer.' He took a long swallow of his sparkling water and sighed. 'I owe you an apology, Charles. I'm sorry I was so snotty and bad-tempered this morning, especially when you were trying to organize yourself for the meeting at TexMax. But Anne . . . well, she just got my goat.'

'I've know you since you were seven years old, Harry, and if I don't know you inside out, I can't imagine who does. No offence was taken, I can assure you of that. I'm only sorry you had to cope with Anne's hysteria at that moment, when we were about to leave.'

'It was tough going for a while.' Harry shook his head, stared at Charles, a look of puzzlement settling in his eyes. 'I don't know why she is always rushing around, doing so many things at this stage of her pregnancy. It's early August and the baby's due at the beginning of September. I'm always aghast, she takes such chances. Falling like that in the street . . . my God, she could have lost the baby.'

'And hurt herself,' Charles pointed out. 'But that's Anne, she's a risk-taker. And by the way –' Charles stopped abruptly, sipped the cognac.

'By the way *what*?' Harry asked, frowning. 'What were you going to say?'

Charles shook his head, and gave a short laugh. 'I was going to ask you how you settled the matter of Catherine's jewellery? You never did tell me.'

Harry let out a guffaw. 'After I'd given certain pieces to my sister, your wife, as you know, and some other heirloom pieces to my daughter Mary, I put the rest in the safe at the Berkeley Square house.'

'You didn't give Anne anything? And after all the fuss she made when you purchased the jewels from Catherine?' Charles sounded astonished, and he threw Harry a quizzical look.

'I gave her a diamond necklace and bracelet, and left it at that. I felt a bit odd about it actually. After all, I'd only just purchased the jewellery from Catherine in February when she had that sudden heart attack and died, and so unexpectedly. No one was more surprised than I.' And guilty, he thought to himself.

'Yes, her death *was* very sudden. I'm glad you allowed Mary to stay with us, Harry. It helped her, I know that.'

'Yes, it did, and you helped me. Mary didn't want to come to the Berkeley Square house, so it was the best solution all around.' Harry looked off into the distance, thinking about Catherine's sudden heart attack, she who had always been so healthy.

He had quickly married Anne at Caxton Hall in March, and she had been relieved that the baby she was carrying would not be illegitimate. He, too, was happy about that, but it had never caused him much worry. He knew he could easily legitimize a child of his simply by adopting it, naming the boy his heir in his will.

The two old friends and colleagues talked for another half hour about business, then finished their drinks, and went upstairs to their suites which adjoined.

'Now that everything's settled with TexMax are we still going back to London at the end of the week?' Charles asked, as he stood at the door to his bedroom.

'I think we might as well stay on schedule,' Harry answered. 'And again, thanks for everything, Charles, and especially for carrying the ball with TexMax.'

Harry found it difficult to fall asleep. Although his bedroom was air-conditioned, he found it stifling on this hot August night. The summer weather in New York always got to him. It was the humidity.

After a while he got up, went and poured himself a glass of water and sat down in the living room of his suite, turned on the television set. An old movie was running, something from the 1930s, a gangster movie with Jimmy Cagney, and he watched it for a while, then turned it off, sat thinking about Anne.

He loved her: she was his wife now, and she was carrying his child. His son and heir. But she was turning out to be an extremely difficult woman. She was tremendously independent, and unusually stubborn, and he had decided she was reckless in the way she insisted on rushing around, going to the shop, seeing clients. The baby was almost about to pop out, and she didn't seem to care. Certainly he felt she didn't look after herself properly.

At least she had stopped rushing over to Paris. He had told her to sell the shop there, but she hadn't paid any attention. He sighed and got up. Once the baby was born he would insist she get rid of her business. It was her duty to be a good mother to their child. His son and heir. He was going to call him Edward, after the great Edward Deravenel. He smiled as he walked back to bed, thinking of the son he had so yearned for, and for so long. He couldn't wait to hold him in his arms.

SIXTY-ONE

London

Harry Turner left his office at Deravenels in the Strand in great haste, immediately after lunch on September the seventh. His wife had just gone into labour and he was on his way to the Westminster Hospital. His driver made it in record time, and once he was finally in the maternity ward he felt a degree of relief.

Anne was still in labour, but at least he was seconds away from her if she needed him. He paced up and down restlessly outside her private room, moving along the corridor and back impatiently. And he paced for several hours, filled with anxiety, his nerves fraying and raw.

Charles had wanted to come with him, and he had turned the offer down, and suddenly he wished he had not. The one person he needed was Charles Brandt, who could always keep him calm no matter what the problem was.

He was on the verge of phoning his brother-in-law at Deravenels when Anne's doctor came out, a huge smile on his face.

Harry rushed over to him, glad to see that the doctor looked happy, that he was smiling. 'How is she? How's Anne, Dr Hargrove?' he asked, already knowing that she was fine.

'Your wife came through very well, Mr Turner. Really well, and you'll be happy to know you have a beautiful baby daughter. She's perfect.'

'Thank God!' Harry exclaimed, meaning it, and smiled back at the doctor, not wanting him to think he was disappointed. But he was. Anne had not given him a son after all; he was still without an heir. A daughter, he thought, with a little stab of dismay. Another girl. However, aware of the doctor's eyes on him, he asked swiftly, 'When can I see them?'

'Very shortly, Mr Turner. The nurse will come and get you. It won't be too long a wait. And very many congratulations!'

'Thank you. And thank you, Dr Hargrove, for looking after Anne so well.'

The doctor nodded, smiled again and was gone.

Harry sat down on a chair and closed his eyes. He had longed for a son, and for such a long time that his disappointment was most acute. But he must now make the best of it. There was another thing also: he must not, under any circumstances, allow Anne to think he was disappointed. That would hurt her dreadfully.

Opening his eyes, he took a deep breath, and told himself he was lucky. He had a baby, one who was healthy; also, the child would bind them closer than they already were. Anne was young, and strong, and she would have more children, and next time they would have a boy. It had to be a boy next time around. Third time lucky, he reminded himself.

The moment he saw his baby daughter Harry Turner fell in love. She was beautiful in every way; she even had a little tiny tuft of red fluff on top of her head.

As he rushed into the room he saw Anne looking at him anxiously, over the baby's head, and he went to her immediately, kissed her, then looked down at the bundle of lacey shawls in her arms and saw that adorable little face for the first time.

'She's going to have red hair like you, Harry,' Anne murmured, smiling at him, even though the anxious expression remained in her eyes.

'That was the first thing I saw,' he said, beaming, and touched her tiny hand, stared at the minuscule nails. He sighed, said, 'She's perfect, just as Dr Hargrove said she was. A little miracle.'

'I know how much you wanted a boy, Harry. I'm so sorry she's a girl,' Anne murmured, and held the baby a little bit closer, protectively almost.

He shook his head, looking at Anne intently. 'No, no, don't say that, sweetheart. We have our very own child. She's part of us. We made her, and I love her. Next time we'll have a boy, I know we will. And you mustn't think I won't love her. I just told you, I love her already.'

'We were going to call our son Edward,' Anne began, hesitated, then went on, 'I was wondering –'

He cut her off when he said quickly, excitedly, 'We shall call her Elizabeth! After my mother: she'll grow up to be as smart and as beautiful as the famous Bess Deravenel Turner, you'll see.'

Anne laughed, relief surging through her. She could see he was happy with their child, and she finally relaxed, the tension slipped away, and she was able to breathe easily again.

'And when can you bring this bundle of happiness and perfection home?' Harry asked, pulling a chair up to the bed.

'In a few days, the doctor said. It was a relatively easy birth, Harry, and I'm very strong, and doing well.'

They talked a little longer and then he stood up, bent over her and kissed her, touched the baby's forehead with one finger. 'I shall come and see you tonight, darling. Now I'm going back to Deravenels to hand out cigars and tell everybody I'm the proud father of a gorgeous girl.'

Only Charles Brandt knew how much disappointment lurked beneath the cheerful exterior Harry was presenting to the world. He walked around the executive offices, handing out cigars, and boasting about his auburn-haired daughter, accepting everyone's congratulations. He was a jolly fellow that afternoon.

It was a stellar performance, and Charles admired Harry for it. Why let the world know what you truly felt? That was Harry's eternal cry, almost his motto, and Charles readily agreed with him. Never let them know when you're hurting, Charles reminded himself as he walked through Deravenels with Harry, spurring him on, helping him to put up a good front.

As the father of two girls, Charles knew how wonderful daughters could be, and he kept reminding Harry of this, not only on September the seventh, but for a long time after that. And as the weeks and months passed Harry did grow to love the little girl with red hair and bright black eyes even more. He treasured her, and her mother, and he wanted nothing more than another child as beautiful as Elizabeth . . . a boy, of course.

'I don't seem able to carry a child to full term,' Anne said in a sad voice that was low and confiding.

A look of concern spread across Mary Turner Brandt's lovely face and her reddish-blonde brows puckered in a deep frown. 'I'm so sorry, Anne, so terribly sorry.' She sighed, pursed her lips. 'You should have confided in me before. It's a hard burden to carry alone.'

It was July of 1973, and in September Elizabeth would be

two years old, and as yet Anne had been unable to give Harry his longed-for son and heir, much to her chagrin.

Mary and Anne were sitting in the breakfast room of the Brandt's Chelsea house, sharing a light lunch of asparagus vinaigrette, to be followed by Scottish smoked salmon with thin slices of bread and butter.

Mary, now thinking of Harry's constant bad temper, his reluctance to socialize and his total dedication and absorption in Deravenels, instantly understood her brother's behaviour of late. Normally outgoing, charming and easy to be with, he had become difficult, somewhat of a curmudgeon. She had, until this moment, believed that Harry's irritability had to do with the way things were going in Britain. He had earlier in the year anticipated the worst recession since the Second World War, and knew the country would be in crisis. He was not overwhelmed by the government under Ted Heath either, and he had sold an enormous amount of property. She acknowledged now that there were other factors at play in Harry's world.

Breaking her silence, leaning towards her sister-in-law, Mary asserted, 'You must have seen your gynaecologist, surely? What does he say?'

'He doesn't really have any answers for me, Mary, because I'm very healthy. However, I do keep having miscarriages.'

'How many?'

'Three over the past two years, and, of course, it's three too many as far as Harry is concerned. He's been extremely disappointed in me.'

Mary was silent, knowing her brother's terrible obsession about Anne having his heir. Finally, she said, 'Look, I don't want you to feel I'm giving you a lecture, because I'm not. However, I do think you are far too frantic most of the time, Anne. Working at the antiques shop in Kensington, designing and decorating for clients, flying back and forth between London and Paris . . .' Mary paused, shook her head, finished, 'Don't you think it might be wise to slow down? Concentrate on having a baby?'

'I do take care of myself, Mary, I truly do. I'm, well, sort of carried around, in a sense, and in great comfort. I have cars and drivers, lots of helpers in the business, and very good domestic staff.'

'Do you really need the Paris end of your business, Anne? And that huge flat in the Faubourg Saint-Germain. Isn't that, in itself, a dreadful burden?'

'No, not at all. I've three assistants in my interior design company, and four people working in the shop on the Left Bank these days. And as far as the flat is concerned, I have a full staff. A houseman, a housekeeper and two cleaners. I don't have any worries about help.'

'But it *all* takes such a lot of management on your part, however much help you have, darling. A business to run – no, *two* businesses now that I think about it, and a very grand flat to run as well as the Berkeley Square house.' Mary shook her head. 'And Harry doesn't seem to go to Paris very often these days, now does he?'

'No, you're right about that, Mary. But I can't give Paris up. I love it too much, the city itself. You know I grew up there, and I'm more French than I'm English in many ways. And I certainly don't want to close either the shop or my decorating business in Paris. I enjoy working there and in London. And what would I do? I'd be so bored.'

'I understand,' Mary replied, and picked up a piece of lemon, squeezed it on the smoked salmon. 'But even if you did give up the businesses in Paris, let's say, you would still have the shop and the design company in London. Isn't that enough for you?'

Anne shook her head, answered with some vehemence, 'I don't want to give Paris up, and most certainly not the flat in the Faubourg Saint-Germain. It's my favourite place to live.'

'I realize that,' Mary murmured, taking a slice of the brown bread and butter, saying not another word. They both ate in silence.

After they had finished lunch, Mary stood up, cleared the plates and asked, 'Would you like coffee, Anne dear?'

'No, thanks, Mary. But I'll have another glass of the white wine, if I may.'

'Of course, and I'll join you.' Mary picked up the bottle of Pouilly Fuissé and filled their empty glasses.

After a few moments, Mary said softly, 'I hope you don't mind my asking this, and don't think I'm prying. But how is your relationship with Harry?'

'So-so. To be blunt, we do still sleep with each other. In fact, he's quite the ardent lover.' She smiled slyly, and added in a cynical tone, 'He must have a male heir, so he must perform, you know.'

Mary winced, said nothing, simply sipped her wine. And thought of Harry's new personal assistant, Jane Selmere. She was really a highly professional private secretary, but these days they all called themselves personal assistants. According to Charles, she was cleverly trying to ensnare Harry, although her husband had no proof that there was anything going on between them. Yet. Charles had simply muttered about the kind of looks they exchanged, and added that those furtive glances were rather suggestive to him. He smelled trouble brewing.

'You've suddenly gone awfully quiet, Mary, is something wrong? Are you angry with me?'

'Of course I'm not angry!' Mary exclaimed, and she spoke the truth. She had lately felt sorry for Anne. After another moment of quiet thought, she put down her wine glass, jumped up, and said, 'Come with me, Anne! I have a great idea, and I hope you agree.'

Anne got up and left the table, followed her sister-in-law out in the entrance hall. 'What's this all about, Mary?'

Coming to a standstill, Mary said, 'Look around, Anne, look

at this entrance hall, and come with me to the library. It's Charles's favourite room, and I love it, too. Come on, come and look.'

Still somewhat puzzled, Anne hurried into the library, glancing around, filled with sudden dismay. It looked shabby. 'It is a beautiful room,' she murmured, not wanting to criticize.

'Agreed. It always has been. And the house has been in the family for over seventy years. And I don't think much has been done to it in all that time, except for a little bit of refurbishing. It's been re-painted from time to time.'

'What are you getting at?'

'I want to hire you to do some redecorating and refurbishing in this house. Our home which Charles and I truly love. God knows it needs it, and I think you would enjoy taking it on, wouldn't you, Anne? It would be a fantastic project for you.'

'It certainly would –' Anne's mouth twitched, and she began to laugh. 'You're trying to anchor me in London, aren't you? It's my guess you want to stop me rushing around the world and back, isn't that it?'

'Yes, *absolutely*,' Mary admitted, as always honest. She laughed with Anne, and added, 'But I do think the house needs perking up, you've got to agree.'

'I do, yes.' Anne walked around the room, her eagle eye catching everything. Then she went and sat down on the sofa next to the grand fireplace. 'Come and sit with me, Mary, and tell me the history of this house. I'd like to know more about it than I do. I want to understand it fully.'

Joining her, Mary sat in the big armchair opposite, and explained, 'The house once belonged to Neville Watkins. I'm sure you've heard his name – he is part of the family lore.'

'Yes, I have, and if I remember correctly, Neville Watkins was the nephew of Harry's great-grandmother, Cecily Watkins Deravenel.' She threw Mary a questioning look.

'That's correct. His father was Cecily's brother. It was Neville who bought this house, and immediately gave it to his wife, Nan Watkins. They lived here for many years and brought up their two daughters here.'

'And the daughters both married Edward Deravenel's brothers, George and Richard, isn't that so?'

'Goodness, you *have* absorbed our family history.'

'Harry has always been fascinated by his grandfather, Edward. I think his mother filled his head with fantastic stories about her father, and he savours them.'

Mary laughed. 'I know he does: we both do. After all, Edward was my grandfather, and his daughter was my mother as well as Harry's. Anyway, to continue, after Neville's daughter Anne Watkins married Richard Deravenel, Edward bought this house from Nan, and then gifted it to his brother Richard. He and Anne lived here during their lifetimes. Of course, Richard died after Anne, he was murdered, you know, on Ravenscar Beach. Anyway, Richard left this house to Bess, his favourite niece. Our mother allowed Grace Rose and her other sisters to live here, until they all got married, actually. And then Grace Rose continued to occupy the house with Charlie Morgan. Until it got a little bit too big for them, as they've grown older. It was then that *we* took it over.'

'How wonderful that it has stayed in the family. And I think its redecoration should stay in the family. Thank you for offering me the job. I accept . . . I'm thrilled to accept, Mary.'

SIXTY-TWO

Paris

Harry Turner was sitting up in bed, eating a boiled egg and reading the financial pages of the *New York Herald Tribune*. At the sound of footsteps clattering on the parquet floor in the adjoining hallway, he glanced up, and saw Anne walking into their bedroom.

He was startled. She looked more beautiful than he had seen her in a very long time. Dressed in a pin-striped pale-grey tailored trouser suit and a white silk shirt, she had a marvellous, gleaming aura about her this morning, a special kind of glow. And she was the picture of good health . . . A sour note crept into his thoughts as he wondered why such a healthy-looking young woman was incapable of carrying his babies to full term. He was sick to death of the miscarriages and stillbirths.

'Good morning, Harry darling,' she said in a light, cheerful voice, interrupting his grim thoughts. 'I just wanted to tell you I'm leaving now.'

'Where are you going at this ungodly hour, it's barely seven o'clock,' he snapped and glanced at the bedside clock as he spoke.

'To the Loire.'

'Why?' He sounded peevish and he stared at her questioningly, suspiciously. He was always suspicious of her these days.

'Harry, if I've told you once, I've told you half a dozen times for the past week. There is a marvellous estate sale at one of the grand châteaux in the Loire Valley, and I'm driving down there this morning. The furniture, tapestries, paintings and *objets d'art* are just out of this world.'

'How do you know that?' he demanded, the sourness echoing in his voice.

'Mark and Philippe have already been down to the preview. Last week. And they came back raving about everything. It's important for my business, you know, Harry. I also want to find the appropriate tapestries and accessories to add the finishing touches to Mary's house. It's almost done, just needs a few things.'

'Why on earth would my sister want French tapestries to put in her house, which is actually from the English Regency period?'

Anne smiled, ignoring his truculence, and answered, 'Because Mary and Charles have great taste, and they both agree with me that the entrance hall at the Chelsea house needs warming up.'

'I hope you're not driving yourself to the Loire. You're a hopeless driver,' he pointed out. 'Most especially in France. You're always on the wrong side of the road.'

'Oh, pooh, Harry!' she said, laughing again. 'Anyway, Mark and Philippe are going with me, and Greg. He's interested in the sale. So one of them will drive.'

'Greg? Your brother Greg?'

'Of course. Why are you sounding so surprised?'

'I just am, that's all. I hadn't realized he was interested in antiques.'

'Paintings, actually, and anyway, he wants to take a break for a few days. He did a lot of work for you on that bank deal.'

'That's true, he did. So, when are you planning to come back to Paris, Anne?'

'The estate sale begins tomorrow morning, Tuesday, and lasts for five days, so we'll be there until Saturday. We'll drive back on Sunday.'

Harry glared at her balefully, took a deep breath, and blew out air. 'So you're not going to be here on Thursday evening, are you?'

Anne, looking puzzled, shook her head. 'No, I'm not. But why do you say it in that way? Is there something I've forgotten? A dinner?' As she said these words, she suddenly remembered that Harry was giving a dinner at Le Grand Véfour. 'Oh, my God, Harry, your dinner . . .' Her voice trailed off: she could see he was a little miffed, put out as only he could be. Irritability was one of his worst traits.

'Yes, my dinner, as you call it. In celebration of my takeover of the French bank. Greg has seemingly forgotten it, too.'

'Can't we do it on Sunday night, darling? I'll have the boys set off early, and I'll be back in time for dinner.'

'Oh, don't worry about it, I'll change it to next week. Charles and Mary won't mind, since they're staying in Paris. Charles and I have work to do on this rather important bank takeover.'

She flew across the room to the bed, gave him a hug and a quick kiss on the cheek, and was gone.

He stared after her, frowning, suddenly in a bad temper. She had that effect on him these days. She was growing more impossible. 'Just go! I never want to see you again.'

Henry walked up the Champs-Elysées, still feeling irritated and upset by Anne's sudden departure for the Loire. He had been taken aback, and taken by surprise, because she really hadn't mentioned the trip before, whatever she had claimed earlier. He had an excellent memory, and because his little celebration was so important to Charles and himself he would have immediately changed the date to accommodate this trip of hers. She had lied to him this morning.

He just wasn't sure of her anymore, and he didn't trust her. He had no proof of any wrongdoing on her part, but she had become skittish, and rather flighty. She was spending more time in Paris than in London, and had become a little indiscreet in her choice of friends. She was with Greg a lot, and in a certain way that pleased him, but then again, Greg had some weird cronies; he could be reckless. He was no longer certain about his influence on Anne.

Harry smiled grimly to himself, wondering if he had clipped Anne's wings and cramped her style by being in Paris so much these days because of business.

Ten years, he thought suddenly: we've been together almost ten years. I was thirty-four when I first set eyes on her, and she about nineteen. I'll be forty-four in July, and she'll be almost twenty-nine. Ten years. Good God, a decade together.

How time flies . . . and to think of all the trouble she had caused him . . . He had fought Catherine for a divorce and probably broken her heart in the process . . . he'd made that poor woman ill, hadn't he? Then he had fired Thomas Wolsen, on Anne's urging, and for ineptitude as his solicitor of all things. How stupid he had been, listening to her. Wolsen had died not long after. Had it been of a broken heart? They had been so close, and for twenty years.

There was no denying that Wolsen had been the most brilliant man he had ever known, and good to him, the best adviser he had ever had. And what about poor Tommy? He had picked on Tommy Morle, quarrelled violently with him, and without genuine cause. All because of Anne Bowles. Their quarrelling had been so violent at times that the rows had obviously made Tommy sick in heart and mind and body, and he had passed away some months after their last most horrendous falling out.

And what of his wife of some twenty years? *Catherine*. Mother

544

of Mary. She had suddenly died, and in so doing she had set him free . . . for Anne to take at last, take as a husband. Anne had been his heart's desire for years . . . but it had all gone wrong.

How could it have gone wrong? Was it his fault? Or hers? Or were they both to blame? He had no answers for himself . . . only sudden, unexpected heartache.

What in God's name was he going to do? He and Anne were estranged, if the truth be told. They were living in a kind of . . . armed truce. He didn't want to live like this any longer. Marriage was supposed to make a man happy . . . that's what he wanted, to be happy, and with the right woman. A woman who could give him his son and heir. Obviously Anne Bowles could not.

He had no son. *He must have a son.*

He had two daughters, yes, and he loved them both. Harry's face now softened as he thought of Elizabeth, who would be three years old in September. And then there was Mary, Catherine's child, a grown-up young woman. She was twenty and studying art history in Florence, and they had become friends at last, thanks to his sister.

Harry had a strong parental streak in him, and he did love his daughters. He thought of them now: it was May, and he would take them on holiday later this summer. He made a sudden snap decision. He would charter a yacht for July or August, and they would go sailing together, down the coastline of France and on to Italy. The girls would love it and so would his sister and Charles. He must make a guest list when he arrived at the office.

His face brightened considerably, and the spring came back into his step. He looked up at the sky. It was varying shades of light and deep blue, filled with huge, full-blown white clouds. The sunlight was brilliant today, but not too hot. It was one of those perfect May days. His spirits instantly lifted. He strode out, heading up the beautiful avenue towards the Arc de

Triomphe where the Tricolor was blowing in the breeze. Harry straightened his shoulders, and increased his pace. Within minutes he would be arriving at the Deravenels building on the corner of a side street facing Avenue George V just across the Champs-Elysées.

Now he couldn't wait to get there. He had just had another brilliant idea. He would ask Jane Selmere to join them on the yacht. She was not only a wonderful personal assistant, most efficient and caring, but a lovely young woman. And of late she had become quite indispensable to him . . . Very important, now that he thought about it.

On Thursday evening Harry went ahead with his little celebration dinner, even though Anne and Greg were absent, off to the Loire in search of antiques.

He took his guests to Le Grand Véfour, the ancient restaurant which went as far back as the French Revolution. It was a landmark, situated under the arches of the Palais-Royal, and a favourite of his.

There were only four of them for dinner, and Harry was now pleased about this. He glanced around the table, smiling at his sister Mary, and her husband and his best friend Charles, the two family members closest to him. Finally, his blue eyes settled on Jane Selmere. She had accepted his invitation to dinner with alacrity, and now, as he looked at her intently, he realized that she was looking really lovely tonight in a soft, gentle way. She wore a simple delphinium blue silk dress and a string of pearls which he himself had given her last Christmas. He had not realized until now how truly fine the pearls were. They looked wonderful on her and they reflected her exquisite English rose complexion. Yes, that's what she was – an English rose.

The four of them were enjoying the setting. It was mellow

and intimate, and there was something quite magical about this most distinctive decor of the eighteenth and nineteenth centuries.

Once the Krug rosé champagne had been served, Harry picked up his flute and said, 'Here's to our new acquisition, the Banque Larouche, and may it prosper. And may we all prosper.'

Charles grinned at Harry, and added, 'And here's to *your* brilliance. You made a great deal, Harry.'

'But I couldn't have, not without you,' Harry shot back.

They all clinked glasses and sipped the sparkling pink wine.

Mary, looking at Jane, said with a warm smile, 'This is like a family restaurant for us, Jane. Harry and I were first brought here by our mother, Bess Deravenel Turner, and she had been brought here by her father.'

'The great Edward Deravenel,' Jane remarked, and looked from Mary to Harry, and added, 'And that's how *you* will be known now, Harry. They'll call you the *great* Harry Turner.' She smiled at him over the top of her crystal flute, her eyes full of promise, her whole demeanour flirtatious, encouraging him.

Harry, smiling back at her, experienced a marvellous rush of excitement, thrilled that she had come to dinner and quite certain he would be extremely welcome in her bed tonight. Certainly he aimed to try. Jane was in her early thirties, and obviously ready for a man like him, he was sure of that. There had to be some experience there, didn't there? She had never married, and this pleased him in a curious way. She moved slightly, turned to speak to Charles and he saw the curve of her milky white breasts as the vee neckline of her dress shifted slightly. He had a terrible urge to reach out and touch them, but he obviously could not. His heart was racing and he was wonderfully aroused by this soft-spoken, serene young woman, in a way he had not been for some time. Still waters run deep, he thought, wondering how she would be in bed. Sensual and willing, he decided.

There were lots of antique mirrors on the ceiling and lining the walls of the restaurant, and as Harry glanced around, seeking a waiter, he suddenly saw a number of reflected Janes smiling at him from various angles. He said softly, leaning across the table to her, 'Wherever I look I see you, sweetheart . . . because of all the mirrors. I can't begin to tell you what a pleasure that gives me, Jane.'

'I want to give you pleasure,' she whispered, and looked at him very directly, her mouth open slightly; when she took a sip of her champagne she let her tongue linger on the edge of the crystal glass, and he knew it was all right. He was home. She would be his tonight. And if it was the way he thought it would be, between the two of them, perhaps it would be forever. A son, he thought. Jane will surely give me a son.

When the waiter arrived, Harry asked for the menus, and then started to tell Jane about the history of the restaurant, how Napoleon and Josephine had eaten here, and many other famous people over the centuries, and she listened attentively. At one moment she slipped her foot out of her shoe, and slipped it onto the edge of his chair, where it rested between his legs.

Momentarily taken by surprise, he then inclined his head slightly, and she smiled at him, began to rub his crotch with her foot. She's a naughty one, he thought. What joy.

'The food here is delicious, Jane: the chef is very famous – Raymond Oliver,' Mary explained. 'I am going to have the sole, it's simply divine, but another favourite of mine and Harry's is pigeon stuffed with foie gras. It's one of their specialities, nothing like it in the world.'

'That's what I shall have,' Harry announced, his gleaming blue eyes fixed on Jane. 'I love stuffed pigeon.'

'Then I shall try it,' Jane murmured, and finally removed her foot, put it back in her shoe, understanding she was tantalizing him unbearably. I'll make him truly happy later, she told herself, excited by the thought.

Charles ordered the duck, and then they all settled back and chatted amongst themselves, enjoying being together. Charles, touching Mary's knee at one moment, signalled to her that he had always been right about Jane. She was after Harry; and he was positive she would succeed.

SIXTY-THREE

'Here are all of the final contracts, Harry,' Charles said, passing the documents to his brother-in-law. 'Once you sign these, the bank is yours.' It was Monday morning, the twentieth of May, in 1974.

'I feel very chuffed about this, Charles.' Harry grinned as he picked up his pen, and began to sign his name. Looking across at Jean-Pierre Larouche, he said, 'It is the first time Deravenels have owned a bank . . . I'm thrilled we've bought it.'

'And I am thrilled to have sold it to you,' the French banker replied. 'I have been wanting to retire for some years now. My wife Claude is also thrilled. And she thanks you most profusely.'

The small group of men in the boardroom at Deravenels all chuckled, and Charles then announced, 'We have booked a small private room at Fouquet's for a celebration lunch, gentlemen. Once these last formalities are over we can walk across –' Charles paused as Jane put her head around the door, and beckoned to him.

He rose, went to speak to her, noticing as he approached that she was as white as a sheet. She whispered something to him, and he caught his breath, then steadied himself. Turning around he said, 'Harry, can I see you in your office for a moment? There seems to be a problem. A personal problem.'

Harry was startled, and he frowned, annoyed by this odd interruption, and then seeing how serious Charles and Jane looked, he stood up, patted the contracts as he did. 'All is in order, gentlemen. Please excuse me for a few minutes. There seems to be a private matter I must attend to before we go across the Champs-Elysées to lunch.'

Jean-Pierre Larouche, speaking for his group of associates, replied, 'Please, take your time, Mr Turner.'

'What is it? What's wrong?' Harry asked once they were outside in the corridor.

'Let's go into your office, Harry,' Charles said, and took his arm, propelled him forward, urgency in his manner.

Jane hung back, not sure what she should do when Charles turned, indicated she should follow them. She did so, shocked by the news she had just heard.

Once they were in Harry's office, he turned around and looked from Charles to Jane, and exclaimed, 'For God's sake, what is it? You both look as if you're the bearers of bad news.'

'I'm afraid we are,' Charles responded a little shakily, and taking hold of Harry's arm he added, 'You'd better sit down here on the sofa.'

Harry did so, frowning in puzzlement. He again stared at Jane, who was a ghastly colour, and speechless, then at Charles. 'Tell me, for Christ's sake!'

Charles sat down in the chair opposite Harry and signalled Jane to sit next to him on the sofa.

'There's been a tragic accident,' Charles began. 'Anne and her brother Greg, and the other two fellows who were with them, were in a car crash in the early hours of this morning. On their way back to Paris from the Loire Valley.'

'Oh, my God, no! I told her not to drive,' Harry cried, his face turning red. 'She must have been at the wheel.'

'I don't believe she was,' Charles answered in a gruff voice.

'Are they in hospital?' Harry asked. 'Which hospital? Where did the accident occur?'

'I'm not quite sure of that, but we'll soon be informed.' Charles swallowed and went on in that same hoarse voice, 'Apparently it was a horrendous crash. Harry . . . Anne's dead. I'm so sorry . . . so very sorry, but they're all dead . . . all four of them.'

'Oh, my God! No! What happened? Tell me what happened, for God's sake!' Harry demanded. All the colour left his face; he turned grey and he was shaking. It seemed to him that all of his blood was draining away. He could not move, nor could he speak, so stunned was he by the news. It was so unexpected and so sudden. Anne was dead. Greg was dead. And Mark and Philippe. It didn't seem possible . . .it was hard to take in. All of them gone . . . just like that . . . in a flash.

Jane took hold of his hand, wanting to console him, but she was in a bad state herself. He simply sat there gaping at Charles, shaking his head in utter bewilderment. It was obvious he was in shock. 'It just can't be,' he mumbled all of a sudden and brought a hand to his face. 'Tell me what you know, tell me all of it, Charles. Please,' he begged at last.

'I don't know much, Harry. But the police are waiting to see you. Jane took them into my office.' He glanced at her and went on in a low tone, 'What did they say, Jane?'

Jane swallowed hard and explained in a shaky voice, 'That the car was hit head on by a lorry coming in the opposite direction. It was on a main road. It seems . . . well, it seems . . .' Jane stopped abruptly; her voice was muffled as she finally took hold of herself, and continued, 'It seems that the impact . . . was very . . . bad . . . Everyone was killed outright, the two policemen said. They want to talk to you as soon as possible, Harry.'

Taking a deep breath, trying to stay calm, steady, Harry nodded. 'You'd better bring them in.'

Jane jumped up and left the room.

Charles rose, went and sat next to Harry on the sofa, put his arm around his shoulder. 'I'm here. Whatever you need, I'm here to help you.'

'It's the terrible shock. What ghastly news –' Harry's voice shook so badly he stopped speaking, totally at a loss. After a moment or two he whispered, 'How am I going to tell Elizabeth?'

'You'll do it, you'll find the strength somewhere, and we're here to help you, Mary and I.'

'I know.' He looked up at his closest and dearest friend, and said, 'I was angry with her, and disappointed, but I never wished her any harm, Charles, you do know that, don't you?'

'I do indeed.'

The two policemen were brought in by Jane, and they sat down, and spoke to Harry in calm, level tones. They explained that the crash had occurred near Brissac, in the Loire Region, and that the four passengers in the car had been killed instantly, as had the driver of the lorry.

Harry listened, nodding from time to time, trying to absorb everything, but he was numb. Charles finally intervened, and took the police to his own office, where they gave him all the relevant details. The bodies were in the morgue of a local hospital near Brissac, and could be brought back to Paris within the next twenty-four hours.

Charles told his secretary to make the proper arrangements with the two policemen; and then he telephoned his wife, Mary.

'Thank you for coming with me, Jane,' Harry said as they walked through the Tuilleries the following afternoon. 'I just needed to get out of the flat, it felt so claustrophobic, and I was feeling so benumbed.'

'You're suffering from shock,' Jane told him, taking hold of his arm, wanting to console and comfort him. 'Anyway, the air and the walk will do you good.'

'Anne loved Paris. The city, the people, everything about it. I used to think she was more French than English.'

'So you've told me.'

They walked on in silence. They were comfortable together, and companionable in their silence; they didn't really need words.

Suddenly Harry came to a halt, stood still, and turned to look at Jane. 'There's something I want to say, actually need to say. I didn't hate her. We *were* having our problems and difficulties, but then you knew we were, didn't you?'

'Oh, yes, very much so,' Jane responded quietly.

'You've known for a long time?'

'I have, Harry.'

'I didn't wish her any harm.'

'I know that.' Jane squeezed his arm.

'If she had to die, I'm glad it was . . . *instantly*. She didn't suffer, as far as we know . . . Do you think she suffered?'

'No. Anyway, the police told you she didn't, because the impact was so enormous. They said she must have died at once. And the Medical Examiner would know the time of death. I'm sure the French police were telling you the truth yesterday.'

'But her neck, Jane – those policemen told us her neck was . . . well . . . partially severed.' A small shudder passed through him at the mere thought of this.

'Don't think about that. Just remember, Anne didn't suffer. You mustn't dwell on the bad things.'

'I know. There's Elizabeth . . . not yet three until September. How do you tell a child her mother has been killed?'

'Gently, Harry,' Jane answered, and there was a hesitation before she said in a soft tone, 'With my help.'

'*Will* you help me, Jane?' he asked eagerly, staring into her eyes, knowing all of a sudden how much he needed her support.

'I will do anything for you, Harry, anything at all. I have

always loved Elizabeth: she's the most adorable child, and so like you.'

'Do you think so?'

'I do.'

He was silent, studying her.

She met his long, intense gaze steadily. She cared about this man, had strong and loving feelings for him. All she wanted was to help him now.

'I've been thinking about the summer, chartering a yacht, Jane. I mentioned that to you last week.'

'You did, and I thought it was a good idea.'

'If I do charter it, will you come with us? There'd be Mary and Elizabeth, my sister Mary and Charles and their daughters, Frances and Eleanor. Would it be too dull for you, do you think?'

'It would be wonderful. Quite amazing, I think. I've always wanted to be part of a large family and, I must admit, I've longed for lots of children of my own, actually. But I don't suppose I ever will have a lovely big brood. It's not on the cards.'

'You mustn't say such a thing, Jane. No one knows what's in store for them, what's going to happen in life.'

She made no response, simply gazed at him, her lovely face open and honest, her eyes clear and sincere. There was no subterfuge in her, and this pleased Harry. She was trustworthy, he was quite certain of that, and he felt a sudden lessening of the sadness as they walked on together. There was an inner peace in her which made her soothing to be with.

'It helps to think about *positive* things – chartering a yacht, for instance. Don't you agree?' Harry asked as they now headed in the direction of the Louvre Museum.

'Going on a yacht, taking a cruise with you and your family, is something very positive indeed. And something to look forward to, for me, Harry. Thank you for inviting me . . . the mere idea of it is magical. I can't wait.'

His spirits lifted, and a small smile tugged at the corners of his mouth for the first time in days. 'I don't know how you managed to stumble into my life, Jane Selmere, but I'm awfully glad you did.'

'And so am I.' Jane took hold of his arm once more, more possessively this time. There wasn't anything better than a truly loving woman to heal a man's troubled soul. And that she fully intended to do . . . if Harry Turner would let her. And she would make sure he had the time of his life.

Epilogue

Harry Turner stood in the middle of the library floor at Ravenscar, staring up at the marvellous painting of his grandfather, the great Edward Deravenel. He had a big smile on his face, and in his arms he held his baby son. His son and heir. Born three days ago on October the twelfth in 1975.

Jane had given him a healthy, beautiful boy, and in a few days' time he would be christened in the family chapel at Ravenscar.

'Here he is, Grandfather!' Harry cried, talking aloud to the masterful painting. 'My son. My heir ... your heir. And he is named for you. He's another Edward. And he's going to be great like you, I promise you that. Another great Edward in our family.'

Smiling from ear to ear, Harry held the child towards the painting. 'He has Deravenel blood and Turner blood, and he's going to rule your empire and take it to even greater heights one day.'

Harry cradled the little boy in his arms, blowing on the little tiny tuft of red hair on top of his head for a second, kissing the bright blue eyes. In my own image, Harry thought, in my grandfather's image. Jane did it for me, gave me what I've yearned for since I first got married all those years ago to Catherine.

I'm forty-five, but I'm not too old to have more children, and I will. Jane will give me more sons, and daughters, as well. She said in Paris last year that she had always yearned for a big brood, and that is what we shall have.

He felt a tugging on his trouser leg and he looked down.

Elizabeth was standing there staring up at him through her bright black eyes. 'Can I see my brother, Father?'

Bending down, Harry showed her the baby, a tiny bundle wrapped in bunch of lacey white shawls. 'Here he is . . . Edward, your brother Edward. My son. My heir.'

Straightening, Harry stared at the painting of his grandfather again, and decided, at that very moment, to have a similar portrait painted of himself. He would do it for his newborn son. So that one day Edward could hold *his* son up, and tell him that here was his grandfather, the great Harry Turner. Bending over the child, Harry kissed his forehead, overflowing with love for him, this longed-for child.

'Can I hold my baby brother?'

'Of course not, Elizabeth. You're only four and you might easily drop him, and then where would we be, eh?'

'*Please*, father.'

'I said no. Now go away, that's a good girl. I'm very busy with my son and heir.'

Elizabeth, hurt and slighted, took a step back, and then turned around and ran to Nanny, who was standing in the doorway of the library.

When Avis Paisley, the nanny, saw the tears trickling down the little girl's cheeks she took hold of her hand and led her away, filled with fury that Harry Turner would hurt his small daughter in this way.

'Don't cry, sweetheart,' Nanny said, 'Everything is all right.'

'No, it isn't,' Elizabeth wailed. 'I'm not a boy. I wish I was.

Then I would be the son and heir and father would love me.'

'He does love you,' Nanny consoled her. 'Everybody loves you.'

'Do they really?' Elizabeth said, cheering up, rubbing her eyes. 'How many people is that . . . *everybody*?'

'Why, the whole of England, Elizabeth,' the nanny answered, improvising. 'The whole of England loves you.'

The red-haired child with the ebony black eyes smiled, brushed her tears away. 'And I shall love them,' she said; and meant it.

Acknowledgements

Although I have accumulated a great deal of historical research over the years, pertaining to the Plantagenets and the Tudors, when I started this series I realized that I needed to know more about the Edwardian era. That was the period in which I planned to set this series of books, from the year 1904 up to the present. In other words, I needed to know a lot more than I did concerning the early part of the twentieth century.

Because I was busy researching the manners, mores, politics, social life, business and fashions of those early days, plus many areas of daily life, as well as the First World War, I needed help. I must now give special thanks to Lonnie Ostrow and Damian Newman of Bradford Enterprises. They helped to make my life so much easier. All I had to do was pick up my phone and ask, 'Was the Savoy Hotel in London already built in 1904?' or some other such question, and no matter how complicated it was I got an immediate answer almost before the words left my mouth. They pulled up all kinds of information I needed, some of it quite strange and obscure, and provided yearly calendars from 1904 up to the present time. These two wizards on their computers must have heard from me at least twenty times a day for the past two years. My gratitude for their help knows no bounds.

I must acknowledge the fascinating novel, *The Sons of Adam* (HarperCollins, London) by Harry Bingham. Apart from being a gripping read, I learned more about wildcatting and drilling for oil in the 1920s than in any of my research books, and in the most enjoyable way. My thanks to this talented author for writing his book in the first place. It was invaluable.

I must say a word here about my two very talented editors who are unfailing in their support of me, and ready to listen and to advise. My editor in London, Patricia Parkin of HarperCollins, has edited twenty-two of my novels and this will be her twenty-third. I am most appreciative of her wisdom, devotion and dedication to my books. In all the time we have worked together we've never had a cross word or a disagreement, something of a record I'm sure.

My editor in New York, Jennifer Enderlin of St Martin's Press, is cut from the same cloth, and is devoted, dedicated and full of enthusiasm, and I appreciate this. Having two such great editors and such splendid support on both sides of the Atlantic is a rare gift. My unstinting thanks to them both.

It is important to me to present a perfect typescript to my publishers, and I could not do that without the help of Liz Ferris of Liz Ferris Word Processing. She has typed many of my books for a number of years now, and my gratitude and thanks go to her for doing this so beautifully. Her finished typescripts are indeed perfect, produced at great speed, in record time, and without one complaint from her when I put the pressure on.

I also want to give special thanks to everyone at HarperCollins in London and at St Martin's Press in New York, all those who are involved in the design and production of my books. Behind the scenes editors, copy-editors and designers are invaluable to an author, and I am grateful for the care they put into my novels, and their hard work.

I have a circle of remarkable girlfriends who are always here for me, cheering me on, asking if I need anything, wanting to help in any way they can, and keen to both cosset and protect me when I'm writing. My thanks and love to them . . . they all know who they are.

Finally, last but not least, I must say that I could not write any of my books without the constant loving care, affection, devotion and 'cheering on' of my husband, Robert Bradford. They threw the mould away when they made him, my very patient Bob.

Bibliography

Edwardian London by Felix Barker (Laurence King Publishing)

The Sons of Adam by Harry Bingham (HarperCollins)

Henry VII by S.B. Chrimes (Eyre Methun)

Victorian and Edwardian Décor: From the Gothic Revival to Art Nouveau by Jeremy Cooper (Abbeville Press)

Great Harry: The Extravagant life of Henry VIII by Carolly Erickson (Summit Books)

The Lives of the Kings and Queens of England by Antonia Fraser (Weidenfeld Nicolson)

Born to Rule: Five Reigning Consorts, Granddaughters of Queen Victoria by Julia Gelardi (St. Martin's Press)

The Edwardians by Roy Hattersley (St. Martin's Press)

Churchill: A Biography by Roy Jenkins (Pan Books)

Richard the Third by Paul Murray Kendall (W.W. Norton)

The Wars of the Roses by J.R Lander (Sutton Publishing)

Queens of England by Norah Lofts (Doubleday)

The Autobiography of Henry VIII by George Margaret (Pan Books)

The Wars of the Roses by Robin Neillands (Cassell)

Victorian and Edwardian Fashion from La Mode Illustrée by Joanne Olian (Dover Publications)

The Edwardian Garden by David Ottewill (Yale University)
Eminent Edwardians by Brendon Piers (André Deutsch) Press)
The Edwardians by J.B. Priestly (Sphere)
Seductress: Women Who Ravished the World and Their Lost Art of Love by Elizabeth Stevens Prioleau (Penguin Books)
Symptoms by Isadore Rosenfeld (Bantum)
Edward IV by Charles Ross (Methuen)
Six Wives: The Queens of Henry VIII by David Starkey (HarperCollins)
Consuelo and Alva: Love and Power in the Gilded Age by Amanda Mackenzie Stuart (HarperCollins)
The Daughter of Time by Josephine Tey (Arrow Books)
Tycoon: The Life of James Goldsmith by Geoffrey Wansell (Grafton Books)
The Princes in the Tower by Alison Weir (Pimlico)
The Wars of the Roses by Alison Weir (Ballantine)
The Uncrowned Kings of England: The Black Legend of the Dudleys by Derek Wilson (Constable and Robinson)
Warwick the Kingmaker (W.W. Norton)